Catherine Cookson

A House Divided

Simon & Schuster

This Large Print Edition, prepared especially for Doubleday Direct, Inc., contains the complete un-abridged text of the original Publisher's Edition.

Simon & Schuster
Rockefeller Center
1230 Avenue of the Americas
New York, NY 10020

Originally published in Great Britain by Bantam Press, a division of Transworld Publishers Ltd.

SIMON & SCHUSTER and colophon are registered trademarks of Simon & Schuster Inc.

Manufactured in the United States of America

ISBN 0-7394-0710-4

This Large Print Book carries the Seal of Approval of N.A.V.H.

PART ONE

Elizabeth Ducksworth walked quickly and quietly along the dimly lit corridor. She had passed four closed doors and was making for the last of the seven when it was thrust open quickly and there came to meet her a figure in a dressing gown. The head was bandaged, covering one eye; the lid of the other was blinking rapidly, and the patient turned his head to one side as he addressed her, saying, 'I was just coming for you, Ducks—I mean, Nurse. I think the captain needs attention. Well, what I mean is . . .'

'Yes . . . yes.' The night nurse turned him gently about, saying, 'You should have rung the bell, Lieutenant.'

But the answer she got was, 'He always

seems to know when I do that and starts his growling.'

'Has he spoken?'

'No; no . . . not a word. Just those sounds.'

She opened the door of the end room, at the same time taking his arm and steadying him as she said, 'You shouldn't get out of bed; I've told you.'

'I'm all right. I only wish he felt half as good.'

'Get back into bed; I'll see to him. Would you like a drink?'

'Later. Later, thank you.'

She now went quickly to the end bed where, to her surprise, she found the patient's head buried under the clothes and the whole of the large form shaking so much that the bed itself quaked.

In a way she was pleased at what she saw and heard, for generally she would find him sitting up at all hours of the night, staring into a blackness that he couldn't accept . . . wouldn't accept. Not since the great outburst of rage that had filled this particular section of the hospital and beyond it with his shouting, raving and blasphemy had he uttered one word, nor had he made any movement towards anyone. Not even to his mother and members of his family had he given a sign of recognition.

What would have happened if he had been able to get out of bed was another question, but the blast that had deprived him of sight had also stripped off the skin and some flesh of his left calf and hip. By rights he should have been on the surgical ward, but because of his unpredictable behaviour it was considered advisable to leave him in the eye section and near his friend, although since that same outburst he had refused to recognize even Lt Fulton.

She knew it had been suggested that as soon as his wounds would allow he should be moved to a psychiatric ward. There was one thing sure in her own mind now: he needed help of some sort, poor devil.

Gently she touched his shoulder and attempted to draw the bedclothes back, and at this Matthew Wallingham's body became still for a second before he buried his head further under the covers.

Nurse Ducksworth sat down slowly on the edge of the bed. Then, her hand going out to the thick tumbled hair showing above the bedclothes, she stroked it softly, saying, 'It's all right. It's all right. It's the best thing that could have happened. Cry it out. There's nobody here but me and your friend. Don't worry. Nobody'll know.'

She paused a moment and bit on her lip. That's what they were all afraid of, anyone knowing they couldn't take it.

'There now . . . there now.' She had her hand on the top of the bedclothes again, and there was no resistance to her turning these slightly back, so revealing his face. The unmarred face. No sign of an injury on it. There had been a deep cut on the other side of his skull but that had healed. There was even hair beginning to grow around the scar.

In the dim green glow from the light on the wall above the bed she saw he was gripping the pillow and thrusting the edge of it into his mouth.

When her hand covered his fist and pulled it gently away from his mouth his sobbing became more audible, and quickly now she bent her face down to his, whispering, 'There now . . . there now. You're all right. I'm with you.'

She put her arm about his shoulders, and at this he started visibly. Leaning on one elbow, he edged himself on to his side and the next moment, it seemed, both his arms were about her and his face was buried in her neck.

She felt she was about to slide from the bed, but his grip kept her there. Then she found herself holding him and patting his back while she whispered, 'There now . . . there now. No more . . . no more. You've done enough. Come along. Come along. You'll be all right now. Believe me, you will . . . you'll be all right now.'

'Oh, Mama.' His grip tightened on her and his wet face moved against her chin and she felt the movement of his lips on the edge of hers as he said, 'It was a dream. It was a dream. I thought it was, and then I knew. Oh! Mama, I'm sorry . . . I'm sorry . . . I mean . . .'

'It's all right. It's all right. I know what you mean. I'll be your mama for tonight.'

'No . . . no . . . I need . . .'

'Please! Please! Now listen to me. I have to do one of two things: either send for Sister—and you know what happens: she'll give you a needle. Believe me, she gives

me the needle, but in a different way.' She
gave a small laugh and patted the cheek
close to hers, then said, 'The alternative is
two sleeping tablets. Now I know your old
trick: you keep them under your tongue,
don't you? Oh now, you can't say you
don't because I've found them in the bed.'

The sobbing had ceased, as had his crying, but now, his head raised, he was taking in great gulps of air, while he still held
her closely; and so, taking her arms from
around him, she pulled them behind her,
bringing him slowly forward; and then, gently laying him back on the pillow, she
cupped his face for a moment while peering down into the sightless eyes and saying, 'It's to be sleeping tablets then, yes?'

He made no movement in response; but
as she made to rise from the bed he said
something, and she put her head down to
him again and said, 'What's that?'

'I'm sorry.'

'Oh, my dear boy, you have no need to
say you're sorry to me. But I'm going to
say something to you: you've turned the
corner. You're back on the road. You'll be
all right, you'll see.'

She paused, her thoughts racing. You'll

see, she says. Do people ever think what they're saying? You'll see . . . and, he's back on the road. What road? She had held his face, she had held him close. He had thought she was his mama—but that was just for a moment—and she had called him boy. Twenty-four! and she had called him boy.

'Open your mouth, and don't try the tongue trick; I'm going to hold your nose.'

After this operation was over and she had returned to her uniform pocket the small box in which she always kept two sleeping tablets, she looked down at him as his head drooped to the side away from her and he said quietly but clearly, 'Please don't report this.'

'I had no intention of reporting anything, except that you didn't get to sleep till about one o'clock.'

'What's your name?' This question came in a whisper, and it was some seconds before she answered, 'Well, in these distinguished rooms I'm generally addressed as Ducks or Ducky . . . that is when Sister isn't about, but my birth certificate states that I am one Elizabeth Jane Ducksworth. Now I don't especially like the name of Elizabeth, nor Jane, but I'm not averse to being called Liz by my family and friends.'

There was another pause. 'How old are you?'

'Old?' Her voice sounded surprised. 'Well now, some say I'd be in my fifties, but I'm not, I'm merely forty-nine.' As she finished speaking she thrust her arm out and back, towards the bed on her left, and a sound like a hiccup came from there as she went on, 'And now you've got the picture of me, I'm what you would call a motherly-looking type. Go to sleep now. I'll see you in the morning before I go off duty—that's if you're awake. Good night.' She pulled the clothes up about his shoulders and for a moment allowed her fingers to rest on his cheek.

As she quietly moved away she bent low down over the other bed and whispered, 'Leave it like that. You understand?'

'Yes, Ducks,' the voice came in a low whisper. 'But what about giving *me* a bit of your motherly attention?'

Her answer to this was to straighten up and give the bed's occupant a playful slap on the face as she said, 'Get to sleep. Good night.'

'Good night, Ducky.' The name came soft and endearing from his tongue.

2

Three weeks later Matthew was sitting up in bed. The orderly had just finished with him. He was washed and shaved and his hair was combed and, as had been usual for some days now, he was sitting waiting. Then there she was, he smelt her. She wore some special kind of scent, a perfume that was warm, elusive; and yet there was nothing elusive about the warmth of her personality. He didn't know how he would have carried on without her, especially at night, although she had never held him since that one occasion. But there had always been her hand to hold, and sometimes grip, as she soothed him out of a nightmare.

Now here she was. He heard her talking

to the new fellow in the end bed. He had
come in only yesterday.

Now she was talking to Jerry. Laughing
with him. Jerry was leaving today. Oh, he'd
miss Jerry! Yes . . . Jerry knew so much
about him, and he about Jerry. And there
was a third party in the know. Fox. Corporal Charlie Fox. He'd have to find out
where Charlie was, because neither of
them would be here today if it hadn't been
for old Foxy.

She was walking again; he knew her
step.

'Good morning. By! you do look spruce.
You've got new pyjamas on. Blue suits
you.'

'What colour blouse have you got on?'
He knew she was dressed for off-duty. But
why, he asked himself, couldn't he speak
pleasantly? Why did he always have to use
a gruff tone towards her? She had been
so wonderfully kind to him, and he didn't
think of her as an older woman—her tone
was so light, her step was so light. She
brought a kind of lightness . . .

Something inside him snapped off the
word and a portion of his mind yelled,
Light . . . light . . . light. It was like when

Jerry would persistently say, 'You see what I mean.' He knew he was only meaning to be careful, but it annoyed him. You see what I mean. If only he *could* see what they meant.

'You'll be having your family here today, and I understand it's your turn to try out crutches. The next will be two walking sticks, then one. Then . . .' her voice trailed off as she asked herself why she was talking like this. She was feeling awful, and she didn't really know why. Usually she was over the moon when her term of night duty was finished. But she knew he had come to rely on her in a way; and they had warned her—well, Sister had warned every one of them. She could hear her voice saying, 'Watch yourselves. You can be attracted to a wounded man; it's natural sometimes, but it happens more so when they are blind. All the stupid instincts of youth come to the fore and you see yourself as a ministering angel, but let me tell you it has been proved you would soon lose your wings if you were married to one, because the blind can become dominant. Unless you are very strong and independent characters in yourselves, they will want to possess you, suck you dry.' And she recalled that Sister had ended, 'I know some of you go out of this room saying, "She's a hard-hearted bitch," but I'm speaking from experience, twenty years of it, and I'm not blaming any one of you for your emotions; I'm only warning you against them and of the consequences of giving them rein.'

And now, on a small laugh, Elizabeth said, 'Well, I suppose I'll have to be going; and this is, I'm sorry to say, farewell, good-bye; see you at the 'Sizes. That's a saying of an old aunt of mine.'

'What are you talking about? Farewell, goodbye? You're leaving?'

'Night duty. I've had three months of it. That's more than enough. Of course I've had weekly breaks, but you always know you've got to come back to it.'

'And you didn't like it?'

'Not particularly.'

Seeing the look on his face, she added, 'Except in some cases, where I think I might have been of help.'

'Where will you be going?'

'You mean straight away? Oh, I've got

a week's leave, then I go on day duty. But first, I'm going home.'

The hand nearer to her was gripping the iron edge of the bed. When she prised his fingers open, the hand clasped hers and in a low voice he said, 'How tall are you?'

'Too tall, five foot seven and a half.'

There was a pause while his hand moved over her fingers as if massaging them. 'Tell me, are you really forty-nine?'

She laughed now, that chuckle that he had come to know. 'Worse, I've put on one year since then. I had a birthday last week.' She now went to draw her hand away from his, saying, 'I must go. The day staff are on their rounds, but I thought I'd like to say goodbye and wish you the very, very best of luck.'

His voice was no longer rough, but low and warm as he said, 'I'm going to miss you—Ducks.'

At this she laughed outright, saying, 'That's the first time you've called me that. Now I *know* you are well along the road.'

'I . . . I want to say thank you and I don't know how.'

'The only way you can thank me is to get on your feet and hit out at life.' Her voice had a serious note as she added, 'Now, I mean that. You've got a lot to live for, so much. But I must go.' There was a slight break in her voice. 'Goodbye, Captain.'

She had forcibly to take her hand from his, and then she was gone, and he was left with two hands gripping the counterpane . . . Oh God! There it was again. He could see it. He was hugging it close, the dead body without a head . . .

He was in hell. They were all in hell. Why? Why now? They had crossed the Senio River, and now it was the Saterno. The 2nd New Zealand Division was already across, but they had come up against those bloody stubborn German rearguards defending the bridge. All the winter up in the hills they had been fighting the buggers, but now, on the plain, everything was looking up. Oddments of different companies had joined them, some from the North-East, and he had welcomed the sound of their voices. They had been camped on the plain for a time, and Foxy had turned out to be a good scrounger. And then there was Jerry Fulton. Oh yes, Jerry. It was those two, Fox and Jerry, who had stopped him running wild. But the headless body in his arms; there it was

again. And all round him the dead. Dead.
Their blood had splashed those mountain
slopes, German blood, American blood, Ital-
ian blood, British blood, oh yes, British
blood. And now it was running all over him.
Was it Ferguson's? Had they killed Ferguson? He had never liked Ferguson. Oh
my God! He threw the torso from him but
he couldn't see where it fell. The tank was
on fire but he couldn't see it, he could just
feel the heat. His head was numb. He was
running now, tripping over bodies. He fell
but couldn't save himself, one hand was
gripping his gun and the other a grenade.
There was noise all around him. He was
deafened by it. Where was he? It was black
dark. It hadn't been dark. Words yelled in
his head: No! No! . . . The thought brought
him to his feet and running. He had to get
away. Away from the bridge. They had lost
the bridge. Why hadn't they sensed those
buggers would be waiting? He became
aware again of his gun and hand grenade.
What use was a gun now he couldn't see?
The bridge had gone, they were all dead.
The bridge. He lifted his arm and flung the
hand grenade and as he did so he felt himself being grabbed on both sides and

brought face downwards into slime and mud. A voice was yelling into his ear: 'Stop it! Stop it!' He recognized the voice: it was young Jerry Fulton's. Then another voice, a remembered voice, Fox's: he was telling him to stop yelling. He wasn't yelling, it was the barrage, but Fulton was shouting, 'If the barrage stops he'll pinpoint us, sir.'

What was he on about? What were they all on about? He wasn't shouting, his mouth was full of blood and mud. He would swallow it; he was choking. And why were they in the river? They were dragging him along the edge of the river. They were going to drown him. By hell, they weren't. He would die his own way.

His arms began to work, flailing at his captors. That was it: he had fought them off, yet they were dragging him uphill. Why couldn't he feel his head? Had he lost it, like Ferguson or whoever that was? His mind gave him no answer, for at that moment it seemed he was lifted straight up into the sky and he knew that now he had only half a body . . .

Had he found that out straight away or did he learn of it later, when they kept sticking needles into the part of him that felt as though it wasn't there? It was then he hit out and yelled at them, at those voices that kept saying, 'He shouldn't be here. We can't sleep.' They were fools, all fools; no one slept in hell. You had to work if you were in hell. Stand up for yourself. Tell them you weren't a coward, you hadn't run away. But that was another thing. He couldn't speak, only yell . . . and then his mother had come and held him.

'You all right, Matthew?'

Matthew blinked his sightless eyes, and then replied, 'Yes . . . yes, I'm all right. I . . . I wanted to see you, Jerry. You're . . . you're off today, I hear.'

'Yes . . . yes, I told you.'

'I . . . . I'll miss you.'

'And me you; but you're getting along fine. Amazingly well. And your family are so happy about it.'

'Jerry?'

'Yes?'

'What does Nurse Ducksworth actually look like?'

Jerry bit deeply on his lower lip and, after drawing it in between his teeth, he said, 'That's a question that's going to be difficult to answer.'

'Why? Why should it be?'

'Because . . . well, she's not what you think. I mean . . . you . . . well, the night that you were upset she played the mother, and in her helpful way she went along with it by saying she was fiftyish.'

There was a pause before Matthew said, 'And she's not?'

Jerry's laugh was clear now. 'No,' he said; 'no, she's not, Matthew. She's twenty-four years old.'

'What!'

'I said she's twenty-four years old.'

There was a snap in Matthew's tone as he said, 'And you'll be telling me next she's a long-legged blonde.'

'No; she's long-legged all right, but she's not a blonde. Brown hair, brown eyes and a lovely face that matches her nature.'

'Why the hell couldn't you tell me this before?'

Jerry bent towards the angry counte-nance. 'Just because, if I had, she would not have bothered so much with you. You wouldn't have got her holding you and prac-tically rocking you that night as she did. And stroking your hair and holding your hand since. She could do it because you thought she was a middle-aged woman, in fact you took her for your mother. Have you forgotten that? You called her Mama in your nightmarish condition, or whatever it was, and the way she looks she can't afford to act her age, particularly with fellows like us who crave sympathy. You know we do.'

Matthew's jaws were grinding now, and when he said, 'I've been made to look a blasted fool,' Jerry answered:

'Yes . . . yes, of course you have, but only to yourself and me.'

'I've told my folks about the motherly nurse, and Mama said she was going to write to her; and if I know anything, when they meet the motherly nurse, if ever they do, they'll have a damn good laugh because—'

His self-pitying tirade was interrupted by Jerry's quiet rejoinder, 'I'm telling you this, chum: she saved your bacon that night because you were ready for going over the edge again. Although you were crying it out you were in a hell of a state, and had been for weeks. They were to send you for special treatment, you know, but then she took you on; and I know she only did it because you imagined she was a middle-aged woman. If she had given half the attention to some of the fellows here that she gave to you they would have eaten her alive. So I say again, you should be grateful . . . By the way, I said goodbye to Charlie Fox a while ago. He wants to come along and see you. That all right?'

'Yes . . . yes, I'd like to see him . . . But about yourself. What're you actually going to do?'

'Oh, go back to where I left off. Old Beeching has kept my job open. I'd done my last year in accountancy, and the agreement was I'd be taken on in the firm and he's kept his word. I'll have an office of my own, and one day, some day . . . well, say twenty years' time'—he laughed now—'I may become a partner.'

There ensued a silence between them until Matthew asked quietly, 'Can you see well with your one eye?'

'With glasses, yes, very well; without them, it's a different bag of tricks. I can make things out, but only through a sort of mist.'

'The other eye . . . what happened?'

'Oh, they put a glass one in. Everyone says it looks natural and all right, but you have only to stare into a mirror . . . You know, I can't say you're lucky, I'm not meaning that, Matthew, because it's damned awful the set-up you're in, yet nevertheless there's not a blemish on your face and no one on God's earth would think you're blind. And you know something? There is a possibility, I understand, that you could get your sight back, if . . .'

'Oh, shut up! man. You should know better than to talk to me in that fashion. My sight is blown to hell.'

'It isn't blown to hell. You've still got your eyes. They say it's the nerves at the back have gone, or some such.'

'Yes, or some such. Now shut up about it. Anyway'—his voice altered—'let me say again, Jerry, I'm going to miss you.'

'And me you, Matthew. I'll never forget how decent you were to me when I first entered . . . the "drawing room". I'd heard about you further back in the lines. Bit of a devil you were, some of them said, but on that day when I almost fell into your tent your hand came out and steadied me; then you shook hands with me and you said, "Welcome to the drawing room"; and this greeting and your manner to me in the days ahead helped me to ignore Lieutenant Ferguson, who was ignoring the second lieutenant who was neither Eton, Harrow, Oxford or Cambridge, yet *was* from the same town. People imagine that the war killed snobbery. Well, I think it killed everything but. That was the second time I had been posted into his company, so he knew all about me; and right from the beginning I didn't speak his language. I got a shock, I may tell you, when I saw him that day, but you helped me through that patch and I'll always be grateful.'

Matthew wanted to reply, 'Don't talk such nonsense. You know you repaid anything you felt you owed me on that particular night that neither you, Fox nor I will ever forget . . . and the reason why.' Instead he held out his hand, and Jerry gripped it, saying, 'I'll find out where they're sending you. They'll be wanting to fix you up in some kind of profession fairly soon, you know. Whatever happens, I'll look in on you.'

'Thank you, Jerry. They tell me I'm due for a month's leave once I can manage the sticks. Why not come for the weekend? It isn't all that far from Carlisle. Take down

the address: The Beavors, Little Fellburn.
It's about two or three miles outside the
town. You can get a train from Carlisle to
Newcastle, then one from there to Fellburn.
A bus'll take you along the main road. It
stops at Manor Grove, and five minutes
walk along the towpath from there will
bring you to our gates. You can't miss it.
We've got a small farm attached but the
house lies some way beyond. You might
find it interesting. It's rather an odd place
and I know you'll be very welcome. You've
captivated my mother, I feel sure of that.'

'She captivated me; she's a lovely
woman.'

'And my father talked to you. That was
something. He can't bear strangers, not
since this other business hit him. I don't
know how on earth he got here, for he refused to come in his wheelchair.'

'I found him a most pleasant man,
kindly. What is actually wrong with him?'

'Multiple sclerosis, but it's attacked him
late in life, and so, I understand, it's a
slower business; nevertheless it's hellish
both for him and Mama. He was so active,
so full of life. He was in the army, too, you
know.'

'No! In the army?'

'Oh yes; colonel, no less. That's why I had to take over from him. I didn't want to. No . . . but then my elder brother William scooted off to America just like that; walked out one day, leaving a letter, and that was that. He's been in the car business there ever since and doing well. There's five years between us, and Father didn't seem to notice me until he lost William. Then it was about that time, of course, that the illness struck him. So, for me, it was Sandhurst instead of Oxford. And that was a mistake.'

Jerry put in, 'No it wasn't. It certainly wasn't; you were a splendid officer. And you stuck it for four years . . . well, practically to the end, when we were all unlucky. And you had only one leave in all that time, I understand.'

'That was my own fault, Jerry, for I knew that once I got home I'd never go back.'

The words had been spoken low and slowly, and Jerry made no answer to them for some time; then he said, 'Most of us felt like that. I know I did. I was petrified at times and scared that the men would notice it.'

Matthew made no comment; he knew that Jerry was being kind, as always, trying to make him forget the sight of his gun spiraling through the fairy light.

'Goodbye, Jerry.'

'Goodbye Matthew. Be seeing you soon.' He was about to add, 'Keep your pecker up,' but you didn't say things like that to a fellow like Matthew Wallingham; and on this thought he could hear Lt Ferguson saying, 'Inanities grate on me.'

Oh, to hell with memories of Ferguson and all his type! He himself was out of it, he was free. All he had to do was to get on with his job, find a nice girl, get married and have a family. He wanted a family, to be of a family. He had been brought up by an aunt and uncle since his parents died when he was seven years old, and they were kind. They were good, God-loving, God-fearing, but they weren't like a family. Now the captain back there, he had a family, marvellous people. His father, mother, his younger brother and two sisters. He had heard there was also a grandmother somewhere, a grandmother whom they all laughed about, an old terror she seemed. Yes, in a real family there was al-

ways an old terror. And now there was another brother in America. He envied Matthew. He stopped in his striding along the
corridor. Did he envy Matthew? No! dear
God, no! Because all the families in the
world couldn't make up for sightless eyes.

3

The house would have appeared square in shape, and uninteresting, were it not for an annexe jutting out from the left side, which could have been a bungalow but for the two dormer windows protruding from the roof like two enormous eyes. These windows were almost buried in clematis *montana rubra,* which had crept from the base of the house and clawed its way on to the main building and up to the high group of ornamental chimneys. But there it must have been checked, for the large slate roof of The Beavors was clear of creeper, as were the twin chimneys on the right side of the house.

The main house was built of stone, large blocks of it, each facing stone having been specially trimmed before finding its place in the structure, and the whole presented a warm creamy texture which, like the roof, was in no way marred by any greenery. The low stone-flagged terrace ran the length of the house. There was no rail to the terrace, nor step, for it lay flush with the deep green lawn, beyond which, and facing the front of the house, were well laid-out flow-erbeds.

On the ground floor were six windows, all large with sloping sills, and symmetri-cally placed between them stood the door. It was made of dark brown oak reinforced with six iron hinges stretching the width of it. On the upper floor were eight windows, four the pattern of those below, the rest smaller and flat-faced. There were no other windows to be seen at this side of the house.

There was no approachway for any ve-hicle to the front of the house, other than perhaps a bicycle that could be pushed, but beyond the right side wall was a large area that contained a stable block consist-ing of three loose-boxes and a barn-like structure, the entrance to which would take two coaches abreast if the yard it faced on to had been accessible. But it was no longer so, the drive to it having been cut off three hundred feet from the house. The trap and other vehicles were housed at the farm.

It was an early November morning. The countryside lay under a white frost but, inside, the house was warm. The heat from the open log fire in the hall, together with the smell of cooking coming from the kitchen, was rising to the first landing and to Matthew, standing for a moment, warily feeling with his foot for the first stair.

He hadn't descended more than three stairs when the sound of a piano note being struck three or four times brought him to a halt, and he hesitated again while tilting his head down and towards the door from behind which the sound was coming.

When the notes formed a little trill he almost hurried down the remainder of the broad staircase. Reaching the bottom, he immediately put his stick into his right hand and thrust out his left as if searching for something, and like this he made his way towards a corridor and the first door in it. Thrusting it open he demanded, 'What are you doing with that, Tommy?'

The small man, with very short legs but

a large head, turned towards him, saying, 'Well, what d'you think, Mr Matthew? I'm tuning her.'

'Who told you to?'

'The old 'un'—his large head bobbed backwards—'the old lady along there. Get at it, she says, no matter what he says. And I'm doing just that.'

'Well, you can stop doing just that because I have no intention of using it. I've told her.'

'Oh, she said you have. But d'you think she takes any notice of you or anybody else, or ever has done?' He now struck two notes, saying, 'Anyway, use it or not, it's a sin to let an instrument like this rot. It's five months since I last laid hands on it.'

'Well, you can stop laying hands on it now and get yourself out.'

'Not me, Mr Matthew; I wouldn't dare go back to the old 'un. She's a good customer. Not many of them have their instruments tuned twice a year, sometimes more; but then, she uses it. Eeh! my. Use it she did, during the war. She used to knock hell out of Wagner every time there was a ship sunk. You could have heard her in the town, never mind the village. But then, I don't think she's ever played a soft piece of music in her life. She really should've been in a percussion band. I wouldn't have put it past her many a time if she had got one of those constructions that play a dozen instruments themselves. Hands, feet and boomps-a-daisy!' He now ran his fingers right up the keys of the piano, and when Matthew moved nearer he said to him quietly, 'You know, Mr Matthew, I'm being serious now: it would do you the world of good if you got your hand in again. You were always good at it, you know. Oh aye; not right up to concert-platform stuff, but you were good at what you did. You had a touch. So why don't you have a go, eh?'

Matthew's voice was quiet too: 'It's no use, Tommy. I could never play much by ear anyway.'

'Well, once you started you would find it coming back like natural. Look at Art Tatum, blind as a bat. Rachmaninov said he had the quickest fingers on the piano he had ever heard. It would give you a pastime, something to aim at. You don't want to be Middle C all your life, do you? Even handicapped as you are.'

He now banged on the C. 'You know, I've learnt about life from these keys, and I feel that half the population don't know they're born. They never look inside themselves—well, if they do, it's just to envy somebody else making money or getting on in life. They don't think that they could have done much the same in some way or other if they'd made the effort. All right, a lot of them have had a bad start like meself. You know what they were going to do with me when I was ten? Put me in a home for the neither-here-nor-there, because I couldn't read. And they would've done it. Me own dad. But I had an aunt and she had a piano, an old thing with a fretwork front and green baize behind it, and if ever a piano needed tuning that one did. Apparently from the time I'd been a small child, every time I went to her house I got at those keys and I dinged out a tune; so it was she who said to my parents, if you keep him at home I'll pay for his lessons. So they kept me at what you would call home, but I had a hell of a life because I had four brothers and two sisters. And you talk about Germans being cruel! You don't have to go any further than your own family at times. But anyway, me Aunt Ethel had her way and I ended up playing in a band. Well, it was sort of playing at half-a-crown-a-night do's. But I was still going through hell. I was a funny little man, you see, but not in a comedian's way, else I would've made a fortune. I couldn't tell a joke, I couldn't make people laugh. When people laughed I died inside. Anyway, I didn't remain Middle C. D'you get what I mean? I'll never reach Top C, I knew that from the beginning, but I left that band, determined to have a profession. Although I wasn't a good pianist I loved the piano; I loved it for itself.

'In the end, one day I got my chance to help build a piano in the factory I was working in. I was living with me aunt at that time, had been for some years, and I'd been six years in the factory when she said to me, "You'll never be a Paderewski, but you love the blooming thing so much it's like a baby to you, so you could go out and nurse other people's babies, become a piano tuner."

'Candidly, I'd never thought of it, but that's what I did, and from the first visit I made I learnt about people, those in the

Base and those in the Top Cs, and the multitude in Middle C.'

'Well, you can put me down for one of your Middle Cs because I won't be playing that, Tommy,' said Matthew gravely.

'You never know. You never know, Mr Matthew. You can't sit doing nothing all your days. The army, I suppose, will put you into some kind of a job; they always do.'

'Not in this case; I'm going to stay on the farm and learn to milk the cows and the rest.'

'Oh well, that'll be something, but I can't see that satisfying you.'

'No? Why not?'

'Well, because I remember you before this business started. You were going places: you were a rip, just like Mr William used to be before he went off to the States. But there you are: once I get going on family records I forget to stop. I must get on.'

Matthew went out of the room, actually laughing now. It was a long time since he had laughed to himself. Tommy was a character: he and his Middle C. Well, he had joined that majority, because there was nothing else for him, because he would never leave this house or these grounds again. He would learn some way to farm; and that would be his life and he would accept it. There was nothing else for it. It would be a quiet, peaceful life.

He now made his way to the end of the corridor, into a small hall, off which went four doors. Standing just within the hall, he called, 'Where are you?'

And a voice came back to him, 'I'm in the sitting room.'

He put out a hand and made his way, still tentatively, towards the door next to the one leading into the conservatory, and opening it, he said, 'You're up early.'

'No; you're up late, it's a quarter to ten.' Then he realised that to someone standing beside her she was saying, 'Take the tray, Mary, and don't rattle it; you'd think you were getting old.'

The answer he heard was, 'Huh!' And when the elderly woman passed him with the tray, he said in his usual voice, 'She was always so gracious for a good deed, wasn't she, Mary?'

'You've said it, Mr Matthew. Never changes.'

Then the gruff voice hit him again, saying sharply, 'Sit down! Matthew. Don't tell me, I know why you're here. And yes, Tommy will go along there and tune that piano every six months. He's early this time. What d'you expect to do with your days? Sit picking your nails?'

'No, Granan, I've told you. I've told them all. I want to try my hand at farming.'

'Farming be damned! Teaching was what you had set your mind to before all this started: history and the piano. That might have been a youthful choice, but nevertheless it was there. Bleeding army! Why the devil I married into it I'll never know! But once I was in, I let them know what I thought of it. Your grandfather'—she laughed abruptly here, a deep, almost manly sound—'your grandfather used to shake in his shoes every time there was a drawing-room night. He used to say he'd rather face a battalion of conscientious objectors any day. But I can tell you something—the men loved me, but the women hated my guts, even though they made excuses for me, because I didn't come of military stock. Then what happened to your father when he was born? He was put

down for the army before he was chris-
tened.

'Then, years later, old Bertie, your great-
grandfather, baptized your brother William
with champagne. Poured it over the child's
head. Here was another victim to be
trained to blow somebody's brains out; and
what did William go and do? You know,
Matthew,' her voice dropped to an even,
soft note now as she said, 'even your
mother doesn't know this. But the day William walked out, just left that note to say
he wasn't going into any army, he was going off to the States, I came into this room
and I laughed until I cried, 'cos I liked William. I could talk to William, like . . . well,
like I can to you. William and you were very
alike. Rodney's the odd one out.' Her voice
froze now. 'There's a farmer for you, hand-
made. I don't know what he would have
done had he been made to join up. Because the job he was doing was helping
to feed the nation, he was left alone—and
now he thinks he owns the blessed place.
Well, the farm anyway. He can talk of nothing else. I'm going to tell you something,
Matthew.' She put out her hand, and he
took the bony fingers between his own and

gripped them as she went on, 'No matter how he appears, he's not happy about you wanting to take over.'

Like a crack of a whip his voice came back, 'I don't want to take over, Granan, last thing in my mind. All I want to do is to work for him, for him to teach me what to do.'

'You're the eldest now, Matthew. And don't forget, one day you will be in charge. It'll all be yours, and it's a nice little estate. None better for miles around. Anyway, Richard might live for a long time yet. He contracted this MS business late in life, and they tell me that because of this the disease will not gather pace so quickly. So he could live another two or three, or even ten years, and like you he's stiff-necked and doesn't give in easily.'

'Oh! Granan.' Matthew was shaking his head at her. 'I've given in; I did some time ago. You know . . . huh! . . . Tommy has been telling me where I stand. He has a theory about the piano and our various places in life.'

'Oh yes, Middle C. And where did he put you? Don't tell me Middle C, just because you won't play?'

'That's right.'

'Nevertheless, he's a very wise man, is Tommy. He was from Bog's End, you know, in the town, but he was brought up mostly in the village down there. His own parents were scum. They're both dead now, I understand; it's a pity they didn't die earlier. But his aunt lived on until about five or six years ago. He was in his forties then, and what d'you think? He got married.'

'He's married? I never knew that.'

'No. Well, you wouldn't. It was about the time you went overseas. And she's a nice little body, a widow, and a bit younger than him. But he's come into his own since he took her on. Couldn't get a word out of him, you know, years ago; now he talks the nose off a brass monkey.'

'I'm glad to hear that,' said Matthew, softly now, 'because he always made me feel sorry for him in some way, he seemed so lonely.'

'Well, he was lonely. It's an awful thing, loneliness. It's like a tapeworm, keeps eating at you. Anyway, he hasn't got it any more; it's as if the wife acted on him like a dose of salts.' And she let out a deep rumbling laugh as she said, 'That's a good simile, isn't it?'

Matthew got to his feet. He, too, was laughing, and bending towards her he said, 'No, Granan, that wasn't a good simile; it was a piece of unladylike crudeness. I'm sorry for all those women in that drawing room years ago who had to suffer you.'

'So am I, boy. So am I'—she patted his arm—'at least I was. But not any more, because I met some of them after they came back from India. They were worse. They had been used to so many damned servants that they treated the ones here like serfs. As for morality! I could tell you some tales.'

'I bet you could, and when it snows and I can't get out, I'll come along and keep you to your word.'

As he made for the door, she stopped him, saying gently, 'Here a minute, Matthew.' And when he turned about she said, 'I worry about you. You keep sitting in that room up there too much. What's happened to you has happened and nothing can cure it. If you want to talk about it at any time you know who to come to, and it'll be better getting it out of your system than brooding on it. Look upon me as that old night nurse Lucille said was so good to you. In fact, she said she pulled you round.'

'Well, I suppose you could say that, she pulled me round; but I've got a surprise for you. You would never be able to play her part, not now, not at your age, because what d'you think? She wasn't what I took her to be, what she gave the impression she was: kicking fifty, a middle-aged nurse, very motherly, oh yes, very motherly. Guess what I felt like when, just before he left, Jerry Fulton told me that my savior, so to speak, was no motherly figure but a long-legged beauty of twenty-three or twenty-four? Brown hair, brown eyes, lovely skin. From how he described her, she had everything. Now guess what I felt like.'

'Well, how did you feel?'

'An absolute fool.'

She flapped his hand away from her, saying, 'Then you *are* a fool. She must have had some feeling for you to look after you as she did and keep up that pretense.'

'Well, as it was explained to me, if she

had shown the same attention to the other fellows in the main ward they would have eaten her alive. I couldn't see her, and that made the difference.'

The old woman slid back into her chair, asking quietly, 'What's her name?'

'Ducks.'

'What?' It was a loud enquiry.

'Well, her name is Elizabeth Ducksworth, but she is known as Ducks.'

'Well, where is she now?'

'The last I heard of her, she was at the other end of the hospital on day duty; and apparently nurses were not encouraged to visit old patients, especially blind or near-blind ones. It had something to do with emotions,' and he stressed the word.

'Well I never! Does your mother know, I mean that she wasn't an elderly woman, this nurse?'

'I don't know; I've never discussed it with her.'

'I'm the first one you've told?'

'Yes.'

'Thank you, dear. Have you got her address?'

'No; and I don't want it. What can I offer her?'

'Get yourself out! Go on! Get yourself out.'

The voice was hoarse and harsh again, and he went out smiling ruefully.

4

'Why don't you sit down a minute, Lucille, and talk to me?' said Colonel Wallingham.

'I talk to you all the evening, dear,' said his wife, 'and sometimes half the night, but there's so much to do. Cook had Rosie in tears this morning. She forgets that we're lucky to have Rosie. These days most young girls of sixteen don't like going into service and, at times, she's such a help to Mary and Bella.'

'But what is there to do?'

'There are two more bedrooms to see to for one thing. Don't forget you've got two daughters coming with their husbands, and two grandchildren. I'll have to ask Rodney to go along to Granan's part of the house, because the children must have a room to themselves. She won't like that, but I can't send the children along to Granan's, she can't stand them. She makes so much noise herself yet can't stand anybody else making it.' And saying this, she pushed her husband's shoulder where he sat in a deep armchair near the fire, and then she added on a laugh, 'Anyway, there's the party. You'll love the party.'

'Go on with you; get yourself away.'

She bent over and kissed his brow, saying, 'I'll be back as soon as I can, dear. But there's another thing: I'm worried about Matthew. He's so taciturn: he can sit there for half an hour and not open his mouth. Of course if you mention the war or anything to do with it he's on his feet and out. Do you understand that?'

'I do. I do, Lucille . . . Well, in a way I do.'

'You know, he never wanted to go into the army; it was never his choice, it was yours. Now you must own up to that.'

'I don't and I won't. He was a man.'

'He was not a man, not really. He was just coming out of boyhood. You know something?' She burst out laughing now. 'I sometimes feel like Granan. Yes, I do. She was, to use her own words, bloody well thrown into this army gang because she was the eldest of five daughters. As she said, in those days if you weren't married you might as well go and shoot yourself. So she thought it would be better to go and watch others doing it, and your father, you know, was army-mad. Long after he retired he imagined he was still in command. You remember him bawling from the top of the stairs, "ANN-EE! ANN-EE! Here this minute, woman!"? Then Granan would go to him and say, "What d'you want?" And he, just like you, would say, "I want to talk to you."

'But you must admit I'm more polite than Granan was, because more often than not her answer was, "Go to hell and take a couple of guns with you." '

He said quietly, 'I'm not like him, am I? Well, not as bad?'

'No, Richard; you're not as bad.' Then bending towards him again, she said more loudly now, 'You're worse sometimes.' And with this she hurried from the room, her laughter making him smile.

It was four o'clock in the afternoon when Peter Carter brought Matthew back from a visit to his colonel. Peter Carter had been Colonel Wallingham's batman in the army, and when the colonel had to retire early, once multiple sclerosis was diagnosed, Peter too had asked for his discharge in order to continue to look after him. It had been no hardship for him to take on Mr Matthew too, although at times it was a difficult task as the younger man disliked assistance of any kind and managed mostly for himself, except when he left the grounds. These he knew like the back of his hands. As yet the colonel did not often need night attention once he had settled him in bed, and so Peter kept to his rooms at the top of the house, which were well furnished and comfortable. He had two pastimes that were assets to the colonel: he was an excellent chess player and he loved crosswords. And in a way it was fortunate that his younger master was of the same mind, although as yet he was not so expert in the former as either his father or Peter, for with chess he had to speak his passes. With crosswords, though, Matthew was way ahead of both Peter and his father, his answer to most clues coming sharp and crisp. They could go through four papers a day with crosswords, and once a week the men of two neighbouring families, the McArthurs and the Hendersons, would drop in and form a four for bridge. Naturally special cards had to be used, and Mr Matthew was becoming expert at it . . .

Bella had opened the front door to the two men, saying, 'What a day! It's a snifter, and there's flakes coming down.'

'Well, you wouldn't expect them to go up, would you, Bella?'

'Oh, Peter!' She had almost said 'Mr Peter', because it seemed he was treated as one of the family; but in the kitchen the others said he wasn't really, and he was no better than the outside men because he had been just the colonel's batman before the war, nothing else. But he was nice and well liked.

'You look froze, Mr Matthew.'

'I am, Bella, and you know what that spells.'

'Yes, Mr Matthew, a pot of hot tea.'

'You're right, Bella,' and in a lower tone, he added conspiratorially, 'and ask Cook if she has a drop left of her medicine to put in the teapot.'

Bella's reaction was a high giggling laugh as she answered, 'I'll tell her that, Mr Matthew. I will.'

'You do, and see what she says.'

'Oh, *there* you are, dear'—Lucille had now entered the hall—'You look frozen, both of you.'

'So we've been told, Mama; and it's all right, Bella's had her orders, hot tea and', he added in a low voice, 'a little of Cook's medicine.'

'Oh, you didn't!'

'Yes, he did, mistress,' Peter put in, 'and that'll put Cook on her high horse; it'll be a skinty dinner we'll all get.'

As Peter made for the stairs, carrying Matthew's coat, hat and scarf, Lucille led her son towards the drawing room, and as his hand brushed the prickly leaves of the Christmas tree beside the door he paused and said, 'That in already?'

'Yes, it is, because I'm sure we're going to have snow for Christmas, probably well before, and it's an awful job bringing it in when it's wet.'

Matthew could smell the extra warmth of the drawing room and in it the scent of his father's cigar, and Richard's voice came at him, saying, 'Oh, hello there. So you've got back. You saw your colonel?'

'Yes, Father, yes, I saw the colonel.'

'How is he?'

'Oh, as usual: polite, diplomatic, kindly and inane.'

'Oh, Matthew, you're too hard on him. A bit dull, I admit, but he knows his job, and he was a good soldier. Still is, although I understand he's retiring next month.'

'Yes, he told me, and it seemed with deep regret.'

'Well, what did he say, dear? What did he suggest?'

'Oh, just what has been suggested before, Mama, that I take up an occupation. I have a choice: I can train to be an osteopath. And then there's the piano.' He laughed and added, 'Oh yes, Tommy should have been there when he was on about the piano. He recalled when I first joined the unit that I dinged out for them at impromptu dances in the mess, so couldn't I take that up again, seriously that is? Lots of men did. Oh, and just think, I could become a psychiatrist. He thought I'd have deep insight into that, and when I couldn't help adding, "And become madder than they were, sir?" he informed me very stiffly that people didn't go mad with shell-shock, they were only deeply troubled people who had lost their way for a time. At the end I thanked him warmly, but said I had already got a niche, I was going to learn farming.'

It was Lucille who now asked quietly, 'What did he say to that?'

She had to wait for his answer. ' "I think you'll find that more difficult than the other three suggestions." '

'And he's right there. Yes, he is.' His father's voice was loud. 'Definitely he's right. You forget you'll be dealing with animals, and they don't move out of your way when they see you. And neither does the bull; remember, he'll greet you head-on.'

'Well, I'll have to work that out. Oh, here's tea; thank the Lord for that.'

When he heard the tray being placed on the table he said, 'Is that you, Bella?' And she answered, 'Yes, Mr Matthew; it's me.'

'Did you give Cook my message?'

'Well . . .' Bella paused, then glanced at her mistress, saying, 'I don't think it would be wise of me to repeat what she said, Mr Matthew. She finished up by saying that if you could find any special doctor's medicine kicking around her kitchen she'd be glad to share it with you.'

They were all laughing now, Bella too, and as she made her way towards the door, she muttered on a giggle, 'She didn't mention anyone searching her bedroom, sir.'

The incident had lightened the atmosphere, and Lucille, still laughing, said, 'We can laugh, but what she calls her medicine will ruin her liver, if it hasn't already.'

'Well, she's been drinking for at least thirty years, to my knowledge,' Richard put in, 'so what's done is done, I should think, and it hasn't spoilt her cooking. She's the best cook in these parts, in spite of rationing. The Hendersons and the McArthurs jump at the invitations to dinner, not forgetting the Marshalls and the Taggarts.'

'Yes. Yes.' Lucille sighed now, then began to pour out the tea. She handed a cup first to her husband, and then to her son, before sitting down with her own and saying, 'Let's get back to the career business. Are you really set on trying your hand at the farm, Matthew?'

'It isn't that my heart is set on it, Mama; it seems the only right thing for me to do. I know every inch of the grounds and the house; I can find my way about; I can handle a horse; and what's more I feel I could be of real help to Rodney.'

When neither parent made any remark on this Matthew said harshly, 'Well; I could give it a try, couldn't I? and if I feel I'm going to be in anybody's way or upset the routine then I'll give it up and think again.'

'Yes. Yes, I think that's the best way: give it a try first. But let's get Christmas over, then you can really make up your mind what you're going to do,' said Lucille. Matthew noted that his mother had ended her suggestion on a long sigh.

He did not have to wait until the new year to make up his mind what he was going to do. Two events the following day settled his future.

5

The sky was heavy, the air biting, and the ground was still white with a heavy frost when Matthew stood in the courtyard with his mother and Peter, and said for the third time, 'Look, I'm all right. I'll keep on the verge, and if there's anything coming I've just got to hold up this thing'—he lifted his white stick—'and they'll keep out of my way, that is, whoever is trying to pass in a vehicle; and once I get to the far end of the drive I'll give a shout for Rodney or whoever's about.'

'It isn't the drive that's worrying me,' said Lucille: 'it's the animals and things in the farmyard, and machinery and such.'

Matthew turned to Peter. 'Take her into the house, will you? She'll freeze out here, and in that thin coat.' He plucked at the material of his mother's sleeve, adding, 'We must get Father to buy you a sheepskin coat for Christmas.'

'I have a sheepskin coat, thank you. Come along, Peter; just leave him. It's not a bit of good. He doesn't care whom he upsets so long as he gets his own way.'

'She's right, Peter. I don't care whom I upset, so take her indoors, for goodness' sake! I'm off.'

He now turned from them and, with out-stretched arm, walked smartly in the direction of the stables; at the end of them, he turned into the drive and, more slowly now and keeping to the verge, he made for the farm.

From the sounds ahead some minutes later he knew he was nearing the yard, and he slowed his pace until he came to the end of the grass verge. He knew where the farm buildings began: first the workshop, then the tack room.

He was about to call out his brother's name when he heard his voice. It was coming from the tack room and was loud, almost shouting. 'You'll have to see to him, Benny. As for getting another man, as you suggest, we can't afford it unless you want your wages dropped.'

'I could see to him, Mr Rodney, I mean, show him the milking. I'd keep an eye on him and . . .'

'You have your hands full already, Joe, with one thing and another, so, as I said, it's Benny here who'll have to take him in hand.'

'And I can take him in hand, Mr Rodney, I've already said that. But I've also said that since most of my work is now done in this room—mending the tack, and watering and feeding and mucking out—the poor fellow's not going to learn much from me. So, as I dared to say before . . .'

'Well, don't say it again, Benny. Don't make use of your age, like Joe here, and position to tell me what I should do. Two-thirds of my day is taken up with work in the office filling out forms. It's all a damn nuisance.'

A quiet voice came in answer to this, saying, 'I don't suppose Mr Matthew himself finds it much of a picnic; to find yourself like that's enough to drive you round the bloody bend. You weren't in the war, were you? Well, I was. Two years of it, and

I suppose I was lucky because I was behind the lines most of the time, bringing up supplies. I think those who weren't in it would be wise to keep their mouths shut and help the poor beggars . . .'

'You said something there, Taylor. It would be wise to keep your own mouth shut for a start. It opens a bit too much at times. You should remember there are men calling in for jobs every week.'

'Oh, I could say to hell with you and your job any minute. I know you only keep me on because I can do twice as much work as the rest, and drive the bloody tractor and such. And I've heard your opinion of me: more brawn than brains, you've said. Well, I'm telling you, I work because I like work, and to my mind good farming comes of good work, not sitting on your arse most of the time, not figuring out how much you're going to make over and above a decent profit. So any time you like, Mr Wallingham, I'll have me cards.'

As he banged the door closed behind him Jim Taylor caught sight of the figure walking away along the grass verge, and in a second he was running after him. Suiting his step to Matthew's, he said, 'Sorry, sir. You likely heard all that. Look, don't worry, I'll stay on and give you a hand.'

'Thank you, Jim, but . . . but I had come down to tell my brother I wasn't going to take up the farm business.'

'You had?'

'Yes.'

'Honest?'

When there was no response, Jim Taylor stared at the stiff countenance, and through him ran a wave of intense pity that softened his rough Northern voice as he said, 'You're too good for farming, sir. There's dozens of jobs men like you can take up. All kinds of things. There's that new hospital outside Newcastle. One part of it is for men whose limbs are broken, bad backs and things, and there are blind men attending to them, masseurs and people like that.'

They were well along the drive now and out of sight of the farm. Matthew stopped and, turning to the man, he said, 'Thank you very much, Jim; you're a good fellow. Do me a favour, will you? Don't say anything about finding me outside; I'll just tell my brother when I see him later that I've changed my mind. Understand?'

'Yes, sir. Yes, I understand.'

Matthew did not move, and it was as if they were looking at each other when he said, 'What were you before the war?'

'I lived with my family on a farm; but I was in cars. I love cars, sir. But you can't get work in them now for love nor money. Two places in Fellburn have girl mechanics, if you can believe it. Although they're as good as any man at the job, it isn't right, I think; and so when this job was going I was glad to take it. But it's like this, sir: if your father and mother ever think about getting a driver, now your father's not well, you can call on me.'

Matthew noted wryly that his own need to be driven hadn't been referred to, but he knew what was in the man's mind, and so he said, 'You will be the first to hear about it if they do, Jim.' He put out his hand, and Jim Taylor grabbed it, saying, 'I take that as a promise, sir.'

'Goodbye, Jim.'

'Goodbye, sir; and the best of luck, and . . . and it'll come your way, you'll see.'

There was a lump in Matthew's throat as he walked on. Once again there was that terrible feeling that he was about to cry. That his own brother didn't want him hadn't brought on the feeling; it was the kindness of that man just gone.

He was like Charlie Fox. Briefly, he wondered what had happened to Fox. He's have to enquire. Lately, he had been so eaten up with his own predicament that he'd forgotten about Fox and what he owed him . . .

Realising he was nearing the house, he told himself he mustn't go in yet; he'd walk in the garden, then in a roundabout way make his way to the annexe and Granan.

Yes, he'd go to Granan. At this moment, he needed somebody to talk to. Not his mother: she'd get so upset, and when she was upset his father would know, and the reason why.

He walked until the lump in his throat subsided; but then he began to feel cold, because there was no hurry in his walking: each step had to be tapped out and measured.

When he opened the side door into the annexe Mary met him with, 'Oh, Mr Matthew. You did give me a shock. I . . . I understood you were down at the farm.'

'No. I've just been walking round the garden, Mary, but I'm frozen to the bone; I hope you've got a good fire on.'

'Well, would you find your grandmother ever sitting in a room that hadn't a good fire on? Now I ask you!'

He laughed as she helped him off with his overcoat and scarf, and when, with a tug, she dislodged his cap he said, 'Hang on a minute! I've just had my hair set; you'll take all the curl out of it.'

'Go away with you! Would you like a coffee?'

'I would, Mary. Thank you.'

A voice now greeted them, calling, 'Stop that jawing out there and come in and get warm.'

When he entered the sitting room his grandmother was on her feet and saying, 'I thought you were going to start at the farm this morning?'

Matthew didn't answer until, taking his arm, she said, 'Sit down; your hands are frozen. Weren't you wearing gloves?'

'No.'

'Well, you're stupid.'

'I know that.'

They exchanged no further words until

they were alone, when she said, 'What is it? You're troubled.' Receiving no answer she asked, 'Something happened at the farm?'

'You could say that.'

'Yes, and I could say that, because I fully expected it. He doesn't want you there.'

His head jerked up and it was as if his gaze were fully on her because she said, 'Yes, you can look at me like that, but he's come to think of that place as his own. Mind, he put a lot of work into it during the war. But he's got too big for his boots of late, and I think your father's aware of it, because when Rodney keeps on about the milk and the extra lambs born and one thing and another your father never opens his mouth. But I must admit he was never very interested in the farm. Yet one feels when listening to Rodney you can get too much of a good thing: there are other topics in the world. So Richard hasn't gone down to the farm. His legs have got worse, we know, yet Peter could have pushed him down if he had wanted to go. What happened to you?'

'I don't want this to get to Mama or Father, Granan. You understand?'

'Of course I understand. By now you should know I'm no fool, and that what I want is a peaceful household, and of late it hasn't been quite that.'

'You mean since I came back into it?'

The words were sharp, and the answer was just as sharp. 'No, I don't, but long before that. Well, you could say, since the war started Rodney's acted as if the family's independence depended on his keeping the farm going. If we never get a penny from the farm we'd manage very well. Your father's got a good pension, your mother's got her own bit of money, and—' she ended on a quiver of a laugh—'my bedroom floorboards are well supported, and the mattress too.'

'Oh, Granan.' He leant forward and caught her hands. 'What would I do without you?' His voice was a mere whisper and her reply was just as low as she said, 'It's what would I do without you? I liked William, I liked Hazel when she was a child. I didn't care much for either Rodney or Amy but I loved you. Likely it was because you were the replica of your grandfather.'

'Oh, Granan. You're a wonderful woman. You act like a salve on a bruised soul.'

'Oh, I like the sound of that, quite po-
etical. A salve on a bruised soul, and yours
is bruised at the moment, boy, isn't it?
Anyway, tell me what happened at the
farm.'

Before he could start the door opened
and Mary came hurrying in with a cup of
coffee, saying, 'There's somebody on the
phone for you, Mr Matthew.'

'For me?' He got to his feet. 'Who is
it?'

'Lieutenant somebody. I didn't catch the
name. He said you would know.'

A minute later Matthew picked up the
phone, saying, 'Hello! there,' and Lieutenant Fulton's voice said, 'Guess who!'

'Oh, Jerry. Jerry! Oh, how pleased I am
to hear you! How are you?'

'Me? Oh, fine, couldn't be better. And
you?'

'Getting along, you know. Getting along.
Where are you speaking from?'

'Where d'you think? Your city, Newcastle.'

'No! What are you doing there?'

'Oh, it's a long story. The company's set
up another business there. One of the part-
ners is heading it, and I was very fortunate

that he chose me for an assistant. So I'm over here for a few days looking round for a flat.'

'You mean to live there?'

'Yes. Yes. But not only for the business. Wait for it. I'm . . . I'm going to be married.'

'No!'

'Yes. Somebody's fool enough to take me on. She was one of the secretaries in the office in Carlisle, in fact. Oh, it caused a stir.'

'Well . . . Well, I'm so glad. And you're going to live in Newcastle?'

'As she's from Middlesborough originally, we thought it better to have a house . . . well, it'll be a flat . . . near the job.'

'Oh, I'm so glad for you. All round, I am, Jerry.'

'I'm very glad for myself, I can tell you, Matthew. I never thought it would happen. But wait, I have another piece of news. Guess who I bumped into yesterday in Newcastle?'

'I wouldn't know.'

'Ducks.'

'Nurse Ducksworth?'

'Her very self. She's working in the new

hospital here on the outskirts, still among the wounded blokes. And, she tells me, Charlie Fox has a job there too. In fact, she and I are having a snap lunch together today. She's off for two hours then, she tells me. I have an idea. Could you join us?'

'You . . . you mean today? I mean . . .'

'Yes. Yes, that's what I'm saying. I mean today. I've got to go back first thing tomorrow.'

There was silence before Matthew replied, 'Oh, I don't see how I can get in so quickly. What time is it now?'

'Ten minutes to eleven. How long does a taxi take from your place to Newcastle?'

'Oh, about half an hour . . . less.'

'Well, what's to stop you taking a taxi?'

There was another pause before Matthew said, 'Yes. What's there to stop me taking a taxi? Yes, Jerry, I'll be with you. Where shall we meet?'

'Outside the station. I'll be on the lookout for you.'

'I can't wait. See you later then, Jerry.'

'Fine. Fine. Oh, it'll be good to see you again! So long for now.'

'So long, Jerry.'

Matthew replaced the receiver, then

stood awhile before turning and, almost at a shambling run, crossing the hall and making for the corridor leading to the annexe again.

'That was Jerry on the phone, Granan. Jerry Fulton, you know, who was with me through all the grey days, and in the next bed. You've heard of him.'

'Oh yes. Yes. Of course. What about him?'

'He's . . . he's in Newcastle. Going to work there. In fact, he's going to be married and live there, and he would like to see me, so I'm going in.'

'Good. It'll do you good. And why don't you bring him back with you? He could stay the night.'

'Oh, he's got to return home early tomorrow. But I'll invite him when he's settled here. You'll like him. He's a good chap.'

'Well, if you like him I'll like him. I'm sure of that. So go on, get yourself changed. Make yourself look smart. But don't try getting to the farm gates on your own. You don't want to bump into a runaway pig in the yard, do you? Get Peter to take you down. You have a taxi coming?'

'Oh Lord no! I forgot to phone.' As,

laughing, he turned from her, she nodded towards his back, thinking to herself: Must be some kind of a fellow, this Jerry, to make him look like that. He sounded excited too. Well, well. And I haven't heard what happened at the farm, but I will, I suppose, before the night's out.

She turned now to where Mary was lifting up the tray from the table and remarking, 'His coffee's cold. I'll get Bella to take him a fresh cup upstairs.'

'No; don't bother, Mary. I don't suppose he wants one now.'

'No, I don't suppose he does. He sounded excited, didn't he, madam? And he looked a bit like his old self. He must be very fond of his friend.'

'Yes.' The old woman nodded at the elderly Mary, whom, within herself, she claimed as having been a friend over all the past years. 'Yes, Mary, he sounded excited and he looked different and he must be very fond of his friend; and that's all I know at present and that's all you know at present. So don't go down to that kitchen expressing your views on Mr Matthew's changed attitude over a telephone call. You know what I mean?'

'Yes, madam; I know what you mean all right.' Then she added as if on an after-thought, 'I should do by now, shouldn't I, madam?'

'Yes, Mary, you should do.' They nodded at each other, which signified the session was over; and Annie Wallingham, sitting back in her chair, wished that the day was over and it was evening and her grandson was back and giving her some idea of what had made him as near happy as she had seen him since before he had put on a sol-dier's uniform.

6

It was a quarter to twelve when the taxi stopped outside the station and Jerry, pulling open the door, helped Matthew on to the pavement, where they stood shaking hands. The taxi driver, leaning forward, smiled at them, saying, 'That'll be twenty-two shillings, sir.'

'Oh yes, yes . . . sorry.' Matthew put his hand into his pocket, brought out a wallet, felt in the compartment and drew out a pound note; then, putting his hand back into his trouser pocket, he took out two half-crowns and, adding them to the note, he handed them to the taxi driver, saying, 'That'll cover it, eh?'

'Thank you, sir. Thank you. Do you want picking up again later?'

'I'm not sure. But I'll give your office a ring if I do.'

'Good enough.'

As the taxi drew away, Jerry, looking into the lean, almost haggard face of his friend, said, 'You're . . . you're looking fit.'

'I can't say the same to you, Jerry; but you sound more than fit . . . exuberant.'

'That's the word, and that's how I feel. The thought of starting a new life away from God . . . Oh, I shouldn't say that because my aunt and uncle have been very good to me, but prayers before and after meals get a bit too much, following on the army life. Added to which you always feel a stinker on Sunday because you won't go to chapel three times.'

'As bad as that?'

'Oh yes. So . . . so as soon as I come across a flat I'm moving into it and getting it ready for June. That's when Jackie and I are going to be married . . . Look! We're blocking the pavement. Let's walk along to the hotel.'

As they walked, Jerry said, 'Isn't it odd, the three of us coming together again, you, me and Fox . . . and then there's Ducks.'

A few minutes later, Jerry caught sight

of Nurse Ducksworth, but before he could say, 'There she is!' Matthew had already imagined he could smell her scent, the scent that wasn't a scent.

'Oh, hello there.' She took his hand in both hers. 'How lovely to see you. You're looking fine.'

Matthew's tone was actually cheerful when he spoke. 'If I remember rightly, Miss Ducksworth, you have taken lying to a fine art. Since I saw you last I've lost a stone in weight, what hair I had left is falling out, I've just this morning lost my farm job, and tomorrow I'm going to the labour exchange.'

Their joint laughter rang out, and in a like vein she remarked, 'Poor soul! What you need is a nurse, a motherly one.'

'You've said it. Definitely, that's what I need, and I'm going to put an advert in the paper. But she must have money; I need to be kept.'

'Shut up! Shut up, both of you, and get a move on, Liz. I've a table booked in there for half-past twelve, and we'll want a drink first.'

When Elizabeth's hand slipped through Matthew's arm, he caught at it and held it tight, even while he thought, Jerry called her Liz. But then he couldn't have called her Ducks; they no longer had the camaraderie of the hospital routine. Her hand was soft and firm, but it was cold, and he said, 'Haven't you any gloves?'

'Yes. Yes, of course I have. But I rarely wear them. I don't like gloves; I like my fingers free. Are you still serious about going into farming? I understood that's what you meant to do.'

'I did, until I found that horses kick, that chickens don't like being trampled on, and cows are such stupid things. They never get out of your way; they're like tractors and walk over you without compunction. I won't mention what pigs can do—when one gets loose, that is—nor bulls.'

They were laughing again as they were led to their table a little later. When seated, she said, 'Well, if it's not to be farming, have you thought of doing anything else?'

'Oh yes, I have a list; the only thing not on it is taking up the piano again. But we've got a very good tuner who tells me that if I put a handle on it, and four wheels, there's no reason why I shouldn't join a theatre queue.'

'Don't be silly!' Jerry said. 'You were a dab hand at tickling the ivories in the mess, if I remember rightly.'

And now it was as if they were back in hospital and the kindly middle-aged nurse, too, was saying, 'Yes, come on, Captain; don't be silly.'

'Yes, yes, I am being silly,' he said quietly; 'but then, what else d'you expect of me? I was always a trouble, you know that.'

'Yes I do, only too well; you were the worst patient I'd ever had.'

There was a pause before he said, 'You really mean that?'

'Yes, I really mean that. You were unruly, obstinate and ungrateful. And that's not all: I, too, could write a list.'

'Oh! Liz,' Jerry put in, 'he wasn't as bad as all that. There were times when he even spoke civilly to me; just occasionally.'

When they laughed across at him he did not join them. Then Jerry said softly, 'We're just pulling your leg, man; aren't we, Liz?'

Elizabeth's answer was to reach out and squeeze Matthew's hand as she said softly, 'Well, if he doesn't know that now, then he never will.'

Some seconds passed before Matthew said, 'I know you were joking, yet at the same time much of it is true. Looking back, I see I must have been a hell of a patient. Only this morning I had to pull myself together again when I realised I would only be a hindrance on the farm, and that now I really have to find out what I can do.'

'Well, we'll talk about that later,' said Jerry, 'when we have something hot inside us. Here comes the waiter, anyway. And I think it's a day for champagne. What d'you say, Liz?'

'I agree with you, Jerry.'

It had been a very good meal, spiced with lively conversation; and perhaps it was tact which made Jerry say, 'Will you excuse me a moment?' and then make for the men's room.

Left to themselves, there was an embarrassed silence before Matthew, groping for her hand across the table, said, 'It's wonderful to see you again, Nurse.' And he could see her: she had brown hair and beautiful brown eyes; he couldn't get the shape of her mouth in his mind yet, but he knew that her skin was soft and would be cream-tinted. He added now, 'Must I still address you as nurse? I notice that Jerry calls you Liz. That's very familiar, isn't it?'

'Not really. We became very friendly over you, when you were both in that little ward, and when he wasn't calling me Ducks he would call me Lizzie. And I don't like Lizzie. You see, I made the mistake of once telling him my Christian name. I don't know whether you realise it or not, but he was a great help to you during that difficult time.'

'Oh, I do. I do. And I'm very fond of him.'

'Good. And he's very fond of you, I can tell you that. He said you were the best man he was ever under.'

'Oh well, I can tell you'—he was laughing gently now—'there weren't many who shared his opinion. It was said, laughingly perhaps, that some of the young subalterns weren't so afraid of a skirmish as they were of being transferred to my company. So you can take it that Jerry was an exception.'

She made no remark on this, but said,

'Seriously, what are you thinking about doing?'

'Well, I haven't had much time since this morning.'

'I think you want to look at that list again; you could take up something like . . . well, osteopathy, I would think. There's one man taking psychiatry, and two partially blind fellows doing osteopathy—I mean in my hospital; and they'll be setting up practices of their own, once they're certified.'

'Who's going to be certified?'

Jerry had come back to the table, and Elizabeth said, 'You! We think it's necessary. But we've kept it quiet up till now.'

'Well, so long as they put me in your psychiatric block I won't mind.' He sat down, saying, 'Let's have another glass of champagne.'

'I'd better not,' said Elizabeth quickly. 'I'll get the sack if I go back tipsy, even smelling of it.'

'Well, if you'd rather not, Liz, Matthew and I will finish off the bottle.'

There was a moment's pause in the conversation until Elizabeth said, 'I was talking to the captain . . .'

'My name is Matthew.'

She bowed in acknowledgement towards him as if he could see the expression on her face, and her tone seemed to convey her smile as she said, 'Matthew.' Then she added, 'I was thinking of his list and suggested he take up osteopathy.'

'Yes, yes, or much worse, he could be a psychoanalyst.'

'Be serious, Jerry; that's if you can.'

'Oh, I can. I can, Liz. Go on. But just a minute. I . . . I recall now there's . . . there's a fellow in the same condition as you, Matthew. He has set up on his own as a physiotherapist; I can't see why you shouldn't do the same, after training, of course. Does it appeal to you?'

'Well, Jerry, I only know that something's got to appeal to me; I can't sit in the house all day. I thought I could, when I was in hospital, that is. All I wanted was just to get home and sit in that house all day or walk round the garden, for I knew I could do that on my own. It's only recently I've had to own up to the fact, and painfully, that I'll never again be able to do some things on my own. By that, I mean everything that I want to do. Your idea's worth thinking about.' He couldn't say he had already decided; but he had.

'You never know'—Elizabeth's voice was low now—'people talk of miracles happening . . . but they're not really miracles, merely the nerves readjusting themselves. Just as in your case, the retina wasn't damaged. The eyes themselves are still all right, it's what's behind them that's damaged. It's been known for something to happen to rectify that kind of damage.'

'Such as being hit on the head with a brick?'

'There you go again,' said Elizabeth, a note of irritation in her voice now. 'But yes, you're right, being hit on the head with a brick or something like that, something to cause a shock.'

'Well, it would have to be as strong as the one that caused the damage in the first place, I would think. Wouldn't you?'

'I don't know. I just go by what I used to hear the doctors saying in the ward.'

When, fifteen minutes later, they were standing in the street again, Elizabeth said, 'It's been a wonderful lunch. Thank you so much, Jerry. It doesn't seem just on two hours ago since we all met. I feel I'm back in the old place and going on night duty again. Oh, and it's been good to see you, Matthew, and to see you getting back into life.'

She was holding his hand once more. He had to repress a strong urge to pull it to him and press it into his chest; and his voice conveyed his emotion as he said hesitantly, 'Thank you. Thank you, Liz; and . . . and for all you did for me. Not only then but . . . but seeing you now, because I . . . I shall think strongly about your advice . . . And perhaps we'll repeat today with Jerry?'

'Yes . . . yes, we'll do that. Especially when I come to live here, and so near you.'

'That's a point,' said Matthew. 'Where are you living, Liz? In a nurses' home?'

'No, I have a little flat, but I just seem to use it for sleeping; I have to save up for the long journey home.'

'Where is your home?' asked Matthew, eagerly now.

'Hastings.'

'Hastings? That's miles away, in Sussex.'

'Yes, that's where it is.'

'I never knew that,' put in Jerry.

'How often do you get home?' Matthew asked quietly.

'As often as I can; in fact, I'm going home the day after tomorrow. I have Christmas leave.'

'I bet you're looking forward to it,' said Jerry now, 'spending Christmas at home. Change from hospital.'

There was a long pause before Elizabeth answered, and then her voice was soft as she said, 'No, Jerry, I'm not looking forward to it, not this time.'

'Why?' The word came over almost as a command from Matthew, and again there was a pause before she answered, 'Oh, I have some business to finish off, and it's not going to be pleasant. I only have a week, so I should be back for the new year.'

'Would . . . would you mind if I phoned you?' Matthew's tone had changed; there was a plea in it now.

'I'm sorry, Matthew. I'd rather you didn't, not this time. Another time perhaps. But now,' she put in quickly, 'I must get back or I'll have Sister wielding the big stick of punctuality, as usual.'

Again they were shaking hands.

'Have a happy Christmas, Matthew.'

'And you too, Liz. I hope I see you when you return.'

'Oh, yes, you will. We'll get together again, like today.'

She had to withdraw her hand from his; and now looking at Jerry, she said, 'Thanks again, Jerry, for getting in touch. I'll tell Charlie Fox all about it.'

'Do that. Will I get you a taxi?'

'No, of course not!' she laughed, 'not with the station next door; and it's only a stop up the line. Bye-bye, then. And bye-bye, Matthew.'

'Goodbye, Liz.' He 'looked' along the street as if he were watching her walking to the station.

After a moment or so, he turned to where he felt Jerry was standing. 'Thanks, Jerry. It's been wonderful meeting her again. You can do me another service: you can get me a taxi, will you?'

'Yes, yes, of course . . . Are you going straight home?'

'No, no. I think I'll go and see the colonel.'

'The colonel?'

'Yes, the colonel, Jerry . . . the job fixer,

you know. By the way, have I got your number?'

'No; but I have a card here. There are two numbers on it: my firm's and my aunt's.' And he pressed it into Matthew's hand, then turned to hail a waiting taxi from the station rank.

A minute later, when Matthew was seated in the cab, he said, 'Thanks again, Jerry, particularly for what you have done for me today.' And on this enigmatic farewell, he waved to his friend.

7

It was on the day Elizabeth went home to her parents that Matthew returned late in the evening and made straight for the annexe and his grandmother, to be greeted with 'Where have you been all day?'

'Well, let me get in and I'll tell you.'

'Your mother's been worried. You went out, not saying where you were going or anything, not even to me. And I can tell you, I'm not very pleased.'

'Poor dear.' Matthew stretched out a hand to feel her face, then cupped her wrinkled cheeks, saying, 'Sit down! you old worrit, and I'll tell you, and right from the beginning.'

When they were seated, he began: 'You remember the day I went down to the farm, and afterwards I decided I wasn't going to be a farmer?'

'Yes, I remember. That was the day your friend Jerry phoned, and you went and had lunch with him and came back like a dog with two tails. And yesterday, you were flitting about, and today again. We knew you were up to something, but what?'

'Well, Granan, I'm coming to that. Give me a chance. I went to see the colonel again—he had always been very understanding—and I told him I had been thinking over his suggestions and I had taken up the idea of becoming a physiotherapist, not a psychoanalyst. I couldn't see myself listening to sad life stories.'

'Oh no, nor could I,' put in his grandmother on a laugh. 'Your temper would get the better of you in five minutes and you'd tell them where to go.'

'Oh! Granan. I'm not as bad as that, am I?'

'Oh yes, you are, my lad, and always were. You're a chip off the old block. Growler was the same.'

He now laughed outright. 'I remember Grandfather, and was always amused by your nickname for him.'

'It was no nickname, it was the right one, suited him down to the ground. But enough about him; go on with your telling.'

'Well, the colonel agreed with me, and to cut a long story short, he immediately got me fixed up to be trained as a physiotherapist at the new Hillcroft Hospital. It just happened that the Chief Medical Officer, Dr John Venor, is a relation of his. The hospital is quite a big place, I understand, with a large handicapped and training section. Anyway, the colonel did some phoning, then was kind enough to get one of his aides to take me along there. And I met the great man. I don't know whether he was short or tall, but his voice was deceptively quiet. One imagined he was weighing up the applicant very closely. The outcome was, I was introduced to the matron.' Here Matthew paused and laughed, and then said, 'It's odd, Granan, how a name can work. That doctor knew the value of dropping them, because he introduced me to the lady in question as Captain Wallingham, son of Colonel Wallingham and grandson of the old general, as if she had heard of Grandfather.'

Annie Wallingham laughed outright now,

saying, 'Well, laddie, besides a doctor, you also discovered a diplomat. Did it have the intended effect on the matron?'

'Well, she was very civil. But from her voice, I can imagine her being otherwise. Anyway, she suggested she would take me down to the Sister Tutor. And she did— Sister Grace Foster. And this woman I immediately felt I could like. I think it was because she was used to dealing with people like me. When we were left alone, she sounded so natural I felt I could ask her if a Mr Fox worked in the hospital. Quite cheerily, she said, "Yes; he's a porter. Do you know him?"

' "Oh yes; very well, he was in my company," I said. "We were wounded at the same time."

' "Really!" she said. "How interesting. You must look him up. But to get down to business. When do you think you will be able to start?"

' "Any time that is convenient to you, Sister," I said, and she answered, "Well, as we are nearing the holiday, we'll leave it until the new year. The class starts in earnest on the third. But we will meet again and have another talk before that."

' "Very good," I said. Granan, I was as excited as a young lad.'

It was a moment or so before his grandmother spoke again: 'Just because you're going to work in that hospital, is that all?'

Matthew did not answer her. He felt he was looking straight at her and she at him; and he was aware, as always, that nothing ever escaped her.

Her voice now came at him tartly as she said, 'Well, don't answer, but get yourself upstairs and tell the others. That's what you really should have done in the first place. You don't make things easier, you know, by hob-nobbing with me. We all have our feelings kept tightly under control here. Oh, how often have I damned the stiff upper lip! Go on, get yourself away; you've given me enough to think about.'

What Matthew did now was to grope towards her and, bending over, kiss her on the brow, saying softly, 'You're the most wonderful woman in the world, bar none.'

'Bar none? You can't fool me. Bar none! What about that nurse, Ducksworth? She's on your mind, isn't she? Remind me what she looks like?'

Matthew heaved a big sigh and said

slowly, 'According to Jerry, Granan, she's tall and beautiful.'

'Oh, that all depends upon what you mean by beautiful. I've known really ugly women be called beautiful because their character shone out and obliterated their features.'

'Well, as far as I know,' he said, 'she has brown hair and brown eyes; but what I myself can speak for is her voice, which is—' He did not say lovely, but explained it as, 'Well, it sounds to me a warm voice. Not deep, but not light; and sometimes there's a note of laughter threading it, and through it I can tell her mood, and whether or not she is telling me off. Oh, you can't explain a voice, Granan.'

'You like her?'

'Yes, I like her.'

After a long pause: 'Do you more than like her?'

Another pause. 'Yes, nosy old woman, I more than like her.'

'Does she like you?'

There was no pause now before he answered, 'Yes, she likes me. I know she likes me, but if she more than likes me, I can't say. I can only tell you that I'm quite aware I'm heaping up trouble for myself in letting my wishes and hopes run ahead of me, because I would normally say that no person in their right mind would take on a blind man. That is, for life. Live with him for a time, yes, until he found his feet, but not marry him.'

'Why don't you invite her to stay?'

'I don't know her well enough to do that.'

'What! Somebody who had looked after you for months and you say you can't, by way of thanking them, invite them to stay?'

'I couldn't ask her; it would put a different meaning on things. Anyway, I don't think she has much free time. I think she saves it up to go home to Sussex occasionally.'

'She lives in Sussex?'

'Yes.'

'Then what on earth is she doing working up here? Aren't there enough hospitals nearer home?'

'I don't know, Granan; but the next time I see her I shall say to her: "My grandmother wants to know why you couldn't get a job nearer home, and whenever she asks a question she brooks no shilly-shallying, she wants an answer, so please tell me, Miss Elizabeth Ducksworth, why are you working in the North-East when you come from Sussex? Hastings, to be exact." '

'Go on with you! You must have thought about it yourself. Anyway, what you have to do now is, as I've just told you, go upstairs and inform your father and mama what you intend to do with your life.'

'Yes, all right, Granan, I'm going.'

'Why *did* you pick on that name for me: Granan? I suppose it was because your grandfather would split my name when he was yelling for me: Ann-ee! But d'you know of another grandmother who's called such a name as Granan?'

'No; because I don't know another grandmother like you. It was William who gave you that name, because "Grandmother" was too big a mouthful for him.'

'Well, "Grandmother" or "Granan", you'd better get yourself away and inform your parents that you have settled your life ahead, and if I were you, at the same time I would tell your brother what he can do with his farm.'

'No Granan! Better let that matter drop; it would only upset Father if . . .'

At this point the door opened and Lucille Wallingham came in, exclaiming, 'Oh, there you are! Peter said you were in. Where on earth have you been? We've been worried to death. Why did you go off like that?'

At this, the older woman answered, 'He was just on his way to tell you all about it. Anyway, if you wanted to know where he had gone you should have come and asked me.'

'I did,' said Lucille, testily now, 'but you were up in the telescope room.' And with an impatient movement of her hand she gestured towards the short, narrow spiral of iron stairs at the end of the room. 'And Mary said you were dozing, as you always do when you go up there.'

'Mary's a fool. To her, everyone who has their eyes closed is asleep. I go up there to view the Mount and the land and to sit and think, and there's a lot to think about these days.'

When his mother said, 'Oh dear!' Matthew knew that this would have been accompanied by a shake of her head, which he could well understand because, although his grandmother lived what seemed a separate life in the annexe, she still appeared to rule the house, being kept informed of everything that went on, through Mary, no doubt.

'Come on, Mama. Let's go,' he said; 'I've news for you.'

And at this, without further word, Lucille took his arm and led him from the room. But once in the passage, she said, 'We have been worried, Matthew. Why didn't you let me know where you were going?'

'How could I? You had gone down to the village.'

'You could have left a message. I went along to see if Granan knew, and you've just heard what happened. She'll be found dead in that telescope room one of these days, or fall down the stairs and break her neck. She's much too old for those stairs.'

'Nonsense, Mama. She's a wonderful old girl, you must admit.'

'Yes, I admit she's wonderful at times, but at others she's a great irritant. What I do know is, she considers that you belong to her, always has. She never had any room for Rodney. As for the girls, she liked Hazel as a child, but later they were a nuisance. But you . . . well, you were different: you looked like your grandfather, and at times, when in one of your tempers, you acted like him.'

'Oh Mama!' He squeezed her arm now. 'You're letting your imagination run away with you. She loves us all. And, you know, I can recall one day when she was having a go at Father about something, she said you were too good for him.'

'Did she? Did she indeed. That's news to me.' She hugged his arm to her side, then added, 'I'm dying to hear what you've been up to.'

A few minutes later they were in the drawing room, and when his mother led him to the side of the colonel's long basket chair, he held out his hand, enquiring, 'Not too good today, Father?'

'I'm fine . . . fine, Matthew. It's just these blasted legs: they won't do as they're told. Anyway, I think, by the sound of the weather, I'm in the best place.'

'Yes, you are, for I'm sure we're going to have snow by morning.'

His mother had pushed a chair towards him and now, sitting by his father's side, he said, 'I've been a bad boy; I've been told off for not explaining my whereabouts these last three days.'

'Well, the last I heard of you, you had gone down to the farm to make a start, but Rodney said you never put in an appearance. He came up before lunch to find out what was wrong.'

'Well, I did go, at least part of the way; then . . . well . . . it must have been what Flossie did to me. She saw me from a distance and came bounding up and nearly overbalanced me, and I knew then that this kind of thing could easily happen in the yard unless I had someone with me all the time; and that immediately knocked the farming business on the head. I made her go back to her kennel, and I turned about and went walking in the garden to clear my mind. Then as usual I made my morning call on Granan. But I wasn't there a minute or so when the phone rang; it was Jerry Fulton.'

'Oh . . . Lieutenant Fulton?'

'Yes, Mama, and he was in Newcastle, where his firm's setting him up in a new office, and he was looking for a flat—a flat for two because he's going to be married.'

'Oh, how wonderful!'

'Yes, Mama, wonderful'—he nodded in her direction—'and he asked me to meet him there for lunch.'

He paused here, asking himself should he mention Liz. Well, they would know sooner or later about her, so perhaps this was the best time to introduce her. But no: they would think it was because of her that he was taking up this other position, and that would surely give them ideas; so he went on, 'And I jumped at the opportunity of meeting him again and carrying out the decision I had made while pondering in the garden, and that is to seek training in physiotherapy.'

'Physiotherapy?' The word came from his father. 'Well! well! Now that is sensible. And I can see myself getting expert treatment in the future.'

'Could do, at that, Father. Anyway, I went to see the colonel.'

'About this business?' his mother questioned.

'Yes; and he was most helpful, as always. In fact, he got on the phone and put me in touch with the new hospital on the outskirts, called Hillcroft. It has a wonderful orthopaedic section. Anyway, to cut another long story short as I've already had to tell the details to Granan, he made arrangements for me to be taken along there to meet the senior physician, who happened to be a relation of his, and who turned out to be a very nice fellow, a bit of a diplomat, I would say. In his office I met the matron; and by! his name-dropping, you wouldn't believe. You came high on the list, Father. One thing became evident, he knows women. Anyway, I was taken round, and the top and bottom of it is, I am starting work on the third of January.'

'Oh, that's splendid,' said his father. And his mother added, 'Good. Good. But how are you going to get there and back every day? Rodney won't have time to drive you.'

'There's Peter,' put in his father shortly.

Lucille Wallingham bit back the words 'Peter takes half the morning to see to you, dear.' As it was, she had no need to give any answer, for Matthew said, 'I'm going to buy a car, Father; I don't relish using a taxi every day.'

'A car?' His father's voice rose. 'What are you going to do with a car?'

'Well, one thing, Father,' replied Matthew tartly, 'I won't be driving it; so I'll hire a

driver, and . . . and . . . Wait a minute!'
He held up his hand as if he could see
the expression on both their faces. 'That's
something I was to discuss with you, Father. In this case I'll need your permission
regarding a driver. Jim Taylor, on the farm,
used to be in cars; and one day when I
was having a word with him, he laughingly
said that if I ever thought of getting a car
and needed someone to drive it, would I
remember him.'

'Oh, wait a minute,' said his father. 'Rodney won't like that. Taylor is a very good
worker—Joe pointed that out to me—although I also understand the fellow's got
a sharp tongue.'

'Well, he's no worse for that; and the
days of "Jump to it!" are over, and that's
what Rodney forgets. Still more, he's never
been in a position to take orders himself.'

'That wasn't his fault,' put in Lucille
quickly.

Matthew made no response to this, but
addressing his father again he said, 'There
are plenty of fellows who would be glad
to take Jim Taylor's place. And I would be
happier to be driven by someone I know,

so would you put it to Rodney, please? I'd like the matter settled soon.'

There was a long pause before Richard Wallingham spoke, and it was not to answer the question, but to say, 'It'll be a course you are going on, so how long will it take?'

'Two years, I understand.'

'What! Two years? You could be a doctor in that time—well, practically.'

'I doubt it, Father. I think you'll have to add on another four to really get anywhere. But beggars can't be choosers, as the saying goes, and what is more, patience comes into it. And, like yourself, I'm rather short on this quality. So besides anatomy and physiology and using my hands, I'll have a lot to learn.'

'Good gracious!' his mother said. 'One doesn't realise the preparation people have to go through for these things.' She paused, then saying, 'Oh, excuse me,' she left the room without any explanation. She had just heard Rodney's voice from the hall, and knew she must have a word with him.

She did not manage to have the first

word with him, however, for he straight
away greeted her with, 'He's back then?'

'Yes. Yes, of course. Look, Rodney, I
want to speak to you. Come in here a minute.'

She took his arm and drew him gently
along a passage and into the sitting room,
but before she could speak he said, 'And
what's his explanation? He could have
surely stayed in the yard when he left the
taxi and told me why he hadn't turned up
as arranged the other day.'

'There . . . there was a reason, my
dear.'

'Oh, there's always a reason. He's always had a reason for taking things into
his own hands.'

'Now, now, Rodney! You'll be pleased to
know he's given up the farm idea.'

'Oh, has he?' These brief words did not
convey the feeling of relief his mother's
message had given him.

'And he did make his way to the farm,
my dear, but he said Flossie stopped him.'

'What d'you mean Flossie stopped him?'

'Well apparently she came bounding up
the drive towards him and nearly upset
him.'

'He's a liar, Mama. He was never near the farm. As for Flossie, she's got an abscess on her foot from a thorn or something and she's been shut up in the little barn for days.'

'Oh! dear. Really?'

'Yes, really.'

'Well, why on earth would he say that?'

'You'd better ask him.'

'No, dear, no, don't say anything about it. He has a reason.'

'There we go again, he has a reason. He's always had a reason for everything, and no one knows anything about it until he carries the reason out.'

'My dear Rodney, you mustn't feel like that. Look how he's handicapped; it's dreadful, after all he went through, and he's borne it so well.'

'Oh my God, Mama! Don't start the hero business again. I'm sick of it.'

'My dear'—Lucille's voice now was harsh—'he's your brother and he's stone blind. Don't you understand? Stone blind.'

'Oh yes, Mama, I understand all right. It's been rammed down my throat since he came back, and before that. I know practically every hour of the four years he spent at the front.'

'Well, you didn't get it from him, dear. He doesn't talk about it.'

'No, but he lets others, all of you, blow his trumpet. And you know something that irks me? There are hundreds of heroes like him in the country, but there's no such name tagged on to men like me, and there were hundreds of us. No glory for the farm worker. Oh yes, the land girls: how wonderful the land girls were. But fellows like me, running their particular shows without any bugles blown for them, what do we get? Snide remarks: "You weren't in the army, then?" I want to yell at them, as I did at Frank Robinson's the other night at the table: "Your belly wouldn't be so fat if it hadn't been for the likes of us." '

'I . . . please! Rodney, don't keep on. You are appreciated; you have been appreciated, and by the whole family. And it wasn't only because of the farm that you couldn't join up; you failed your medical because your feet were flat. And don't forget, my dear, that your father lost two brothers in the previous war . . . your two

uncles. Your grandfather lost many rela-
tions in the first war.'

'For God's sake! Mama, stop it. Be
quiet! will you? I'm bloody well sick of the
talk of war.'

'Rodney!' Lucille's voice was low and
very firm now. 'Please don't speak to me
in that tone of voice, or use that language
to me. And since you're talking so plainly,
I shall too. You never wanted Matthew on
the farm, and you could have used him in
some way. I know it would have been awkward, but it could have been done. One
of the men could have been spared to see
to him. Old Joe would have loved to do
just that. And, what's more, it both hurt and
surprised me when I found out that you
did not even want him to be brought home.
What you expected them to do with him,
I don't know. Stick him in a home for blind
men? Now, Rodney, we're speaking plainly,
so I shall say I know how you think, I
mean, what you think about Matthew, because you never hit it off when you were
younger.' She refrained from adding, 'You
were jealous of him because, although you
are tall and well made, you haven't his
looks or charm'—not that his looks would

do him any good now. As for his charm,
that seemed to have been blown away
from him even before his embarkation
leave for North Africa. Even then he was
a changed man. His manner was short,
even taciturn, and he seemed to have
completely lost the art of conversation.

'Well'—Rodney's voice had a bitter note
in it—'I know where I stand. Up till now I
thought you were for me.'

'I am, Rodney'—her voice was soft—
'you know I am, but your brother is handicapped in the worst possible way, for, to
my mind, to be blind is worse than losing
a limb, even two in fact. So all I'm asking
of you is a little more understanding; and
you can show that right now, when you
go into the drawing room and hear what
Father has to say to you. Matthew is going
to take up physiotherapy, so you can dis-
pel the fear that's in you that he might try
to take over the farm. Because that's what
you have been imagining, isn't it? In practical ways or otherwise, he knew it was impossible, as did we all, without a great deal
of help.

'What he has wanted to do for some
time now is to walk up to the Mount. He

wouldn't ask Peter, for it would have meant taking him away from Father, and so it would be a nice gesture if you offered to take him up there. You know he used to love that walk, especially this time of the year when the air is clear and the views are wonderful.'

'Mother, talk sense. What view is he going to see from up there? And the top of it'll be like a skating rink in weather like this.'

'Well, he knows the view,' Lucille came back sharply at him. 'I know the view; but it's the feeling he'll get from it. Anyway,' she said, impatiently now, 'forget about it; Amy's Walter will take him up sometime during the holiday.'

'Oh, all right. All right, Mama. I'll do as you ask, but when there's time.'

'There's always the weekends.'

'Well, there are very few what you would call weekends on the farm, Mama. It's seven days a week.'

'Only because you make it so, Rodney,' she snapped back at him. 'That place has become an obsession with you. And remember this: the farm will be there when your father won't, and he's still master of the house and all it stands on. Even when he's gone, it'll still—' She stopped abruptly, screwed up her eyes tightly and bowed her head. There was silence between them for a moment, until his voice came in a low rasping tone, saying, 'You were going to say, I still won't have any real say in the place because it'll pass on to your dear Matthew, weren't you?'

She shook her head in a sort of bewilderment, then said, 'No, I wasn't, because by then he'll have a career of his own.'

'Yes, he might have, but you'll still consider him the head of the house, not William, he's too far away in the States.'

'Stop this, Rodney! Stop it. What has come over you?'

When he didn't reply but continued to stare at her, the answer to her question was loud in her own mind: he was jealous of Matthew. Even now, blind as Matthew was, Rodney was jealous of him and would always remain so. Then his next words startled her when he said, 'I'm not going to lie down under this, I'm going to have a talk with Father and have it put in writing that should anything happen to him the farm is mine. I've worked for it, Mama; if anybody has, I've worked for it. I left school when I was sixteen because I wanted to be on it, and I've made it into what it is, a thriving little business, and . . .'

'You'll do no such thing. You will not upset your father by approaching him on such a subject. Now, I'm warning you, Rodney: if you do that you will never get any support from me one way or another. Let things bide as they are. Your father has always been fair and he will continue so to the end. He knows the situation more than you think.'

As he flung round from her she said, 'Don't go in there in this frame of mind, Rodney, please! Go along and have a talk with Granan.'

'What! And hear more about the conquering hero, or be told there's a wall down on the hill field needs seeing to, or that I should have attended to the open gate into the west field sooner because the sheep have got through? She and that damn telescope, she's always spying on me with it.'

She could have answered this with: 'She uses the telescope because she doesn't go out much, and she likes being up there because it seems to bring her nearer to

Grandfather.' But he was already making for the door, saying, 'I'm having a bath.'

With a sigh, she sat down on the arm of the couch. Life was difficult now and seemed to be getting worse. It was the war, it had changed everything: her children weren't like this before the war started.

Immediately a voice seemed to jump into her mind, contradicting her thought, saying, Oh yes they were; they were always at it. Just go back to the school holidays. You dreaded them, especially as the children all got older and took sides, Rodney and Amy against Hazel and Matthew. The arguments used to be ceaseless. That was, of course, when Richard wasn't present. But if Granan was at the dining table she was as bad as they were. Yet the only one, Granan would point out, who kept up the huff would be Rodney. The others would be speaking to each other the next day, but not he; he could keep that stiff face and silent tongue for days on end. And now she was forced to admit that that trait had remained, in fact had been accentuated since Richard's retirement from the army. It was quite true what Granan had said more than once when referring to Rodney's possessiveness over the farm. You would think Richard was already gone, and Matthew too, and that he was running the show alone; in fact, if anyone had enjoyed the war, he had. He would have been glad if Matthew had been wiped out altogether. This was an awful statement to make, but it was, nevertheless, true.

She sprang up from the arm of the couch, saying, 'Oh dear me! I must stop brooding . . . I've forgotten to see Cook about the dinner.'

The war had been over for a few months now but it had made no difference to rationing. They had, of course, been better off than most because of the farm, yet one still had to be careful: you couldn't kill a pig without a license, or even a lamb. In any case, the news would have reached the village. Her butcher had intimated as much only a short while ago.

Perhaps things would be better after Christmas when Matthew was settled in this physiotherapy business and when Hazel and Amy and their irritating husbands had returned home. You would think that those two men had won the war between them, but neither had been out of the country. Walter had been something in the War Office; he was still there, clearing up. Hazel's husband Harold was a solicitor, exempted because of short sight.

She knew she shouldn't be thinking like this, but she couldn't help it. She didn't like her sons-in-law, which was one thing she and Granan had in common. Oh, Granan had summed them up right away, and hadn't been reticent about speaking her thoughts aloud. There were times, she found, when she liked Granan, liked her very much, which was strange because generally she irritated her. Oh yes, she did. Perhaps mainly because of the love she had for Matthew and, more irritating still, he for her.

She must go to the kitchen! She was dreading the next hour or so when Rodney would be hearing from his father about Matthew getting a car and the farm losing Jim Taylor to drive it. Oh, dear, dear, there would be ructions!

8

Some days later Matthew's euphoria over his new vocation was slightly dimmed.

He was in an armchair alone in Granan's sitting room. She had gone for her afternoon's rest. He lay back in the chair, half musing as he went over in his mind all that had taken place on his second visit to the hospital and Sister Grace.

She had started with 'Do you know anything about anatomy and physiology?'

'Not a thing, Sister—except you soon learn a lot about your body when you're blown up.' As they laughed together, he recalled thinking, Good gracious! I've made a joke.

'Have you a good memory?'

'Pretty good.'

'Well, if that's so you'll soon pick up the theory. Let me look at your hands.'

He had held out his hands towards her and she had remarked, 'Broad and firm. Yes, good hands. They'll come in very useful. But first, before you can use them properly, you must have a thorough theoretical knowledge of anatomy and physiology.'

He remembered replying gallantly, 'Oh, there won't be any suffering in that, I'm sure, Sister.'

But she had come back at him: 'Don't you believe it. I'm known as Sister Disgrace, as well as the Iron Hand in a Velvet Glove, especially when it comes to tests.' And she had ended, 'But now, we'll have a quick run round the wards that are in your section. There are three male wards and two female. You'll be pleased to know there are two other trainees in much the same condition as yourself, but they are a little further on in the course, having been here three months. The whole section is under the care of Sergeant Mullen. I must warn you, Captain or Mr Wallingham, as you wish to be addressed, our sergeant demands to retain his title. Oh yes indeed!'

The ridicule in her voice should have warned him.

He next recalled her drawing him to a stop outside what she termed the main ward and bringing up the sergeant's name again, saying, 'I must repeat what I have already suggested. Sergeant Chip Mullen imagines he is still in the war and on the barrack square. He'll take a little getting used to, but he does know his job.'

From the moment he was introduced to the man as Captain Wallingham and his outstretched hand was grudgingly taken, he knew there was trouble ahead. And before the end of the day this was made clear to him.

He had been introduced to all the patients, some of them long-term, and had met his two associates, Henry Cook and Bill Branston, both of whom could see just a little, and he had taken to them. They too had suggested he would initially be in for a rough time with the sergeant; they themselves had been through it.

It was nearing four o'clock in the afternoon, and Sister Grace had left him in a side room to enjoy a cup of tea, when he heard the voices outside in the passage.

'Oh, you don't need to rub it in, Sister. I've heard all about it from Dr Venor and Matron. A bloody hero, he's been, but he's no longer a bloody captain.'

'I'll thank you not to use swear words when you're speaking to me, Mr Mullen.'

'Oh, Sister, I'm sorry, but it would make a saint swear. Look, I've got two blind fellows, isn't that enough?'

'No, it isn't.'

'Well, I'll tell you for nothing, Sister, he's not coming the captain with me. The war's over.'

'Well, you're the one who seems to have forgotten that, Mr Mullen; you insist on being addressed as "Sergeant." You revel in it. And I must tell you your bullying barrack-square ways have been noted. It's a wonder you haven't been reported, but there's still time, and I warn you that if I hear any more I shall do the reporting myself. Anyway, I don't think your manner will affect Mr Wallingham as it did Cook and Branston, for they had been privates.'

'Well, it's clear whose side you're on, Sister, isn't it? It's the same as ever: bloody title counts, in the army or out of it, with women at any rate.'

'Stop it! this moment, and get about your work.'

It was some minutes before the door opened again and, now in a light voice, Sister said, 'It's been a long day for you, Mr Wallingham; I'm sure you'll be glad to get home.' He recalled just checking himself from saying to her, 'I don't think I shall be able to do this course, Sister,' when she took his hand and squeezed it gently, saying, 'Forget about what you might have overheard. You're strong enough and able enough to stand up to two or three of Mullen's breed. If he comes over too strong, there's always our friend Charlie Fox. And what's more, we need men like you to take on this work. There is a waiting list of patients needing our attention.'

Now his thoughts jumped to Liz; and he knew that had he not taken up the work it would have been difficult for him to maintain a close relationship with her, which was what he wanted, even desired, so much he could not get her out of his mind. She had become like a beam of light in the darkness ahead.

PART TWO

9

She had set off from Newcastle at seven o'clock in the morning, and from then onwards she wasn't really aware of the long and chilly six-hour journey to King's Cross, for her mind was continually jumping ahead to the disagreeable, very disagreeable, task before her, the outcome of which she knew would be equivalent to the breaking-out of another war, a private one this time.

It was drizzling with rain when she crossed London to Charing Cross to catch the train for Hastings, and during this almost-two-hour journey her agitation grew, only to subside somewhat when, coming down the second flight of stairs and into the booking hall of Hastings Station, she could see, as was usual, her father standing near the ticket collector. She went straight into his arms, saying, 'Oh, Dad, Dad. It's so good to see you.'

Presently, he placed a hand on her cheek, saying, 'You're getting thin, my girl,' to which she answered as they walked from the hall and into the street, 'I'm no thinner than I was three months ago, and anyway Mum will soon attend to that.'

'She will too, girl! She's been baking this last couple of days as if she were preparing for the five thousand. And Mike's mother will be doing the same, ready for when you get along there. She'll be out to beat Mum at her own game. You know what she's like.'

Oh yes. Yes, she knew what Bridget McCabe would aim to do. But this she passed over by suddenly stopping and taking in deep breaths of the fresh air, saying as she did so, 'It's different, every time I come home. The first thing I notice is the air. The smell of ozone. It's different, so clean, so fresh.' Then, as they walked on, she added, 'Have they cleared the sea-front, Dad?'

'Oh, give them a chance; you know what it was like by the end of the war. But the town's getting back into shape. It's simply marvellous what they're doing. The White Rock is at its usual musical best again, and the pier has its players, and they've made a start on renovating quite a few buildings. Oh, it'll soon be back to what it was, only'—his voice saddened—'it never will be, not really, because there are so many depleted families. Those with empty sleeves or in wheelchairs consider themselves lucky. Ah well. What am I talking about? *You* don't need to be reminded of empty sleeves and wheelchairs. I hope you've got some new tales to tell us when you get in.'

She did not give an answer to this but said, 'How are you feeling now?'

His reply came quickly, too quickly: 'Oh, fine. Fine. Well, I . . . I mean, I've not had a turn for . . . what? three, four weeks.'

'What does the doctor say now?'

'Well, they don't say anything more than they've said before, because actually they don't know. Only one thing they're sure of, I'm not skiving.'

'Oh, Dad . . . you, skiving! You've never worked less than a fourteen-hour day in your life. Anyway, you know the cure: it's

rest you want, and Phil manages wonderfully.'

'Oh yes, he does, and his leg doesn't
seem to bother him so much now: he's
tackling all kinds of jobs I never thought
he'd be able to. The only thing wrong with
him is he's so stubborn, he just doesn't
like accepting help, especially from Mike.
Joseph, yes, but not Mike.' He could not
bring himself to add, 'Any more than I do.'
The McCabes had been such good neighbours, during the war, and were still, but
he wasn't looking forward to Mike McCabe
becoming Liz's husband. 'Ah! here's the
bus. We're lucky.'

They hurriedly crossed by the memorial
in the town centre to the trolley-bus stop.
The bus meandered through Ore village
and along the Ridge to the cemetery,
where they got down and turned into the
road leading towards Westfield. They soon
passed the large McCabe farm—she knew
it to be seven hundred acres—and came
to a much smaller one, with its adjoining
house and buildings.

This was Elizabeth's home, a place she
had never wanted to leave, until six years
ago. But now, although she still loved it,

she could never see herself living in it again. And after this short holiday even her visits would have to be curtailed.

Jane Ducksworth ran across the clean farmyard to greet her daughter, and as they hugged each other, she whispered, 'Oh my dear, my dear. It's so good to see you.'

'Well, let her into the house, Mum. Let her in! She looks frozen.'

The voice had come to them from a young man limping from a barn at the far end of the yard. Liz turned from her mother and, holding out her hand and laughing, she said, 'Phil! It's always the way, they never invite me in.'

Her brother was peering at her by the dull gleam of a wall light, and he exclaimed, 'My word, you're thinner than ever!'

'Shut up! you.' She pushed him, saying, 'I'm sick of hearing that. Every time Dad greets me it's with the same words. I must look like a skeleton.'

'And you feel like one, dear.' Her mother was helping her to take off her coat and scarf. 'You're pretty near a skeleton. You are, dear. Aren't you eating?'

'Of course I'm eating.' She stood in the

hall and looked about her. 'It's lovely to be back.'

'And I hope it's for good this time.' This came from her father as he, too, was taking off his coat and scarf.

When she didn't answer, the three of them turned and looked at her, their silence asking a question; and now she did answer it by saying, 'We're going to have a talk, but that'll be later; for now let's get into that kitchen and have a cup of hot tea, with cream in it, please. Then I shall have a bath, because that journey makes you feel as if you've been down a coalmine.'

'I'll take your case up first,' said her father.

'You'll do nothing of the sort,' and Phil grabbed the case from his father, saying, 'I'll see to that,' then turned with mock-servility to his sister and said, 'Would you like me to lay out your evening gown, madam?'

Picking up her brother's tone, she answered him from high in her throat, saying, 'Yes, Ducksworth. You may do that, but be careful, please, how you handle my undies.'

'Oh, girl!' Her mother put on a shocked

expression, and her father laughed as he dropped into an armchair near the side of the blazing fire, saying, 'Ah! Now I know we're all back home.'

Elizabeth had had at least two cups of tea, then gone upstairs; and now Jane and Dan Ducksworth and their son sat close together and talked in lowered tones. Jane was saying, 'Well, what could she have meant? She said she would talk to us. You know, when she left the big hospital and came home that time I thought her mind was half made up to get into one of the hospitals here. You know, we talked about it. There's plenty of them: the East Sussex and the Buchanan and the General, not forgetting the TB hospital up on the cliffs along at St Leonards. She could have got a post in any one of them. I said that to her, and she said she had been thinking about it. But then the next thing I knew, she wrote and told us she was going into this new hospital—quite a flash place, cost the earth to build, and it's a teaching hospital too.'

'I don't think', her father said now, 'that she's anything to learn about nursing. By what she tells us, she must have had all the experience that anybody would ever need when she was in that other place. What was it called?'

'Rockstone House,' put in Phil, 'and by what she said to me she had gone there just for a few months to sort herself out. Now I ask you, Mum'—he looked at his mother—'what could she have meant by that? I should imagine all her sorting out had been done before she decided to marry that one along the road.'

'Now, now, Phil,' his father put in quickly. 'Don't forget they've been a great help to us.'

'I don't, Dad, I don't. They might have been before I came back on the scene. And he wasn't pleased to see me, I know that. We've never hit it off. I've always looked upon him as a bully.'

'Now, now'—Jane was patting his arm—'don't . . . don't say that. He's a big fellow and, like his mother, he talks loud, but I think he's good at heart. He means well and he's always loved Liz. In fact he's looked upon her as his from the beginning.'

'That's it, Mum. That's the trouble, he's looked upon her as his. He's bullied her into this engagement. Now if it had been Joseph . . . But then he didn't stand a chance.'

'What d'you mean?' said his father.

'Well, Joseph was in love with her, and he's a decent chap, but whenever he went near her he got it in the neck at home from the big brother. Once he punched Joseph silly, and he had a black eye to show for it, but his dear mother put out that it had been a boys' scrimmage.'

'This is upsetting me,' said Dan, softly now. 'I didn't realise this.'

'No, Dad. To put it in plain language, our dear Mike is a clever bugger, and he's a devious bugger.'

'Phil! Phil!'

'All right, Mum. All right. But I've been dying to speak my mind for some time. And you, Dad'—he turned to his father—'you're not to worry. My leg's fine.' He patted the side of his knee. 'I have hardly any pain there now, and they said it would take time. Well, it's had two years to do that and it's showing progress.'

'You're lucky to have your leg,' said his father quietly.

'Nobody knows that better than I do,

Dad.' And now his son smiled at him and added, 'And it's very fashionable, you know, to have a slight limp these days.'

'Oh you! Phil,' said his mother, slapping his hand and smiling fondly at him. Then her expression changed as she said, 'Well, you know, as soon as she's had a bite to eat you'll have to take her along the road.'

'Yes I'll do that, Mum, but I'll not be going in, because Mrs Bridget McCabe irritates me as much as her son does. I can never understand why a quiet fellow like James took her up.'

'Likely', his father replied, 'in the same way as you suggest her son has taken up Liz. But then Liz won't stand being taken up; she has too much character.'

'Oh, Dad! Character counts for little when you're up against the Mike McCabe's of this world. You find them on the barrack squares. But you know something? I'd like to bet ten to one at this minute that what she has to tell us has something to do with him.'

'Oh, don't say that, Phil,' his mother appealed; 'it's all settled for Easter.'

'And who settled it, Mum? Dear Auntie Brid. The only reason they weren't hitched last Easter was because Liz refused to change her cloth and go over to Rome; Brid couldn't bear the thought of her dear boy being married outside the fold. I don't think she's given up hope yet.'

'Oh, I think you're wrong there,' said his mother now. 'She's had to accept that there's no moving Liz on that point, and that she'll have to witness her son being married either in that awful Protestant church'—she emphasized the last words—'or the registry office.'

'Oh, that would be living in sin,' put in Phil.

Then his father said, 'Shh! Here she comes.'

Elizabeth entered the kitchen wearing a soft green woollen dress. It had a large collar and a row of buttons down to the waist, where it was clasped by a brown suede belt that took up the colour of her hair, which she wore in a long bob.

On the sight of her, her mother exclaimed, 'Oh! that's nice. It's a long time since you wore that. That's the one that Connie got you from that "nearly new" shop in Brighton during the war, and it still fits you like a glove.'

'Well, that's something, Mum. It proves I haven't got all that thin. Anyway, I'm hungry. When are we going to eat?' She looked towards the long table laden with food and said, 'Oh, isn't that a sight for sore eyes! I can't wait to get at it.'

'You'd better go steady,' put in Phil now; 'there'll be a banquet waiting as usual along the road, you know.'

'I won't be eating there tonight. All right! All right!' She waved her hand from one to the other. 'Let me get something into me and then we'll talk.'

During the next half-hour it could be said that the meal was plentiful but the talk was meagre—'forced' would be a better word, touched not a little with anxiety. Afterwards, each of them bearing a cup of coffee, they went into the sitting room, and there, after he had replenished the fire with more logs, Phil lifted up his cup from a side table on which he had placed it and, almost emptying it in one gulp, exclaimed, 'Put us out of our misery, Liz; what d'you want to say?'

Sitting on the couch next to her mother, Elizabeth drooped her head for a moment; then, raising it, she looked from Phil to her father before turning to her mother and saying, 'I'm not marrying Mike.'

For a full minute no comment was made on this statement; then her father, using his favourite phrase, which could have expressed either love or reproach, said, 'Oh, girl!'

Jane Ducksworth was now making sounds in her throat as if she were trying to swallow, and then she brought out, 'But why now? Is it just something new? Have . . . have you met somebody else?'

'To answer your first question, Why now?, I can only answer it with the second, is it something new? No, it's nothing new. I have wanted, even tried, to put him off before, but you all know him.' She glanced from one to the other now. 'He won't be put off. As to the last question, Have I met somebody else? Yes and no.'

'What d'you mean?' said her mother. 'You have or you haven't.'

'Well, Mum, I have; yet I can't say it will come to anything. What I mean is, marriage.'

'He's married?' Her mother sounded utterly shocked.

Liz replied quickly, 'No, he's not married, Mum.'

'Then why? There must be a reason.'

'Yes, there is a reason, and a good reason.'

'Is it the fellow you talked about that you looked after in that ward for so long, who thought you were a middle-aged woman?'

'Oh no! No!' The exclamation again came from her mother. 'He's stone blind.' She was looking fully at her daughter now. 'You couldn't . . . you couldn't do that. I've heard before about girls doing that, and you'll regret it. They think pity is near to love. It isn't. It isn't.'

'Be quiet, Jane.' Dan's voice was low, heavy-sounding as if weighed down with actual pity, and now he said, 'It would be a very grave step to take, my dear, and it would be for life. In the present state of things these days, you can marry today and be divorced tomorrow, so to speak. There is a new liberty, a new morality that is without morality, but that is between two able people. What I mean is . . .'

He faltered here, and Elizabeth put in brokenly, 'We-ll, I know, Dad, what you mean. I know quite well. I've been through all this in my mind and it's still not made up. If I take him on, it will be for life, and I know that; but as I've tried to put to you, that isn't the main point that I have to face tonight, and not only face but ram home. I've known for some time I can't go through with this. That's why, Mum'—she turned and looked at her mother—'I haven't come home as often as I really could, because I didn't want to see him.'

'Have you thought about writing to him?'

Her mother's voice still had a plea in it and it caused Elizabeth to give a rueful laugh as she said, 'Oh, Mum, write to him! What would he do? He'd land up at that hospital and throw his weight about. Oh, not only throw his weight about but create such a stir that I'd be out of a job, one that I'm growing to love.'

'Is this blind chap in the new hospital?' asked her father.

'No, Dad, he's not.'

'Well, if he's blind, girl, how d'you know he cares for you?'

When she drooped her head and made no reply, his voice became unusually harsh and he cried at her, 'I've never been in such a situation, so I don't know, and that's why I'm just asking you.'

'Well, Dad'—her voice was now as harsh as his—'I just know, that's all.'

'He doesn't know what you look like?'

'He's made it his business to find out, Dad.'

'Well, if that's the case'—her father's voice was still grim—'he's going to make it his business to tie a beautiful young girl to him for life, knowing that he's ruined her chances. Oh . . .' He stopped here and bent his head deeply forward to hold it in his hands as he said, 'I'm sorry. I'm sorry, girl.'

'Have you been to his house?'

Elizabeth turned to look at Phil, and quietly now she said, 'No, Phil, I haven't.'

'You gave the impression that the family was out of the top drawer, his grandfather a general and his father a colonel, and all that. Is that right?'

'Yes, that is right. But . . . but I didn't say they were out of the top drawer, I just said they were nice people. The thing is, I've never met them.'

'You haven't?' It was her mother now,

her voice again high. 'You've gone this far and you haven't met them?'

'Mum'—there was a long plea in the word—'I haven't gone any far! I've seen him once since I left the hospital. I had lunch with him and his friend, Lieutenant Fulton.'

'And you mean to say you're going on that and have decided to marry him?'

'Oh dear God!' Elizabeth sprang to her feet, her hand across her eyes. 'I nursed the man for months. I felt I knew him in-side-out. I got to know him as no one else did, I'm sure not one of his family. I can make it my business never to see him again. It all depends on how I feel, but at the moment he isn't the point. The point is telling Mike McCabe that I am not going to marry him, and I'm going over there now to do it.'

They were all on their feet, and as Eliza-beth went out of the kitchen her mother said to Phil, 'You'd better go in with her; you don't know what'll happen.'

'Mum, I daren't go in with her because if I heard him yell once at her or go for her, I'd hit him. I mightn't be as quick on my pins as I used to be, but I've still got a fist on me, and I've used it before today.'

Phil took his sister's arm as he stumbled along the half-mile of rugged lane that lay between the two farms. With his other hand he kept flashing the torch ahead of him, and they were nearing their destination when he said, 'As I said, I daren't go in with you, Liz, but I'll hang around outside for a little while, just in case.'

'Oh no, Phil. No; you'll be frozen. And he wouldn't dare do anything. His father and Joseph would see to that.'

He left her at the kitchen door and she waited a moment before she knocked on it; and then it was opened by James McCabe himself, who, on seeing her, cried, 'Oh! Liz. Come away in, girl. Come away in.' Then, looking beyond her, he said, 'You didn't come on your own, surely?'

'No. Phil brought me, but he's gone back.'

'There's a queer lad for you. Never seeks company, except his own. I suppose it was the war that did it. How are you? How are you?'

'Fine, Mr McCabe. Fine.'

Now the tall man with the grizzled hair

and long, sharp-featured face called, 'It's Liz herself has come.'

Into the hall from a far door now bounced a very large woman. That was the only description for Bridget McCabe's walk, because she didn't walk, she bounced. Her whole large, fleshy frame seemed to rise and fall from one step to the other as she approached Elizabeth, who had got out of her coat and was handing it to the farmer whom she had known since childhood and liked; she didn't feel the same way about his wife.

She was being enfolded in that lady's arms and kissed with her large soggy lips, because soggy was how Liz had always thought of her future mother-in-law's mouth. She recalled that when she was a small child, having yet again suffered this lady's embrace, on one occasion she had been shocked into silence by a quick slap, for she had remarked aloud, 'Auntie Brid has a very sluggy . . . sluggy mouth, hasn't she, Mum?'

Bridget McCabe was now leading the way back into the kitchen, talking loudly as she went: 'He's not home yet; we're expecting him any minute. He's best man, you know—Harry Weldon is being married today. It's all taking place at Brighton. Such a big affair. Four bridesmaids, pages, the lot. But we'll show them, won't we, dearie? Won't we?' She turned to Elizabeth again and squeezed her arm.

On their entrance to the kitchen two young men rose from the settle and moved towards them.

Joseph McCabe was the second son. He was almost four years younger than his brother Michael and the only resemblance between them was the colour of their hair, which was almost black. Joseph was five foot nine to his brother's six foot three and his body was slim. You could put the word 'wiry' to it, whereas Michael McCabe's body seemed built as if specifically made for a rugby forward, though the eldest of McCabe's sons had never been inclined towards athletics of any sort. Moreover Joseph McCabe's features were those of his father. His face was longish and his nose thin, as were his lips, and like his father he had a pair of large brown eyes that gave off a warmth denied by the rest of his features. He now held out his hand, saying, 'Nice to see you again, Liz. How goes it?'

'Not too bad, Joseph. And you?'

'Oh me, Liz. Worked to death, badly paid and downtrodden into the bargain.'

'My God! listen to him!' cried his mother. 'As if anyone could tread him down. Too big for his boots, always has been.'

'Hello, Liz, how are you?' She was now shaking Sam McCabe's hand. He was a young man of twenty and like no one else in the family. They said he took after his great-grandfather, for he, too, had had trouble with his eyes. His round pleasant face was marred by his having to wear spectacles with almost bulbous lenses, because without them he was almost as blind as the man who was always in her thoughts. He was saying, 'I don't know whether it's me, Liz'—referring to his eyes—'but you seem to get thinner every time I see you. Don't they feed you back at that heathen end of the country?'

She could laugh with Sam—he had always been easy to get on with—and she said now, 'Feed you? They don't only feed you, they stuff you up with food. And, Mr Samuel McCabe, don't you dare call it a heathen end of the country. That's if you don't want one of those heathens to give you two black eyes and a broken nose.'

He laughed, as did his father and Joseph, but not his mother, and the young fellow said, 'You like it up there then, although from what I am told there's nothing but pits, slagheaps and shipyards?'

'Then you've been told wrong, Sam'— her tone was serious now. 'There is the most beautiful country just outside any town along the river, and Newcastle is a marvellous city. Of course, it's still industrial, but not so much as it used to be; and that's a pity, because many are out of work.'

'Poor souls. You'll have me crying in a minute, suggesting that there's no poor and no out of work in this area,' put in Bridget McCabe.

'There isn't any comparison'—Liz's voice was sharp now. 'This town has been blessed. Thinking in terms of money, there will be pockets of poor here, but nothing compared with the type and amount of poverty in the North-East. I know now that I've been fortunate in being born and brought up here. We're all fortunate, let me tell you.' And she looked round at the three men who were staring at her in silence.

It was the woman who broke into it: 'It sounds as if you like them,' she said in a tone that was full of meaning. 'Perhaps you'd like to live up there.'

'I don't know about living up there, but yes, I like them. They're a very friendly lot of people; yet the same as here and everywhere else, there are the big-heads, the big-mouths, the bumptious and the up-starts among them. But you'll find *them* wherever you go.'

What Bridget McCabe's answer would have been to this wasn't to be known, for at that moment they heard the front door being pushed open, then banged shut, and they all turned towards the door that led into the hall. Through it now came striding Michael McCabe, and immediately the room seemed to be taken over by his presence.

His yell on sight of Elizabeth certainly shattered the silence for, rushing to her, he picked her up under the armpits and swung her round twice before saying, 'A sight for sore eyes! Sorry, love; I expected to be able to meet you.' He now kissed her full on the mouth, and at this she turned her head away from him and pushed at him with both her hands.

'Oh ho! What's up?' He turned from her and looked round to his father and brothers, then to his mother, and there was no laughter in his voice as he said, 'What've you been up to, Mrs McCabe? What's this? My future wife is pressing me aside.' He now pulled Elizabeth closer to him and when she again turned her head away from him the laughter went completely from his face and he said, 'What's up?'

'Nothing much, except that you stink of whisky.'

'Huh!' He was laughing again. 'I've been to a wedding, woman. What d'you expect me to stink of? I was best man and had to give a speech. I had to . . .'

Before he finished, Elizabeth, pulling herself from his hold, said, 'And of course you had to wet your whistle before you could blow it.'

At this rejoinder there was a snort from Sam and a 'Huh!' from Joseph, and it was his father who said, 'You asked for that, and . . .'

But his voice was cut off by his wife yell-

ing, 'You're taking the mickey out of me,
aren't you, Miss Elizabeth?'

'Well'—Elizabeth looked at the woman—
'it seems to be a saying of yours: there
have been times when I've asked about
how the boys are and you've said, "Oh,
wetting their whistles down at the pub,"
and you've always told me that every man
should be allowed to wet his whistle at
least once a week.'

'I did and I mean it, and if you want to
keep your husband happy you will allow
him a night out to do what he likes—that
is, within reason. But now, if you don't
mind, it's about time we ate. We've been
waiting long enough, so let's go to the dining room. It's all spread out and awaiting
us this last hour or so. Come on now.'

'I'm sorry, Mrs McCabe, I'm very sorry.
I know how wonderful your spreads are,
but I'm . . . I'm sorry, I can't stay.'

They were all staring at her, and it was
Mike who demanded, 'You can't stay! Why
can't you stay?'

She didn't answer him but looked at his
mother and said, 'May I go into your sitting
room, Mrs McCabe? I'd like a private word
with Mike.'

'Dear God in heaven! Asking if you may go into my sitting room. How many times have you gone into that sitting room, you and him, and no need to ask? Is it such a private word you can't say it before the family?'

'Yes, it is, Mrs McCabe.'

'Leave it, Brid!' It was her husband speaking now. 'Go on, girl. If you talk privately with Mike he'll be only too pleased to hear you out, I'm sure.' And now he looked straight at his son, and for a moment they exchanged a hard glance; then Mike, about to turn away and follow Elizabeth into the hall, was checked again by his father saying, 'Listen to me: go steady. You get me? Go steady.'

'D'you know what this is about?' Mike now asked his father.

'No, I don't,' said James, 'yet I've a good idea.'

Mike asked his mother, 'Have you been up to any of your preaching again? You know she won't turn.'

'Dear God and his holy mother; the things I'm blamed for. I've never set eyes on the girl until a few minutes ago, and she's been strange all the time. Go on and find out what she's about, because she's about something, that's sure.'

He went out quickly now, across the hall and into the sitting room; and there he closed the door none too gently behind him.

She was standing on the hearth rug before the fire. He did not attempt to take her into his arms but demanded, 'What's the matter with you? What's all this about?'

'May we sit down, Mike?'—her tone was very quiet. 'I want to talk to you.'

'Yes, we can sit down.' He went to sit on the couch and immediately she said, 'No! No, not there, please,' and at this she took one of the four straight-backed chairs lined along the far wall and brought it towards the hearth; and there she seated herself.

He gazed at her in amazement, then, making a great play of it, he crossed the room and lifted the heavy straight-backed chair with one hand and almost crashed it down on to the floor a few yards from her, saying in a sarcastic tone, 'Is that far enough away from you, madam?'

'Mike'—her voice was pleading—'I'm feeling awful. I'm sorry about what I'm going to say, but it's got to be said. For months past I've tried to tell you, but you've put me off one way or another. It's simply this: I . . . I can't marry you.'

The marble clock on the mantelpiece seemed to tick louder than ever as the seconds passed. He hadn't moved; and he made no move when she said, 'Mike, I can't help it. I . . . well, to tell you the truth—' At this the anxiety went out of her voice and it was firm as she went on, 'You pushed me into this, you know you did. You made yourself indispensable to Father when he was sick and Phil was still in hospital getting over his wound, and Mum appreciated you so much that she too did the pressing. I was sort of payment for your kindness. I tried to get out of it last year, you know I did, by refusing to go over to the Catholic Church. You should have realised then that there was more to my attitude than just the question of changing my religion.'

Still he did not speak, but the colour of his face had changed. There had always been a ruddy tint to it, but now it wasn't only red, it seemed to have taken on the tone of his hair. Then he spoke.

'You're sitting there, telling me that it's all off, all the preparation, all the looking forward. It's all off, you're not going to marry me.'

'I'm sorry, Mike. I am . . . I'm really sorry.'

'Sorry!' It was a scream. He was on his feet now and with one back thrust of his leg the chair went flying. 'You're sorry! There's somebody else, isn't there? I've seen a change in you. There's somebody else.'

'No! No!' she lied.

'You've fallen for one of those bloody blind buggers, like the one who thought you were a middle-aged old wife.'

Oh dear God, dear God. She was praying inside herself now. She had told them about the captain, but thank God she hadn't told Mike how he had acted that night when she first took him into her arms. She had merely said that he thought she was a middle-aged woman and no one had disabused him of the fact.

'It's one of them, isn't it? It could be him.'

'Don't be silly.'

'Silly, am I? Now hear you, Liz Ducksworth, and I say again, now hear you and listen to me. We are getting married at Easter if I've got to dope you and drag you there.'

She too was on her feet now but backing from him as he went on, 'You're not going to make a bloody idiot out of me. Oh no. And to think that all this time I've stood off because you didn't like me touching you, did you? Oh no. I thought you were waiting for marriage. You've had me burnt up inside, like a cinder, wanting you. But no. Miss Elizabeth made it clear she didn't like that kind of thing . . . well, not until after we were married, because she didn't want to be like those girls in the war who are now left with kids when the troops have moved on. And I went along with you. When I think what I've put my body through because of you. You made me go whoring, d'you hear? But now we can rectify all that, can't we, Liz? Can't we?'

He made a spring, but not towards her, it was towards the chair that he had kicked away; and going to the door, in which there was no key, he stuck the top rail of the chair underneath the doorknob, then wedged the back legs of it against the bottom of a bureau that had been standing against the wall.

To say that Elizabeth was frightened was putting it mildly. He had gone mad. Somehow she had been expecting it, but . . . but not like this. Not what he intended to do. Oh no! No. No.

She looked around the room. The only escape would be through two French windows that led on to the back lawn, and they were rarely opened. In a panic, she dashed towards them and shook the handle, but it didn't give. When his hands gripped the neck of her frock, pulling her backwards, she screamed at the top of her voice, 'Joseph! Joseph! Mr McCabe! Joseph!'

'Don't! Don't! Mike!' She was yelling at him now. 'Don't! Don't!'

As if she were a bundle of hay he threw her on the couch, but as he went to undo his trousers she twisted about and grabbed at the brass poker that was resting against the top of the filigree brass fender, and she would have brought it down on his head, but he was too quick for her and, grabbing it, he flung it across the room. When it hit the china cabinet there was the sound of breaking glass, and now she was screaming again, 'Help! Help! Joseph!'

The blow of his hand that came across her face made her head reel, but at the same time the very fact that he had struck her brought into her being a force that was almost equal to his own. As part of her training she had learnt to deal with de-mented men, and now this came to her aid, and her strength increased for a mo-ment. When he tore the front of her dress open and his big hand clutched her bare breast she brought her fingers on to his face and her knees up into his exposed groin. This brought him rolling from the couch, but she was still within his hold when, in the fall, the side of her head caught the edge of the fender. She knew she could do no more, and as the strength left her she willed herself not to faint. She didn't, not actually, she just blacked out for a moment or so, to come round to a great noise and the weight being lifted from her body, and someone pulling her dress down. The room was full of people: she could hear Phil's voice—he seemed to be screaming. How did he get in? He was saying the same words over and over again: 'I'll kill him, I will! I'll kill him!' Then someone turned her gently about on the floor until her back was against the couch.

Through her blurred gaze she took in the fact that Joseph and Mike were fighting, and Mike's arms were flailing at his brother. Then, as if she were watching a play, she saw her own brother get to his knees from the floor and grab the poker where it lay among the glass. Still on his hands and knees, he brought it down heavily across the back of one of Mike's legs, and instantly there followed a loud scream; then another and another and another; and these were from Bridget McCabe as she bounced from one end of the room to the other, her words unintelligible but conveying that this night not only her beautiful room had been made into a shambles, but also their lives. And in this she was right.

There was someone on each side of her: it was some time before she realised it was Mr McCabe and Sam, and Mr McCabe was saying, 'It's a cut at the back of her head. I don't know how bad it is, but it's still bleeding. Get on the phone and ask

Dr Hill if he'll come at once. Tell him it's urgent.' He looked along the room and saw the two figures, one lying and one sitting on the floor. The prostrate one was his eldest son, for not only had Phil Ducksworth brought him low with that poker but a last punch from Joseph had caught on a vital spot at the side of the jaw. As for Phil, something must have happened to his lame leg, for he was unable to stand.

'Oh, Mr McCabe.' Elizabeth's voice was a weak whisper, for now she knew she really was going to faint.

10

Christmas had come and gone but there had been no festivities. It was the middle of the week and Dan was helping Elizabeth down the stairs, saying at each tread, 'Be careful now, be careful, girl.'

'I'm all right, Dad. I'm all right.'

When they reached the hall she stood for a moment and took a deep breath. She had said she was all right, but she felt she would never be right again, not in her life. Her father, still holding her arm, turned her about and towards the sitting room, calling over his shoulder as he did so in a voice he attempted to make cheerful, 'We're down, Mother. Coffee up!'

When he had seated her on the couch and put a footstool under her feet she smiled at him, saying, 'Oh, Dad, I'm not an invalid, I'm all right.' And his answer was, 'Well, just as you say, but we'll take the doctor's word for it when he comes along today.'

'Well, I hope he takes this lot off.' She touched the ring of bandages circling her head. 'It wasn't all that deep, I'm sure.'

Her father did not reply, but turned to where his wife was entering the room carrying a tray, and she repeated to herself: Not all that deep. No, the cut wasn't deep, but the feeling that had accompanied it was deep, so deep. It was filling her body, making her feel dirty; she would never feel clean again. She had heard of girls being raped. She had even had one under her care on the ward, early on in her training, but the real meaning of it had never penetrated her mind until now, when she herself had been almost raped, had gone through most of the process of what it was like to be raped. Her right breast was still sore where his nails had dug into it, and she could still feel his hot flesh on her thighs.

As she shuddered violently, her mother's voice, soft with concern, wafted over her, saying, 'What is it, dear? What is it? Are you cold?'

'No, Mum; it's like people say, someone's walking over my grave.'

'Here, drink this coffee, girl, and don't
say it tastes funny, because it's bound to:
I've laced it.'

She smiled up into the two faces hov-
ering over her, and as she took the cup
from her father's hand she said, 'How are
you managing without Phil? Where is he?'

It was her mother who answered now,
and with apparent brightness: 'He's in the
kitchen peeling potatoes. As for how we're
managing, Ronnie Stoddart from the village
is helping out. He's always ready to give
a hand, is Ronnie, and he likes to think
he's still young enough to do it; and at this
time every year things are quiet, as you
know. So everything's fitting in; there's
nothing to worry about.'

'How is Phil's leg really, Dad?'

'Truthfully, dear, it's fine. What happened'—he paused—'on that particular occasion was that the false part came adrift
and the sinews in his Achilles tendon
stretched a bit too much, and when that
happens apparently the rest of the foot
won't do what it's told. And there you have
it. But it's all been put back in order, and

the only thing he has to do now is take it easy for a couple of weeks or so. He wouldn't let them put it in plaster again because that would mean a crutch, but he's managing fine with a couple of sticks. And there's nothing wrong with his arms, so once in the cowshed he can still milk. There's plenty of work to be done in the harness room,' and he added ruefully, 'though how long any of us will need a harness room, I don't know. It's tractors, tractors, tractors now.' His voice was cut off by the sound of a sharp rapping on the window, and they all turned to look towards where the old leathered face of Ronnie Stoddart was pressed against the glass, the while he was thumbing over his shoulder as if indicating someone.

Dan left the room to go to the front door and opened it to Ronnie, who was now exclaiming, 'It's Big Bridget, Dan. I was on the hill'—he pointed upwards—'seeing to the fence and I could see her tearing along the road. I think she's making for here. I thought you should know, be put on your guard, like.'

'Thanks . . . thanks, Ronnie. But look, go into the barn and fetch me a pitchfork, because if I know anything, the rage she'll be in, that's the only thing that'll keep her at bay.'

'Aye, I'll do that.'

But it was too late. As the elderly man hurried across the yard Bridget McCabe entered it. She was at the front door before Dan could close it and, her voice at its loudest, she yelled, 'I've come to see that trollop of yours, and see her I will. Get out of me way!'

And with a thrust of her great fat forearm she almost pushed Dan on to his back. He just saved himself from overbalancing by thrusting out his hand and gripping the top of her coat, and she cried at him, 'Take you hands off me, Dan Ducksworth, else I'll floor you! Begod! I'll floor you! I'm here to speak to her and tell her what I think of her and what she's done to my family, and do it I will.'

From the sitting room there now came a voice saying in seeming calmness, 'Let her in, Dad. Let her have her say.'

After a moment's hesitation, Dan took his hand from the woman's shoulder, and with her usual bounce she made for the sitting room and, thrusting its door open to its widest, she stood just within the room and looked towards Elizabeth, very upright now on the couch. For a moment it appeared that Bridget McCabe was about to bounce towards her, for her body leant forward, but she was halted by a voice that was no longer quiet and contained, but more of a roar, as Dan cried, 'You move another inch into there and I'll stick this hayfork into your fat lazy arse.'

This last word showed the extent to which Dan Ducksworth's temper had risen, and it stilled the woman's action, but not her tongue, which she leveled, screaming, at Elizabeth. 'You know what you are, Elizabeth Ducksworth? Nothing but a dirty slut. You've egged on my son for years, but now some other fellow has tickled your fancy: likely one of the blind buggers you've coddled, going on your talk of late about compassion and such. Compassion be buggered! For two pins I'd come over there and throttle you with me own hands, I would that, for you've wrecked my family. Not only is my son, my big fine son, in hospital with a broken shin, but now you've taken the other. It's a whore you are.'

Her body did bounce now as the pitchfork was thrust none too gently against the back of her coat, and she swung round on Dan, screaming, 'You dare do that again and I'll come back up here, not with a pitchfork but with a gun, and I mean it, mind. I mean it,' and she thrust out a fat finger almost into his face as if she were actually firing a gun.

Another voice came, this time from behind Dan: 'A gun, did you say, Mrs McCabe? You would never handle a gun. You're like your son, all mouth, wind and water, and yellow inside. He was petrified of being called up, wasn't he? So much so that he wrote to the head of the Agricultural Office with marvellous ideas of how he could provide food and double the yield and God knows what; and you wrote a letter too, didn't you? saying how much he was needed on the land, for his father wasn't well. My God! Fetch a gun, you say? All your son is capable of is using his mouth in the same way as his mother does; he hasn't the guts to face the fact that a girl doesn't want him, has never really wanted him. Instead, he's tried to bully her into it, the same way as he's bullied his brothers. So what does he do? Something he's quite used to doing, and he thinks nobody knows. Of course, he had to pay for that kind of raping, whereas this was free.'

When Bridget McCabe made a dive at him, Phil jerked his lame body to the side and, lifting up one of his sticks, he brought it across her outstretched arms, causing her to spring back from him, hugging them now tightly against her bulbous breasts. And it was Phil who was now shouting, even screaming, as loud as she had ever done: 'I broke your son's leg with a poker. It should have been his neck. But I tell you, woman, if you don't leave this house this minute I'll do the best I can on you with this stick, for you're a loathsome woman.'

What might have happened next will never be known, for bursting through the doorway came Joseph, to stop in the middle of the room, panting. Looking from Phil to Dan then on to Jane who was now standing in the doorway of the sitting room, her face held tightly between both hands, he said, 'I'm sorry. I'm sorry. What has she done?'

It was Dan who answered and quietly

now, 'Just opened her mouth too far, Joseph. Take her home.'

As Joseph now made towards his mother, she cried at him, 'Take me home you'll not, until I finish the job I came to do. It was to wreck this place as mine has been wrecked.'

Joseph stood before his mother and, his voice shaking, he said, 'All right. If you don't come with me this minute I leave to-day and I'll go to the Boxalls, your dear friends, and ask them to put me up until I sail for Australia next month. Now, you've got your choice, and I mean it. You know me, Mum, I mean it.'

Another woman's head might have bowed at having to capitulate, but not Bridget McCabe's. What she said was, 'I'll go if you promise to give up your plans and stay where you are.'

'I'm sailing on the fourteenth of February, Mum; nothing will make me change my mind. It's all settled anyway: Uncle Ned is expecting me. So there you have it, the choice is yours. Come quietly home and your friends will know nothing whatever about your eldest son being such a swine as to attempt to rape Liz because she was turning him down. And there are a few other things regarding my dear brother I'd be very pleased to inform them of. Otherwise you can leave things as they are: poor Mike, coming back from the big wedding in Brighton and, having had one too many, taking the short cut across the back field where lies the rusting hayrake, with the result that he fell and cracked the bones of his shin and landed himself in hospital. And as you've already bought the doctor's silence—he's a very mercenary fellow, our dear Dr Hill—so you would have nothing to worry about scandalwise, and your favourite son could come back into the fold and take up his pose of the big-mouthed, anything-for-a-laugh, gentle giant again.'

There ensued a moment's silence until Joseph took his mother's arm, only to have his hand knocked from it with a short jab from her fist and to be dismissed with a growl as she marched towards the door, saying, 'At bottom you're like the rest of them.'

It was some seconds before Joseph followed her: now his head was down and shaking from side to side, but as he passed Dan he murmured, 'I'm sorry, Dan. I'm sorry.'

The door closed. Dan stood leaning his back against it for a moment before saying to his son, 'You all right, Phil?'

'Yes. Yes, Dad, I'm all right.'

Together now they walked into the sitting room, to see Jane sitting beside Elizabeth, whose body was no longer straight but was lying in her mother's arms as she sobbed uncontrollably.

'Oh, my dear. My dear.' Her father was patting her shoulder, and Jane said to him, 'Let her be. Let her be. It's better this way; she'll cry it out. It had to come.'

She cried it out for a full five minutes before lying back on the couch exhausted.

Her father now put a glass to her lips, and she coughed and choked on the raw brandy. Then, wiping her face with the small towel her mother handed to her, she murmured, 'I . . . I've caused havoc.'

'You've caused nothing of the sort,' Phil said from where he was sitting on a chair to the side of her. 'I'll tell you something, Liz. The day you married him I would have done the same as Joseph is doing now, I would have got out. I couldn't have stood it to see you giving yourself to that big-mouthed bully, for that's all he ever was, and a coward into the bargain.'

'Was it right,' asked his father now, 'what you said about his going to the agricultural people and her writing to them?'

'Yes, it was, Dad. You remember I was in the Young Farmers' Club at the time, and I heard it there. I always knew he was yellow. He never stood up to anybody his own size. It was always the little fellows he went for, such as Joseph was in those days. Joseph never sprouted, you know, until he was about sixteen, and not over-much then. And as for what happened that night, let me tell you, Dad, if I'd been able to get on my feet and had that poker still in my hand he wouldn't be in the hospital now—he'd be six feet under.'

'Oh, don't say that, Phil,' pleaded Jane. 'You would never do a thing like that.'

'You weren't there, Mum; you didn't see what I saw, as did his father and Sam, and of course Joseph. And his mother saw it too. So yes, I mean what I say, that I would have used that poker on his head. He's got off lightly. And you, Liz'—he put out his hand and laid his fingers gently on her discoloured cheek as he spoke—'you're free. That's all you've got to think about, you're free of him. You now have a future life you can look forward to, because your past has been tied to him through pressure.' Quietly now he repeated, 'Nothing but pressure,' as he gripped his sticks. Then, pulling himself up, he limped from the room.

Now it was Jane who was crying: 'He blames me too,' she whimpered.

Elizabeth did not reply, 'No, no, he doesn't, Mum,' because in her heart she knew her brother was right. She had been pressed from all sides, with her mother doing her share in order that they should keep this farm going. And so she remained silent, swamped with a sickening feeling of degradation.

For nights now she had woken up struggling and wrestling with the bedclothes, the sweat pouring from her; and now for the hundredth time she asked herself what would have happened if Joseph hadn't dashed back into the kitchen and got the keys for the French windows. His quick action had certainly stopped Phil from breaking down the glass door.

Her father was now saying, 'I suppose

this business has put the lid on any idea you might have had of coming back here to nurse,' which opened up a further road for questioning.

Elizabeth closed her eyes. She would have liked to answer him, 'I've never had any idea of coming back here to nurse, Dad, at least not since the war ended, not even earlier.'

'Don't bother answering, my dear, we understand. But we don't want to lose touch with you.'

'Oh, Dad'—she pulled herself forward on the couch—'that will never happen. In spite of everything, I'll come and see you. Phil can always bring me in the long way round. But what is more, I'd love you to come north for a holiday, or for just a long week-end, whatever could be arranged. So don't worry, Mum.' She turned now and took her mother's hand. 'I won't lose touch. I'm too fond of you all. You've had such hard times, and you've been so good to me through them—let me go my own way.'

'Well'—her father sounded almost cheerful now—'you'll be with us for the next few weeks, and that is something.'

'Oh, Dad. No . . . no, I feel I must get

back as soon as possible. And . . . and I'm all right now. After all, there were only five stitches put in.' She looked from one to the other now pleadingly. 'It's the feeling it's left on me; I need to work it off. And another thing'—her voice faltered—'I've got to confess that I'm . . .' she paused, then stammered, 'I'm afraid of that woman. I really am, Dad.'

'My dear.' He sat down beside her and put his arm about her, saying, 'She can't do anything to you.'

'Oh, she can, Dad. I didn't really think so until, well . . . I saw her and heard her. She would mark me for life, and without a second thought for the consequences. She would. I know she would. I tell you, she is dangerous. I feel it. As a nurse I've seen women fighting like tigers over a man, a husband. Faces smashed, pregnant stomachs kicked. I know. I know what can happen. I've seen it all. You do in a hospital. But I've never seen anyone look like she did, not with so much venomous hate, evil hate. Phil told me that I scored his . . . I mean Mike's, face with my nails, and that was something he'll have a job to explain away. But she'd do the same to me when she got near me, only worse. I saw it in her eyes. So, please, my dears'—she looked from one to the other—'let me go back as soon as I can.'

'We'll see what the doctor says.' Her mother's voice came as a mere whisper now. 'We won't keep you back if he says you can go, dear; will we, Dan?'

'No. No, of course not, so don't worry, my girl. Now that's settled.'

But it wasn't settled. When the doctor came that afternoon he said, 'Apart from the cut on her head she is still in a state of shock, and the long journey she proposes to take might act on her in such a way that she could find herself in another hospital. Take another week,' he advised, 'and then we'll see.'

It was on the fourth of January, in the afternoon, when the phone rang and a female voice asked, 'May I speak to Nurse Ducksworth, please?'

'Who's speaking?' asked Jane quietly.

'Sister Fowler from the hospital. Matron has had a certificate and note from her doctor. Also a letter from her father. I understand she's been in an accident and I was just enquiring as to how she is. But I would like a word with her, if possible.'

'Yes. Yes, of course. Just a moment.'

Jane hurried into the kitchen where Elizabeth was setting the table for tea. 'Come quickly, there's someone on the phone for you, it's Sister Fowler.'

'What! Sister Fowler asking for me?'

'Yes. Yes; what am I saying, girl? Come along, quick!'

When Elizabeth picked up the phone she said, 'Hello, Sister. How nice of you to get in touch.'

'Not at all. Not at all. I . . . I was just wondering how you were.'

'Oh, I am much better, thank you.'

'Was it a bad accident?'

'Well,' Elizabeth hesitated and looked round to where her mother was standing near the kitchen door, and she moved her head slightly as she said, 'not all that bad, you see I . . . I slipped and fell on my back and my head caught on a piece of iron that was lying about. There's always odds and ends lying about a farmyard, you know.' What was she saying? There were never odds and ends lying about *their* farmyard, but what else could one say?

'I'm very sorry to hear that. Was it a bad injury?'

'No, not at all, but . . . but I was concussed for a time.'

'Naturally. Naturally. But . . . but you will be coming back to us?'

'Oh yes, of course, Sister. Yes.'

'Oh, that is good to know. I thought once away from this area and in that lovely town again, where, as I know, there are a number of quite good hospitals, you might have decided to stay. You see, I was born in Kent, but I was brought up from the age of two in Eastbourne, so you can understand I am very cognisant with that part of the country.'

'Really, Sister?' Even as she spoke she was thinking, How like her . . . 'very cognisant with that part of the country'. But she heard herself add inanely, 'It's a very small world when you come to think of it, isn't it, Sister?'

'Indeed, it is, Nurse. And it's amazing how one meets up with old associates. For instance, one of our porters—Mr Fox, you know—he was delighted to find his captain, Mr Matthew Wallingham, coming into this very hospital for a course of training in physiotherapy. Apparently they were wounded at the same time and I understand from Mr Fox that you helped to nurse the captain when they were first taken to Rockstone House.'

Elizabeth could not quell the excitement in her voice as she said, 'The captain, I mean Mr Wallingham, is going to train at our hospital?'

'Yes. His colonel is a relation of Dr Venor, you know. Mr Wallingham is a very imposing-looking man, and it's such a tragedy—I mean his condition. But Sister Foster, who had a long talk with him, thinks he will do well in his new vocation.'

Elizabeth wanted to laugh, loudly, hysterically, not only because the 'fowlpiece', as the nurses termed Sister Fowler, should phone her and enquire about her, even hoping that she would soon return to duty, but also because this tall, thin, stiff-necked, forbidding individual who put the fear of God into young nurses was showing herself to be a very ordinary middle-aged woman, besides being a snob and a name dropper. At times Elizabeth herself had been slightly afraid of her censure, for she had a mania for punctuality: promptness,

promptness in everything from answering a question to jumping to her command. This was one of the reasons why she herself was glad she lived out. Some of the trainee nurses weren't so fortunate.

Her surprising caller was now saying, 'The patients in B Ward were asking kindly after you, and that in itself spells a great deal, Nurse; you will know there are a number in that ward who are very testy customers, so to speak.'

So to speak, thought Elizabeth. There she goes again, forgetting her preciseness, using clichés. My! My! But it was nice to hear that the B Ward fellows were missing her.

'When do you think you will be able to return, Nurse? At the moment we are very pushed for competent staff. Nurse Armstrong does her best, but she hasn't had your experience, I mean war experience, and so one is kept over-busy having to attend to trifling matters. You know what I mean?'

'Yes, yes, Sister; I know what you mean. I understand. So shall we say I'll be back within the next week?'

'Oh, that is good to hear. But of course

you must not come unless you are feeling quite up to it. It's a long journey and a very tiring one. Don't I know!' There was even the suspicion of a laugh, and Elizabeth confirmed her statement, saying, 'It can be very tedious, but I think it would be wise to return this time by sleeper. Don't you, Sister?'

'Oh yes. That is a good idea. So we can hope to see you next Monday then?'

'Yes, Sister. Next Monday. And thank you, Sister, for phoning. You have been very kind.'

'Not at all, Nurse, not at all. I can say, and truthfully, I shall be very pleased to welcome you back. Goodbye, Nurse.'

'Goodbye, Sister, and thank you again.'

Elizabeth put down the phone, then pressed her hand tightly across her mouth. She wanted to laugh, but she knew if she did she would become hysterical, which would end in tears again. Sister Fowler was pleased she was coming back. The truth was, Sister Fowler was having a hard time with Nurse Armstrong. The two women were very much alike; it was as her dad would say: 'You can't knock an oak tree down by hitting it with a brick.'

Her mother was by her side now, asking, 'What did she want?'

'Just to know when I was going back, Mum. D'you know something? I've told you about Sister Fowler, the old warhorse. She's not really old, not yet fifty I would say, but just now she proved herself'—she nodded towards the phone—'to be a very human individual.'

Her mother was smiling, but her voice was sad as she said, 'You look happy, dear, for the first time in a long while.'

'Well, as I said, Mum, I want to get away. I must get away.'

'When have you arranged to go?'

'Oh, I've told her I'll start next Monday. But I'll leave on Friday and get the night train up; I'll have to see to the flat and get myself settled in again.'

'But the place will be damp, my dear.'

'No it won't. I've told you before that Mrs Baker goes in every day and puts the electric fire on for a while.'

'Yes, that's when you're away for a weekend; but now you will have been away more than a fortnight.'

'I wrote her a note last week, Mum. In any case, I know she'll go in every day;

she's on her own in the upper flat and it gives her something to do.'

'Well, that's all right,' Jane nodded. 'As long as the place will be warm. But . . .' her expression had changed and her voice had an edge to it as she went on, 'your dad will be upset at your leaving so soon. He is inside, you know, very upset about all this. We've . . . we've got to live near them for the rest of our lives.'

'Oh, Mum—' There was a break in Elizabeth's voice, and an accusing look in her eyes as she said, 'In your heart you're still blaming me.'

'No, I'm not, girl. No, I'm not. I'm just stating facts, and I know what Dad will do: he'll do what Phil has suggested and start looking for another place well away from here. Well now, I don't want that. I was born here, and you and Phil were born here. It means everything to me. But if they decide to move, what can I do?'

Elizabeth sat down heavily on the kitchen chair. She couldn't speak; what she would like to do was to go upstairs and pack her things, and take a taxi to the station. In her mother's eyes it was all her fault. If she had married Mike McCabe, none of this would have happened. But then, if she had married him her life would have been hell. She knew now that she couldn't bear his physical presence, and would have been forced to do something drastic. And then he wouldn't have stopped at rape, he would have murdered her.

It was awful to own up to the fact that her mother would have sacrificed her to save the farm and her way of life.

Her mother said, 'I'm sorry, dear. I'm sorry, but I'm worried about your father: he's not well, you know, and if anything happened to him . . .'

Elizabeth sprang up from her chair, saying, 'Oh, Mum! Please don't keep on. I can't stand any more,' and she hurried from the room to go upstairs and into her bedroom and there, immediately, she was pulling two cases from under the bed as if her departure were imminent. There came a tap on her door, and as it opened Phil's voice said, 'Are you all right, Liz?'

She got up from her knees. 'Yes . . . yes, I'm all right, Phil. Now why did you try the stairs?'

'I've got to try them sometime,' he said, then he added, 'She's been at it again.

She's crying in the kitchen. Now listen to me, Liz. Don't let her deter you in any way. Get yourself out of this as quick as possible. She says you're going on Friday; well, it's a pity it isn't tomorrow, because she'll not face up to facts until you are gone. She still imagines she can hold you here out of pure pity, all the time plugging Dad's condition. Now Dad isn't as bad as she makes out; he has these turns, yes, and they're debilitating, but who hasn't been debilitated in some way through this war? And I can tell you this: although Dad hates to lose you, he is all for you going because he's afraid of what that damned woman will get up to next. And I'm going to tell you something else: Michael McCabe's shin will mend, but not his mind. You've dealt him a blow that he'll never be able to stomach: no girl is going to leave him in the lurch and get away with it. So I'm not going to frighten you, Liz, but for the next few months keep on your guard because in his head I'm sure he knows there must be somebody else, and nobody's going to take over what was rightly his. You've got a flat, but you're there on your own, I understand. So see you're well locked up at night. I know that fellow better than most. I know him inside-out: I went to school with him, I've listened to his yapping at the club. God! how I've wanted to shut his mouth; and when I knew you were engaged to him, I tell you, Liz, the things I thought of doing, you wouldn't believe. Accidental death was in every idea I ever had.'

'Oh, Phil.' She put both hands out to him, and he, after laying his sticks by the side of the bed, put his arms round her, saying softly, 'I'm going to miss you, Liz. I know you won't make the journey back here very often, if at all, but perhaps you won't have to because there are other places besides this, and who knows'—he laughed shakily now—'we could end up on Tyneside.'

Her face was wet as she released her hold on him and handed him his sticks; then with a break in her voice she said, 'There's many a worse place you could land, Phil. It's . . . it's a different life there, so different you can't compare it.'

As he went to leave the room he half turned towards her and said softly, 'Whoever he is, Liz, I hope he compensates for what you've gone through for him.'

To this she made no answer; there was nothing to say.

The following evening, she was packing the last of her oddments; she was taking back with her much more than she had brought. It had been a trying day. Her mother's manner towards her had changed entirely: there was now blame in every look and gesture; it was as if she were unable to hide her feelings, and it had made Elizabeth aware of one thing: she would return to her home only in an emergency. Yet the thought made her want to cry out against it, for she had loved her parents, still did, but mostly her father. The only light on the whole situation was the hope that Phil would carry out his plan to move north.

She had heard the phone ring but had taken no notice of it until her father, without ceremony, opened the bedroom door and said, 'There's a man on the phone who says he wants to speak to Nurse Ducksworth. His name is Matthew Wallingham. What about it?'

'Oh!' she exclaimed as she felt the colour rising in her face; then she passed him hastily, adding, 'I'll see to it.'

In the hall her hand was shaking as she picked up the phone. She said, 'I'm here.'

There was a pause, then his voice came, his words rushed: 'Hello, Liz. It's good to hear your voice. How are you? They say you've had an accident. Are you all right?'

'Yes. Yes, I'm all right, and yes, I did have a bit of an accident. How . . . how did you get my phone number?'

'Oh well'—she could hear him laughing now—'men like Charlie Fox are born to carry out not just one purpose in life, but many. Jerry could tell you some of his exploits. He was the best scrounger in the company. Anything from a wheelbarrow to a tank, you just had to mention it to Fox.'

'Yes? Well', her voice was flat, 'that doesn't explain how he got my number.'

'By devious routes, I must tell you, my dear. We had a talk. It was he who told me you'd had an accident, and . . . well, I was worried, Liz. I was worried. I . . . I went to Sister and asked for your number and was refused it. In spite of my connection with colonels and generals, she stuck to hospital rules, and the giving of nurses' telephone numbers is very taboo. But then, there was Fox. Well, Fox was friendly with a cleaner. And the cleaner did Sister's office. Apparently she was as good a hand at snooping as was Fox himself, and this morning the dear fellow pushed a piece of paper into my pocket, saying, "For bedtime reading, sir." '

When his laugh rang out again she had to smile and say, 'He'll end up in jail one of these days.'

'That'll be nothing to him, Liz. By all accounts he spent most of his war years in the glass-house. And even there he seems to have had friends.'

There was silence now on the line for a moment; then she said, 'I . . . I heard from Sister Fowler the other day. She said you were starting on a course.'

'Yes. Yes, I have started.'

'And how are you finding it?'

'Rather extraordinary, somewhat irritating. That's because I'm not used to taking orders, at least from a barking sergeant who forgets he's out of the army now. But I'll tell you all about this later. When . . . when are you coming back, Liz?'

'Tomorrow night.'

Her voice was low, merely a whisper, but his was loud as he said, 'Tomorrow night!

Oh good . . . good. I'll . . . I'll meet you at the station.'

'No. No, listen. I'm coming on a sleeper; I won't be in until Saturday morning.'

'Oh well, I can still meet you. You see, I've got a car now, and a driver.'

Her voice rose and she actually smiled into the phone as she said, 'A car and a driver? Really?'

'Yes, really. A wonderful fellow. Used to work on the farm, but cars were his job. We get along like a house on fire. Oh, I've a lot to tell you. And . . . and Liz . . .'

He waited until she said, 'Yes?'

'I'm . . . I'm dying to see you again.'

When she did not answer, he said, 'We'll be working in the same place.'

Now she did answer, and quickly. 'Oh yes, we might be working in the same hospital, but let me tell you there are rules, and one of them is that nurses don't fraternise.'

'Oh well, rules are made to be broken.'

'Not in this case,' she replied quickly. 'I don't want to lose my job or . . . leave my job. You'll have to understand.'

'I'm sorry. I'm sorry. I get carried away. This new life seems too good to be true. The very fact that I'm working and perhaps going to earn my own living has gone to my head, I think.'

Her voice was soft now as she said, 'Yes. Yes, I understand, Matthew.'

As she spoke she was aware of her father standing at the foot of the stairs, and she now said, 'I must go, but I'll see you later.'

'Yes, Liz. Yes. I'll be there.'

'No! please.'

'Don't you worry. Just get yourself back. Goodbye, my dear.'

He was gone. There was no sound but that of her breathing. She stared at the mouthpiece for a moment before laying it down; then, turning, she looked at her father. He was waiting for an explanation as to who the caller might be, but she didn't oblige him. She merely said, 'I'll finish my packing, and then I'll be down to tea.'

He did not move aside as she went to pass him, nor put his hand out to touch her, and for a moment she felt as alienated from him as if he had gone wholly over to her mother's side.

11

It was eleven o'clock on Friday night when Elizabeth boarded the sleeper at King's Cross. She was weary and sad.

The night attendant had introduced himself and brought her a cup of cocoa and a plate of biscuits. Then he told her that they would get into Newcastle at about six in the morning, all going well, and that she could stay aboard until seven-thirty. He asked her the time she would like to be called.

'Half-past six, thank you,' she replied.

After drinking the cocoa she undressed, washed her face and hands, then got into her bunk-bed, expecting now to turn her face into the pillow and to let go and cry, cry out the sadness that was deep in her.

But she didn't do that. She found herself

lying on her back, her hands behind her head, and thinking of tomorrow morning when she would reach Newcastle and be starting a new life. And it must be a new life. Whatever was to happen couldn't be worse than these past two weeks. But it was no use telling herself she must try to forget what had happened, for it had embedded itself in her so deeply that she could not imagine ever being rid of it.

She thought back to her mother's last embrace. It had not been loving. As for her father, she had felt he was about to cry as he held her. It had only been Phil's terse voice saying, 'You'll miss your train if you don't make a start' that had made him release her and push her away.

Phil had led her to the waiting taxi, and there he kissed her and said softly, 'Don't worry. Stick to your guns. Just keep in touch. Let me know what's happening.'

She had been unable to answer him, and the door closed and the car sped away into the dark night, away from the home that she had once loved but now never wished to see again.

What about Matthew? her mind asked now. He was moving fast. Too fast. She must have time to think. But did she need to think? No: in one way she did not need to think at all, yet there would keep coming into her mind the words of her former sister's warning to all new staff, that sympathy was not akin to love, the special kind of love expected by a blind man from a sighted partner. She had always ended, 'I know what I'm talking about.'

It was on this depressing thought that she went to sleep.

She entered the large booking hall of the station at just turned seven the next morning. Although it was Saturday the place still seemed full of working men going hither and thither. She was accompanied by a porter, carrying her cases, one in each hand, the weekend one tucked under his arm.

Suddenly, she brought him to a stop, saying, 'Wait a minute! please.' She was staring over the heads of the throng to where a man was holding up a large card on which was written her name, Miss Elizabeth Ducksworth. She turned to the porter quickly. 'Can you wait a minute?'

As he dropped the cases, he said, 'Aye, miss. Is that your name?'

'Yes.'

She approached the man holding the card and as she tapped him on the arm she said, 'Who are you? What do you want with me?'

'Oh.' The card was pulled down and a thin, perky face smiled at her, saying, 'There you are then, miss. It was . . . well, Mr Matthew, you see, he didn't want to miss you and you would have likely walked straight out, and this was the only way to get your attention. He's over there.' He pointed to where, between the moving bodies, she could see the tall figure of Matthew, standing as if he were looking towards her.

'Oh dear.' The words were said aloud; then others came quickly: 'I have a porter here with my luggage.'

'Is that him over yonder?' The man nodded towards the waiting porter.

'Yes. I have three cases.'

'Well now, miss. You go to Mr Matthew there and I'll see to the fellow. Our car's outside.'

'Oh . . . wait a minute—' she opened

her bag and drew out a coin, saying, 'Give him that.'

'I will, miss. I will.' He smiled at her, and she turned and walked slowly towards Matthew, and as if he knew she was coming he half held out his free hand and she greeted him with, 'What d'you mean, doing this?'

'Oh, hello there. Had a good night?'

'Never mind about me having a good night. This is a silly thing to do.'

'Silly? Now I ask you, how else was I to get in touch with you? I'd have had to wait until Monday.'

'Dear, dear! That would have been a trial.'

She half smiled at him now, and he answered, 'It would for me. Anyway, come on, take me outside. Jim's got the car there.'

Jim's got the car there, she repeated to herself. Things were moving fast again, too fast. She took his arm and walked him slowly out of the station hall into the street, there to see Jim packing her luggage into the boot, and she just stared: it was a large car, a beautiful car.

'Do you like it?' He seemed to know that she was staring at it.

'Did you have to get such a big one?'

'Yes. Yes, I had to get such a big one. Cars aren't that easy to find these days. At least I didn't get it, Jim here'—he nodded as if his chauffeur were standing by his side—'he got it. It's a Daimler.'

'Yes. Yes, I know it's a Daimler. I've seen one before.' She didn't add that it was in a magazine.

'Come on, miss. Let me help you in; we're holding up the traffic.'

She allowed herself to be almost lifted into the back seat, which felt as if she had dropped down into a luxurious cushioned armchair. Then she heard the man say, 'You getting in the front or the back, sir?'

'Where d'you think, Jim?' Matthew was now stepping over her feet and into what she thought of as the other armchair, for there was a padded armrest between them.

She also noticed there was a glass plate separating this part of the car from the driver's seat, and when one of the glass panels was pushed back and the man called Jim said, 'What's your address, miss?' she paused, then said on a sigh, 'Twenty-three Beaulah Grove.'

'Oh, Beaulah Grove. Oh, I know that; that's Jesmond way, isn't it, miss? Jesmond way. My family lived round there once—not in the upper section of course.' He laughed. 'So it is twenty-three Beaulah Grove. All right, Mr Matthew?'

'Yes, Jim, I'm all right, carry on.'

The panel closed and Matthew said on a low laugh, 'He's a lad, is our Jim Taylor. There's no place in this town that he doesn't seem to know of, or anything he doesn't know about its main residents.'

'Is he married?'

'Was; but, as he says, it was one of them war do's: marry in haste, repent for the rest of your life. By the sound of it he was well rid of her. He's from a large family, nine of them. Five sisters and three brothers, and from each one he was given details of his wife's amours. He'll make you laugh when telling you about his family. Apparently four of the girls are married and, as he states, proper and aboveboard . . . you know, no two and a half kneeling on the altar steps . . . they're Catholics. His father drinks like a fish, but never misses mass on a Sunday morning. As for his three brothers, two of them, to use his own words, have turned up trumps, but the eldest, he's got himself into jail because, and again to use his own words, he can't bear to see ladies' jewelery lying about on dressing tables, it looks so untidy.'

She was actually laughing now, but silently, and she could see how this Jim Taylor was going to be very good for Matthew.

'It was he who got me this car,' Matthew said. 'I'd never thought of a Daimler, but he heard of it going second-hand. It had been wrapped in cotton wool all the war years and he got it for a song, really. Only fifteen hundred. I can imagine him beating them down.'

Only fifteen hundred, she thought. Fifteen hundred pounds! For a car! When you could buy a nice little new one for four to five hundred pounds—if you could find it; but then of course it wouldn't be like this.

It seemed no time at all before she realised they were running into Beaulah Grove. A few moments later, the car had stopped and the driver was out and holding open the door, saying, 'Here we are, miss, number twenty-three.' He helped her out, then, picking up Matthew's white stick where it had been lying on the floor, he handed it to him and carefully helped him down on to the pavement. Then he stood waiting, looking from Matthew to Elizabeth, who was now thinking, Oh dear me. Of course, I'll have to ask him in.

Matthew was holding out his hand to her, and she took it and led him towards the door, while Jim Taylor's voice followed her, saying, 'Your luggage will be with you in a minute, miss.'

The door was painted bright green and had a shining brass knob in the middle of it. She fumbled in her bag, took out her key, then pushing the door open, she said, 'There's a slight step here,' and with that she guided him into the hall. They were met immediately by a past-middle-aged lady coming down the stairs, crying, 'Oh, there you are, Miss Ducksworth! I didn't expect you till this evening, but I thought I'd just look in on my daily visit to your flat. It's all nice and warm and welcoming.'

'Thank you, Mrs Baker. By the way'— she hesitated on introducing Matthew— 'this is Captain Wallingham. He was kind enough to meet me at the station. He's . . . he's an old patient of mine.'

'Oh, I am very pleased to meet you, Captain.' Mrs Baker's hand went out towards him, but when it did not meet his she looked enquiringly for a second at Elizabeth, who pointed to her eyes; the next second the woman was gripping Matthew's hand, saying, 'How d'you do?'

'How d'you do, Mrs Baker?'

Elizabeth had opened the door of her flat and it was Mrs Baker who led him into it, followed now by Jim Taylor carrying the luggage. Placing the cases on the floor and grinning from ear to ear, he said, 'That'll be four and six, sir, but Lady Golightly'll likely settle the bill,' and on this he turned away on a laugh and left them all slightly embarrassed. It was Matthew who explained, saying, 'Lady Golightly is the name he's given to my car; it alludes to her smooth running, I think. I'm afraid his sense of humour will be hard for many people to understand, but it's his way of brightening the day, you know.'

He had been speaking to Mrs Baker, and that lady replied, 'Yes. Yes, of course, I understand.' But she didn't. Elizabeth could read her mind: she felt the man was presumptuous, taking too much for granted. Indeed, she had been surprised at how familiar Jim appeared to be with Matthew.

Matthew was thinking along the same lines. The middle-aged lady wouldn't understand a man like Jim Taylor being tolerated. How could she understand such a relationship? But Jim wasn't stupid, he knew how far he could go. The colonel would have eaten him up, and his mother, too, would have been on her dignity. As for Rodney . . . well, they had crossed swords already, and not in a jocular way either. But Granan would have understood the man: she'd have met him on his own ground. Liz too, would understand him; she was used to people like Jim in the hospital. Oh, if only that woman would go.

As if Mrs Baker had read his thoughts she said, 'Now I must leave you to get on with your unpacking, but I'll pop in later, my dear, and we'll have a chat.'

'Oh, please do, Mrs Baker. I won't be going out. It'll take me some time to settle in again because I've brought a lot of things from home with me this time.'

'Yes, of course. Goodbye . . . Goodbye, Captain Wallingham.'

'Goodbye, Mrs Baker. But I expect we'll be meeting each other again, at least I hope so.'

Mrs Baker flashed a quick look at Elizabeth before she answered Matthew brightly, 'I'm sure we shall. I'm sure we shall. Goodbye then.' She too was gone.

The audible sigh from Matthew caused Elizabeth to say, 'Oh sit down . . . Here,' and she guided him to a chair.

Once seated, he said, 'And you too, quite near, please.'

She pulled up a chair, but not too near him, and as he held out a hand to her she hesitated before taking it.

'It's wonderful to hear you again, Liz. It seems years. What happened . . . I mean what kind of an accident did you really have?'

'Oh.'

He could feel from the movement of her arm that she was shaking her head, and her voice had a sharp note to it as she went on, 'It . . . it wasn't an ordinary accident. I'll have to explain it to you sometime.'

'Explain it now.'

She answered him in a voice that was definitely heightened in tone: 'No, I won't. I can't. It's something I . . . I've got to get used to. I mean, the thought of it.'

There was a silence before he said, 'Some other person implicated in it?'

Again she allowed a silence to fall on them before she said, 'Yes. Yes, there was another person in it, and I'll say this much: I went home to clear up the matter, but it didn't work out as I had planned. One could say that it had devastating results. Now, that is as much as I'm going to tell you. Understand?'

He was thinking that yes, he understood. There'd been a man in this, and the accident. What had he done to her? Dear God, what had he done to her?

She broke into his thinking by saying, but quite brightly now, 'How are you finding work?'

'Oh, very, very good in parts, but the thought of going at it for two years daunts me.'

'Don't worry; I'm sure you'll have a great deal of help.'

'I won't.'

'What d'you mean?'

'There's one in particular who is not out to help, and he's more or less told me that from the beginning. He's in charge of me, and he's got to deal with me every day. That's Sergeant Mullen. The man's a bully and he still imagines he's in uniform. I've tried to point out that the war's over now, that all men are in a way equal; but he refused to accept that, especially when Fox insists on addressing me as "captain". Of course he himself still likes being addressed as sergeant; in fact, he demands it.'

It had struck him as he was speaking that this business of all men being alike after the war was by no means a universal view. There were people, older people, who were like his father. He was still a living personification of the army, with its demanding divisions of rank, and he would not have tolerated Taylor's chit-chat, or that of Fox, in or out of the forces. He was a colonel, the man who gave orders and saw that they were carried out. But had *he* ever carried them out himself while crawling through mud side by side with men like Taylor or Fox? Or lain in a shallow homemade trench during a bombardment, huddled against another man—a private, a corporal or a sergeant—so close that they could have been embracing? Or had he been hauled out of snowdrifts so frozen that he had had to be tightly clasped back and front by two men aiming to warm him back to life? But then he had to admit there had been many like his father, and often younger, holding lower ranks than colonel. There was Lieutenant Ferguson. Ferguson . . . don't let him think about Ferguson. What was the matter with him?

He was brought to himself by Elizabeth saying, 'Well, I know who'll come off second-best in that fight.'

He felt she was smiling and said, 'Don't bet on it, Liz. I might lose my temper and hit him . . . "The officer struck out blindly." Huh!'

He laughed at himself, and she said, 'Don't talk like that, Matthew.'

'No, you're right, Liz. It's a cheap kind of comeback on one's feelings; but tell me—' Then he added quickly, 'Oh, don't take your hand away, Liz, not for a minute. I know you want to get settled in, but it's the weekend and I've got two boring days ahead of me. The only light relief at home is my grandmother, and she gets too much of me, and that upsets my mother. So, can I call on you this afternoon, and we'll take a trip in Lady Golightly out into the country and have tea somewhere? That would be lovely, at least for me. Will you?'

What could she say? She had wanted time to think, but that plea of his a few moments ago, 'Don't take your hand away', even that small action foretold the future. But she said, 'All right. That is if the sun stays out; I'm not going for any drive if it rains.'

'No, of course not. If it rains you'll make tea for us here, won't you?' He was standing on his feet now and actually laughing. Then, his tone changing abruptly, he leant towards her, saying, 'Please don't think I'm jumping the gun, Liz. I suppose I am but . . . but I do so want us to be friends, and there's no one I can talk to like I do to you. You brought me back to life, and just talking to me or letting me talk to you keeps my mind from jumping back into the past.'

He turned from her now, groped for his stick, which she placed into his hand, then

stepped forward as if he knew the whereabouts of the door, which he didn't, and
so she was forced to take his arm and turn
him about. He then surprised her by putting two fingers into his mouth and giving
a long low whistle.

'Will he be able to hear that?'

'Yes. He has what my grandmother, and
I'm sure his grandmother, would term
cuddy's lugs . . .'

Before she had guided him into the hall
there was Taylor at the open door, saying,
'OK, Mr Matthew?'

'OK, Jim,' he replied; then, addressing
her, he said softly, 'Be seeing you later
then, Liz?'

'Yes. Yes.' She let him go at that. She
did not walk to the car with them, but
stood on the step until Jim Taylor had settled Matthew in the front seat. After closing
the door, he did not, however, immediately
take his own seat, but returned to where
she was standing.

'You think I've forgotten my place, don't
you, and you've taken me for one of these
fast-talking Northern galoots. Well, you're
mistaken, miss. I've taken on a mission in
me life and I'm carrying it out in the way

I see best. Another thing. Nobody knows their place better than I do, and when to use it. Understand, miss?'

His mouth was wide and there was a smile on it, but none in his eyes. She answered, 'Yes. Yes, I do,' while at the same time being taken aback by his forthright words.

'Good. Be seeing you, miss.'

It was from that minute that she liked Jim Taylor, and anything he did with regard to his master became right with her. But what was she going to do about . . . his master?

She went back into the flat, but didn't start unpacking her cases; she simply dropped on to the couch. She found she was shivering, as if with a chill, and she asked of the air, 'What am I going to do?'

Then came the question, Do you love him? and she answered it with fervour: 'Yes; oh yes, I do.'

Then why was she afraid of admitting it, of him knowing it? She knew that he loved her, that what he was feeling was not some passing fancy. She knew he saw her as a helpmate and a good companion; no, she knew he loved her. Then there came into her mind the picture of their joined hands and his voice begging that she shouldn't release her hold on him. The incident had acted as a preview of what their life would be together. He would always want her close and need her all the time. She would have no life of her own. Evidently, too, he could afford to keep a wife, and therefore he might object, at least inwardly, to her continuing with her career. He'd want a family, and although the timing of it could be arranged these days she knew he wasn't the kind of man to put up with half-measures: if there were children he'd expect there to be a full-time mother to see to them. He was from an old military family. There'd be rules to be kept, not enforced but taken for granted. She had met one or two families from the same sort of background during the course of the past five years, and with the exception of one would-be lady they had all been very nice, very pleasant—but they didn't fraternise easily.

She sat up swiftly. What was the matter with her? Why was she going on like this? Talk about *him* moving too fast, *she* was flying too fast! The man hadn't asked her to marry him. All right, she knew he loved her. Yes, and so had Mike McCabe. Oh dear God! Don't let her mind go back to that! Whatever was to happen, Matthew had two years' training to do, and her own aim was to become a sister. So why didn't she tell him how she felt and let them enjoy the future weeks, months, or even years together before they decided on marriage? And anyway, how would his people take this? Yes, that was another point. They had never met her; they knew of her, if at all, only as a middle-aged woman who had nursed him.

So leave it, her mind cried out, and let things take their course, whichever way that goes.

12

After driving the car into the small barn that had been cleared to act as a garage, Jim helped Matthew out of his seat, then took his arm and led him across the farm-yard, the only sounds being those of a dog barking and the lowing of cows in their stalls.

'Nobody about yet,' he remarked. 'Are they all about their business? I've been thinking, Mr Matthew: having to leave the car in the farmyard, even if it is in the barn, annoys Mr Rodney, when with a little change to the lawn and the terrace, and it wouldn't be much, we could continue up the drive and straight into the first of the wood-barns. It's only half full of wood, bags and oddments—the lot could be stacked next door—and both barns set well back from the end of the house. Well, what I mean to say is, cut away about four to five yards of the lawn—that wouldn't disfigure it, as there would be plenty left to front the terrace—then make a pair of doors in the side of the wood-barn, and it would be a simple matter of going from the drive straight into it. I've never been able to see, Mr Matthew, why the lawn should stretch so, because at one time there must have been room for traffic up there, horses anyway, seeing that the loose-boxes are still intact further along.'

Matthew gave a small laugh now as he said, 'You've touched on a very sore point, Jim. It was my grandmother herself who had the lawns made like that to block any vehicle going up there. It was when she was living in the main house, and she considered the working buildings were much too near. She didn't like the to-ing and fro-ing. At that time, too, she had recently returned from India and there her home wouldn't have been so near to the outbuildings. Nothing was the same as in India; and anyway, what was the farm for? Her orders were that vehicles had to stop there. I often wonder that she didn't give the order for the stables and barns to be pulled down. I think it must have been my grandfather who drew the line there.'

'You could get round her, sir.'

'Now, now, Jim. What are you suggesting?'

'Just that I understand, Mr Matthew, that she has a very large soft spot for you, always has had.'

'Well, I can tell you, Jim, it isn't as soft as all that.'

'You could but try, sir.'

'You're a bad influence on me, Jim Taylor, you know that? It's been said in the house. And I don't know what impression you have made on Miss Ducksworth as yet, but I'll soon find out. I think I can vouch that the neighbour, Mrs Baker, didn't appreciate your one-liner, "That'll be four and six, sir." '

There was a chuckle from Jim Taylor now as he said, 'Oh, I don't know, sir. It's good to take some people's hair down, you know. Which door d'you want to go in by?'

'The front door, please, Jim.'

'Right, the front door it is.'

Matthew had to smile to himself. When anything serious was to be said he was given the title of 'sir'; otherwise it was 'Mr Matthew'. He was a card, was Jim Taylor, but a good card to break the monotony of the days, particularly the weekends. That was, up till now, when the black horizon was showing a streak of light.

When he entered the house his mother was crossing the hall and she greeted him with, 'Where on earth have you been? Why didn't you leave a note to say where you're going? Have you had any breakfast? We've cleared away now.'

'I've been to the station, Mama, to meet a friend coming off the sleeper. No, I haven't had any breakfast, and I didn't leave a note because I expected to be back before this.' And he *had* expected to be back earlier; though now he thought it was stupid of him to have imagined that she would leave the train at six o'clock when it came in.

His mother was saying, 'I must get you something. What would you like, bacon and egg, or a boiled egg, or . . . ?'

'Toast and coffee, Mama; that'll do me fine.'

'Who were you meeting at the station, dear?' she asked. 'Jerry?'

'No, not Jerry, Mama . . . A lady. A nurse. In fact my old nurse, the middle-aged one, you know.' Lucille knew all about the story of his middle-aged nurse. 'I thought you had met her, Mama, or at least seen her.'

'Have I? I don't think so, because as far as I remember she was on night duty, wasn't she?'

The subject was changed immediately by her saying, 'Your father's had a bad night. He's very down. He needs cheering up in some way.'

'If he's able to get downstairs we could take him for a run. I could whistle Jim back and we could go out this morning.'

'I wish'—his mother's voice came to him now with a petulant note—'I wish you would stop calling your chauffeur Jim. He's not on the same standing as Peter. You haven't known him five minutes and the man, although I have nothing against him, seems to act very familiarly towards you. It isn't as if he had been . . . well . . . like a batman to you in the forces. He was merely a farmhand, a new farmhand.'

Matthew found himself getting angry: 'There has been a war on, Mama! Did you know anything about the war other than that you couldn't go up to Harrods for your Christmas shopping? You've lost no one belonging to you: you still have Father, and he didn't have a scratch on him from his war work; the illness he has affected him before then. But the vital point is that there's no real working class, as you understand the words, left. Many of the men are lying dead somewhere in France or in the bloody desert, and the women have turned themselves into their own fighting force; they're having no more of the "Yes, ma'am, no, ma'am" of domestic service. You're damned lucky you've still got people like Mary, Bella and Cook.' He was shaking with agitation.

A hand came on his free arm and her voice, conciliatory, said, 'Please . . . please, Matthew, don't excite yourself. And please do stop tapping that stick on the tiles!' She had said tapping when she meant thumping, and she ended, 'Oh dear me! Getting into a state like that just because I expressed an opinion. Surely I can have an opinion about standards?'

When, without any reply at all, he freed himself from her hold and made his way to where the door led out of the hall and into the connecting corridor between the house and the annexe, she knew he was making for his grandmother and that she would be given the whole story, and, of course, agree with all he said. And in her own defense she thought, But then, why doesn't he understand *me* and *my* feelings? He isn't a bit like his father. Well, she had always known that, and Richard had always known that. Like his grandfather and his grandmother, he was a law unto himself, at least he had been when sighted, and in a way was still. Oh dear! At its best life was a trial with one thing and another. She wished, oh how she wished she had never been inveigled into an army family as an escape route . . .

Annie Wallingham stared at her grandson, who was sitting opposite her still holding on to his stick, and as she said, 'Put that thing down,' he lifted his hand as if he weren't aware that he was still holding the walking stick, which he then threw to one side.

'What's the matter with you? Got out of the wrong side of the bed?' When he made no reply, she said, 'I understand you left early, had an appointment with the dawn.'

He now made a sound in his throat that could have been a derisive laugh and he answered her, saying, 'Something like that,' then explained, 'I went to the station to meet the night train.'

'You mean, you went to the station to meet somebody coming *off* the night train.'

'Yes, precisely that, Granan, precisely that, and before you go any further and ask more questions I'll tell you who it was.'

'You needn't bother, I know. It was that nurse you made such a fuss about, the one who lifted you out of the doldrums the day Jerry phoned asking you to lunch. Right?'

'Right.'

'But . . . but the uplift didn't last . . . did it? Over Christmas you were like a bear with a sore skull, and there was fur flying over your pinching Jim Taylor from the farm and him advising you to buy a car that drinks petrol by the gallon and costs a fortune to keep up. Daimlers are like tender débutantes: they're mostly beautiful to look at but expensive to maintain.'

'That's a very poor simile, Granan, very poor. Not worthy of you. Anyway, I have quite a generous petrol allowance. It's one of the few advantages of being disabled.'

'Well, we can't all be brilliant, not continually anyway,' she said on a low chuckle; 'but on the first morning that car was put to the use it was bought for, you went off to work, as Mary said, like a lord of the manor; but when you came back you were for telling me that you were going to give up the whole scheme, you wouldn't be able to stand it. Something to do with a sergeant who didn't know his place.'

'That's quite wrong.' It was a shout now. 'There was nothing about place in it from my side, and I've just had a lecture from Mama about place, so don't you shout, Granan. I don't give a damn about place.'

'Oh dear! Oh dear!' Annie Wallingham's voice was very low. 'What has she said that's upset you so much?'

'Just that I've dared to call my driver Jim instead of Taylor.'

'No!'

'Yes. I should know my place as a captain and a colonel's son and the grandson of a general. She didn't say all that, but she put it into a few words, and I can tell you here and now, Granan, I wanted to say,

"Damn you, woman!" I really did: "You're still in India playing the great memsahib." All those bloody women who have lived in India are the same.'

'Are they? Well, I was one of them for a time.'

She watched him toss his head from side to side, fidget in his chair, throw one leg over the other, then drum his fingers on an arm before he said, 'You're different. You're one in a thousand, and you know it.'

'Well, if that's the case, your mother's one in a thousand, if *you* but knew it. She's had a great deal to put up with. All right, she's got rather old-fashioned ideas about class, but I can tell you this, my son is no easy man, no easy husband to get along with. He never was an easy boy. If anybody's to blame for her attitude to what she would call the working class, it's him. Strange, too, because his father wasn't like that. In his younger days Growler hob-nobbed with all and sundry and was more at home with the ordinary Tommy than with the brass hats at the top. In fact, he loved the ordinary men, and to be among them, and they adored him. Many of them died for him. One gave his life by dragging him to cover from a filthy battlefield. He never forgot that. And he made sure the man's wife and family were provided for.

'And I'll tell you another thing, he was disappointed in his son because, as he said, Richard was the army ABC by the book; but you can't always go by the book. And another thing he said was that battles had been lost by the buggers on top sticking to the book.' And, now sadly, she said, 'Richard didn't love his father. Perhaps, as I see it now, there was his side to it because, one day, Growler went for him hammer and tongs. I recall exactly his words: "You'll never know what the bloody war's about until you yourself lead your men and crawl, sweat and vomit your guts out with them, because no soldier alive is worth his spit if he doesn't experience fear; in the end it's fear that is the spur that makes the hero".'

When Matthew dropped on his knees beside her, she held his head in her bony arms and said, 'Don't worry, my love; just try to remember we are all very human beings, but in every walk of life there have to be leaders. Whether they sit on leather chairs behind big desks or get out into the field and rough it, they've got to have the power in them to lead. Half of them might be wrong. They often are; oh yes, they are. Look at this last war. Churchill made mistakes, but nevertheless he was a leader. To my mind he saved this country; to my mind he won the war. Not everybody would agree with me, but what they would agree on must surely be that he was a leader.

'But, to get back to your mother, don't hold it against her that she cannot let go of the old customs. Although I haven't moved away from this house or grounds for years I am well aware we'll never enjoy anything like the pre-war years again. There is a new freedom, and whether it will bring good or ill I won't live to see. They say now in the newspapers and on the wireless, at least its implied there, that class is dead, we are all equal. To me that is the talk of unthinking men and women, because there'll always be class distinction. And, you know, it'll be more prevalent in the working class—oh yes, it will—than among the upper, because most of those in the upper class have a background to hang on to, whereas in the working class there will be a fight for position. They imagine they are fighting the upper class, but in reality they are fighting their own kind. As Mary says, some of them would take your eyes out and come back for the sockets to get one over on you, and Mary knows her own kind. Oh yes . . . yes, she does that.'

He was actually laughing when he rose to his feet, and he was hardly seated again when the door opened and Mary herself appeared carrying a tray on which there was a plate of thin bacon sandwiches, a rack of toast, butter and marmalade, and a pot of coffee.

Putting the tray down on the small table, she said, 'Cook says, Mr Matthew, you've got to eat those sandwiches, all of them, 'cos she's not having your death at her door through starvation and there's not enough good food about now to waste any.'

'I bet that's not all she said.'

'No, it isn't, Mr Matthew, and I can tell you the rest. She said you've got to stop picking at your food like a cock in moult—you know, when it's losing its feathers.' And Mary laughed.

For a moment he listened to his grand-mother's laugh joining Mary's before he said in mock-indignation, 'As soon as I've finished this I'll go down into that kitchen and I'll tell her what I think. A cock in moult! Mary, just you tell her I'm coming down there to give her what she would call a mouthful.'

'Oh, I'll do that, Mr Matthew, I'll do that with pleasure. And I'll be there to hear her answer.'

'Get yourself out!' her mistress barked at her.

As the door closed behind Mary, they could still hear her laughing, and Annie Wallingham repeated on a chuckle, 'A cock in moult.' Then she added, 'You know what that means . . . Mr Matthew, sir?'

'No, Mrs Wallingham, I don't know ex-actly what it means.'

'Well, it refers to a man in love pining for his dear one . . . likely'—she laughed aloud now as she ended—'a Rhode Island Red.' Before he had time to remark on this she asked abruptly, 'Are you in love?'

He almost choked on a mouthful of ba-con sandwich; then, turning his face to-wards her, he said, 'Why do you ask that?'

'Because, my dear fellow, you show every sign of it.'

He did not speak for a time; when he did it was to say, 'Is it so plain?'

'It is to me. It's that nurse, isn't it?'

'Yes, it's that nurse, Granan, it's that nurse.'

'And you met her off the train this morning?'

'Yes, I did.'

'Am I to gather she works in the same hospital?'

'Yes, you may gather that.'

'And that was one of the main reasons why you've taken up this career?'

'Yes, again you could say you're right.'

'Then why hasn't she been back at work since the holidays?'

'She had an accident.'

'What kind of an accident . . . knocked over?'

'I'm not sure. I've just got the idea there was some trouble back at her home.'

'Man trouble?'

'Granan!' His words came slow now. 'I don't know, and I'm not going to press her to tell me, but if and when she does you will be the first to hear about it, I can assure you of that.'

'Thank you. Thank you kindly, Mr Matthew; I'll look forward to that. But of course you may forget to tell me, like you did about what happened on your second visit to the hospital.'

'My second visit?'

'Yes, what happened between you and the sergeant? Because something dire happened for you to come back and say you thought about giving up the work; what is more, that same night you had one of your nightmares, didn't you?'

He said nothing, but poured himself out a cup of coffee, and as he was doing so she rose to her feet, saying, 'I'll let you finish your breakfast in peace; I'm going upstairs, because I'm following a fox.'

'You're following what? A fox?'

'Yes; with the telescope. She comes out about this time. And she's got young and they have to be fed: yesterday I saw them playing round about ten o'clock. My vixen passed along the top of the Mount. That's why I can make her out so clearly: she usually takes the sledge path at the end of the quarry.'

He made no remark on this, but listened to her pulling herself slowly up the spiral stairs into the observatory above. Her husband had spent most of the last years of his life in that room. It was he who had had a large window built into the end wall. From it there was a view of the so-called Mount, what was left of the wall of a deep quarry. Its jutting rocks and ledges were mostly covered with lichen and stunted shrubs, and on the floor of the stone quarry was evidence of storms, frost and snow in the boulders that lay about. The nearer side of the quarry didn't rise to any great height and the viewer could see most of the floor and the moorhens' pool towards the end of it. There was no other homestead between the quarry and the house, merely grazing-fields and a small area of woodland to the west of it.

Matthew finished his breakfast. Then, pushing the small table to one side, he sat back in his chair and thought of what his grandmother had said about his second visit to the hospital.

It was a while before he pulled himself up from the chair, shook his head as if he had been dozing, then picked up his stick and went to the foot of the stairs and called up to her: 'I'm away to see Father, Granan.' 'Good,' she called back. 'Try to get him to go out.'

He made his way to his father's room, but there his suggestion was received brusquely: 'Go for a ride,' his father said, 'when I can hardly get on my pins this morning? Don't be silly!' Then, softening a little, he said, 'Another day perhaps; yes, another day. I'd like to see the new contraption anyway.'

'Very well,' Matthew said, and without further ado made his way across the landing to the main staircase, where Peter caught up with him.

'Don't take any notice, Mr Matthew; he's had a really bad night. By the way, no matter what anybody says, I must tell you I think you made the right choice of a driver. He's a lively fellow, and I'm sure he keeps you amused.'

'He does, Peter. He does. I'm glad somebody understands.'

'Oh, it takes all types to make a world; you know that. Go careful now.' He guided Matthew to the stairhead; then he returned to his master's room, where later that same morning he was to repeat his opinion about Mr Matthew's choice of a chauffeur.

It had already been agreed it would no longer be suitable for Jim Taylor to continue to lodge in the village; the man should be at hand, not only to take Matthew back and forth to work but also at other times, such as weekends. He should be there to attend to Matthew's needs, few as they might be, for as things were now this task fell on Peter's increasingly heavily burdened shoulders.

So it was arranged that the new man should clear out a room above the stables at the side of the house. At one time it had been used as a bedroom for the groom, but it had latterly become a store room for odds and ends of gardening implements. Jim cleared it out, scrubbed the floor and put in an oil stove to get rid of the damp. The next step was the carrying of oddments of furniture such as a single bed down from the attic in the house.

This morning he had left the room and was about to make his way down the drive to the farmyard, there to wash the car, when he saw the old lady walking along the terrace. She was muffled up to the eyes and leaning heavily on her two sticks.

Raising his hat, he said, 'Lovely morning, ma'am, sharp but nice.'

'Yes, it is a lovely morning.' She added, 'Are you settled in your new abode?'

'Not quite, ma'am; just got to bring a few more things down from the attic.'

'I see. Do you prefer your new position to the farmwork?'

'Oh yes, ma'am. To be honest, yes. I was brought up on a farm, you know, but never took to it, not really. I was always for cars, like.'

'Well, you've picked on a good one now.'

'Yes, ma'am, she's a spanker.'

'I agree with you, a Daimler is a spanker, equal to a Rolls any day.'

'Oh yes, ma'am. Yes, equal to a Rolls . . . I'll say.'

'And Mr Matthew is enjoying it?'

'Oh, he's enjoying it, ma'am. Given him a new lease of life. The only fly in the ointment is, I can't drop him at his door.'

The old lady did not speak; and then the new man voiced a piece of homemade philosophy: 'You can't have everything you want in life, can you, ma'am? It would make it too easy for you then. You wouldn't know you were alive.'

He heard what could have been a chortle from her, then she said, 'What is it you're wanting in life, Taylor, at the present moment? Something special?'

'Yes, I could say that, ma'am, but I don't want it for meself. It's for Mr Matthew I would have it; but then, as my mother used to say, if you know what's good for you, keep your mouth shut and you won't swallow flies.'

She had stepped nearer to him now and said, 'What is it Mr Matthew wants and can't have?'

'Oh, I couldn't say, ma'am. Anyway, it's none of my business, and he'd skin me hide off with his tongue if I even suggested it.'

Her voice was low now as she said, 'On our short acquaintance, Taylor, I see that you're no fool, so don't take me for one, please, but tell me what you would like to suggest that will be of help to Mr Matthew.'

There was a long pause before Jim Taylor said, 'Well, taking the bull by the horns, ma'am, it's this piece of grass I'm standing on.'

'Piece of grass! What d'you mean?'

'Well, if five yards or more could be taken off it, the old drive could be continued and the car could come straight up and be driven into the barn here.'

'Driven into which barn?' Her voice sounded puzzled.

'Well, the wood-barn, ma'am. There's not enough room for such a car to be driven straight into it as it stands, but if the side where the window is were taken down and a couple of doors inserted there, well, there you have it, Bob's your uncle! a garage.'

'Really? Really. And you expect all this alteration to be made just because Mr Matthew doesn't want to walk up that short piece of grass?'

'Oh, he's not complainin', ma'am, but others do, you know, when they have to park in the farmyard.'

'There's space left to park there.'

'Yes, ma'am, but people have still got to walk from there up to the house. There's old Dr Peel. He got drenched the other morning.'

'Oh, Dr Peel!' Her voice was indignant. 'That fellow should have a ward to himself. He has every illness of all his patients. Either he's got the illness or he's had the illness, or his wife's had it. The only thing that man hasn't had is a miscarriage.'

When Jim Taylor's laugh rang out she silenced it quickly with, 'Hush! man. Hush! You'll have them here in a minute and get me into trouble. I shouldn't be out, that's what they'll say, and it's right, I shouldn't be out standing here listening to your stupid suggestions. The reason why I had that lawn put there was I couldn't bear the sound of traffic rumbling by the side of the house most of the day. Horses, horses, horses. Get yourself away, man!'

'Yes, ma'am. I'd go in now, ma'am, it's getting chillier.'

'Don't you dare tell me what I should do. Get away out of my sight; and I want to hear no more about your suggestions. Away with you!'

He got away, but he was still laughing, silently now. Eeh, she was a tartar!

He had no sooner disappeared than the front door opened and Peter came out, crying, 'Madam, what on earth are you doing out on a morning like this? It's enough to cut you in two. Do come inside . . . please!'

'I will when I get along to my own abode; and I'm all right, Peter. I'm quite all right. I've had a most enjoyable walk. Yes, and conversation too. Close that door, then help me along to my home.'

He quickly pulled the front door behind him; then, his hand gently on her arm, he walked beside her along the terrace. At the annexe she said, 'Come in a minute.'

Once in the warm room, she pulled off her fur hat and scarf and sheepskin cape; then, sitting down on the sofa, she held out one foot, saying, 'Pull off that blooming overshoe. I don't know how I got the damned things on anyway. Where's Mary?'

'The last I saw of her, madam, she was in the kitchen having a cup of tea with Cook.'

'And a gossip no doubt. And my grandson?'

'He was in his room, madam.'

'And my daughter-in-law?'

'She's with the colonel.'

'Well, that's them all set. Now you have two or three minutes free, I want to ask you something. What d'you think of this new fellow?'

'You mean Mr Matthew's new driver?'

'That's who I mean, and you know who I mean. Don't waste words.'

'Well, madam, I think he is the right man for the right job. Not only can he drive well but he's a very amusing chap, and I think because of this he will be a great help to Mr Matthew.'

'Amusing be damned! You know what he really is, and let's speak plainly: he's a cheeky young bugger, that's what he is. He knows too much, more than is good for him, and his tongue causes havoc.'

'What has he done, madam, to annoy you?'

'Who said he had annoyed me? He hasn't annoyed me. Though I've listened to more free speech in a few minutes from him than I've done for a long, long time.'

'You mean this morning, madam, when you were out?'

'Yes, this morning when I was out. We met at the end of the terrace, he standing on what he termed my grass and telling me what should be done with it so that the car could be driven straight into a garage made out of one of the wood-barns.'

'He did?'

'He did. But he put it over in such a way that I thought of all those heads in the diplomatic departments. If that fellow had only had education he could have prevented the last war!'

They were both laughing now.

'Well, one thing, he has certainly impressed you, madam.'

'Impressed me? Not only has he done that but he has made me think about altering my mind, a mind I made up years ago when I first came back to this house. I was having no traffic up there; you know the story as well as I do. And now, five yards off the lawn! Oh, you wouldn't believe it, and all in a few minutes and cleverly put. He even brought that old fool Dr Peel to his aid. Said he got wringing wet or something coming from the farmyard up to here. And you know what I told him?' She leant towards him, then whispered, 'Well, you know my opinion of old Peel, don't you?'

'Yes, madam.'

'Well, he's always got something wrong with him, hasn't he?'

'Well, he does complain, madam, or tell you about complaints.'

'Complain! I told that young man he needn't be sorry for Dr Peel and that the only thing that man hadn't had was a miscarriage. I should have added, and an abortion.'

Over the years Peter Carter had had to train his countenance to meet all occasions. He smiled when necessary, he spoke when necessary and always tactfully; in fact, he knew he had become a kind of automaton in the family. But he was highly respected because he gave respect where it was due. But now the automaton was lost under the man and he put his head back and laughed out aloud. He couldn't remember the last time he had laughed out aloud, not like this. She was a star of stars, this old lady!

'Be quiet, Peter! You're the second one I've had to hush up this morning.' She was laughing herself though, but quietly, saying now, 'I'm a very vulgar woman. In fact if my son heard me he would say I was acting like one of the common herd, as he would describe them, and that's where he'll put poor Jim Taylor when he hears my suggestion, right back in the middle of the common herd. Anyway . . .' her voice was quiet now as she said, 'I've always liked ordinary people, Peter. I feel I have something in common with them, even though they're all scared of me. And you know something else? Matthew takes after me. He likes them too, and from the little I gather from his talk he lived with them during the war and came to honour the men under him, even love them. No wonder he went off his head for a while. You know, I understand he never opened his mouth for weeks on end. It was that nurse who brought him round, acted as a sort of mother to him, I surmise, saying that she was in her fifties or some such. But, old or young, he must have fallen for her. Men do fall in love with older women, don't they, Peter?'

'Yes, indeed they do, madam. Oh yes,' said Peter with feeling.

'But she isn't an old woman. I understand she's young and beautiful, and his mind is full of her. But what about her? We know nothing of her, only the little he lets slip now and again. She's been off ill, you know: she is supposed to have had an accident, but I have my own ideas about that. There's something fishy there, but we'll get to the bottom of it.'

'I'm sure you will, madam. If anyone can you will, especially through Mr Matthew, because he thinks the world of you.'

She made no reply to this, but went on, 'He's not like his father, you know. Nor yet can I see anything of my daughter-in-law in him. As for Rodney, they are poles apart. Matthew was very like William. You didn't know William, did you?'

'No, madam, but I've heard of him.'

'They're both like their grandfather.'

He put in now, 'The post has just come and there are two letters from America. They'll be from Mr William, madam.'

'Oh, that's good. I'll have to go up there and find out what they're all about. The last letter he wrote was from his place in Detroit. His work's there, but he also tells us he's taken a house on Lake Erie in Canada, just across the border. It's a beautiful place, he says. Well, he's done better for himself than if he had gone to Sandhurst. My! That was an upset. His father had them all down for the army and the first one who should have gone in refused flatly. William was going to have nothing to do with the army. As he said, he had been brought up in it and it wasn't for him. He left for America, you know, when he was just nineteen, and he's never talked of coming home once since. Personally, I think that's wrong of him but . . . but he had his reasons. His father and he didn't see eye to eye about anything. Anyway, after I have my coffee I'll make my way along there and find out all the news and give them some of mine, which undoubtedly will cause a stir . . . in some quarters anyway.'

Peter did not say, 'You always cause a stir, madam, wherever you go'; he just smiled at her and said, 'Do be careful of the stairs, madam. If you will give me a ring I'll help you up.'

'Yes, I'll do that, Peter.'

13

It was about half an hour later when Annie Wallingham entered her son's room on Peter's arm, to be greeted by the colonel from his couch, saying, 'Why on earth do you attempt those stairs, woman?'

'I haven't attempted them on my own, I've been helped up. What d'you think Peter was doing? Anyway, I've come to hear the American news.'

'Well, get off your feet,' said her son. 'And Peter, go and tell Mr Matthew there's a letter here for him.'

As Peter left the room Annie Wallingham looked at her son and said sharply, 'He won't like that. Why couldn't you let Peter take it to his room?'

'Oh dear me! Mother. Doesn't he need it to be read to him?'

'Yes, he needs it to be read to him, but Peter could have done that, or he could have asked me. It's his letter. Anyway, what does William say in yours?'

Lucille, who hadn't so far spoken, took the letter from a side table and read it aloud. It began: 'Dear Mama and Father', and went on to say he was at the lake for a few days. The weather was vile there, as it was in Detroit; the business was thriving and he was now on the board of the company. He hoped they were both well and also the rest of the family. He sent them his love as always.

To this, the old lady's response was, 'Well, well! Such an exciting letter! He's on the board. The only piece of news in it was he's on the board, but I'd had the impression he had been put on the board years ago and was running the whole concern.'

'It's a very large concern, Mother.'

'I know that. I was hoping this letter would say he was going to be married. He's past thirty now, isn't he? He should be married. But there is no doubt he will be well provided with a mistress or two.'

'Mother-in-law!'

'Oh! Lucille, don't be so pious! Your son

is a man. He's in a country that moves fast, big and fast. Everything from America is big.'

'Ah! All the family at once.'

Peter came in leading Matthew, and behind them came Rodney, and on the sight of him his grandmother said, 'There's a saying on the South Tyne, "Aall together, like the folks o' Shields, and it early in the morning." '

'There's a letter here for you, Matthew.'

'So I understand.'

Matthew's tone was terse and his grandmother just refrained from saying, 'I told you he wouldn't be pleased at his mail not being sent up to him.'

When his mother handed him the letter Matthew fingered the long envelope for a moment, saying as he did so, 'From William?'

'Yes, dear,' said his mother. 'It'll be from William. Shall I open it for you?'

'Please.'

Lucille opened the envelope, then, smoothing out the two sheets of fine notepaper, she paused a moment before she began to read, her voice soft: 'Hello there, Brother.' Another pause, during which she glanced quickly at her husband before she repeated, 'Hello there, Brother, how are things in the backwoods? I hear you've taken up a career. Good for you. But two years is a long haul. I do wish you were over this side of the water. They work miracles here, you know, and as you've still got your eyes, under the right man you could be right near to one—a miracle I mean.'

Lucille's tone had a sharp edge to it now as she went on, 'How is the old warhorse, still bossing the show? She would go down well here, plenty to get her teeth into. I often think about her, and you. Yes, I do, boy, I often think about you and the dirty deal that's been handed out to you. By the way, you've never said, but have you got a secretary or a batman or somebody like that to read to you? The only two letters I've had from you were written by Granan.' Lucille paused again here and glanced at her mother-in-law, who was lying back in her chair staring ahead.

'Anyway, old lad, I have the opportunity of playing the market now and again, and from the time I heard of your accident I bought a bit of stock for you which soon trebled its value, and so I sold and reinvested your gains in another firm. This paid off as well, but I'm not keeping all your eggs in one basket. All I'll say at the moment is you have seven thousand dollars floating free and I'm sending this on to you through the bank. I suppose Father's still with the old branch? I'm not doing this because I imagine you're broke: they'll have given you a decent pension, at least I hope they have, and our battling old grandfather didn't leave you penniless. But I understand that after this training of yours the idea will be to set up your own practice, and there's one thing you've got to learn and that is you can't have too much money. You were never business-minded, but you must realise if you want to set up an establishment of your own you'll need quite a bit of help, and as I've found in life, help has to be paid for in all kinds of ways, but the easiest way is with cash.'

Lucille Wallingham took in a long deep breath as she took the second page of the letter and put it on top of the first; then it was with a definite effort that she went on: 'Before I finish I'll just say I'd love to see you, Matthew, and I can't see any reason why, with a manservant, you couldn't do it.' Lucille paused here before going on, 'It's too much to think that our parents would move out of their shell. Oh, I know Father isn't well, but a sea voyage, as I see it, would be one of the best things for him. Anyway, Matthew . . .' again Lucille paused, then, wetting her lips, she repeated on a louder tone now, 'Anyway, Matthew, keep in touch. More than that, write me a long letter full of the real news, and you can, you know, because I understand there is a kind of lined paper, sort of ridged, for people who are in your state. So let me hear from you, because, believe it or not, there are times when I miss my family. Bye for the present. Yours ever, William.'

There was silence in the room until Rodney spoke. 'Misses his family? Like hell he does!'

'Rodney!' It was his father's voice, speaking as a colonel. 'That is enough!'

'No, it isn't, Father. That letter is an insult. No real mention of you or Mama, or reference to the fact that he's got another brother. All it's about is Matthew going over there.'

Matthew's voice now broke sharply in on the tirade, 'It isn't the contents of the letter that's narking you, Brother, it's the fact of the seven thousand dollars, isn't it? As William said, I never had a head for business, but you had, and you have now. Oh, very much so now. And to think he is sending me seven thousand dollars . . . my goodness!'

Now it was his mother who cut in on him, saying, 'Money or no money, I think the whole letter was rather hurtful, and in this case Rodney is right.'

It was Annie Wallingham's turn to interrupt. Turning to her daughter-in-law, she said, 'I don't see why you're so upset. It was a letter from brother to brother, someone he could speak to openly; and Matthew was right about the money. If the same amount had been sent to you, Rodney'—her head was bobbing now towards her younger grandson—'you wouldn't have found anything wrong with the letter, now would you? Well, while there is a private war going on, I'll join in and tell you something else that will disturb you one and all, but mostly you, Rodney. And Matthew, I might say, as yet knows nothing about it.

I'm going to have the end part of the lawn taken up and the wood-barn turned into a garage, so that Matthew's car can come straight up to the house. Now, you can all chew on that.'

'The lawn taken up?' This cry came from Richard Wallingham. 'Take the lawn up, Mother? It was you who made all that fuss about laying it down. My father went nearly mad because he couldn't bring his horse past the house, and now you're saying you're going to have it up so that Matthew's car can be brought practically to the door?'

'Yes, that's what I'm saying, Richard. And you needn't remind me of the fuss I made. I had enough noise and shouting to put up with from your father at that time, never mind horses tramping back and forth when down the road was a big farmyard all equipped with stables and such.'

'But not for horses, Mother. They were for the farm animals. Oh'—his two hands went to his head—'I'll never be able to understand you. Never!'

'Well, that's no news to me, Richard.' She now pulled herself to her feet, saying with quiet dignity, 'Will you see me down the stairs, Peter, please?'

'Yes, madam.' And, gently taking her arm, he led her from the room.

Richard Wallingham was speaking again, and to Matthew: 'You knew nothing about this, Matthew?'

'No, sir, nothing whatever.'

'I don't believe you.' This came from his brother, and Matthew turned on him, his voice high now and angry: 'I don't care a damn whether you believe me or not. I would never have dreamt of suggesting such a thing to Granan. Anyway, what you forget is that this is Granan's house, all of it, not just the annexe. The farm and every square inch of land is hers. Grandfather left the whole caboodle to her and not to you, Father.' Matthew turned in what he thought was his father's direction. 'He made no reference in his will to a son inheriting, and that has upset you, too, for years, hasn't it? Because you couldn't understand, with your military heritage, why you weren't named as his successor to the whole estate. No, he broke all the rules: he worshipped Granan and knew she had a head on her shoulders; he left everything in her care. And so, as she has just pointed out, she can do what she likes with any part of it, and that, Mr Rodney Wallingham, includes the farm. Perhaps all this is news to you. It was to me until I had reason to visit our solicitor, and it just slipped out. He spoke as if I knew all about it, which I didn't.

'We were too young at the time Grandfather died to have wills explained to us. And you, Rodney, are afraid that if anything were to happen to Father I would naturally take over. Wouldn't it be funny if the old lady were to leave the whole bang shoot to William? She was very fond of William, for the simple reason that he took after his grandfather.'

Into the silence that followed, he said, 'Please, Mama, let me have my letter.' And when she handed it to him he added, 'And I would be grateful if, in future, my mail could be sent to my rooms.'

His father's voice came rasping back at him now, saying, 'The mail that comes into this house will be delivered into my study as usual.'

'Well, Father'—Matthew paused—'we'll have to go into that matter, but later.

Enough for the present.' And on this, he tapped his way to the door, which Peter was already opening from outside. As he led him across the landing to the top of the stairs, Peter said under his breath, 'I'll see what I can do, Mr Matthew.'

'Please don't bother, Peter. By the way things stand, the best thing I can do is to get a flat of my own.'

'Oh, don't say that, Mr Matthew. You'd break at least two people's hearts and touch a lot of others at the same time. Oh, don't think along those lines, Matthew.' This time he did not add the 'Mr' to his plea but spoke as if to a friend. 'You will break up the family because, whether you realise it or not, you're all your mother's got left. She's a very lonely lady at bottom.'

Matthew made no reply to this statement, but patting Peter's arm he said, 'You're a very good fellow, Peter, always have been. This house owes you a lot.'

'No one owes me anything, Matthew. I am pleased to be here and to help in any way I can.'

On this they parted, and Peter, having gone back into the colonel's room, was greeted immediately with, 'This fellow Taylor. He must be at the bottom of this! Get him up here! I want to know what he thinks he's about.'

Peter hesitated for just one moment, and this brought the colonel's voice rasping at him, 'Well!'

'Yes, sir, I'll tell him.'

Peter had not far to go to find Jim Taylor, for he had just brought a small table down from the attic, and as he rested at the back door leading from the kitchen into the yard, Peter said quickly, 'Leave that! The master wants a word with you.'

'With me? The . . . the colonel?'

'Yes, the colonel.'

For a moment the men stared at each other, until Cook called from the kitchen, 'What have you been up to now, me lad, eh?' and Jim answered her flippantly by saying, 'Likely somebody's split on me for pinching your cakes.'

'Wouldn't be a bit surprised.' Cook's thick body wobbled with laughter as she added, 'And what else? Aye, what else?'

Jim was stroking back his ruffled mop of sandy hair as he followed Peter up the stairs, but they hadn't reached the landing when Peter, turning to him, said quietly, 'Mind how you go.'

'What d'you mean?'

'Just what I say.'

There was a friendly note in Peter's voice, and Jim said, 'Trouble?'

'Could be. It all depends how you handle it.'

They exchanged glances but said no more. Then Peter, opening the colonel's door, ushered Jim in, saying, 'Taylor for you, sir.'

Jim took in the situation at a glance. A man with greying hair was sitting upon a couch. He hadn't seen the colonel before now, and straight away he knew he didn't like the face, for it bore no resemblance to Mr Matthew's. Then also in the room there was his late boss, staring at him with that look he remembered vividly, as if he would like to strike at him if only he dared. And lastly, there was the lady of the house. He had seen her about the place a number of times and wondered why her face always held a worried look, which at this moment was emphasized.

'What have you been up to, Taylor?'

For a moment Jim did not answer, but

then he said, 'Up to, sir? I don't know what you mean, up to.'

'You know fine well what I mean. How dare you interfere with my household arrangements?'

'Me interfere with your household arrangements, sir? I don't know what you're getting at.'

Jim now turned his head and glanced at Peter, who was standing slightly to the side of him. It was to him Jim spoke now, saying, 'I've never interfered in any household arrangement.'

'Look at me! man.'

'I'm looking at you, sir.'

The colonel snapped back, 'It's about you daring to go to my . . . the elder Mrs Wallingham and suggest that she has the lawn removed from the end of the terrace and a garage made so that you could drive the car up to the house.'

'Ooh, that. Well, let me tell you, sir, I never went along to the old girl . . . lady, and said any such thing.'

'Don't stand there lying, man. You had already spoken of this to Old Joe.'

'Yes. Yes, I had, along the lines that it was a pity the car had to be left down in the farmyard when there were these barns, like, on your very doorstep. But as for going to the old lady, this I never did.'

'Well, would you mind telling me how she came to know about your idea, then present it to me not half an hour gone?'

'Yes, I'll tell you. It was when she was walking on the terrace. She came right to the end of it and I was standing on the grass.'

'She what! She was walking on the terrace? What are you talking about, man? My mother would never walk the terrace in this weather.'

'Well, she did, sir, and this very morning.'

The colonel now turned to his wife, and Lucille shook her head and said, 'Well . . . well, how was I to know? She can't be chained up.'

'But to walk the terrace in weather like this! It could kill her.'

'She was well wrapped up, sir.' Jim's tone held a note of placation. 'Yes, she was wrapped up to the eyes; and she said she was out for a breath of fresh air and . . . and it was a lovely morning and . . .'

'Never mind what she said about a

lovely morning. Why did you put your idea to her?'

'I never did, sir, not like that. She talked to me and I did say, I confess, that it was a pity the car couldn't come right up to the house because in bad weather you could get soaked making it from the farm. Dr Peel had spoken about it, and that made her laugh and she made a joke about him . . .'

'Nonsense! You must have already worked out a scheme how this could be done.'

'Yes. All right, sir, yes, I had. When she asked me an outright question I gave her an outright answer. I said the only way it could be done was by taking four or five or so many yards off the lawn. Yes, I did say that.'

'You dared to say that to her?'

'Yes, I did, sir, and then I asked her about a garage or such, and I told her what could be done. I didn't actually put anything to her, it just came about through her questioning and . . . and, at bottom, what was best for Mr Matthew; and as I'm out to get the best for him I told her what could be done with the wood-barn and . . .'

'Get out of my sight, and at this moment!'

Jim did not immediately do as he was bidden, but rather he dared to say, 'You're not my boss, sir; Mr Matthew is, and he's a man on his own. I'd go through hell and high water for him, but not for anybody else in this establishment.' And now he looked from the almost convulsed face of the man on the couch to his youngest son, who was standing rigidly now, that same look on his face as if he could kill him. Lastly, he spoke to Lucille. 'I'm sorry about this, ma'am. It all came about through the old lady speaking kindly to me and our joint interest in her grandson. Now I will go, sir.' And on this he actually elbowed Peter aside and marched from the room.

'Oh! my dear, don't upset yourself, please.' Lucille was holding her husband by the shoulders. 'I . . . I suppose the man meant well. I . . .'

'*Shut up,* woman, will you!' Then, as his wife almost sprang back from him, he cried to Peter, 'Get me a drink, man, and quick!'

After Peter had hurried from the room,

Rodney said, 'I told you, Father, what he was like; he should never have been taken on.'

Now it was his turn to be lashed by his father's tongue, for the colonel turned on him: 'If you knew how to keep your men he would never have left the farm.'

'My God!' said Rodney. 'How have I kept things going all these years?'

'Because the old hands were there, that's how. You're dealing with a new generation now; they've got to be handled, and properly.'

'Well, I'll be damned!' Rodney was on his way to leaving the room when he stopped at the door and said, 'Well, to my mind, Father, your manner wasn't one to be copied.'

'Rodney!'

The door banged on Lucille's amazed cry, and again she went to her husband, saying, 'Please, Richard . . . don't upset yourself further. You know what'll happen, you'll be in bed for days.'

'Yes'—he now turned on her—'and you'll hate that, won't you? Oh, don't tell me that you love being at my beck and call, I'm no fool, never have been. You've done your duty, and that's that. Altogether I can tell you, now we're private for once, that I consider I've had a dirty deal all round: from my father; from my mother, who never showed any interest in me; from my eldest son, now throwing his weight about with his money—he didn't think about us, did he? We might have been having it hard. And then there's Matthew. There's been no peace in the house since he returned. I can't help saying it, it's true. And, too, there's the one who's just stalked out. I understand him because he's going through a similar process to the one I had to put up with. He is given no credit for his capabilities, such as they are.'

Lucille said nothing; she just stood looking at the man whom she had indeed put up with, and those were his words, put up with for years. Yet she could understand his feelings, and everything he had said was true. His own mother hadn't shown much love for him; for his sons, oh yes; yes. And this very love for William and Matthew had been like salt on a sore to him because in Matthew his own father had been reborn. The colonel suddenly slumped back on his couch and, covering his eyes with his hand, murmured, 'I'm sorry, my dear. I'm sorry.' She could not go to him, nor could she speak because her throat was full of tears which were now forcing themselves down her cheeks. When Peter came in carrying a tray it was with a sigh of relief that she left the room. He had stood aside to allow her to pass, and her bowed head and tearstained cheeks wrung his heart.

She was running for her room when she saw Matthew making his way along the gallery, and when he called out, 'Mama! Is that you?' she stopped but could not answer him.

When he reached her he put out his free hand and touched her shoulder, saying, 'What is it? You're upset. Peter has just given me a quick word. He says there's been hell to pay along there, and Father's had Jim up on the carpet, blaming him for telling Granan of his idea for a garage. It is true?'

'Yes, yes, dear.' She opened her bedroom door and he followed her in. He knew she had dropped down into a chair and he stood beside her, his arm about her shoulders, saying, 'And you as usual have come in for the brunt of it. I'll . . . I'll have to speak to Jim. He had no right.'

'It wasn't the man's fault, I'm sure. You know what your grandmother is like for worming things out of people and'—she now wiped her face with her handkerchief—'the worst of it was—or the best of it was, it's how one looks at it—the man stood his ground for which, as your grandmother would surely put it, Richard let him have it.'

'You mean he answered Father back?'

'Oh'—Lucille sighed sadly—'answered him back? He went for him. Not only him, but for the rest of us in this establishment, as he called it. Only one good thing came out of the scene, the fact that he'd give his life for you. I have never taken to the man, as you know. I've said before he doesn't know his place, but if it hadn't been for the fact that he ripped your father's military self-esteem from him I could have admired the fellow for standing his ground and refusing to be intimidated or bullied.'

Matthew took his arm from his mother's shoulders, and standing apart he said, 'I think, Mama, it would be the best thing for everybody if I took a small house or flat in town. Jim would see to all my needs, I know that. And I must admit I like the fellow. I understand his language and his way of looking at things; I met so many like him, when I was in tight corners, men like him and like Charlie Fox. Now, *he* would take me on tomorrow. He could come too and be my houseman.'

She was on her feet now, holding him, imploring, 'Don't . . . oh, Matthew, don't. Don't even think of such a thing. Don't you know you are all I have left? and although I am jealous of your feeling for your grandmother and hers for you, you're a link between us. We both have your welfare so much at heart. There is no one I can talk to except you and Peter. Oh yes, dear Peter. What we'd all do without Peter I don't know, but he isn't you.'

'All right. All right, Mama. But somehow I feel that my condition caused so many changes in the house that no one seems happy any more.'

'We were never happy before: we all lived behind façades. The only happy couple in this house as far as I can recall were your grandmother and grandfather.'

'Oh, Mama.' His arms were about her now. 'I didn't know, didn't guess that . . . that you weren't happy.'

'Why should you? If . . . if you should marry, Matthew, and . . . and I know you will . . . oh yes, I know you will—and in your case and hers, whoever she is, I know it will be out of love—keep it alive by speaking of it. Don't take any emotion for granted. All emotions should be voiced, although it's only those of anger and frustration that are usually given air.'

'Oh, my dear Mama. Come, sit with me. Where's the couch? I want to talk to you.'

She led him to the window, below which a two-seater couch was placed, and when they were sitting side by side and he was holding her hand tightly, he said, 'I'm in love, Mama.'

'That isn't any news to me, Matthew,' said Lucille, giving a little laugh. 'Ever since Granan told me that your night nurse was not a middle-aged mother at all, and that she was working in the new hospital like you, I've been waiting for something like this.'

'I'm not just in love; I love Elizabeth, Liz

as I call her, enough to risk asking her to marry me. But I need your help.'

'My help? Well, my dear, what can I do to help you with this affair? She is a nurse and, I understand, a very capable one. She must have been to bring you through your difficult period.'

'I want you to ask her here for a meal, or better still for a weekend.'

'Well, I can't see why not, if that will be of any help.'

'Not in the ordinary way, Mama; but I feel she'll need persuading.'

'If that is the case I don't think your feelings are really reciprocated.'

'They are. I . . . I feel they are, and to a great extent, but there is something holding her back, and it isn't only her career— she hopes to become a sister—but what happened at Christmas. She was supposed to have had an accident, but of what kind I don't know. However, whatever happened during the holidays and the time she was away has changed her somewhat.'

'But, my dear, how could you detect a change in her in that short time?'

'I don't know, but I do, Mama.'

'What are her parents?'

'What little information I have about them is from Jerry. They have a farm, a small one, but her father isn't at all well. She has a brother who was wounded in the war, a leg wound I understand. He's at home, but they have good friends in the people from the much larger farm next to them. Apparently the families went to school together or something like that. Jerry said she wasn't very forthcoming about the set-up, and whatever happened I fear it's still troubling her.'

'But what good, my dear, would a visit here do, even just for tea?'

'I don't exactly know, Mama, I just get this feeling. But, you know, when you can't see you're very aware of atmosphere or of the slightest change of tone in anyone's voice, and all your other instincts are heightened: hearing, touch, smell. It's a weird experience. I know whenever she's near or coming to me, I can smell her.'

'That's probably scent. Perhaps she uses a special kind.'

'No, it's nothing like that, Mama.' And gravely he added, 'It isn't scent that emanates from Rodney, but I know when he's near.'

'Oh, don't say that. I know he's jealous but . . . but you've got to try to understand he hasn't your nature or looks.'

'Looks, Mama?'

'Yes, looks, dear, because no one would ever take you for . . . well, for being blind. It is the movement of your hands that gives that away. Anyway, my dear, if you think it will help, of course invite her, but don't, don't I beg of you, talk of leaving us and setting up on your own. Yes, yes I know'— she patted his hand—'if you marry, that will have to happen, but you have two years' training to do in your profession. But in the meantime, do . . . do, my dear one, give a little thought to me.'

His arms were about her again and he was kissing her cheek, which was still wet with her tears, and he said, 'I do, Mama; I do give a lot of thought to you.'

And now there was a plea in her voice when she said, 'And be kind to your father, please, for my sake. He needs help. This muscular business is very trying and there's no good end to it. He knows it, and I know it, and'—her voice dropped—'the unfortunate thing is that he's not a happy man, never has been.'

'I'll do my best, Mama,' he said. 'I'll . . . I'll visit him more often and learn to chat. I'll tell him about all that goes on in the wards, especially about my dear sergeant. That'll rouse him.'

'Don't worry, dear. Just go and see him now and again and do as you say. You told Peter about the sergeant, didn't you?'

'Yes, I did.'

Why did Peter have to tell her what Matthew had told him? But why not? He was like one of the family.

She was saying now, 'Would you like me to drop a note, a little invitation to your nurse?'

'Yes, I would, but not for, say, a week or so. She'll . . . well, she might think I'm jumping the gun. You know what I mean. But I just wanted to know that I could invite her when the time is right and that you would welcome her.'

She took his hand again, saying now, 'I'd do anything to please you, Matthew, and to keep you here.'

'I don't deserve such love,' he said as he put his hand on her cheek. 'I only hope

I never disappoint you. But now, where's that damn stick?'

She placed the stick in his hand, and as he made for the door he said, 'I'm off to find that fellow of mine and give him the length of my tongue for causing this uproar.'

'Oh, don't blame him entirely, dear; the Queen of Uproars had something to do with it.'

He laughed heartily and repeated, 'The Queen of Uproars. It's a good title for her, I must admit.' . . .

He did not, in fact, go and find Jim and tear him off a strip, but returned to his room and sat down at the desk that had been placed there for him—for what purpose? he had once asked himself. He now took out from a writing case a sheet of fine paper indented with lines a third of an inch apart. It had been a present and he had barely used it before, but his brother's letter had reminded him of it. He groped for his fountain pen, then began to write.

Only once before had he attempted this task, when its slow progression had irked him and he had given up in disgust. But after listening to the warm and generous letter that his mother had read to him with such chagrin, he wanted to express himself in the same vein as William had used. And he couldn't see himself doing this through an intermediary.

He had just finished it and placed it in a long envelope ready for Peter to address when there was a tap at the door and a voice said, 'It's me, Mr Matthew.'

'Come in, Mary,' he called; and when she entered the room and saw him at his desk she exclaimed, 'Oh! You're writing, Mr Matthew. That's good; that's a good sign. The mistress has sent me to tell you that she thought you would like to have lunch with Madam today, and she's had it sent along and it's all ready for you.'

'Oh, that's nice, Mary. Thank you, I'll be down in a minute.'

'Well, don't keep Madam waiting, because you know what she's like if things get cold, and there's Cook's Scotch broth the day.'

'Good. Good. I'll be down immediately.'

He went into the bathroom and washed his hands, thinking, That was nice of Mama. She knew that lunch with Rodney would be intolerable. To think that she must have been unhappy all these years. Why?

Hurrying from the bathroom, his thoughts were saying, Why am I asking? She told me the reason. But I'll never make that mistake with Liz . . . no, never. In an hour or so's time I'll be seeing her again. Funny about that, *seeing* her again.

When he entered the annexe his grand-mother's voice greeted him from her small dining room, saying, 'I'm not waiting another minute for you. This soup'll be stone cold.'

He found his way into the dining room, to be met by Mary, who led him to a seat, saying, 'It's scalding hot, Mr Matthew; mind it doesn't burn your tongue.'

'Get on with it,' said her mistress, 'and mind you don't bite your tongue. What has Cook botched up for us today?'

'Well, madam, there's the broth; then cutlets with creamed potatoes and braised parsnips; and if that isn't enough she's made you your favourite pudding, plum duff, although as she says it's not what she could call a suitable finish to such a meal.'

'Well, you can go back and tell Cook from me she doesn't know what she's talking about.' Then, without pause, she leant towards Matthew who was sitting opposite her and said, 'You all right there?'

'Yes, dear, fine; and this is excellent broth.'

'Oh, there're one or two things she's not bad at; but she can never cook pancakes.'

'Oh, madam! They're paper-thin.'

'Well, they must have grown to magazine thickness by the time they reach this room.'

And so the meal went on, with chaffing between the two women while they exchanged surreptitious signals as to how Matthew's meal should be arranged before him.

And when the tray of empty dishes had been passed to Bella, who had been standing outside the door, and Mary was saying, 'I'll bring the coffee right away, madam,' Matthew said, 'Tell Cook, Bella, I thoroughly enjoyed the meal.'

'Well, that's your opinion,' his grandmother muttered, to which Mary came back with, 'Everybody's allowed their opinion, madam,' only to be driven from the room as the old lady yelled at her, 'That's got whiskers! Be off with you now!'

The door closed on a giggle from Bella and Mary's 'Huh!', and Matthew, laughing too, said, 'You treat her dreadfully, Granan.'

'Of course I do. She expects it, she loves it, and so does Cook. I know my people, Matthew. Oh yes, I know my people like you know your men, especially that mischief-making Jim.'

'Yes, I want to talk to you about that. He's really not the one to blame. But that will have to come another time because'— he had taken out his Braille watch—'it's ten-past one now and I have an appointment at two.'

'Oh, have you? You come and stuff your kite, then you're away.'

'I'll pop in when I get back, I promise.'

'You're off to see her, aren't you, that nurse?'

'Yes, I'm off to see that nurse.'

'Why don't you bring her here?'

'I will. I will soon.'

'Well, if you're going, get yourself away. I hear that you just whistle for that fellow.'

'Yes. That's how I call him, by a whistle.'

'That's no way to give orders, treating the man like a dog.'

'Huh! Nobody in this life will treat Jim

Taylor like a dog, you can take it from me. He was summoned to . . . the colonel this morning to be shredded; but I think Father got a surprise. Have a word with Peter and you'll probably hear what really transpired. For once Father apparently picked on the wrong man, someone who isn't afraid of rank and has little respect for it. Having spent half his war service in the cooler—as my friend Fox did, too, but for other reasons—Jim Taylor is not a person to be cowed. A whistle will bring him running, but not crawling on his belly.'

'My! My! We have another strong-minded person attached to the house.'

'Well, you could say that, but by all accounts he doesn't give a damn about the house or its inhabitants.'

'Just you.'

'Yes, Granan, just me; and I am sincerely grateful for his concern. It's a good feeling to have someone behind you when your front is blurred, if you follow me.'

'I follow you, Matthew'—her voice was low now—'and I can tell you my opinion of him is much the same as yours, following our conversation this morning.'

'Well, that's what we'll talk about later

on, your conversation this morning. Now goodbye, my dear.' He groped for her out-stretched hands, then drew her towards him, saying softly, 'I love you, you know, you old faggot.' He hugged her for a moment before turning away and leaving the room.

14

It wasn't until the car was well out of the grounds that Matthew said, 'I should tear you off a couple of strips for the rumpus you caused this morning.'

'I caused no rumpus, Mr Matthew. All I did—'

'I know all you did. You got ahold of my grandmother and inveigled her into seeing things your way.'

'*Sir!* It would be a brave man who could get hold of your grandmother in any way, physically or mentally. Huh!'

'Don't come your funny stuff with me, Jim Taylor. I know you and you know I do, and I can hear you putting your point, as you would say, straightforward like and with the finesse of a bull.'

'Meaning to say, sir, I ain't got tact. Well,

there you are wrong, and if I ever used that quality I used it this mornin'. The bull description is on your grandmother's foot. But I can tell you, I liked the old girl and I got on with her and, excuse me, Mr Matthew, she's the only one in your lot that I can say that about, with the exception of Peter. But he isn't family, is he?'

'He's as good as. He's been with my father for years.'

'Well, that speaks well for his patience, if nothing else.'

'Now, now, that's enough! If my father ribbed you, you deserved it.'

'No, I did not, sir. No, I did not. Not to be spoken to like he did to me. He's an army man and can't forget it. You're an army man, too, sir, but you treat folk like people. Well, what I mean is . . . human beings.'

'Yes, yes, I know what you mean, Jim. But we are all made differently. Circumstances carve us out. Even your folk, going on what you say, are different. It's the environment that carves the character, high or low.'

'Meaning, how you're brought up?'

'Yes, meaning just that.'

'Well, sir, I don't agree with you, because by environment you mean the background, the family life, like. Well, our lot was brought up decent, but one of us had to end up in the clink, as I told you, and he was livin' in the same . . . environment.'

'Well, Jim, think about it. That bears out what I said, we are all different.'

'What you said, Mr Matthew, was that the background carved your character, like puppets on a production belt.'

'Oh, be quiet! man. I don't want to get into your mental depths again, I've other things to think about and arrange, and with you. It was spitting rain when we came out; what's it like now?'

'Coming down in sheets.'

'Oh Lord! Then there'll be no country trip.'

'I shouldn't think so, Mr Matthew, not today; it looks in for it. But there's no reason I can see that Miss shouldn't make you afternoon tea and . . .'

'Will you kindly allow me to make my own arrangements, please?'

'Well, I was only suggesting.'

'As usual. But I will put it to Miss Ducks-

worth and let her decide. We'll leave it at
that.'

Matthew leant back against the head-
rest, and smiled wryly as he thought of
how his father would react to hearing such
an exchange. Of course it would never
happen between him and Peter. Peter
wouldn't be so brave, or foolhardy. His father, he imagined, would have choked to
death before now with frustration, irritation
and the desire to have the man shot,
whereas Matthew enjoyed these ex-
changes. And now he asked himself
whether he had been so tolerant of others
while at Sandhurst, or did the change happen during the campaigns in North Africa,
Sicily and Italy? Was it the battles and skir-
mishes that had changed his character or,
rather, not the events themselves but his
close contact with the so-called ordinary
men who had come through it with him,
and especially those who had died?

'Well, here we are, sir, and it's coming
down cats and dogs.'

As if coming out of a doze, he sat up
stiffly and as Jim helped him out of the
car the front door of the house opened and

Elizabeth, standing there, called, 'Hurry in before you get drenched.'

He was standing in the hall now, holding her hand, saying, 'So much for our joy-ride. You don't feel like going out in this, do you?'

'No, I certainly don't. Come along in. Come along.'

As she took Matthew's arm Jim said from behind them, 'I won't be a minute; I must shut her up else she'll be swamped.'

When he returned to the flat and the sitting room, it was to hear Elizabeth saying, 'Well, we can have tea here: I can provide toasted tea-cakes and strawberry jam. How's that?' She looked towards Jim now, and he said, 'That sounds very tasty, miss, but if Mr Matthew's going to stay a while I could ask him if he would mind me slipping off to see my folks. They don't live ten minutes' run away. I'll be back whatever time you arrange. How about it, sir?'

Matthew smiled to himself as he answered, 'That will be all right with me, but I don't know how long Miss Ducksworth will allow me to stay for?'

At this Elizabeth answered lightly, 'Until I get bored with you. Say, somewhere between four and five o'clock, if that will suit you.'

She was looking at Jim again, and he said, 'OK by me, miss, say half-past four. What about it, sir? Will that suit?'

'Yes, Jim, that will suit me fine, only be sure that you park Lady Golightly in some decent garage.'

'Oh, you leave that to me, sir. I'll take her to the garage where I bought her.' He gave a 'Huh!' of a laugh and lapsed into a refined tone, saying, 'I shall house her in the garage from which she was bought. How's that, sir?'

Both Elizabeth and Matthew were laughing at him, and Matthew said, 'From where did you pick up that piece?' And the answer came back on quite a serious note from Jim, 'Four months of evening classes in English at the tech, sir.'

'No!'

'Yes, sir.'

'Then why didn't you keep it up?'

There was a pause before Jim answered, 'They all scoffed me lugs off in the house, and me da said it showed I was getting too big for me boots. Only me ma was for it.' Neither of them was smiling now; and Jim, looking at their faces, said, 'Well, sir, look at it this way. If I had kept it up, I wouldn't be here now doing a job I like and'—he laughed—'keeping you on the straight and narrow.'

Sensing this clever man's feelings, Matthew said, 'Well, you are here now, but I want rid of you, at least for the next two hours; so, to use one of your own terms, skedaddle!'

'Will do, sir. Bye-bye, miss.'

Elizabeth smiled back at him and said, 'Bye-bye, Jim, for the present.'

Left alone, they stood for a moment; then Matthew said, 'Damned shame! You know what I mean?'

'Yes; but I also know he's in the right place.'

'So do I, Liz. So do I.'

She helped him off with his coat and scarf, then led him to an easy chair; and when he was seated she brought another chair forward and placed it about an arm's length away from his; and not until she had sat down did he speak. 'This is nice. How big is your flat, Liz?'

'It's enormous: two rooms, a kitchen and bathroom. This room is twenty by fifteen, the other room's smaller; the kitchen's smaller still, and the bathroom . . . well, it's a bathroom with no space for press-ups or beautifying exercises.'

'Well, don't expect me to be facetious and say you don't need any limbering up.'

'No, I wouldn't expect you to pay me compliments of any kind.'

'Oh, Liz.' He almost bounced to the edge of the chair, and thrusting out his hands and not finding hers he gripped her wrists and rose, drawing her to her feet as he repeated, 'Oh, Liz. I'm a fool of a man. Stupid, ungracious, but . . . but you don't understand what it means to me, just to be able to sit with you and talk. Quite candidly, I'm all het up inside. There's a conflict going on, and I can't fight it, and yet I'm terrified of bringing it into the open and frightening you away. All I seem to be able to come out with are silly platitudes or ungracious remarks which have nothing whatever to do with my feelings. I tell myself that I'm no prize; in my condition everything is against me. Yet I persist and refuse to believe it.'

She now pulled her hands into his and, joining them together, she held them to her breast, while the voice inside her cried loudly, No, no! not yet. Think more about what it means . . . Well, what *does* it mean? I go on burning up inside with love for him. Why? Why? It'll come out some-time; it'll have to. I need him. Oh, how I need him. Face up to it.

She took a deep breath, then said qui-etly, 'Matthew. Matthew. Listen to me. I . . . I love you. Oh, how I love you.'

It seemed as if he were pushing her off when he drew his hands away from her, and for a full ten seconds he did not move. When he did it was as if his body were acting in slow motion, as his arms went about her and drew her to him, it was done so quietly, so softly, as to puzzle her for a moment.

His next movement was to take her face between his hands, and his words came out on a long, low tremble. 'Oh, dear God, if I could only see your face for one flash-ing moment I would be content for life.' His arms were now about her again and he was pressing her fiercely to him, as if to make their bodies one. He did not kiss her, but buried his face into her hair, muttering over and over again, 'Oh, Liz, my love . . . my beloved Liz.'

She was gasping for breath when his lips found hers, and she returned his kiss with a passion now equal to his own.

How long they remained like this they were not aware; then their faces drew apart and, as if slightly drunk, they both staggered to the side, and Liz spoke for the first time, saying, 'Darling! Darling Matthew.' Then on a slight laugh, she said, 'We've made ourselves giddy. Let's sit on the couch.'

She led him to the couch that was set against the wall opposite the electric fire, and, once seated and their arms again round each other, he said to her, 'Oh, my dearest, along with my love I have to give you all my gratitude; you are sacrificing so much for me.'

'I am sacrificing nothing, my love, only gaining a great deal. I'll tell you something. I think now I must have first loved you when I held you in my arms the night you took me for your mother, but I was sure of it three weeks later when I finished my turn of night duty and said goodbye to you. It was that that decided me to do something I'd been putting off for more than a year, something I knew would cause havoc, and yet I didn't really connect it with you. It must have been this, though, that gave me the courage to take that particular step.'

He was holding her tightly now and her head was on his shoulder when he asked, 'Did it concern a man?'

'Yes.'

'And was that linked with the accident you had at Christmas?'

It was a long moment before she answered, 'Yes. Yes, it was; but I'm not going to speak of it now and spoil this wonderful moment. I'll tell you sometime.'

'But it's over? I've got to ask this, my love. It's over . . . I mean with the man?'

'Oh yes, it's over, irrevocably over. It never should have happened; but as I said, I'll tell you all about it sometime later. The only thing I can say to you now is that I wasn't in love. I have never been in love until now.'

Their lips met again and once more she was lost in the wonder of love and being loved. That was until he said, 'I hate the idea of any other man ever being near you or coming near you now.'

There it was again. That feeling of doubt, pervading even this ecstasy. The sister's words were loud in her ears. Married, she would always have to be on her guard not to sound too cheerful in other company, especially male company.

He felt the slight change in her and he put in quickly, 'What is it, my love? What is it? I've said the wrong thing? But it's natural, isn't it, that I should hate any man who has ever held you in his arms?'

'Not when I tell you, Matthew, that I wasn't there voluntarily. What I mean is, it was something expected of me between two families. Oh, you mustn't probe this, because it upsets me so much. I'm too close to it. It . . . it was a dreadful time for me, and for others too.'

'I'm sorry, darling. Oh, I am sorry. I promise you I'll never ask you again. You'll tell me sometime, I know, so we'll leave it at that, and I'll ask you now, Nurse Ducks'—he laughed and hugged her tightly—'when can I announce our engagement? We could do it next weekend. You could come and meet—'

'Matthew! Matthew, please!' She put her fingers across his lips. 'It's . . . it's too soon. Well'—she laughed gently—'you haven't asked me to marry you yet.'

'Oh, I can put that right now: Miss Ducksworth, will you please marry me? I can get a special license at any time; we are both over the age of consent.'

'Be serious, darling, just for a moment. Yes, I'll marry you, and yes, we can become engaged, but . . . but not just yet, please.'

After a moment, he said, 'You know, we should drink to this. I bet you haven't a bottle of anything in the house, have you?'

'No, but I do have plenty of tea and coffee, even cocoa and Horlicks, I think. What would you like?'

'Well, I'll have to plump for tea, I suppose. Anyway, I've been invited to tea, haven't I?'

'Yes, you have. And what you can do is come in the kitchen and help me make it. There's just about room for you to sit there and for me to keep you at arm's length until I set the table. Right?'

'Right, but under protest.' After kissing

her again, he said, 'Will you always love
me, Miss Ducksworth?'

'Yes, I shall always love you, Captain
Wallingham.'

Laughing, she led him to the kitchen . . .

It was just turned half-past four when
the doorbell rang, and he knew that Jim
had arrived. He said quickly, 'Let's tell him,
darling, shall we?'

'Oh, my dear, I don't know.'

'He won't say a thing until I tell him, I
promise you.'

She let Jim in, and when he entered the
room he looked at Matthew and said,
'Sorry, sir, if I'm a bit late.'

'You mean a bit early.'

'Well, have it which way you like. It's still
coming down cats and dogs; you've been
in the right place.'

'Yes, definitely,' said Matthew; 'we've
been in the right place and each with the
right person.'

Elizabeth took Matthew's outstretched
hand as he said, 'Meet my future wife, Mr
Taylor.'

At this Jim beamed on them and gave
a low whistle as he stepped forward and

shook Matthew's hand and then Elizabeth's, saying as he did so, 'Well, I've never in me life wished anybody as much happiness as I do the both of you. But mind, miss'—he nodded at her—'you've taken on something. You'll be forever at his beck and call. He'll be whistling for you now, like he does for me.'

'Does he whistle for you?' Elizabeth asked.

'Oh yes, miss. It's like the song me ma sings at times, "Whistle an' I'll come t'yer, me lad".'

'Well, Jim, if I have to whistle at all for *him,* it won't be any hardship to me because I like whistling. I can't sing a note but I can whistle practically any tune.'

'You can whistle?' put in Matthew now.

'Yes, I can whistle. My father trained me from a child to whistle for the dogs, like this.' She put her two fingers up towards her mouth and said, 'I can demonstrate because Mrs Baker isn't in,' and, sticking her fingers between her lips, she let out a long clear whistle; at this Jim exclaimed, 'By aye! miss, you *can* whistle.'

'Well, well!' laughed Matthew; 'that's

something we've got in common. Aren't we lucky?'

'So long as you don't whistle inside the house. That brings on bad luck, so me ma always says. And she's been proved right. She had been out and she came back to hear our Cissie whistling. She scudded her lugs for her, and two hours later she said, "There, what did I tell you?" That was when the polis came to the door to say that her dear eldest son had got himself nicked climbing down a spout, the one who doesn't like to see untidy dressing tables. And he was then only fourteen. Mr Matthew will tell you all about it.'

A short while after Jim had tactfully removed himself out to the car and Elizabeth had stopped laughing about the tidier-upper, they kissed and held each other tightly once more; then Matthew said, 'This has been the most wonderful day of my life. As I walked into this room today, my love, I didn't imagine for a moment that I would float out of it in this ecstatic state.'

'Oh, sweetheart, sweetheart, I'm floating too.'

He softly touched her cheek and whispered, 'You called me sweetheart, and I say to you, good night my darling.' . . .

. . . It was to be some time before she called upon her whistling talents again.

15

It was nearing the end of February. At ten minutes to eight on a Friday morning, Jim had just left Matthew in the changing room of his department at the hospital. He had taken off his outdoor things and hung them in the cupboard allotted to him, donned his white overall, then groped his way to the end of the room where there was a table with what he knew was a mirror over it, and as if he were gazing into it he took a comb from inside the pocket of his coat and combed his thick hair well back from his face. There was no one but himself in the room as yet, so he knew he had a few minutes to spare to stop and savour the radiant happiness that he could imagine was shining from him, evidence of what he had been experiencing these past weeks. And there was more to come, for tomorrow Liz would meet his family.

He was sure they all knew what was coming, for as Granan had said only last night, it was written all over him and all he had to do was to translate it. His mother had been kind, and even his father had said, 'I understand we're having a visitor on Saturday; you're bringing a young lady to lunch.'

Peter had said, 'Roll on Saturday, Matthew, that's what I say.'

The only one to have given no response was Rodney. Yet in a way he had done so, when his mother had brought it out casually at dinner that she must tell Cook to make something special for lunch on Saturday as Matthew was bringing a young lady to visit them.

The response had been silence. Matthew imagined that Rodney had stopped eating, because it was some seconds later when he heard his knife touch his plate. His mother had, as usual, filled in the awkward gap by saying they'd soon be in March when, Jones had said, they'd be able to plant the beds of the rose garden again and stop using it as a vegetable patch.

But what did it matter what Rodney thought? At lunchtime today he'd be seeing Liz again.

When he heard the door open he turned and said, 'That you, Henry?'

Henry Cook, one of the physiotherapy trainees, replied, 'Yes, it's me, Matthew; and it's Friday and here's one that's damned glad it is. It's been a week. He's like a bear with a sore skull. What did you think about the test yesterday?'

'I think I mixed up my anatomy with my physiology.'

'I wouldn't worry. It'll come all of a sudden. When I first came what I knew about anatomy and physiology you could write on a postage stamp. I've learned a bit since; it suddenly comes. It's the nerves and sinews that are getting me now.'

'What d'you think about Danny's leg?'

'Dreadful, poor little chap, and all he's looking forward to is playing football again. Oh dear.'

'D'you think he knows?'

'Yes and no, because for a twelve-year-old he's got a head on his shoulders, and his chattering covers his feelings very well. Well, you're on B Ward this morning and so is Nurse Murphy. Oh, and if she starts to mother him and the tears come as they often do, Bull's Skull will tear her apart. He's been looking for trouble all week. He gets worse. Well, here we are. I'm on C with the ladies, average age seventy. Can you manage?'

'Yes thanks, Henry. Be seeing you.'

Matthew made his way to the first bed of the ward. The long broad room held twelve patients, six on each side. All but two were sitting up in different positions, and the remaining two were lying flat on their backs. He said aloud, 'Good morning, all!' and received a chorus of 'Good-morning, Mr Wallingham.'

'Good morning, Nurse.'

And there came the answer with a strong Irish accent, 'Good morning, Mr Wallingham,' followed immediately by a voice from a bed on the other side of the ward, which murmured in a good imitation of the nurse's accent: 'Good morning to yerself, Mr Wallingham.' As the laughter rippled around the ward the nurse replied, 'And you won't yerself see another morning, Mr Paul Smarty, if you don't strap down that tongue of yours.'

'Oh,' came back the cheeky reply, 'you're letting me off lightly the day, you are, Nurse . . . just strapping it down, when yesterday you said you'd take a brace and bit to it. Now what d'you think of that?' Again there was laughter in which Matthew joined, and he knew that Nurse Murphy too was laughing. But ignoring the clever mimic, she said to him: 'It's going to be a busy day, Mr Wallingham. There are six ready for the gymnasium. Charlie Fox will be here in a minute or so to get them down. The sergeant will be back shortly and will be seeing to Frank and Bill.' He knew she was inclining her head towards the two prone figures, and she went on, 'You can start with Leslie . . .' Her voice dropped to almost a whisper as she added, 'And work down to Danny. He's in a very low state. I . . . I think he's aware of what's before him. Poor laddie. Anyway, let's make a start.'

She took hold of his arm, adding, 'Give most attention to Leslie's shoulders. He's finding it difficult to raise his arms to the pulley grip. Anyway, you know what to do.'

'Yes, Nurse. Thanks.'

And so Matthew's day began. He saw to Leslie, massaging the patient as he had been instructed, then after ten minutes or so went on to the next bed, to an elderly patient named Joseph. As he massaged the old man's back he listened again to the tales of the man's life, spent mostly at sea. Then on to the bed next to that of the twelve-year-old boy.

This particular patient had very little to say ever. He was a young man and had a grievance against life for crippling his body with arthritis when, as far as he was concerned, it was only old people who should have such a disease. It was when Matthew was just starting on his routine work that he heard the sergeant's voice for the first time that morning. He hadn't heard him enter the ward, but now he was saying to the nurse in no small voice: 'The night nurses should have seen to him. Don't tell me again, Nurse, what they said or what they wrote down. He shouldn't be in this section at all. He is surgical, purely surgical.' He did not hear the nurse's answer to this, but the sergeant's reply was, 'All right, all right don't keep on, but let's get

on with it. It's one of those days—we've
got to make room for another one here.
Where's Cook?'

'I think . . . I think he's in C Ward.'

'Well, go and get him; tell him I want
him. I need help here.'

'Oh, I think we could manage between . . .'

'Am I talking to meself, Nurse? What you
think and what I think are two different
things, always have been. Now, will you get
Cook?'

Matthew had to restrain his fingers from
turning into a fist. That man. Oh, he got
under his skin. It was with an effort that
he kept his body slightly bent over his patient, for he had the greatest desire to
straighten up and, as Captain Wallingham
would have done, shout at the fellow, 'Remember it's a nurse you are speaking to,
not a dog!' It was as well the patient he
was attending now had no small talk,
otherwise he would have been unable to
answer him, so angry did he feel.

By the time he reached Danny there was
a lot of commotion going on at the end
of the ward, groans and comments and the
sergeant's voice rising above all.

Danny was sitting up in bed now, and he said softly, 'Hello, Captain.'

'Hello, Danny.'

'He's in a tear this morning, isn't he?'

'Is he ever in anything else?'

'He doesn't like you.'

'I'm well aware of that, Danny.'

'D'you know why?'

'No, not really.'

'Well, it's because I like you and I call you captain.'

'Is that the reason?'

'Yes—well, most of it, and I told him that I liked you and I thought you were a nice man for a captain, that is because as me ma says, "Them lot are hoity-toity".'

Matthew actually smiled now, and as he began to massage the boy's right leg from the hip downwards he said, 'Well, you tell your ma we are not all alike, and we're not so bad when people get to know us.'

'Oh, she knows that, 'cos she said she could have a soft spot for you, you're good-lookin'.'

'Oh, Danny, don't spin yarns.'

'I'm not. I'm not. Captain . . .' His voice was very low now.

'Yes, Danny?'

'I'm . . . I'm for the long corridor this afternoon.' Matthew could make no immediate comment on this, because he knew in this moment that his throat was as full as the child's own. Then Danny's voice came with a break in it, saying, 'They . . . they won't take me leg off, will they, Captain?'

How did one lie convincingly? He kept his voice steady as he said, 'Well, I shouldn't think so. As far as I know they are going to try to straighten it out.'

'But it's straight as it is, Captain.'

He was thinking, Dear God, but he heard his voice saying, 'That's on the outside, Danny. There are things on the inside that . . . well, the doctors work miracles these days. I mean . . . I mean with the nerves and sinews and things. You see, as you know, I'm new to the job, but I know that whatever they do to you down there will be for the best because everybody is . . . well, very fond of you. Even if you are a . . . a cheeky young devil.'

There followed a short silence, then Danny said, 'Me ma's comin' this afternoon. She said she's goin' down with me and she'll hold me hand. Would . . . would you come down with me on the other side? Mr Fox will let you; he'll be pushin' me.'

Matthew's hands were actually fumbling with the leg when the bawling voice behind him seemed to hit him in the head and nearly knock him over the foot of the bed.

'What the hell d'you think you're up to? Learn them, they say, learn them. My God! Get out of me way, you big fumbling-fisted idiot, you!'

What happened next took only seconds. When the sergeant gripped the back of Matthew's collar and swung him round Matthew must have sensed he was immediately facing him, for both fists shot out, one catching the sergeant full in the face, the other in his shoulder, and the blows sent him reeling and brought him on to his back full-length on the floor.

Matthew was trembling from head to foot. He was no longer in the ward, he was out there somewhere running with his men, and they were yelling and shouting. And Henry Cook must be one of them, for he was yelling in his ear, 'It's all right. It's all right, man. Steady yourself. He's had it coming to him. Don't you worry; we all heard what he said.'

Then Matthew knew that Henry was speaking to Danny, his voice gentle as he said, 'It's all right, laddie. It's all right. Leave loose of the captain. He's all right now.'

'I like the captain.'

'I know you do, Danny.'

'Will he get the push?'

'No, no, he won't get the push.'

'He's bleeding . . . the sergeant's bleeding.'

'Yes, I know. Leave loose of the captain's arm, that's a good fellow. He'll be all right. He'll be all right.'

At this moment all Matthew knew was that he wanted to sit down; and then he realised that he was sitting down already. He hadn't been aware of being led out of the ward by Sister Foster, but he knew now he was sitting in her office and she was saying, 'Thank you, Nurse,' then, 'Drink this cup of tea, Captain.'

He drank the tea, swallowing it down in gulps. And now she was saying, 'Nurse will take you to the rest room and I'd like you to stay there quietly for a time.'

'No, Sister. I . . . I'm finished here and I would like to leave.'

'Well I'm sorry, Mr Wallingham'—Sister

Foster's tone had changed—'you can't do that yet awhile. You have struck the sergeant. As yet I don't know what damage you have done to him. This matter will have to be gone into. So kindly do as I ask. Nurse here will take you.'

He did not protest further, and the nurse, taking his arm, led him from the room; but they had not gone very far before her voice came to him, saying softly, 'Don't you worry your head about what you've done. He had it coming to him. He's a pig of a man. I only wish I'd been there to see you do it.'

He made no answer to this. He didn't recognize her voice but, his mind clearing, he asked, 'What is the usual procedure in a case like this?'

'Oh'—she gave a small laugh—'I wouldn't know because it's a very unusual case. Likely the big heads will get together, such as the matron and Dr Venor, and hear what you've got to say.'

And then suspension. He did not voice this thought aloud but it brought him a tinge of regret, because he knew he would have liked to carry on and become qualified to run his own practice, and of late he had seen himself doing this with Liz by his side.

He was in the rest room now; the nurse had seated him on the couch and was saying to him, 'I would put my feet up, if I were you. I'm not going to add, "Take deep breaths and try to relax," but I will say, try to unwind, at least physically, because at the moment you're like a ramrod. Bye-bye for the present.'

'Thank you.'

He sat for some time, looking towards where his joined hands hung tightly gripped between his knees. The room was full of silence. There was no sound from the corridor. There was an emptiness all around him, and he was slipping back into it.

No! No! He literally shook himself, then, bending, took off his shoes and did as the nurse had suggested, put his feet up and lay back on the couch. He hadn't felt like this since the beginning, the awful beginning of the awareness that he could no longer see. He'd had nightmares, yes, but they happened in the night, not in the daytime, as now. As he had cried that night for his mother and had got Liz, so he wanted her now: the reassuring grip of her hand, her voice telling him that everything was all right, not only all right but that she loved him, actually loved him.

For a moment he had the feeling that she had come into the room and she was near him, but he could not smell her. Yet she was there. He actually felt his limbs relax. He became aware of the slight pain in his thigh that he sometimes felt where the skin grafts were stretched over the flesh and bones. He was actually taking deep breaths, but natural ones, not forced. The nurse had been right, his body had been like a ramrod. Anyway, he had done what he had wanted to do for weeks now, hit that swine. He knew that one fist had landed full in his face, the other somewhere on his shoulder, and he had knocked him down. He knew he had knocked him down. Yet what good had he done himself, for the incident had almost taken him into the silence again. But no, he had fought it; he was back on level ground.

He now let out a long slow breath as he muttered, 'Thank God . . .'

He didn't know he had been asleep until he became aware of the voices, one saying, 'It's a shame to wake him. Battle fatigue, I'd say. Boy, was there a stir! I wanted to laugh at the great man lying there with his bloody nose, the great sergeant knocked out by a blind man; and after they'd taken him out you should have heard them in the ward. They'd never enjoyed anything so much for years. But now the execution committee is waiting; we'll have to wake him.'

Then Matthew felt Henry Cook shake him by the shoulder and heard him say gently, 'Come on, old chap. You're needed in the committee room.'

Matthew yawned. 'Where?'

'Matron and Venor want to have a word with you.'

Matthew pulled himself up into a sitting position, put on his shoes, took hold of his stick, then rose, saying, 'Where are they?'

'In the committee room, and Nurse Murphy's here. She's been off duty this last half-hour and has sat keeping watch on you.'

'Thank you, Nurse.' He turned in what he imagined to be her direction, and she put her hand on his sleeve and said, 'Don't thank me, Captain, and I can call you that now openly, for you've repaid a number of scores for me alone this very morning. Oh, I'd give a month's pay to see it over again, I would so.'

As they approached the door it opened and Charlie Fox stood there saying, 'How are you, sir? I've been trying to have a word, but I've been kept at it all morning; Sister Foster has been on the warpath. Anyway, I hear you did a fine good job, as usual, sir. I've wanted to do that meself for a long time.'

'Then why didn't you do it, Charlie? You would've saved me the trouble.'

'Where're you off to now, sir, back on the ward?'

'No, Charlie. As I understand it I'm going to an inquisition.'

'Oh aye.' Charlie laughed. 'There's bound to be an inquiry but they'll likely give you a medal.'

'Yes, of course, nothing less.'

'Your driver will be here shortly. I'll tell him to hang around, will I, sir?'

'Yes, do that, please.'

'Move yourself, Charlie,' said Nurse Murphy.

As they moved away the nurse said to

him, 'I've been told to wait, and Henry has too, I suppose for questioning'—and now she laughed softly—'as witnesses, you know, to the scene of the crime. There's a saying in our religion—I'm a Catholic, you know—"There is joy in heaven over one sinner who repents." Well, I'll twist it about a bit and say, there is joy in our ward in particular over one bastard getting his deserts and if there was ever a bastard of a sergeant in this world, he's one.'

'Oh, Nurse, I don't want to laugh,' said Matthew. 'Because if I go in there laughing on this particular occasion they'd have the white-coat men out for me.'

'You're right. You're right. I wouldn't put it past some of them, because I could put a name to one here and there who needs psychiatric treatment. But here we are.' Her voice dropped. 'Stand still and I'll straighten your tie, and you rub your hands over your hair, it's standing up as if you've had an electric shock.'

He did as he was bidden, and she said, 'Just stay there a moment until I announce you.'

He heard her knock on the door, open it and say, 'Mr Wallingham's here, Matron.'

There was no reply to this, and now the nurse led him into the room and placed him in a seat, and he knew immediately there were a number of people at the other side of the table for, besides the rustle of paper, he heard separate coughs and throat-clearings.

'I shall point out to you'—he recognized Dr Venor's voice—'that those present are Matron Johnson, together with Assistant Matron Evans and Sister Tutor, with whom you are well acquainted, and last but not least Dr Hamilton.'

At this point Matthew wanted to burst out with, 'I'm not in need of a psychiatrist, sir,' but as if Sister Foster knew what he was about to do her voice cut in, saying: 'We . . . we just want your version of the event, Mr Wallingham.'

His retort was sharp: 'I think you already know my version. I struck the sergeant, and not, I may add, before time. That man has treated me as no delinquent private in the army would have been treated.'

'In what way? Explain please, Mr Wallingham.'

This was Matron speaking, and now he turned his head slightly in the direction of the voice and answered, 'Just that he has laid physical traps to trip me up, literally trip me up.'

'How do you mean, literally?' It was the doctor's voice now.

'Well, a long-handled sweeper, supposedly accidentally laid in my path, or a biscuit tin, or at his last attempt Sister's waste-paper basket full of odds and ends.'

'How do you know this?' It was now Miss Evans speaking. 'You cannot see.'

'No, I cannot see, otherwise there would have been no need for his subterfuge, but in each case I was warned by a patient.'

For a moment no one spoke, then the psychiatrist's voice came at him, saying, 'You have never got on with this man since you took up the training, have you?'

'No, I haven't; nor has anyone else, I imagine, got on with him. He is a bully, the worst type of bully. The kind that would never stand up to anyone who could strike back. But on this occasion he gave me the opportunity by yelling at me that I was a big fumbling-fisted idiot; then, gripping me by the collar, he swung me up and around from the bed. I knew I was facing him and instinctively I struck out, blindly you could say, against such treatment and the insults he was yelling aloud at me.'

'We understand from Sergeant Mullen that he was incited to act as he did because you weren't doing your job properly. Were you aware that you weren't working correctly?'

'Yes. Yes, I suppose I was.'

'And why was that?'

The doctor's voice was crisp, and Matthew's tone matched his as he said, 'Because, sir, I was emotionally troubled at that moment.'

'Emotionally troubled? Why?'

'Because, sir, the patient I was working on was young Danny Fairclough. You are quite aware, aren't you, that he's going to have his leg off today? He had been talking about it and asking me questions.'

'What kind of questions?'

'Oh.' Matthew shook his head impatiently. 'All kinds of questions.'

'About his leg?'

'Yes. Yes, about his leg, and . . . and other things.'

'And you answered his questions?'

'Yes, but with lies. You don't shoot the truth at a boy like that, who is still really a child and, in spite of his brash manner, is highly sensitive. Our conversation was such that I had been . . . well, touched already by it. But when . . . when he said that his mother was to go with him down to the door of the operating theatre, and then suggested that I go with him, too, I forgot what I had been taught and instead of carrying on massaging it I recall clasping the boy's leg in both hands. The rest you know about.'

After a moment's silence Dr Venor said coolly, 'This is not the place to let one's emotions have rein.'

'No!' Matthew's voice was almost a bark now. 'Then tell me where is the place, and would you advise at the same time that all those attending patients should act in the manner of the sergeant?'

'Mr Wallingham, calm yourself, please.'

Now he turned towards Matron, saying, 'I'm as calm as ever I shall be when I hear statements like that. I think this interview should end here. I am not staying in the hospital and if the man wants to take the case up, then by all means let him do so.'

Again there was a short silence before the quiet voice of Sister Foster said, 'Mr

Wallingham, don't be silly. Dr Venor was right, in a way: one can't afford to show emotion; and let me tell you that patients would be difficult if they thought they could affect one in such a way. As for the sergeant taking the case up, that would certainly be a stupid idea, and whatever the man is he's not stupid. He certainly wouldn't want it to be made public that through his bullying ways he had been floored by a . . . well . . . a blind man. Anyway, now calm yourself. As for leaving the hospital, again I say don't be silly. You are really in my charge and I know you have it in you to make a very good therapist. Now let Matron or the doctor tell you what has happened.'

It was as if she had taken charge of the meeting, her position at the moment seeming to indicate that it was well above that of Matron, her assistant, the doctor and the psychiatrist.

But no one spoke, and there was a feeling of uneasiness until Matthew, sitting back in his chair, sighed heavily and said, 'I'm sorry, Doctor. I apologise.'

It was some seconds before he got an answer and when it came it was in the same vein as his own, for the doctor said quietly, 'I understand. And I haven't been unaware of Sergeant Mullen's general attitude. He will now be placed under Mr Quinton. Mr Quinton, as you know, is a martial-arts man who teaches judo and karate. Paul Jenkins, Mr Quinton's current assistant, will be taking over the sergeant's position in your department and I'm sure you'll be pleased to hear'—there was even a touch of humour now in the doctor's voice as he went on—'that the sergeant will not be able to carry his title into the gymnasium. There he will become Mr Mullen and I think, speaking frankly, this will be a worse blow to him than his demotion.'

Matthew was unable to speak. The doctor was right. The loss of his title would be a dire blow for Mullen, as well as the fact that he was being demoted. God, for a moment he felt sorry for the man, but just for a moment. This news had lifted a great load from his shoulders, the last obstacle to his happiness.

Outside the hospital he had felt his happiness was already assured, but once he entered the gates in the morning there had always been the sergeant and the difficulty that lay before him of coping with another day under the man's bawling and hatred of him.

Slowly now, he said, 'I'm . . . I'm sorry I've caused all this upheaval; yet it had to come in some way or another.' And now more quietly he added, 'I thank you all for your forbearance. I can assure you that I will do all I can . . . I mean, make the best of my training.'

'Well, I think that's all that need be said.' This was Matron once again, taking over. 'This has been a very unusual morning and as it is near lunchtime I'm sure we are all ready for a break of some kind. Will you call the nurse for Mr Wallingham, Sister, please?'

Matthew stood up. He felt that Matron was actually smiling; as for himself, he felt weak, drained yet elated. He'd be under Paul Jenkins. He had already talked to him a few times and he was a nice fellow.

As the nurse took his arm, he turned towards the table and said simply, 'Thank you,' then allowed himself to be led out.

They were halfway down the corridor when the Irish voice whispered, 'You told

them. Good for you! I've got good ears—
lugs, me ma calls them. I'm taking you
now', she went on, 'to your man, who's in
the waiting room. Charlie Fox has just told
me he seems to be in a bit of a stew about
you. But Charlie assured him there wasn't
a scratch on you.'

A few minutes later Jim greeted him,
saying anxiously, 'You all right?'

'Yes. Yes, Jim, I'm all right.'

'What happened? Did they give you the
push?'

'Push? No, no, everything's fine. I'll tell
you later. Is Li . . . Miss Ducksworth waiting?'

'No; it's only ten to twelve.'

'Well, just take me to the hall, and then
wait for her; I want to slip back to the ward
and have a word with Sister Foster.'

'I'll do that. Sure you're all right?'

'Shut up, man, and do what you're told
for once!'

'Well! Well!' exclaimed Nurse Murphy.
'Did you hear that? You were like the sergeant himself.'

'Oh, I can be worse than the sergeant
any day.' Then his tone changed suddenly:
'No, I can't. I'd hate to be linked with him.'

'Aye. Aye, indeed; it's me mouth, it should never have said a thing like that. But come on, I'll get you along to the ward and then, Mr Captain Wallingham, I'll finish me time off, if you don't mind.'

'Oh, I'm sorry, Nurse, if I've taken up your free time.'

'Don't be. I wouldn't have missed it for all the tea in China. Come on now.'

When Matthew saw Grace Foster in her office she took both his hands in hers and said, 'Oh, I'm glad that's over and settled with.'

'It's only thanks to you, Sister, for calming the troubled waters. The doctor could have turned nasty.'

'Oh, it does them good to be told the truth sometimes; and at bottom he's not a bad sort. A bit stiff-necked, but fair; and he was fair with you. That was, after you apologised. Mind, I was surprised at that, knowing of your temper.'

'Oh, Sister!'

'Don't Oh Sister me! Now get yourself away. Your man will be waiting for you in that little car. By! it's a spanker! You do things in a big way, don't you?'

'No, I don't, Sister. That was Jim, my

driver. You know how scarce cars are, and he saw it going second-hand and got it for me. I knew nothing about it until there it stood; but I'm very glad of it, and him. And there's something else I'd like to tell you, Sister: I'm . . . I'm engaged to be married.'

'You're what!'

'Engaged to be married.'

'When did this come about? Who to?'

'Well, I'm sure you've met her. She's on B Ward. Her name is Ducksworth, Elizabeth Ducksworth.'

'Ducksworth. Yes, of course. Elizabeth Ducksworth. Isn't she the one that nursed you through some bad patches?'

'The very same.'

'But how has all this happened without my knowing anything about it, and me with a nose on me like a ferret?'

Matthew laughed, saying, 'Oh, you sounded just like Nurse Murphy there.'

'Well, I have so much to do with her, is it surprising? But anyway, when did this happen?'

'Well, our engagement hasn't been made known to the family yet, that's to be done tomorrow.'

'And nobody in here knows about it?'

'No, I'm sure she hasn't said a word to anyone.'

'Oh. Oh'—her tone had risen—'wait till I tell Isabel Fowler, the sister on B Ward, that her Ducksworth is engaged . . . and to whom, does she think? Oh—' She pushed his arm, saying now, 'Aren't we all human, wanting to get one up on somebody else?'

Jim met him halfway along the corridor, saying, 'Miss is in the car waiting. She can't believe it. She had heard a rumour about somebody giving it to the sergeant, but never imagined it was you. Oh! lordy, I wish I'd been there. Straight left, Charlie said, blood all over the place.'

'Shut up! and let's get out.'

He was seated in the car, holding her hands and kissing her before she had time to say, 'You actually hit the sergeant and you've been up before a board? What'll you do next?'

'Put my arms around you and keep you there until tomorrow.'

'Be quiet, and tell me what happened.'

He gave her a brief idea of what had taken place, finishing with, 'I feel elated, but it's not right really: he's been demoted, and what is worse, he can no longer use his rank. But oh, the thought of being able to go to the wards and no sergeant. Happy days. "Happy days are here again",' he sang and Elizabeth laughed.

A voice through the window now interrupted them, saying, 'Same place?'

'Of course the same place.'

A few minutes later Jim dropped them off at a small café in a side street that he had found for them a few weeks ago.

Just before he closed the car door he said, 'Will you be telling them back at the house about it tonight?'

Matthew laughed as he said, 'I just might.'

'Well, if you don't, sir, I shall, and I mean that, especially to your grandma. I wouldn't miss her reactions for anything.'

And as Matthew laughed he thought, Neither would I.

Jim wasn't there to witness Annie Wallingham's reaction, but it was along the lines of what he had imagined: it actually brought her up from her chair and across to where Matthew was standing, and she put her hands on his shoulders and said, 'You actually punched him and knocked him down?'

'Yes, that's what I did, Granan, I actually punched the fellow, between the eyes, I think. But whatever part it was, his nose did some bleeding. However, my second blow missed and hit his shoulder.'

'My God! Well I never! Give us a kiss.'

He kissed her wrinkled lips, then held her as she leant against him murmuring tearfully, 'Oh, how I wish your grandfather were here at this minute! He would thump you on the back and drink a whole bottle of port off at one go, glass after glass raised to you, handicapped as you are. You hit that bully of a man who, even from the little that you've given away, was bound to bring you to breaking point sooner or later. Are you going to tell your father?'

'What d'you think? I mean, should I?'

'Yes. Yes. I'm sure he would enjoy it. And another thing, he's felt a lot better to-day. He's up and down, you know, like a yo-yo, with this business of his; but he's coming down to dinner.'

'No!'

'Yes, he is. And your mother is so

pleased. And I tell you what.' She thumped his chest with her small fist. 'I'll tell you what, I'll come in to dinner, too, tonight; and you can leave the telling to me. Let me break it. I'd enjoy that. There's not much fun in life now of any kind, but I'd enjoy that. I want to see the look on their faces. I wish the girls were here, and those stupid men of theirs. Oh, I do wish that! Still, surprising the family, as it is, is something to look forward to.'

'You're an imp of a woman, Granan. You know that? An imp of a woman. You never grow old.'

'Don't be silly. I'm doddering on my feet now; I can hardly make those stairs over there. That's the day I dread, when I won't be able to go up into that room and look at the only bit of the world that's left to me. Go on! Get yourself away else I'll get morbid. You have a smoking jacket, haven't you, velvet? You've never had it on since you came back. Put it on tonight. This is an occasion. It's not going to outdo tomorrow, but nevertheless it's an occasion of a different kind. I want them to realise that you're not handicapped, and I want you to realise it too. You are not handicapped, understand? The next thing you must do is play that piano. I won't rest until you do. D'you hear me?'

'I hear you, madam. I hear you.'

'Well, get yourself away and have a bath and spruce up. We'll meet later at dinner, sir.'

The last words were said in a high-toned, refined twang; and on it he went out laughing.

They were through the soup and had started on the fish when the old lady, looking towards Matthew, said, 'You'd better have a double helping of everything tonight if you want to keep up your boxing habits,' which brought the expected reaction from her son, saying, 'What d'you mean, Mother, boxing habits?'

'Hasn't he told you? Well! Why be shy about it, you down there?' She thumbed towards the other end of the table where Matthew was sitting to the right hand of Lucille. 'Shouldn't leave it to me to spread such news. He's had that hospital raised this morning. He hit the sergeant plum between the eyes. Knocked him flat. Bloody nose, black eyes, the lot.'

'Mother! Mother! What are you saying?'

'Don't ask me, Richard, what I am saying. Ask your son.'

'Matthew, what is your grandmother talking about?'

Matthew chuckled now as he said, 'She's doing her drama bit again, Father. But she's right. As she stated, I hit the sergeant plum between the eyes.'

'Good God!'

Everyone had stopped eating; even Mary and Bella who were seeing to the meal on the sideboard turned and stared towards Matthew who was, as Bella had related earlier to Cook, looking lovely in his velvet jacket. He was saying now, 'Well, Father, he shouted at me, then manhandled me, and in doing so swung me round to confront him, and my reactions were swift. That's all there was about it.'

'And . . . and you actually knocked him out? I mean, on to the floor?'

The question had come from his mother, and he said, 'Yes, Mama, I actually knocked him out and on to the floor.' He gave a short laugh and added, 'I'm not fully aware of much more because there was a great deal of commotion in the ward.'

'Oh, Matthew, how dreadful. I mean . . . well . . . to cause such an upset in the hospital.'

'Don't be silly, Lucille!' said Granan. 'For weeks now Matthew has been on the point of leaving that job, and all because of that sergeant, who had a hatred for rank of any kind but his own.' She turned now to her son, saying, 'You understand the type, don't you, Richard?'

To this Richard answered quietly, 'Yes, Mother, yes, I understand the type,' and addressing his son he asked, 'What actually happened to bring it about?'

Again his mother was to the fore. 'He won't tell you, he won't go into it all again, but he told me.' And so she related what Matthew had told her about Danny and his leg, finishing the account with the sergeant's calling Matthew a big bloody fumbling-fisted idiot.

Matthew, who had been unable to check her tirade, now wanted to laugh at her addition of the word bloody, but the desire froze as he heard his brother's voice saying coldly, 'The man could make a case of it and have you up.'

'Yes, Rodney, he could have me up if doing so wouldn't show him in an even worse light than the one he already stands in. He is clever enough not to advertise the fact that he had been knocked out by a blind man, him, the great sergeant who was out to put the fear of God into all those under him.'

'Well, you'll probably have to go back and face him on Monday.'

'Oh no, I won't, Rodney. He has been sent to another department where he will be under a very tough man, a black-belt judo expert, who'll see that he doesn't come the sergeant any more.'

The merriness had disappeared from the meal and Lucille said suddenly, 'We're ready, Mary.' But the old lady was determined to finish her story: 'And that isn't all. He had to go before a board.'

'A board?' her son repeated.

'Yes,' Granan said, 'and he tore the doctor off a strip or two.'

'Granan, please! Don't exaggerate.' Then, addressing his father, he said, 'It was a small exchange. Questions had to be asked. You understand that, don't you?'

'Of course,' said Richard.

'Well then, Granan, let it end there. You've had your bit of fun, as always.'

'Oh! Well, if that's how you feel, I'll keep my mouth shut, and when you bring your future bride here tomorrow, I won't open my mouth to her.'

Matthew heard his father actually laugh, then joke as he said, 'Mother! Mother, don't sin your soul any further by promising to do the impossible. You, who should have been a reporter on the gossip column of a magazine, promising not to open your mouth!'

'Well I never! And this from my own son.'

Even Lucille laughed aloud now, for it was rarely that she heard her husband joke with his mother, or anyone else for that matter.

She looked across the table. The only one not smiling was her younger son. She thought: He's an unhappy man, and so jealous of Matthew even though he is blind. I wonder what'll happen tomorrow when he sees this girl; he himself has never had a girl, not even as a friend.

She wished tomorrow were over, because she didn't know how she herself would react to the girl, the woman, who was taking Matthew away from her.

16

It was Saturday morning; the sun was shining and the car was on its way to The Beavors. Elizabeth was excited yet fearful, and finding it somewhat difficult to fall in with Matthew's light-hearted mood. Yet overall, she was happy . . . except for one niggling matter. She had phoned home last night, as she always did on a Friday, and her mother's voice had sounded more plaintive and accusing than usual. Her father had had one of his bad turns at the beginning of the week and Phil was irritating him by pressing the need for a quick move. In fact, he'd had someone there already to view the farm. How was she? her mother had asked. Liz's answer had been merely that she was all right and keeping busy. She had not mentioned her engagement, for she knew that her mother would be really up in arms at the thought of her getting engaged to a blind man so soon after she had wrecked their lives—because that's how she knew Jane Ducksworth looked on the situation.

But she had been more disturbed when, at eleven o'clock, she was awakened by the sound of the phone ringing. Getting up and going into the sitting room, she had been surprised to hear Phil's voice speaking in a very low tone and saying without any lead-up, 'Liz, will you be in on Sunday morning about eleven? I can't say any more now as they are both awake, but I've got to talk to you.'

'What's wrong?' she had asked.

'I'll tell you when I ring. I can't talk now. Goodbye, my dear.'

Matthew's voice was saying, 'What is it, darling? You shivered.'

'Well, anyone is allowed a shiver before going into battle.'

'Oh, don't look upon it like that, darling. They won't be able to help themselves: they'll fall for you, and you look so lovely. Jim says so.'

'You're judging me on Jim's taste, and

I wouldn't say that was taken from London or Paris.' Yet as she spoke she knew she looked good, and Jim's exclamation on the sight of her a short while ago of 'By, don't you look the goods, miss!' had heartened her.

She was wearing a grey corduroy dress, which she had bought in '39 when she was a stone and a half heavier than she was now. But the alterations made it appear that her whole outfit was a new purchase: the corduroy skirt was calf-length and the bodice was made up of a pale rose jersey material with a collar and small reveres picked out in the grey corduroy. She was wearing a small-brimmed, deep blue felt hat, and her black leather shoes, with their two-inch heels, gave her the appearance of being tall, almost Matthew's height. They looked well matched.

Matthew's voice came to her again, saying, 'You have nothing to fear, my dearest. They'll all welcome you, I'm sure of that. But just one little hitch: you might find my brother Rodney not very communicative. He has very little to say at any time, and I must confess we haven't been the best of friends over the years. My older brother

William and I were always very close, and so, as he grew up, he must have felt like an outsider. I am told that William and I are very much alike and take after our grandfather, the general who made a lot of noise. He was a terror of a man, I can remember from the time I was a child, but, as I think I told you, he loved his wife, and . . . and it was his way of yelling "Annee!" that made us children add "Ann" on to Gran, so she's always been known as Granan. You know, the old lady is what today would be called a stirrer, but she's a wonderful stirrer. She's been my confidante since I was a child, and I'm afraid this, at times, has annoyed my dear mama. Anyway, minutes now and you'll meet the gang . . .'

Lucille met them in the hall. She came from the direction of the library and Matthew called to her, 'Is that you, Mama?'

'Yes, dear, it's me.'

'This is Elizabeth.'

'Oh.' Lucille held out her hand, saying, 'How d'you do, my dear?'

'Very well,' answered Elizabeth politely, 'and I'm so pleased to meet you.'

'Let me have your coat. The sun is shining but it's very nippy still, isn't it?'

'Yes. Yes, it is.'

With the coat and hat gone, Lucille took
in the trim, even elegant, appearance of
her future daughter-in-law. Her immediate
thoughts were, At least she knows how to
dress; and she has no Northern accent.
But of course she wouldn't have, coming
from the South. I suppose you could say
she's beautiful. She covered her thoughts
by saying, 'We're all in the drawing room,
dear. Granan too.' Then, turning to Elizabeth, she added, 'Your ordeal will soon be
over, my dear,' and she forced herself to
be cheerful, adding, 'and none of us bite.
Well'—her voice dropped—'I can't account
for my mother-in-law.'

Matthew laughed outright, and Elizabeth
answered in much the same fashion as Lucille herself, 'Well, I can't say I haven't
been warned.'

They entered the drawing room on a
murmur of laughter, and Elizabeth noticed
that there were four people present: a man
sitting in a basket chair; a middle-aged
man standing by his side whom she pre-
sumed would be Peter, the retainer turned

friend; then there was a young man rising from his chair: this must be Rodney, and her first impression of him was that he had a face like an ascetic priest. He was thin and pale, yet he was the farmer and used to outdoor work. The fourth person her gaze rested on was an old lady. She was sitting in a chair next to her son, and the first impression she had of Annie Wallingham was that she looked like an old bird: there was the beak of her nose and two dark eyes in sunken sockets, a thin mouth with the lips in motion all the while, which proclaimed her years. Yet even so the face did not give an impression of age but of eagerness, the whole belying her years. She was dressed in a soft pink velvet dress, the cut of which spoke of long-ago fashion, in that it was ruffled to the neck and the sleeves were buttoned to the elbow. She took all this in in the first glance; and then she was going forward to the man in the basket chair and he was holding out his hand to her, saying, 'Welcome, my dear,' not 'Nurse' or 'Miss Ducksworth'.

'My name is Elizabeth, Colonel.'

'Ah, well, Elizabeth, you're very welcome.'

'Thank you. And I am very pleased to meet you.'

'Straight out of the book,' came from the bird in the chair, 'but couldn't be better said. I'm the grandmother, dear, and known as Granan. I'm a terrible woman and everybody in this house is afraid of me. How's that for a welcome?'

Elizabeth took the outstretched bony hand and shook it, saying on a gentle laugh, 'Well, I now know where I stand, at least with you, and I can tell you that I've had some experience with intransigent patients.'

'Have you indeed! Well, I can see there's a battle ahead. There's nothing I like better than a battle.'

She was now turned from the old lady's attention by Lucille saying, 'This is Rodney, my younger son.'

Elizabeth now stood looking fully into the face of the young man and found that he was staring at her fixedly, for it was some seconds before his hand came out and took hers; and when she said, 'How d'you do, Rodney?' he did not answer her at first, but after a pause said, 'I understand your family have a farm.'

'Yes. Yes, they do.'

'Well, I'm a farmer too.'

'Yes, Matthew has told me,' and she added diplomatically, 'and how well the farm is kept. I'd very much like to see it.'

'That can be arranged.'

He was still staring straight at her, but again Lucille's voice turned her away, saying, 'This is Mr Carter, Peter to us all. He is the family friend . . .' and, on what sounded like a small laugh, she added, 'the sustainer of us all.'

'How d'you do, Miss Elizabeth?'

'Well, that's over. Satisfied, Matthew?' The old bird's voice was taking control again and Elizabeth wanted to laugh out loud, partly with relief that it had all turned out to be easy. It was so different from what she had expected, and mostly because of that old woman. She would always think of her, though, as the old bird.

Peter passed round a tray of sherry, and quite soon after, Elizabeth heard Granan say, 'Well, let's eat,' only for her voice to change immediately when she spoke to her son, saying, 'Do you think you can make the table, Richard?'

'Yes, Mother, I'll make it, but will you?'

Lucille was amazed at the touch of humour in her husband's voice. It was all put on for the visitor and to please Matthew, she knew, but that Richard would so bend in this way that he could joke really surprised her, and she thought: Don't tell me he has taken to the girl in this flash of time.

Later she was to admit to herself that that was what her husband actually had done, and at first sight. Men were so unaccountable. Take Rodney for instance . . .

Lunch turned out to be a successful meal. There was much cross-talk, in which even Rodney joined. When Matthew suggested that after the meal he would show Elizabeth around the gardens, no one was surprised; but they *were* surprised when Rodney offered to take Elizabeth around the farm before the light went, and it was Matthew himself who accepted the offer for her, saying, 'But don't expect me to accompany you on that trip.'

So the entertaining of the guest was settled until teatime, Lucille thought thankfully, and then later she could go and see Granan . . .

It was as they walked arm-in-arm, Matthew leading her now around the intricate paths of the home garden, that he spoke of his happiness again, saying, 'It was wonderful how you responded to the introductions. I felt so proud of you. And they have all fallen for you. Yes, all of them, even my taciturn brother. I was amazed when he offered to show you round his farm. He looks upon it as his and his alone; you'll have to praise everything he shows you.'

'I won't *have* to do any such thing. You forget that I'm used to animals and the conditions under which they are kept, and I like pigs. I even liked a bull once. He was called Neptune, I don't know why. But that was when he was young. When he grew older, like Neptune he wanted to lord it over everything and everyone. Strangely, storms affected him—I always said it was connected with the name they'd given him—but one day he ran amok. And so Neptune had to go.'

'I can see, if I'm not careful, I might lose you to a farmer.'

She stopped and held his face in her hands for a moment before saying, 'You'll never lose me, Matthew. Never.'

He couldn't answer, but held her close:

her quiet statement had reached the core
of his being, for he knew she had spoken
the truth. He only hoped he could be de-
serving of her love; but he could never live
long enough to prove that.

They had reached the copse at the far
end of the garden when, surprisingly, Rodney's voice hailed them from the end of
the terrace, calling, 'If you want to see the
farm, there's not much light left.'

The only comment Matthew made was,
'Well, well!' then quietly he added, 'Come
on, darling; he's dying to show you his
farm. I'll go into Granan's until you get
back.'

When they reached the terrace Rodney
opened the door into the annexe, saying,
'Can you manage?'

'Yes, yes, I can manage. Go on.'

At this, Rodney turned to Elizabeth and
asked, 'Is that coat warm enough? It's
turning nippy.'

'Oh yes. It's well lined and I'm used to
the cold.'

They were walking along the road that
led to the farm when he said, 'How long
have you known Matthew . . . I mean altogether?'

She was surprised by the question and hesitated before answering, 'Oh . . . well, several months. It must be eight months or more since I first met him in the hospital.'

'He was out of his mind then, wasn't he?'

'No! of course not; he was just in shock.'

'Yes . . . but he was out of his mind.'

'We . . . we don't use that term when men are shell-shocked, because they're not really out of their mind, as you put it, and most of them recover, just as Matthew has.'

'He has nightmares.'

'Well, that's not surprising.'

They were in the farmyard now. A man was coming towards them, and Rodney said, 'This is Joe Platt, one of our oldest workers. He has been here for years. This is Miss Ducksworth, Joe.'

'Oh, I've heard about you, miss, and congratulations. That's what I say. You're gettin' a fine man in Mr Matthew, no matter about his eyes. A fine man.'

'Yes, I know that, Joe; and thank you.'

She thought it rather strange that this old man was the only person who had alluded to her engagement. No one as yet in the house had referred to it, or to the prospective marriage.

'Would you like to see in the byres, miss? They're all busy in there milkin'.'

'I can see to Miss Ducksworth, Joe.' It was a dismissal, and she didn't like the tone of it; but there again, she must remember what Matthew said about his brother and the farm—he considered it his.

So the inspection went on under Rodney's guidance. Everything she saw was very well kept. There were no odd pieces of machinery lying about here. She admitted to her liking for pigs and admired the way the brick sties were built. The only thing, she told him, she wasn't very fond of were hens, for she considered them stupid things in the main. She laughed about this and he laughed with her.

When they came to a kennel, which was more like a small hut, and a dog came from it barking loudly but controlled by a long lead, she remarked, 'I love sheepdogs.'

'Don't go too near her, she can be a bit vicious.'

'Vicious?' She stopped and looked at him. 'And dealing with sheep?'

'She no longer deals with sheep; she is Matthew's dog.'

'Oh yes. Matthew spoke of her. He's very fond of her. What a pity she can't be trained.'

'She's much too old for that.'

'I'm sure she wouldn't bite me, I'm used to dogs.'

'Please don't go any nearer to her, she's a bitch,' and he added, 'in more ways than one; she's been known to bite.'

'Oh! Oh, I'm sorry.'

They skirted the dog and went on. She was shown the barns, the tack room, the boiler room and his office, then walked up the rise beyond the farmyard, from where Rodney pointed out the ridges of tilled land all around him, especially that running up to a disused quarry dug into a steep hillside.

The light was fading fast as they returned up the short road to the house, so when he took her arm as if guiding her she made no objection, although her feelings were telling her that she didn't like the man, which was indeed a pity, since he was Matthew's brother.

When they entered the hall they were

met by Matthew, who said, 'It's almost dark and almost freezing out there. You shouldn't have kept her so long.'

'She's not a china doll, and she says she's not susceptible to cold. What's more, I think she's enjoyed the tour, haven't you?'

'Yes . . . yes, very much, and thank you.'

When Matthew went to help her off with her coat his hands were checked by Rodney saying, 'I've already done it; it's hanging up there.' Then he left them.

'You all right, darling?'

'Yes. Yes, Matthew. Why shouldn't I be?'

He said nothing more until, taking her along a passage, he explained, 'There's a little sitting room here; we can have it to ourselves. I'll ring for Bella to bring us some tea. Mama's upstairs with Father. I doubt if he'll come down again and make dinner tonight, but there's one thing I can repeat, you've made a hit there.'

'And with your mother?'

'Yes. Yes. I'm certain of that too,' he answered, even though, at the back of his mind, he wasn't really sure; his mother's façade of politeness was well practiced. However, he knew she had made a hit with

Granan, and with Peter too. Oh yes, certainly with Peter.

'We'll be all right till dinner,' he said; 'Granan is having her afternoon nap, but I think you should go along and have a word with her before dinner.'

'I will. Yes, I will.'

'And I know you'll pop up and see Father again before we leave.'

She said tentatively, 'I don't think I should stay to dinner; the idea was that I should come to lunch.'

'Oh. Well, it was expected that you would. Anyway, there'll be only Mama, Granan and Rodney. By the way, you've made an impression there all right.'

'You think so?'

'I'm sure of it. That fellow hardly ever opens his mouth to any of us . . . well, not unless it's to complain about something, mostly the things that I do or I want.'

'Then I can be sure of one who will welcome me into the family.'

He added nothing to this, for he had his own thoughts on the matter.

And so had she. Oh yes; so had she.

* * *

They had a pleasant hour to themselves before he took her along to the annexe. Here it was as if Annie Wallingham had been sitting waiting for her, for she greeted them with 'Where have you been?'

'Having a quiet hour to ourselves, Granan. Do you object to that?'

'No; but I didn't think that was in your plans: you were going to get Flossie and let her take you and Elizabeth here up to see the Mount and the view of the whole land and the house from there.'

'Yes, that had been the intention, my dear, but, surprisingly, Rodney offered to show Elizabeth his farm'—he stressed the 'his'—'so, as it isn't often we have any co-operation from my brother, what could I do?'

'No, nothing different, I suppose. I see your point. I'm surprised myself that he should bother trying to make an impression of being a civilised individual. But there, that shows what a pretty woman can do. Sit down, my dear; I want to talk to you. And you, Matthew, go and have a word with your father, or better still a chat with your mother. She mustn't be left out. Don't forget that.'

'Who's forgetting it, Granan?' His voice was quiet now. 'I never forget it.'

'No, perhaps not, but the very fact that, through this pretty piece here, she might be losing you is not going to make her jump for joy.'

'Oh, old woman, you are the limit. The things you come out with.'

'They're better out than in. It's always advisable to know your opponents and find out their weak spots. Otherwise they've got you. Now get yourself away when you're told.'

He moved towards the door and turned there to say to Elizabeth, 'I've warned you, Liz: only believe half of what she says, and then doubt that too. She's prejudiced from her head to her toes.'

'That's what I'm not, sir; I'm prejudiced in no way. I'm a good friend or a bad enemy, and to all classes, types and sizes, whether black, brown or khaki.'

At this, Elizabeth could contain herself no longer; she burst out laughing, to which Annie Wallingham's response was, 'You'll probably explain to me, miss, what you found so funny about that bit, for I meant it seriously.'

'I'm . . . I'm sorry, Mrs Wallingham.' Elizabeth was wiping her eyes as she added, 'Perhaps I've got a warped sense of humour.'

'You could be right there; but anyway, warped sense of humour or not, you can laugh. And now that he's departed we can talk. First, I'm going to ask you a question, but I'm going to give you your answer before you give it. I'm going to ask why you are wanting to marry my grandson, and you'll say it's because you love him. Right?'

'Yes, right. I love him.'

'You love him now, but have you considered what it will be like living with a blind man twenty-four hours a day?'

'I won't be living with a blind man twenty-four hours a day; we'll each have our work.'

'Oh yes, yes, for a time. But all kinds of things can happen in work and play. Sighted, a man with any sense can deal with his life, but a man in Matthew's position will, I tell you, become very possessive: he'll want to own you body, soul and mind.'

'Yes, I know that. I've thought about it. I've mulled on it.'

'You have? Well, in that case you're wise.'

'Thank you.'

'And, being wise,' the old lady went on, 'you will gather from this person's inquisition that I am more than fond of my grandson.'

'I have no doubt of that whatever. The most simple-minded person would soon realise how you feel for him.'

'Well'—the old lady gave a brief laugh— 'what I've already become aware of is that my grandson should consider himself damned lucky he found you . . . I mean, was sensible enough to pick you out of all the nurses who must have attended to him and were probably attracted to him by his handsome face, and so fell in what they imagined was love. How old are you?'

'Twenty-four.'

'Nice age. I was eighteen when I married the Growler. He was my husband, you know. He never spoke, he just growled. Growled at everybody. Growled himself into being a general. But he was lovely.' Her voice softened. 'Oh yes, the loveliest man on earth, and he loved me. He always said I made him. I didn't, of course, but I didn't contradict him. Nobody contradicted him. But he never forgot a kindness, never. No. Deep down he was always grateful for any help he got. He had little grace in manner or speech, yet I always said that he had one grace that outdid all the rest, that was the grace of gratitude.' She did not wait for Elizabeth to comment on the turn of phrase, but went on, 'I coined that expression, you know. You won't believe it, but I used to write books. I once wrote a full book of poems. That was after . . .' her voice seemed to drop back in her throat as she ended, 'I lost the boys.'

The room became quiet and Elizabeth's tone was tentative as she asked, 'You had other sons?'

'Yes. Yes.' Annie pulled herself up further in her chair. 'Two wonderful, wonderful boys. Bill was the elder by fourteen months, and then came Laurie, but so close were they you would swear they had been both born from the same seed. They were closer than twins yet so unlike in looks and manner. Bill was the size and the image of Matthew now, and Laurie only five foot eight, slight as a reed yet with a mind as lively as a cricket. He took after me in that way, whereas Bill took after his father. Oh, and they were a pair of devils. Loving devils. The things they got up to! Wonderful company. This was a happy house then, really happy.

'Then came the war, the Great War, and nothing would prevent them from straight away enlisting. They survived until the first Battle of the Somme. I understand they died within minutes of each other. That was as far as could be gathered. They had been together up till then. Their father saw to that, and also that they were buried in the same grave. They were but two of the thousands that died that day and were buried, many of them unidentified. But for me, you know, my boys are not dead: their spirits are here in this house. The Growler used to feel the same about it. I think that's why he spent most of his last days upstairs with his telescope. There he felt he was nearer the sky where he imagined they were. Yet he was not a religious man, oh no. But he was a spiritual one. Deep down he was a spiritual man.

'Anyway, all I did for months afterwards

was write poetry about my two boys; then one day it came to me that I had another son and that he was being neglected, that in fact he had always been neglected. So I burnt all I had written. It was odd about that awakening to Richard's needs, because from the beginning he hadn't had a square deal. He was between five and seven when the boys came and, to use a common phrase, his nose was put out. He was sent to boarding school and during the holidays he had to listen to the nanny glorifying the escapades of the two young devils; and such was his life until he, too, went into the army. When he married Lucille, they were both on the rebound after unfortunate affairs and they needed love, and my poor Richard had never been given love. He had seen it dished out all round him but had never had his share of it.'

She stopped now and, joining her hands together against her bony chest, she looked at Elizabeth and said, 'Why am I telling you all this? That's what you're wondering, isn't it? It isn't the thing to do. It's the first time we've met, the first time you've been in this house; but the point is you are coming into the family, and not in an ordinary way: you are taking on a handi-capped member of it, handicapped in such a way that his affliction is evident. But there are all kinds of handicaps in people that don't show, handicaps which make them react in a way that annoys the on-looker or the person who has to live with them. So I'm putting you in the picture about the other handicaps you will prob-ably have to deal with, and not so easily as that of our dear Matthew.

'My eldest grandson William took him-self off to America, although he wouldn't say it was as a result of a handicap. But his handicap was having been born into a military family. And there is my youngest grandson, Rodney. He's suffering from the same handicap as his father. He has been not exactly ignored, but outshone by his handsome brothers, first William and now Matthew, who legally one day will own the whole estate, and that will include the farm which Rodney has come to consider as his. You will already have noticed that this afternoon. Speaking of legality, it should all go to William in America, but he doesn't want the estate and has made that plain.'

There was nothing that Elizabeth could

say. At the moment, her mind seemed to have gone blank, bludgeoned into silence by all the confidences being rained on her. That was until Annie Wallingham's voice came to her again, saying, 'I haven't only bored you but I'm frightening you.'

'Oh no. No. Not at all. Neither. I'm . . . I'm only amazed that you could give me your confidence and . . . and put me wise to so much I would not have been able to find out for myself for a long time, if ever. One thing I am certain of, and that is that I have a friend in you.'

The old hands now were patting hers and Annie's voice had a slight break in it when she said, 'You'll bring a breath of fresh air into our lives, I think; and, you know, I find it strange how Rodney has re-acted to you. I never thought he would un-bend in this way, but I could see that he admires your courage and . . . no! don't. Don't shake my hands like that. It does take courage to give your life over to a blind man. No matter how much you say you love him and he loves you, there are going to be difficult times ahead. But as you said, you've already pondered over this and know that you can cope. And I know you can.'

Then, her tone changing, she said lightly, 'If Lucille knew what I've been saying, she'd go, as Mary would say, up the lum. The lum, you know, in North Country jargon, is the chimney. And, speaking of Mary, she is another one who possesses the grace of gratitude, for that woman has looked after me for years, and just because of some simple little thing I did for her family a long time ago. I don't know how long we've been together now, but she'll tell you. And yet, by the way I speak to her, no one would believe that she is my friend. There are times when we talk quietly about the old days, for she, too, knew the Growler and loved him.' Now her tone changed as she said quickly, 'Come and spend a weekend with us sometime soon, won't you, my dear?'

'I will, and be only too pleased to.'

'And it will be your turn to spill the beans and tell me about your life. But one thing I will ask you now: have you ever been in love before? I mean had another man?'

At this, Elizabeth laughed, then said, 'To answer the first part, I will say immediately,

no. Your second part, if I understand your
meaning, I could really only answer by telling you a long tale. It started in my
schooldays when I was five and taken to
school by our farming neighbour who is
four years older than me . . . and ended
last Christmas. I will tell you this story one
day. Now, I shall only say that I did then
what I should have done last year or the
year before.'

'Why didn't you do it before, then?'

'Fear.'

'Oh. Well, what gave you the courage
to go ahead this time?'

'Putting it briefly, the knowledge that I
loved someone else.'

'Matthew?'

'Yes, Matthew.'

'Well. Well. I shall be very interested to
learn your whole story, my dear. And you
know something? I have two granddaughters, both married, and Hazel has two children now; yet I must confess I have never
been able, even felt inclined, to talk to
them as I have done to you today. Now
isn't that strange?'

Elizabeth paused for a moment before
answering: 'Yes, when I come to think of

it, it is strange; but, as I have already said, I am grateful that you have done so.'

The grace of gratitude. Their gentle laughter joined now, and when Elizabeth saw the old lady lean back in her chair and sigh, she said, 'I'm sure you are tired.'

'No, I am not tired, my dear, nor weary. I suffer from both at times, but tonight I'm experiencing a quiet happiness, and it's because I know that my dearest Matthew is happy too. Until you came I wasn't sure about anything in the future concerning him, but now I am.' Then, her voice quickening, she said, 'Speak of the devil and he has arrived; I can hear his stick in the corridor. Thank you, my dear, for this afternoon. I only hope we can repeat it often.'

'So do I, Mrs Wallingham. So do I.'

The day was almost at an end. They were sitting pressed close in the back of the car.

'It wasn't so bad after all, was it, darling?'

'It was wonderful.'

'No, *it* wasn't wonderful, *you* were. You entranced them as you did me.'

'Don't be silly.'

'I am not being silly. For one thing, I have never seen or heard my brother come out of his shell as he has done today. Look at dinner. He actually cracked a joke with Bella about the pheasant. As for Father, well—I never expected him to come down to dinner again. I never heard him so . . . I won't say relaxed, but civil. Yes, I mean that, civil . . . polite, even kindly. Look what he said to you when you said your goodbye to him: "I can understand why some men revive in hospital better than they do at home." That, I can tell you, darling, was something from him. As for Granan, I know she thinks she's found a kindred soul in you.'

'You haven't mentioned your mother.'

'Oh, she likes you—I could feel she does—but she's a reticent kind of person. She is with her own daughters, too. She lets go a little when the grandchildren are about, but otherwise she mostly keeps her feelings to herself . . . until something happens that touches her deeply—emotionally, I mean. Anyway, my dear, dear Liz, I was so proud of you and so thankful, oh, so thankful that you love me.'

She interrupted him by saying, 'One little thing puzzles me. No one mentioned our engagement, except your grandmother, and that was in a roundabout way.'

'Oh, that's my fault, darling, entirely. I had had a word with Peter and asked him to put it round for them not to come out with the usual "When's the wedding?" et cetera. That always follows, doesn't it, on anybody being engaged, and I knew there was nothing decided about the actual date. For me, it could be next week at the registry office, but . . . All right! All right!'—he pressed her closer—'that's something we've got to go into later, I know. About tomorrow, though. If it's fine we will take that trip and have lunch somewhere. Right?'

'I'd like that. Yes, I would like that.'

'Good. Here we are then.' The car was drawing to a stop. 'How is it this journey gets shorter every time?'

She laughed and said, 'It's the way Jim drives.'

'Yes, it's the way he drives; he really needs lessons.'

'What's that you say, sir?'

'I was actually saying you need more lessons in driving.'

'Oh, you're right, sir. You're right. And I'll have to have them, because I'm applying for a job on the buses, and if not that, as a long-distance haulage driver.'

'Shut up! and get us out of this contraption.'

He let them out and saw them into the sitting room of the flat, then went back to the car and waited for the whistle. And when, ten minutes later, it came, he answered its call . . .

Left alone, Elizabeth did not immediately go to her bedroom and undress, but sat on the couch, stretched out her legs, laid her head back, and sighed as she stroked the five-stone diamond engagement ring on her third finger, thinking that no one had referred to it. No matter; it had really been a wonderful day. She had liked them all, although in a strange way she felt that she must be on her guard with Rodney. He seemed an unpredictable fellow, not a bit like his brother. But it was as his grandmother had said, they were all carrying burdens. Oh, what a wise woman that was, and a terror. Oh yes, she could imagine her having been a terror and, in a way, she still was; she must always have dominated the house, and it couldn't have been easy for her daughter-in-law. But at bottom she was a loving, kind, thoughtful woman with a mind as alert as someone half her age.

She was happy, she told herself, oh so happy. She had never imagined such happiness.

Suddenly she pulled herself up to the edge of the couch. There was tomorrow morning at eleven o'clock. Why did Phil want to ring her at that time . . . from a call box? It could only mean trouble of some sort. Oh dear. Nothing ever went smoothly. She tried to guess what his message might be. Perhaps her mother was objecting to his plans for a move. Perhaps her father was really ill. Anyway, she would have to wait until tomorrow morning to find out.

17

It was exactly eleven o'clock when the phone rang and she heard Phil's voice saying, 'That you, Liz?'

'Yes, Phil. Oh, it's nice to hear you speaking ordinarily and not in a whisper.'

'What would you expect me to do, with ears hanging all around me?'

'Are you in trouble?'

Phil paused. 'To answer truthfully, well, no, not me; yet things are not happy at home.'

'Is Dad worse?'

'No worse and no better.'

'And Mum?'

'Much the same, my dear: It's a dreadful world, and what have they come to? and so on. You know the theme. Well now, listen. The great "I am" came out of hospital earlier than was expected. I hadn't done as much damage as I had intended. And now, on doctor's orders, he's supposed to be going away for a change of air. He's going to Ireland to visit Bridget's family. But young Sam met me in the market and said he's sure he's not going there at all, but he'll make for the North. Apparently, in his cups, he was heard to brag again in the pub that nobody had yet been born who was going to get the better of him. And so I thought I would warn you, Liz, because he's dangerous. I only wish I was nearer you.' There was a short silence. 'Are you there, Liz?'

She had to wet her lips and swallow deeply before she said, 'Yes'; then added, 'When did he leave?'

'Thursday. Have you any friends near, who might be of help?'

She thought for a moment, then said quickly, 'Oh yes, yes, and I'll get in touch with them.'

'Well, Liz, I'm not trying to frighten you, but I wouldn't leave it too long. Phone me later, will you, if you have any trouble.'

'I will. I will.' Her voice was now agitated. 'Try not to worry about me. My . . .

My friends will help me. Goodbye, Phil.
And thanks.'

'Goodbye, Liz. Be careful.'

She laid down the phone and now almost fell on to the couch. Her hand was
tight across her face, gripping her cheek-
bones. She thought of Jim and Charlie
Fox. But Jim was never in the hospital except for a few minutes each day, and anyone could enter that hospital unknown to
Charlie. But Mike wouldn't attempt anything in the hospital. No. No; it would be
outside or here. He could break in here.
She would have to warn Mrs Baker not to
answer the door. But then she would have
to tell her the reason why . . .

She got up and began to pace the room.
Why hadn't she defied her mother, particularly over the last year, especially when she
must have realised that she didn't want to
go through with it? But if she had, Jane
would have pressed home what they owed
to their neighbours. She had been willing
to sacrifice her daughter so that they could
keep the farm going and her own way of
life. She could hear her almost whining,
'You know, your dad would never have
been able to get through these past two

winters if it hadn't been for Mike and the others.'

At this moment she almost hated her mother. She hadn't succeeded in sacrificing Elizabeth, but she had succeeded in spoiling her happiness, because now she would be unable to hide her fear. If she could only talk to Jim. The only one who could talk to him and get him to act in some way or another to protect her was Matthew, and that would mean telling him the whole story. Oh dear God; she didn't want to take that all up again, but what else could she do . . .

The minutes till twelve o'clock seemed like hours, yet when she heard the car stop she had to force herself to go to the door.

Even before Matthew had entered the room with her he sensed that something was amiss, and was sure of it when he heard her voice actually trembling as she said to Jim, 'Jim, would you mind waiting in the car for about ten minutes or so? I'll call you then, because I . . . I think I'm going to need your help.'

'What on earth are you talking about, darling? What's the matter?'

Before she could answer Matthew, Jim

said, 'OK, miss, any time you're ready, I'll be in.'

'What is it? What's happened? Oh, my dear, what has happened to make you like this?'

'Sit down, darling.' She drew him to the couch. 'There's something I have to tell you, and it's not going to be easy. I . . . I promised I'd tell you some day, but I never thought I should be brought to my present state to have to tell you.'

'Well, I'm listening; and don't tremble so, please. Whatever's happened can be dealt with.'

'I only wish I could agree with you. Well, I'd better start at the beginning. It's about what happened when I was home at Christmas: the supposed accident, you know.'

'Yes, the supposed accident.'

He waited, then was surprised when she suddenly threw her arms about him and held him to her before pressing him away again, saying, 'Don't hold my hands, my dear; just sit and listen.'

And so she told him. First, of the place-ments of the two farms and the members of the two families. Then the long teens during which the assumption grew that she would marry Mike McCabe some day. She explained that she now realised her desire to take up nursing wasn't out of compassion and in order to help others so much as to get her away from home, at least for longish periods. She also knew that there were one or two other young men in the town, and not in the farming business, who were interested in her, but they would immediately be warned off. She went on to say that she found, to her surprise, that she liked nursing very much and was gratified by the fact that she could help people, especially those who had come under her care during the war. She stopped; then, putting her hands out to his, she pressed them, saying, 'For example, one particular man who needed my help badly.'

All he said to this was, 'Oh, Liz. Liz.'

She now went on to the time when she came off night duty and realised that in spite of Sister's wise warnings she had fallen in love with a patient. 'I went on leave that time determined to make an end of things. But my mother kept pressing at home how much we had to thank the McCabes for because my father had these bad turns so often, and that they would never have managed without Mike's help.'

Elizabeth recounted how, when she told them of her intentions at Christmas, her mother became reproachful. But Phil was all for her—actually, he hated Mike McCabe.

There was a long pause before she went on to the actual scene in the McCabes' sitting room when she feared she was about to be raped.

It was now that Matthew put out his arms and pulled her towards him and held her tightly as he cried, 'The bloody swine! Oh my God!'

It was she now who had to soothe him by saying, 'It's all right, darling; it's all right. But listen. A short while ago Phil phoned and said he is sure Mike is making for here, and me. And I'm frightened, Matthew—more than frightened, I'm terrified of meeting up with him again because I feel he must really be slightly mad.'

He shook her gently by the shoulders, saying, 'Why didn't you tell me earlier about it? We could have done something about him. There's always ways and means to deal with these . . . these big-mouthed bullies.' Smoothing her hair back from her forehead, he said, 'My God! To think that you went through all that at Christmas. But now try not to worry, my darling. You'll not have to be left alone night or day. Look, we'll definitely have to have a word with Jim. He'll work something out, one way or another.

'Wait a minute.' He got up abruptly, felt his way to the door and whistled. Within a few seconds Jim was standing in the room and Matthew, taking his seat beside Elizabeth again, said, 'Sit down a minute, Jim; we want your advice. It's like this.' And so he gave him a rough picture of the situation.

Jim Taylor was looking at Elizabeth now and he said, 'God almighty! To put you through all that. I'd like to take a swing at him. What is he like, miss . . . I mean, how big?'

'Oh. Oh, he's a very big man. Six foot three or more, and broad with it. Yes, broad with it. Anyway, you couldn't miss him, Jim, once you saw him, and he dresses well, mostly in tweeds.'

'Well,' said Matthew now, 'what thoughts have you on the subject?'

'Up to a point, anyway during the day,

we can see to her, sir. If you don't mind
coming in a little earlier, we can pick her
up and take her to the hospital. Then at
lunchtime, that's if miss is on the same
shift next week, I can take you both, as
usual, to your café.'

'Yes, Jim, I'll be on the same shift, eight
till five. But the following week it'll change.'

'Well, we'll fit that in somehow, miss, but
what we must think about now is when we
bring you back here in the evening. It's
from then on you must have somebody
with you. And I've just thought of the very
person. You need someone here to sleep.
That couch there that you're sittin' on
would make a good enough bed for anybody, and I've got a sister. It just happens
that she's out of a job at the moment.
Funny how things fit in, but she's as big
as a house-end and as strong as an ox,
and why she's out of work again is because she can't take orders, not, as she
says, from young upstarts who don't know
their jobs. She's had three different places
in the year gone, but she's never out of
work for very long. Anyway, she'll be only
too glad to come round here and keep you
company. What about it? And I'll tell you

this much, I'd like to see the fellow who'd get past her, because she can use her knees-up-Mother-Brown in the places she aims at.' He laughed, saying, 'Excuse me, miss. Another thing, she's got a pair of hands on her like camel's feet.'

'Oh! Jim.' There was a slight note of laughter in Elizabeth's voice. 'You do me good.'

'Well now, sir, d'you hear that? That should go a long way to me gettin' a raise, shouldn't it?'

'Be serious, Jim. This is a serious business.'

'You're telling me, sir! Because there's still the weekends.'

'Oh, don't worry; I'll see to the weekends. There'll be no trouble about that. But now, my dear, we're going out, and I'm not going to say to you stop worrying and stop being fearful, because I know that's stupid, but you can see that, with the help of this thick-head here, you'll be protected to the best of his ability and mine. Now go on up and see your kind neighbour, and tell her what to say to the fellow should he turn up here.'

When they were left alone, Jim, serious

now, said, 'If that fellow's as mad as you make out, sir, she's in a bit of danger, because fellows of that description will stop at nothing. It doesn't occur to them that they could go along the line, perhaps for life. You read about it, you hear about it on the wireless, even see it happening in your own street. He must be a pig of a fellow.'

'Yes indeed, Jim, a pig of a fellow. Only "pig" is too clean a name for him.'

'I'm with you there, sir. Oh yes, I'm with you there; he's a bugger all right.' He then went on, 'D'you think we could drop in to my home on the way, sir, and tell my sister what she has to do?'

'By all means, Jim, call in at your home, but rather than *tell* your sister, I think you should *ask* if she's willing to take on the responsibility.'

'Oh, she'll be willing all right. She'll do it for me in any case. By the way, her name is Cissie. It's such a soft name for the big bulk of her.'

And that's what Elizabeth thought when, later that day, she was introduced to Cissie, because there was nothing gentle-looking or -sounding about this woman. Elizabeth thought she was almost as big as Bridget McCabe, and her short-cropped hair and broad face gave her a masculine appearance. There, however, the similarity stopped, because her bust and hips showed her femininity. Moreover, her talk and attitude could have been those of Jim himself. Elizabeth liked her straight away and told her how pleased and grateful she was for her falling in with her brother's plans. And, like Jim, she tactfully returned to the car to give the couple time to say good night . . .

Matthew made himself say, 'I have no fear that you'll be interrupted tonight, because that lady, I'm sure by the feel of her hand alone, gives me the impression that it would be a foolish man who would try to get past her.' He left her with, 'Try to sleep, darling. Although the night's still early I want to get home now and have a talk with Mama and work things out about the weekend.'

She did not protest, for she felt she was still drowning in her fear and could refuse no lifebelt held out to her.

18

When Jim left Matthew at the house, Bella came across the hall towards him, saying, 'Oh, hello, sir! You're too late for dinner but the family's at coffee in the drawing room. Have you had a good day?'

'Yes, thanks, Bella, a very good day.' Then quickly he asked her, 'Who's there, Bella?'

'Well, Mr Matthew, there's your father. He came down this afternoon, and your grandmother came and joined him for dinner. And, of course, the mistress. Mr Rodney was there until a little while ago, but he went down to take a last look round the farm as usual. And there's Peter.'

'Thank you, Bella . . . It's all right'—he resisted her touch on his arm—'I'll find my way across.'

When he entered the drawing room, he was greeted with an exclamation from his grandmother, 'My! You're early back to-night, or are you late? You've missed dinner.'

Before he could answer her he knew his mother was by his side, and she said, 'Have you eaten?'

'Oh yes, twice. But I could do with a cup of coffee.'

'Well, it's still hot, dear; but come and sit down.'

She placed him in a chair to the left of his father, who now said, 'What's the weather like?'

'Cold but brisk.'

After a pause it was Richard Wallingham who spoke again, saying, 'Anything wrong?'

Matthew let perhaps five seconds pass before he answered, 'Quite a lot, I would say, Father.'

'What's happened to you? Liz hasn't . . . ?'

He turned in the direction of his grand-mother's voice and on a shaky laugh he said, 'No, Granan, Liz hasn't turned me down, and I'm all right; but she isn't, and it's about her I would like to talk. And you, Mama, I think, are the main one concerned.'

'Me? Why?'

'Well, it'll be for you to decide on what I am going to suggest; but let me have that cup of coffee, will you?'

'Oh, my dear. Yes, yes—I'm sorry; I left it on the table to your hand.'

It was Peter who handed the cup of coffee to Matthew, saying with concern now, 'Has . . . has something happened to Miss Elizabeth?'

'Not yet, Peter, but the trouble is, it might.'

At this Richard Wallingham's voice came at them, sharp-sounding now, 'Stop beating about the bush, Matthew!'

Just as sharply Matthew replied, 'I'll have to beat about the bush quite a lot, Father, if I'm to make you all understand the whole situation.' Again he paused, before going on, 'I'll start at the beginning, as she did, from when she was five years old. It's like this.' Then he went on to repeat all that Elizabeth had told him. But halfway through he stopped and asked, 'Is there any more coffee there, Mama? It doesn't matter about it being cold.'

In silence, Lucille poured out a cup of coffee and placed it in his hands.

After drinking it, he began again: 'You remember, Granan, the morning Jerry phoned and I went out to lunch with him? Well, there she was, the nurse I couldn't get out of my mind since she had said goodbye to me in the hospital. Now, it appears that she had been experiencing the same sort of feelings I had. Later, she was to tell me this, and that it made her determined that when she went home for Christmas she would tell the man she couldn't marry him. This was much to her mother's distress, but not to her father's. Then, accompanied by her brother, she went to this man's house and this is what happened.'

Matthew now went into details of the events that resulted in Elizabeth's being beaten up and almost raped—for this would surely have happened if her brother, who had been waiting for her outside, and the man's own brother hadn't forced open a locked door.

'Unfortunately, a week later, and with

Elizabeth still very unwell, the man's mother, a giant of a woman, actually got into the house, determined to wreak vengeance on Elizabeth by marking her face as she had marked her son, who was now in hospital with a broken shin caused by the poker. And this would have happened had not Elizabeth's father warded her off and out of the house.'

He now came to the point, saying, 'Her brother phoned Liz this morning and said that he had been told the fellow was actually on his way North, because he had been heard in the local pub to say that no one had been born yet who could make a fool of him and get away with it.'

'The police should be informed.'

'Yes, Father, I feel that way too; yet what can they do? He hasn't even been seen up here yet, let alone done anything. But we have taken some precautions: Jim's sister is going to sleep in Liz's flat, and Charlie Fox and I must see to her as much as we can during the day at the hospital. However, it is the weekend I am worried about.'

'Well, tell us what's on your mind. What do you want us to do?' This had come from his grandmother, and again appearing to address his mother he said: 'I was just going to ask Mama if Elizabeth could stay here at the weekends, but now the request goes further. I . . . I wonder, Mama, if you would allow her to live here for a time, until we know what this man is about?'

Into the slight hesitation that followed, Annie Wallingham's voice broke in, 'Well, say something, Lucille!'

'Give me time to speak, Granan, please!' There was an unusual sharpness in Lucille's tone now and there followed another pause before, addressing Matthew, she said, 'Yes. Yes, of course she may stay here for as long as is needed. I'll get a guest room prepared.'

'No need for guest rooms; she can stay along my end, there's a bedroom going begging there.'

'But it hasn't been used for such a long time, Mother-in-law. It is bound to be dampish.'

'A fire or two will soon cure that, and until you feel it's damp-free there's a good chair-bed in the little sitting room. Mary used to sleep on that when needed.'

'Peter'—the colonel's voice sounded weary now—'get me upstairs, will you? But one thing more, Matthew.'

'Yes, Father?'

'Your fiancée is welcome here as long as she wishes to stay.'

Although the invitation had been issued in the formal manner, Matthew was touched by it and he said, 'Thank you, Father; I'm very grateful, and I know Elizabeth will be too.'

After his father and Peter had left the room, Matthew was surprised to hear his grandmother say to her daughter-in-law in a tone that she very rarely used, 'Lucille . . . I . . . I didn't mean to offend you, and I know that you would be only too willing to get a room ready and to have the girl here, if it was only to please Matthew. And I know, like all of us, you were touched by what he had to tell us of Elizabeth's plight. Now, as you are only too well aware, I'm a selfish old woman, and the fact is I liked what I saw of the girl. When I think back to yesterday, I feel ashamed of how I prattled on to her about my own life and sorrows, and so on and so on. It's strange, because that is something that I can't remember ever doing before—and of course, I didn't know at the time what she herself had gone through. So, being my selfish self, I jumped at the chance of doing something for her. No—there I go again. I didn't think like that at all. I thought how pleasant it would be for me to have her along at my end. But I say now, Lucille, if you would rather have her in a guest room . . .'

'No, no! Mother-in-law, I understand. Really, I do. And it would be nice for her to be along there. I'm sure she'll feel . . . well, more at home with you, for, as you have learnt, I'm not very good company. Never was.'

Matthew sat listening to this exchange in some amazement. They seemed to have forgotten that he was there. A deaf patient had once warned him about experiencing this very situation. They pass you over, he said. They wave their hands about and make signs, then look at you because you can't respond to what they are saying, and you can practically hear them saying, 'Oh to hell!' before turning away.

It was strange, but instead of feeling grateful to both of them he felt annoyed for a moment, only to reassure himself by thinking that Liz would never talk as if he weren't there. She'd bring him into the conversation.

But why couldn't he understand that what he had listened to hadn't been just an ordinary conversation? It had been a sort of an opening up between two people who were very dear to him. So what was he being tetchy about? He should be thankful that in some strange way they were being brought closer together by Liz's troubles.

His mother was saying now, 'Will I ring for Mary, dear?'

'No, Lucille. I can manage. She'll probably be along there now, puffing up the pillows. Will you come along, Matthew, and say good night?'

He had to pull himself together before he answered, 'Er, yes. Yes, of course.' Then he heard her voice saying, 'Good night, Lucille,' and his mother reply, 'Good night, my dear. We'll talk more in the morning.'

He heard the drawing room door open, then close, and his mother coming back towards him. 'I am truly sorry for the trouble Elizabeth is in, Matthew, but as you told her story I could not help but think how strange it was that the daughters of a house have always been used as a bargaining point between families for bits of land or great estates. We scorn the marriage arrangements in so many nations abroad, but we practice the same system, with just a little more refinement. You know, my dear, I will confess to you that I've always envied working-class women because they seem to follow their hearts—except, of course, when the religion of their parents thrusts its dogmatic head between them and their choice.'

'Oh! Mama.' He held her gently to him as he said, 'I hate to think of you ever being unhappy.'

'Well, my dear boy, I can tell you I am not unhappy at this moment. I am pleased at your father's attitude towards you and, as he said'—she laughed gently now—'your fiancée. That sounded so correct, even prim, didn't it? And then'—she paused—'there is your grandmother. I can't remember her ever speaking to me so kindly. You know, Mary has a lot of old-fashioned sayings and she recalls her own mother quoting them, and just a short while ago I remembered one of them. It goes, "Trouble can unlock frozen hearts," and Elizabeth's trouble has done that, I think, tonight. For me at any rate.'

'Oh, my dear Mama.' He could find no other words to say.

Patting his cheek, she said, 'Good night, darling. I must go and see to your father now, and I'll get Peter to explain the situation to Rodney.'

Although he kept the telling down to mere details, Peter saw amazement on the younger man's face and heard it in his voice as he queried, 'She's coming to live here?'

'Yes; for the present.'

Resuming his natural self, Rodney demanded, 'Why couldn't he have waited until I came back to tell everyone?'

'Well, you were gone over an hour and that would have meant the family waiting too, your father and mother and Madam, and none of them, as you are aware'—he laughed now—'are known for their patience. Anyway, Matthew was in no state to wait; he wanted the matter settled.'

'Oh yes. Oh yes, I can understand that: everything must be fixed and suited to his requirements.'

'Rodney!' There was a deep reprimand in the voice.

And Rodney came back at him, saying, 'Well, you know it's true, Peter: what Matthew wants, Matthew gets.'

'He didn't ask to be blind.'

Rodney made no comment on this, but after a moment he said, 'And the fellow has followed her here?'

'They think he may, and he is apparently determined to get at her one way or another. All because she turned him down.'

Rodney stood for a moment as if thinking; then he walked towards the dying fire and looked down into it as he muttered, 'Strange how some men let themselves be affected by women.'

Peter could have remarked, 'You weren't unaffected yourself by her, if my observations on your changed manner yesterday were anything to go by.' Nevertheless, all he said was, 'Good night, Rodney, I'm locking up.'

'Oh; good night, Peter.'

The room to himself, Rodney slumped into an easy chair and, as was his habit when thinking, he began to bite his nails.

19

Back in the flat, Elizabeth and her new companion were preparing for bed. Cissie had declared that the couch would be fine, at the same time assuring Elizabeth that she was a light sleeper and that at the sound of any small disturbance she'd be on her feet.

Although Cissie's bulk put Elizabeth in mind of Bridget McCabe, nevertheless she had taken to the young woman; she was so like Jim, she would be reliable.

It was just after nine; Elizabeth was in her dressing gown, but Cissie had not yet undressed, when they heard the front doorbell ring. Cissie looked at Elizabeth and asked quietly, 'Does anybody come to the door at this time, I mean for the woman upstairs?'

'No. No, she has no visitors that I know of, no one that would come at this hour anyway.' She almost stammered on the last words.

'And you told her not to come down and answer the door?'

'Yes. Yes, I did.'

'Well then'—Cissie now pointed towards the window—'that looks on to the street, doesn't it?'

'Yes.'

'Well, it isn't very far from the front door; put out the light.'

As Elizabeth quickly obeyed, Cissie said, 'There's a streetlight further along; I'll be able to make out the shape of who's there anyway.' The room in darkness, she now parted the curtains and pressed her face against the window, then exclaimed softly, 'Well, he's a pretty big fellow. I'd like to take a guess and say it's him, miss. In a dim light he looks like a house-end.'

'Oh my God!'

'Don't you worry, miss. I've dealt with big 'uns before, and drunks. Me da takes after me, or me after him, whichever way you put it, but I've managed him in my day

and him blind drunk. Now look. Stay where
you are.'

'Where're you going?'

'I'm going to open the door.'

'Oh no! Please! Please, Cissie. No! no,
don't!'

'Let me handle this, miss, please. I know
what I'm doing. Leave the light off. I'll put
the hall one on.'

She went out of the room, banging the
door as loudly as she could after her,
crossed to the front door, opened it and,
looking at the huge bulk before her, she
demanded, 'Who're you? What d'you
want?'

'I've come to see Miss Ducksworth. I'm
told she lives here.'

'Ducks . . . Ducksworth? Oh aye. Aye.
Well, she used to. She likely will again, but
she's rented me this flat for a month.'

For a moment, the man did not speak,
then he said, 'Have you her new address?'

'No, mister, I haven't, and if I had I
wouldn't give it to you. What are you after?'

'I want to see Miss Ducksworth. I have
a message from her parents.'

'Her parents? Where're they from?'

'Hastings.'

'My God! Hastings. That's the other side of the country. If they had a message for her couldn't they have got on the phone?'

Again there was a pause before the man spoke: 'She had left home; they didn't know her address.'

'Then where did you get it from?'

'The hospital. I called in there and they said she had just gone off duty, and they gave me this address.'

'They never did, not in the hospital. I've worked in a hospital and behind a desk, and you're not supposed to give any nurse's address away.'

'Well, they did in this case because I explained it was urgent, and I told them that they could confirm my identity by phoning my home. I gave them my number.'

Cissie's thoughts at this moment were that they were dealing with a clever bugger here, so now she said, 'When she left here she must have had a reason, and she's left the wrong address at the hospital—at least, she hasn't left her new one there— and she's been gone now . . . well, I took over on Wednesday. I thought then there was something fishy, she seemed in a hurry to go. But I was in a hurry to get somewhere to stay and so we suited each other, and I don't ask questions. So have you got your answer, mister?'

There was a pause before he answered, 'Not quite.'

She looked down at his foot, which was on the step that led into the hall, and she said, 'Well, I'll say good night to you, and hope you find who you're lookin' for. Would you mind moving your foot from that step?' When the foot remained in place, she said slowly and ominously, 'Mister, I can use my feet very quickly, and they always hit what I'm aiming at. D'you get me?'

When he still did not answer, she brought her heel crashing down on the toe of his shoe. There was a slight gasp, and as he stepped backwards she quickly slammed the door.

Once back in the room she said, 'Switch the light on.' Then, 'Did you hear that?' she said to Elizabeth.

And Elizabeth muttered, 'Yes. Yes, you were marvellous, but I know him, he didn't believe you. He'll . . . he'll come back.'

'Aye, I'm afraid to admit he might do just that. Anyway, he can't get in by the front door and he'd have to scale the wall at the back before he could get to the window of your bedroom, and you say it's all of six feet. A man like him, though, could jump it. He's an enormous fellow. I thought me da was big and that there weren't many women my size, but if his mother's anything like him . . .'

'Oh, she is, and the same type, Cissie; and I'm desperately afraid of them both.'

'Look, sit down. If he's going to try to force his way in, he'll be in that back yard in no time, then I'll phone the polis.'

'It . . . it might be too late then . . . once he gets in.'

'Would you like me to phone them now? Or shall I phone our Jim, and he'll bring your fellow?'

'Oh no. No, I mustn't disturb them. They . . . they've been so kind.'

'Kind! Don't be silly, girl. Mr Matthew'll go mad if anything should happen to you. That's what our Jim says, so don't talk about them being kind. You need them. And your man . . . I mean Mr Matthew. He can't do much, poor fellow, but he'd damn well see that our Jim would. And knowing Jim, he'd need no pushing. By! no.' She now asked, 'Is there not a door leading from the kitchen into the yard?'

'No. The only access to that part of the yard is through the basement, and the rubbish has been left at the top of the basement steps. There's no one in the basement. I understand it's been used as a kind of store room, but it's locked now.'

'Well, come on in the kitchen with me, love, and we'll make some tea.'

She took Elizabeth's trembling arm; but they had no sooner reached the kitchen than they were both stopped by the sound of a slight thud. They stared at each other. Then Cissie darted back into the sitting room, picked up the phone and got through to the police, with Elizabeth standing almost behind her as if for protection. She could make out a voice asking for the address and heard Cissie say, 'He's tried to get in the front way, but I bolted that door. I feel sure though he's got over the wall into the yard.' She could not make out the voice now, but Cissie's reply of, 'In five minutes, thank you. Thank you, sir,' informed her.

Cissie put her arms around Elizabeth's shaking body and said, 'They've got through to the sub-station. It's quite near here, they'll have a couple of men round within five minutes or so. It'll be all right. You'll be all right. But we're not staying here. Once the polis come I'll get them to run us home, but before I do, I'll get in touch with our Jim. Have you got a torch? I'd likely be able to see into the yard.'

Elizabeth hesitated, then said, 'Yes. I'll get it,' and rushed into her bedroom, with Cissie following her, saying: 'Don't put the light on. I can pick him out in the yard if he's there.'

When Cissie opened the bedroom curtains and flashed her light down around the yard, at first she could see nothing except some empty tea-chests and what looked like a dog kennel, but at the bottom of the yard there was a doorless recess. It could have been a coalhouse once, and she concentrated her light on it. She was about to flash it away when she saw the hand. Just a hand gripping the stanchion that had likely supported a door. She took in a deep breath and, closing the curtains, she said quickly, 'He's down there. Now look! Stop shaking, get into your things, and pack a case with your odds and ends

and what you need for overnight. We'll
come back tomorrow for the rest . . .
Hurry up! Hurry up, you polis!'

As if in answer to her cry, the front doorbell rang and Cissie hurried to the sitting
room and looked out through the curtains,
there to make out a van with a policeman
standing before it; on this she flew out of
the room and opened the front door.

The taller of the two policemen said,
'Having an intruder, miss?'

'Yes.'

'Do I understand he's tried the back and
the front?'

Again she answered, 'Yes.' Then she led
them into the kitchen and said, 'Five minutes ago he was in the yard there.'

'You're sure it was the same man?'

'Oh, I'm sure of that. I answered the
front door and let him have it.'

'But how do you know it's the same man
who was in the yard?' asked the other policeman now.

'Well, I just know it was, and Miss
here'—she pointed to Elizabeth, who was
now entering the room, buttoning up her
coat—'she knows it was him 'cos she's
met up with him before.'

'Oh, you know the man?' He was addressing Elizabeth.

'Yes. He was a neighbour of my family.'

'Where was that? On the outskirts?'

'No. Back in Hastings.'

'Hastings, miss? That's a long way off. And what d'you think he wants now?'

'To . . . to injure me.'

'Injure you?' The two policemen stared at her. Then the first one said, 'Has he done so before?'

'Yes.'

'I suppose there's a reason?' said his companion.

'Yes. Yes, there is.'

'Oh. Oh.' The policeman shook his head now and said, 'Well, how can we get into the back yard? Is there a door here?'

'No. The only entry is through the basement.'

'Have you a key?'

'No, I haven't, but Mrs Baker, up above . . .'

Now it was as if her words had wafted Mrs Baker down the stairs, for she was standing in the doorway, exclaiming, 'What is it? What's the matter?'

'The man I was telling you about, Mrs

Baker,' said Elizabeth, 'he . . . he has called and got into the yard. Have you the key to the basement so that the police can look there?'

'Oh yes, yes, I have. But dear me! Dear me! What an upset for you. What are you going to do, my dear?'

'I'm . . . I'm going to Miss Taylor's house'—she indicated Cissie—'for . . . for the present. I can't stay here.'

'No, no, of course not, dear.'

'Could we have the key, madam, please?'

'Yes, yes, of course.' Mrs Baker disappeared, to return within a few minutes with the key, which she handed to the policeman. 'Right!' he said. 'We'll have a look.'

Immediately they had gone Cissie snatched up the phone, saying in an aside to Elizabeth, 'I'm getting through to our Jim; he left me the number.' The conversation that followed after Peter had answered the telephone and fetched Jim went, 'You in bed? Well, that's a good job. Get yourself here quick. He's been both front and back. The polis is here. I'm takin' Miss to our house. Yes, yes, she's all right so far. But I couldn't have managed him alone, I know that.' A pause, then she ended, 'Yes, do that. Do that.' She put down the phone and turned to Elizabeth, saying, 'Go on in there and get your case, because I'm not letting those polis go before they see us home.'

It was a few minutes later when the policemen returned and informed them, 'There's no one in that yard now, and no sign of a break-in in the basement either. What's this man like?'

Cissie answered, 'You could say he's my size only half as big again.'

'Then he must be a big fella,' said one of them, laughing.

'Yes, I'll say he is, six foot four or so, I'd say, and he looked almost as broad, what I saw of him.' Her voice changing now, she asked politely, 'I'd be grateful if you'd see us back to my home 'cos we . . . I mean she, can't stay here. He's dangerous, that man.'

'Why hasn't she reported him before?'

'Well, because she wasn't aware of him havin' chased her to this end of the country until yesterday, when her brother phoned; and he hasn't been long in findin' out where she lives.'

'Where do *you* live?' asked the other policeman flatly.

'The Bishop housing estate. Just off the main road.'

'Well then,' said the other policeman, 'we'd better be going, hadn't we?'

'There's a case.' Cissie now hurried into the bedroom, saying, 'They're waitin'; they're gonna see us home.'

Elizabeth said nothing but tried to fasten down the catch on the case.

'Give it here. I'll bring it. Have you got a scarf? Put it round your head. It'll be cold out there. Come on; they're waiting.'

Like a child doing her mother's bidding Elizabeth went into the sitting room, and there Mrs Baker greeted her with, 'Oh my dear, I'm so sorry for all this trouble you're in. Will you be coming back?'

'I . . . I don't know, Mrs Baker. I don't know. But I'll keep in touch. I'll phone you.'

'Do that, my dear. Do that. I'm going to miss you.'

'If you're ready, miss, we'd better be on our way; time's everything at night in the city.'

Mrs Baker leant towards Elizabeth, kissed her cheek and said, 'Don't worry about the flat. I'll attend to it and I'll look after what things you've left until you're settled.'

'Madam. We must be on our way.'

'Oh yes. Oh yes, Officer, yes.'

It seemed only five minutes later when the two policemen left them in the dim-lit hall of the block of flats, saying, 'You'll be all right now, miss?'

'Yes. Yes, thank you.'

'Oh, by the way,' the second policeman said, 'where will we be able to contact you, miss, after you . . . well, after you leave here?'

It was Cissie who answered him, and not without a touch of upgrade in her voice, 'She will likely be at The Beavors, Colonel Wallingham's estate. My brother is chauffeur to his son, Captain Wallingham, and Miss Ducksworth here is engaged to him.'

Elizabeth almost groaned as she muttered, 'Oh, Cissie!' and the policeman said, 'Indeed! Indeed! Well, that's an address I'll remember. Good night, miss.'

'Good night, Officer, and . . . and thank you very much for your kindness.'

'It was nothing, miss. It's all in a day's

work, or night's, it's how you look at it. But we'll keep an eye open for that fellow. By his description, he'll stick out in a crowd.'

'Thank you. Thank you very much indeed.'

They stepped into the lift and rose slowly. When it stopped at the fifth floor Elizabeth stepped out on to a landing and waited while Cissie brought out the case, then closed the cage door with a clashing bang; and it would appear that this opened the blue-painted door right opposite them. In the bright light from the room beyond stood a woman who exclaimed in a voice not unlike Cissie's, 'In the name of God! what's this? What's up, our Cissie?'

'Let's get in, Ma, and I'll tell you what's up. This is Miss Ducksworth. Don't stand there, Ma, like a stook, let's past.'

'Oh, lass. Oh, miss. Come in. Come in. But we're all upside down in here; they've been out'—she turned to her daughter—'they've been out for fish and chips.'

'No need to tell me that, Ma, I can use me nose. Anyway, miss, this is me ma.'

'Hello, Mrs Taylor,' said Elizabeth. 'I'm . . . I'm so sorry to have to intrude on you like this, but you see . . .'

'No need to explain, lass. No need. Come in. If you'll take us as you find us you're more than welcome. Come in. Come into the sitting room.'

'Where're the others?' asked Cissie.

'Well, where d'you think, Flabby?'

'Eeh! Ma.'

'All right, all right; they're in the kitchen, stuffin' their guts as usual, and that after a big tea. I've told them I'll do no more cookin' in this house, they can live on fish an' chips. Oh, lass, you look all in. Let's have your coat and hat and I'll get you a cup of tea.' Now bending towards Elizabeth, the surprisingly small woman said, 'You wouldn't like a drop of hard, I mean a tot of whisky or something to pull you round?'

'No, thank you, but it's kind of you to offer. I'd love a cup of tea, though.'

Mrs Taylor ushered Elizabeth towards a door, saying, 'This is me sitting room. I don't let them in here 'cos I try to keep it nice.'

'Ma, she's not going in there, it's like an ice-box! I'll take her to my room and she can put her feet up.'

'Oh, lass,' said her mother, apologetically now, 'Fanny's in there. She wanted to stay the night. She thought you'd be away . . . well, at least for a night or two, and she's planted herself.'

'I'll murder her, I will one of these days, Ma, I'll murder her. Look, come on, miss, into the sitting room: there's an electric fire there. It'll soon warm up, at least within the next week or so. I'd keep your coat on. And Ma, bring in the other electric fire from . . .'

'Please, Cissie, and please, Mrs Taylor, don't put yourself to such trouble. Look, I'll go in the kitchen and meet your family, and be pleased to . . .'

'No, lass, no, not the night. They're in there all with cans of beer and the place is like Paddy's market. No, I'll bring the other fire from our room in here. By the way, have you phoned our Jim?'

She was addressing her daughter, and Cissie replied, 'Well, what d'you think, Ma? He should be here at any minute; and, if I know anything, the captain will be with him.'

'Oh my God! no, and the place in such a pickle.'

'Shut up, Ma, and don't be so daft. Anyway, the captain's blind, and it won't be the first time he's gone slumming.'

'My house is no slum, girl! and mind your mouth and . . . oh, miss, I'm sorry.' She turned to Elizabeth, who tried to bring a smile to her lips as she answered: 'Please don't worry, Mrs Taylor; I'm only too grateful that you have taken me in for a while.'

'Oh, lass. Anyway, that tea . . . I'll get it.'

Alone together, Cissie laughed, saying, 'That's me ma, worryin' about appearances, and with a gang like she's got! But it's funny; she's always kept one little cubby-hole that she could put the name of sitting room or parlour to. And look at this one: if I stretched me arms out wide I could push the walls away. It should've been a bedroom, but no; for years I had to sleep with two of the others, and there was always an uproar because I took up too much room.'

She bent over Elizabeth, who was sitting close to the three-bar electric fire, and she said, 'Oh, miss, you look like death. But you'll be all right now. Once our Jim gets here with his boss everything'll run smoothly, you'll see. Jim has a way of gettin' things done, and, you know, he'd stand on his head for that man—the captain. He'd work for him for nothin'. Oh aye, he would.' She pulled a chair up to the other side of the fire and quietly she said, 'By! I can understand, miss, how you're frightened of that fellow. I've always bragged that there's not a man big enough that I couldn't handle, but to tell you the truth I wouldn't look forward to a tussle with him. Although I would use every dirty trick in the book, I still can't see me gettin' away with it. And, from what our Jim let drop, he tried his hand on you. My God! No wonder you're terrified of him . . . Are you any warmer?'

'Yes, I'm all right, thanks, Cissie.'

'Oh, here's Ma with the cup that cheers.'

As her mother placed on a small table a tin tray covered with a crocheted doily and holding three large cups of tea, Cissie said, 'You've quelled the riot in the kitchen then. It sounds so quiet there could be a death in the family.'

'There will be shortly, I can tell you that, and it'll be Fanny who'll be carried out.

That girl's gettin' too big for her boots . . . Here you are, miss. I didn't know if you took sugar or not, but I've put a spoonful on the side there.'

'Thank you. I . . . I don't take sugar.'

'Well, in that case, miss, there'll be more for our Cissie here. That's what's put the fat on her.'

Mrs Taylor suddenly stopped talking and turned her head to the side, and at the same moment Cissie rose from her chair, saying, 'That's the lift. It'll be them.'

It was Cissie who hurried out of the room while her mother, stroking back her hair, muttered something like, 'Eeh! and the house in the state that it is.'

Then the door opening brought Elizabeth up from her seat, and there was Jim leading Matthew into the room, saying, 'We're here, miss! We're here. You'll be all right now.'

'Liz! Liz!'

She was in his arms and he was stroking her face, saying, 'Don't, darling! Don't! Don't tremble so: I'm with you, and you're coming home.'

She hadn't spoken, but now she gently drew herself from him and said, 'This is

Mrs Taylor, Jim's mother, Matthew. She and her daughter have been so . . . so very kind to me.'

Matthew held out his hand, and it was taken and shaken by the small firm one as he said, 'Thank you very much, Mrs Taylor, and your daughter too. And I can't miss this opportunity to say how thankful I am to have your son, not only to drive me around, but to be a good companion to me.'

'Oh, sir. I . . . I'm so pleased to hear you say that, honoured in fact, because Jim's a good fellow. He's my son, and although I say it meself, you'll not find anyone better to serve you. And he thinks the world of you . . .'

'Shut up! Ma, an' let the captain sit down for a minute. Better still, get yourself back into the kitchen. And you too, Cis. Come on with yer now, and let the miss rest for a minute.'

The forceful tact cleared the room, and Elizabeth was once again held in Matthew's arms. 'Oh, Matthew . . . Matthew, I've . . . I've never experienced so much fear'—her voice was trembling. 'I never knew what real fear was. I'm . . . I'm really terrified of the thought of . . . of . . .'

'Listen, my dear. And listen carefully. From now on there won't be a minute, either at work or at home, when you are on your own. Tomorrow, I'm going to have a talk with the police and get them to look out for a man of his description. Also I'm going to see the matron and Dr Venor, not forgetting Charlie Fox, because he will engage the help of the other porters too; and this fellow, as you say, is so big they'll have no difficulty in spotting him. Anyway, his actions so far have proved that he's a wily individual into the bargain, and so he'll know better than to start anything in a hospital. So now, darling, try . . . oh, try not to worry so much because you'll make yourself ill; your whole body is trembling at this moment.'

'But . . . but what will happen if he is arrested? He can be so plausible. He has done nothing so far, only express the wish to see me. So what can they do?'

'They can warn him that he is being watched, and they can also advise him to return home. If not, my dear, you will have to tell the police exactly what transpired

at Christmas and why you are afraid of the
man. I really think that would be the better
thing to do now.'

'Oh no. No, Matthew; don't ask me to
do that. I . . . I couldn't go through that
again, and . . . and to strangers. To you
it was different.'

'Then, my dear, what you've got to do
is to trust me and . . . and I will see . . .'

Of a sudden he let go of her and, with
clenched fist, he thumped his head as he
groaned, 'Damn these eyes! Damn them!'

'Oh, Matthew darling, don't. Please,
please don't say that. Never say that.
Look'—it was she who was now holding
him—'I . . . I promise you I'll try to quell
this stupid fear and stop worrying, especially stop worrying you. I . . . I'll look at
it this way: what has to be will be. Everything that possibly can be done is being done to protect me. I will rely on that.
I am only sorry that . . . that I am causing so much upset in your home.
Does . . . does your mother know that
you're bringing me back?'

'Of course she does. They all know. I
explained the whole business to them tonight, and Father said immediately that

you must come back there and stay with us. I must tell you, though it's the wrong time, that I was a little peeved when Mama and Granan vied with each other as to where you would sleep. Mama suggested a guest room, Granan demanded that you sleep in her quarters. They even forgot my presence; their talk became so intimate that I might not have been there. For a moment, believe me, I was annoyed that I should be left out of this arrangement.'

'Oh, Matthew. What can I say? And I cannot bear to think what would have happened to me in the present circumstances if I hadn't had you and your family.'

'Not forgetting Jim Taylor, his mother, his sister and the rest of the tribe.'

She knew he was endeavouring to make her smile now, and she did so as she said, 'I will never forget them, especially Cissie. Oh, she was marvellous tonight, so courageous. Without her, I think I would've gone mad. And . . . and her mother is a dear. The rest of the family are in the kitchen . . .' her voice dropped to a whisper as she ended, 'and as Cissie said, eatin' fish an' chips and sluggin' beer.'

'Good for them.'

'There was a lot of chatter from the kitchen when we first came in, but Mrs Taylor silenced it and, as Cissie said, it sounded as if somebody had died because the house must never be quiet. So far I've met only three of them, but I'm sure they must be a lovely lot.'

It was Matthew whispering now, 'Even the one in jug who clears ladies' dressing tables?'

It was good to feel a different kind of tremble in her body now, and he went on, 'Look, we'd better be off. Time's going on.'

'Come along then.'

Before she led him to the door he kissed her, but softly and tenderly. Then they went into the hallway, where Elizabeth wasn't surprised to find most of the family waiting. And it was Jim who said, 'This is me da, sir.'

It was a big bony hand that gripped Matthew's as the rough voice said, 'Pleased to meet ya, Captain. Pleased to meet ya.'

'And I you, Mr Taylor.'

'And this, Da, is Miss Ducksworth, who's engaged to the captain.'

'And the same to you, miss; and the same to you. Very pleased to make your acquaintance.'

Elizabeth's hand now was being pumped up and down and she said, 'And me yours, Mr Taylor, and all your family.'

'Well, that's as far as the introductions are going the night. There's two more lasses who dropped in this evening besides Cissie, and their fellas,' said Jim, 'and these, leaving Cissie out, are open-mouthed, goggle-eyed and utterly brainless.'

There was a chorus of 'Oh, our Jim! Just you wait, our Jim, I'll have you for that,' and to this Jim replied, 'Any time. Any time.' Matthew was laughing gently as he was led into the lift, and he squeezed Elizabeth's hand as they stood side by side. And when Jim took Elizabeth's case from his sister, the big woman leant forward for a moment and said, 'Be seein' you again, miss.'

'Yes, yes, definitely, Cissie. And thank you, thank you so much. Good night. Good night, all! And many thanks, Mrs Taylor.'

As the lift made its rickety journey to the ground floor, Jim made a comment on his sister: 'Cissie's a good lass,' he said; 'it's only a pity some fella can't see her from the inside.'

20

All the lights in the lower part of the house were on. Peter was at the open door to meet them, and his greeting was quiet: 'You made it then,' he said.

'Yes, Peter, we made it. But Elizabeth is very tired.'

Following them, carrying the suitcase, Jim said, 'Where'll I put this, Peter?'

'Oh, just leave it to one side for the present, Jim; and look, go on into the kitchen and get yourself something hot. The girls are still all up.'

'I'll do that. I'll do that.' However, he did not go immediately but went to Matthew and, touching his arm, said, 'You'll be all right for the night, sir?'

'Yes, yes, thank you, Jim. Thank you. We'll talk in the morning.'

'Aye. Good night, miss. Feeling any better?'

'Yes thanks, Jim, a lot. Oh yes, a lot.'

'That's good. Good night.'

'Good night, Jim. Good night.'

'There's a nice fire on in the sitting room, Mr Matthew,' said Peter now, 'but first of all I'll slip upstairs. The mistress asked that she be told the moment you arrived. She's with the colonel.'

Holding Elizabeth by the arm, Matthew made his way to the sitting room where he said, 'Oh, it's nice and warm in here. Sit down, darling,' and he led her to an easy chair. 'But let me have your coat off first.'

Elizabeth sat down in the soft-cushioned armchair, but its comfort did not make her feel that she could relax: she was feeling tense and ill at ease, for it came to her that she was disorganising the lives of a number of people, particularly those in this house. Back there, in Mrs Taylor's front parlour, she had felt reassured as Matthew described his mother and grandmother arranging her stay with them, but now that feeling was gone. She was feeling awkward, out of place.

'Oh, there you are, my dear. How are you feeling?' Elizabeth looked up at Lucille Wallingham, who was bending over her, her face full of concern. Somehow, tonight, she looked different. Perhaps it was because she appeared less formal as she was wearing a full-skirted, quilted pink dressing gown.

Elizabeth found that she was unable to make any remark; all she could do was to gaze up stupidly into the face above her. She was also aware that her lips were trembling, and that she couldn't stop them.

Lucille straightened up and, turning to her son, she said, 'Has Bella been in?'

'No, Mama, but Jim is in the kitchen, so she'll know we are back.'

'Well, she should have brought it in before now . . . I mean, Cook is keeping some soup hot. She knew you'd need something, it's so bitterly cold tonight.' Then quietly, she asked, 'Are you all right, Matthew?'

'Yes, Mama, I'm all right. But tell me, where have you arranged for Elizabeth to sleep?'

'Oh . . . oh, tonight I've had the Tulip Room prepared because I didn't want to disturb your grandmother; you know she likes to get to bed early. As yet she knows nothing about . . . well, Elizabeth coming tonight.'

She turned now and looked towards Elizabeth, who was lying back, her eyes closed and the tears streaming down her face. Suddenly she knew what was going to happen; it had happened like that to herself all those years ago.

She now turned quickly to Matthew, who was sitting near the armchair, and taking his hand she drew him to his feet, whispering softly as she did so, 'I want a word with you.'

She led him out to the corridor, where she said, 'Listen to me, dear, and please do as I say. Go upstairs and get ready for bed.'

'What! and leave . . . ?'

'Please! I beg of you, listen to me, and do this one thing I ask, and without question: go upstairs and get ready for bed.'

'But, Mama! Elizabeth . . .'

'Leave Elizabeth to me tonight, dear, please! No! Just wait a minute. Here's Bella with the soup. Thank you, Bella. I'll take the tray. And thank the others very much for staying up so late.'

'Will I not come back for the tray, mistress?'

'No, Bella, don't bother tonight. Just leave it.'

'Very well, mistress.'

There was a note of disappointment in Bella's reply: she had hoped to go back and tell them how the visitor looked, because although Jim Taylor had made them laugh he had mentioned nothing at all about the captain's fiancée having been brought here the night.

'Stay a minute,' Lucille now said to Matthew as she slipped back into the room and put the tray on a side table.

When she was back with Matthew, he demanded, 'What is it, Mama? Can you see something wrong with Elizabeth?'

'Only that she is very tired, dear, and . . . and in an emotional state.'

'Then I should be with her.'

'Not on this occasion, Matthew: your very presence will make her hold on tight to her emotions, and I can tell you, if they are suppressed they can affect her to such an extent that . . . that'—she paused—

'that one goes into a breakdown. I'm speaking from experience, dear.'

'Oh, Mama!'

'Yes, you can say oh, Mama! like that; so will you do as I ask? Go upstairs, and not only get ready for bed but go to bed; and you may see her in the morning, when, I can assure you, she'll be a different girl, very tired, in fact worn out, but relieved. Will you do that for me?'

He gave a long sigh, then said, 'Well, I imagine you know best at the moment how she should be treated. All right, I'll do as you ask, but I do it reluctantly.' He bent and kissed her on the cheek, before feeling his way from her and up the stairs.

Elizabeth had remained in the same position. She was still lying back, her eyes closed and the tears running down her face. The front of her dress was wet with them, and she was making no effort to wipe them away.

Lucille bent down to her, saying gently, 'Come, my dear. Come. Sit on the couch with me.'

Elizabeth allowed herself to be helped from the chair and over to the couch, which was set at right-angles to the fireplace; and when they were seated together Lucille tucked some cushions behind Elizabeth's back, saying, 'There now. There now. Cry, my dear. Don't be afraid of crying.'

Elizabeth turned her face to this woman whom she had met for the first time yesterday, and she opened her mouth twice before she brought out the whimpered word, 'S-s-sorry.'

'Oh, my dear.' Lucille's arms were about Elizabeth's shoulders, were drawing her close, and she was saying, 'There now. There now. Never say you're sorry, not to me. At least not about crying, because I know a lot about crying, my dear.'

'I'm so . . . so very afraid.'

'You have no longer any need to be afraid, dear. That man will not be allowed to get near you, not in any way.'

Elizabeth seemed not to have heard Lucille. Her head was whirling: she was back in Bridget McCabe's sitting room. She was on the couch. His hands were on her thighs, clawing at them. She was about to scream. No! No, she mustn't scream! But she felt she was swelling; her whole body was swelling. Now it changed into a huge lump that forced its way through her throat, choking her, until she opened her mouth wide and released it in a wail which filled the room like the cry of a trapped animal.

Her trembling body shook them both. Lucille's face, too, was swimming in tears and her voice was shaking as she cried, 'Hush! Oh, my dear, don't! Don't! You'll be all right now: it's over, it's out.' She was rocking Elizabeth now. 'You'll never feel so bad again. Come! Come now! Remember you are greatly loved. You have Matthew. There now! There now!' The rocking slowed to a halt, and Lucille laid the exhausted girl back on to the cushions.

Then she herself leant back on the couch, and, taking a white handkerchief from her pocket, she wiped Elizabeth's face. 'I understand you, my dear,' she said. 'I've been through all this myself. And your outburst, my dear, has swept away any feeling of jealousy I was building up against you. When this happened to me, and I did as my mother wished, I had no one to turn to, no one with whom to talk it over with. And so I built myself a remote and austere façade. It was a loveless cage.'

She was holding Elizabeth's hands now. Why was she talking like this? She could never remember speaking so frankly to anyone. She had never spoken like this to her daughters. Strange, when she came to think of it. They hadn't needed to be talked to like this. They were full of self-confidence, in fact at times cool, withdrawn. But hadn't she been like that most of her married life, cool and withdrawn? Yes, on the outside, but not the inside. No, not inside. For inside her had been a great need: a need for a hand to hold; a need for someone to soothe her as she was soothing this girl here. This girl in a way had suffered, as she had, from the insidious sweetness of a selfish mother whose one aim had been to see that her daughter's way of life was not to be deflected in any way from the old pattern of family sacrifice—everyone had to make sacrifices, and daughters in particular. They had to learn to be unselfish and remember all that had been done for them since they were born; but above all, they must learn how to avoid scandal.

Elizabeth shuddered. Then she opened her eyes and looked at the face so close to hers: she said no word, but she turned her head and laid it on the shoulder that had been supporting her.

Whatever kindness Elizabeth would show to her in the future, Lucille knew that it would not evoke the feeling that was in her now, for it was as if a lost daughter had come back . . . an only daughter. She had never felt like this for her own daughters. Again, strange but true. This girl, of whom she had been afraid because she was taking her beloved son away from her, would in the future be a friend. The age difference between them meant nothing. The thought was so comforting that she pressed Elizabeth's head closer to her and let her own face rest on the tumbled hair for a moment.

Lucille did not move her position until the door was softly opened to show Peter standing there, amazement showing in his face at the scene before him.

Elizabeth was conscious of being laid gently back among the cushions. She felt very odd, tired, as if her whole body had been emptied, leaving her limp and dazed.

Later she was to ask herself if she really did see the scene that followed, or if it had been born of the imagination, for she saw Peter, who was a servant but treated as a friend, wiping the tears with his forefinger from his mistress's cheeks, then laying his hand gently on the side of her face, and heard his voice, strange-sounding, saying, 'You'll feel better too, my dear.'

What was real was Lucille's voice saying, 'Help me to get her to her room, Peter. She is riddled with fear.'

Riddled with fear. Riddled with fear. She no longer felt riddled with fear. Where was she? She had been asleep. She felt so rested she wanted to lie here for ever, never to move again, and think, and think. But think about what? About whom? Oh, Matthew. Matthew. Oh yes, Matthew, and Cissie and Jim and all the Taylors. Oh yes, all the Taylors. Then there was . . . yes, yes—her mind was nodding at her yes, there was his mother. What had she said? 'Cry, my dear. Cry. I know all about crying.' She had said that: she had held her and talked to her as her own mother had never done, and yet before she had thought her so stiff and rather prim behind her polished smile. But she wasn't like that at all. She was kind. Oh, so kind. And that torrent that had hit her? She had never before in her life given way like that.

Up till recently she'd had nothing to cry about: be upset about, yes; worry about, yes; but really nothing to cry about. But that hadn't been just crying; that had been the release of something that had been buried in her, shut down, kept at bay—at least over the last few years—the knowledge that she was really being pressed into a marriage that she didn't want, even feared. Yes, she must have feared him even then: she had feared his displeasure, which would make him fling himself about and raise his voice so loud as to deafen one when he was baulked in any way. But now it was over. She was safe. Safe among these wonderful people; for there were a number of men on the farm, and three in this household who would protect her: Jim, Rodney and Peter.

She had a strange memory of Peter. She couldn't quite recall it. She had imagined seeing him wiping Mrs Wallingham's face and talking to her. She must have imagined it, because she certainly wasn't herself at that time; she had even thought, as they

led her upstairs, that she was in the lift
going up to Mrs Taylor's parlour again. She
must for a time have been slightly delirious.
That great torrent of released emotion must
have swept her mind away too.

'You're awake, miss?'

'Oh . . . oh, good morning, Bella.'

'I'll pull the curtains, miss. It's a lovely
day, but cold; I think we're going to have
snow.'

She watched the woman pull back the
heavy brocade curtains from the broad
window, and the light filled the big room.
She couldn't see much of the walls, for
they seemed to be covered with large
pieces of dark shining furniture: a huge
wardrobe, a dressing table, a wash-hand
stand, a writing-desk and a bed. The bed
too was made of wood. The end had miniature posts supporting a carved footboard.
The bedcover was of a soft bluish-mauve
picked out with some kind of flower. The
bed itself felt like a nest. 'You slept well,
miss?'

'Yes, I must have. What time is it, Bella?'

'Half-past nine, miss.'

'What!' The answer brought her straight

up in the bed. 'Half-past nine? But I must . . .'

'Oh! Oh, miss, do lie still. Cook's got your breakfast all ready. I'll bring it up in a minute, but I'll tell you what.' She leant towards Elizabeth and in a low voice she said, 'Before you eat anything at all you'll have to see Mr Matthew, 'cos he's pacing the corridor like a caged tiger.' She gave a little giggle now. 'The mistress warned him not to disturb you, to let you come awake, like, on your own.'

Elizabeth lay back in the pillows, and all she could do was smile back at the smiling woman and say, 'Oh, Bella.'

The door had scarcely closed when it was opened again and there he was, his hands outstretched towards the bed.

She leant forward and caught them as he crossed the room, and brought him down to sit on the edge of the bed. And now he was holding her, talking, his words tumbling over each other: 'How d'you feel? Have you slept well? Are you all right? Did you wake in the night? I said somebody should have been in . . .'

'Matthew. Matthew, darling.' She kissed him, and he clung to her lips, holding her in such a way that she was twisted in the bed, causing her to groan now as, releasing herself, she said, 'Do you want to break my spine?'

'Oh, I'm sorry, darling. I'm sorry.'

She now hitched herself nearer to the edge of the bed and him and, her voice changing, she said, softly now, 'Oh Matthew, I've put everybody to so much trouble.'

'Shut up! Don't talk nonsense. I'll tell you what, though, you've done something that no one else has done. I don't know how you managed it or what happened last night but it would seem that you have brought my mother to life. I mean, in a different way. I'll whisper something to you.' And his next words were, 'She's concerned for my father, but not in the way she's concerned for you. As Peter said, it was as if she had never had a daughter of her own. My sisters, I'm afraid, are apt to take after my younger brother, they're very self-contained, not outgoing at all like William was and I myself used to be.'

'And still are, my love, and still are.'

'Well, that's debatable, for you have only

my long sojourn in hospital to judge on.
But since you've come into my life, Liz . . .'

At this point the bedroom door opened
again and Lucille's voice said, 'I told you,
didn't I, to let her have her breakfast first.'

'She asked to see me, Mama.'

'She did not. How are you, my dear?'

The hand was outstretched past her
son, and Elizabeth took it, saying, 'I
feel . . . well, a different being this morning. And oh, I am sorry for all the trouble
I—'

'Be quiet! I've told you before, you're
causing no trouble here.'

'No; she's a godsend.'

'And you be quiet; and get up off that
bed and get away because she's going to
have her breakfast.'

'Oh, Mrs Wallingham, I'm putting . . .'

'Well, let's get another thing straight, my
dear Elizabeth. Please call me Lucille.'

'There. What did I tell you?'

Matthew's voice had a laugh in it, and
his mother demanded, 'What have you
been saying?'

'Never you mind. You've proved my
point.'

'Get out of the way with you. Here's

Bella with the breakfast. Look what you're doing! Move to the side.'

She pressed her son gently towards the head of the bed; then, taking the breakfast tray from Bella's hands, she placed it over Elizabeth's knees, straightening the legs and saying as she did so, 'There now, I'm going to clear this room so that you can eat in peace. I'll be back shortly.'

'Thank you. Thank you.'

And now Lucille's voice, sounding light and cheerful, said, 'I don't need to tell Bella to go, but I need to tell you, Matthew, to come with me. And now, and without further comment.'

'See what you've done . . . Ordered about like a child.'

'You shouldn't act like one,' joined his mother; and then, her voice dropping, she said, 'Enjoy your breakfast, dear.'

Elizabeth looked at the laden tray. It held a segmented half-grapefruit, a boiled egg in a miniature woollen cosy, a rack of toast, a small jug of coffee, another of milk, and two small glass dishes, one holding butter, the other marmalade.

About to cry again, she checked it, saying to herself: No more of that. No more of that, even though she was aware her tears would have been of gratitude . . .

It was more than a half hour later when Bella came back for the tray, to find Elizabeth up and dressed.

'Did you manage to find everything in the bathroom, miss? I would've run a bath for you if you'd only said.'

'I . . . I didn't have a bath this morning, Bella, thanks.'

'Oh well, you never need worry about using hot water, miss, there's plenty of it because we burn a lot of our own wood here.'

'Thank you, Bella.'

'The mistress is coming up in a minute to see about your case. She told me not to touch it. And the last I saw of Mr Matthew, he was in his room writing. Funny that, isn't it? I mean . . . well, clever is the word, that he can still write.'

'Yes; yes, it is, Bella, very clever.'

'Oh, there you are, my dear; and you're already dressed.'

After closing the door behind Bella, Lucille walked over to Elizabeth, saying as she touched the collar of her dress, 'Oh, this is a nice outfit. Mauve suits you; and it looks warm.'

'Yes. Yes, it is.'

Elizabeth was feeling awkward until Lucille took her arm and said, 'Come along, dear. We must have a little talk. It's about'—she pointed—'the case.'

When they were seated on the deep windowledge, Lucille said, 'It's like this. Granan insists that you make your abode along with her. I would rather, much rather, you stayed this end; I feel you'd be more comfortable, and this is such a nice room, don't you think so?'

'It's a lovely room. Yes, a lovely room.'

'You can't describe it as pretty, the furniture is too heavy for that, but you could say it is rather elegant. We call it the Tulip Room. Oh'—she waved her hand—'there is a story behind that, which I'll tell you some day. Now, Granan's spare bedroom is neither as elegant as this nor as large; one could be kind and say it's a comfortable room. She's had a fire blazing away in it since early morning and hot water bottles in the bed; and, oh dear, what we've all gone through for not informing her that you had arrived last night: why wasn't she woken up? Why are things always kept from her? Fancy, my dear'—Lucille's face was near Elizabeth now as she lowered her voice—'fancy anyone daring to keep anything from her. She has a nose like a ferret's; in fact she seems to know things before they happen. Perhaps she's just very good at guessing; but, my dear'—now she patted Elizabeth's knee—'she is good at heart and, on short acquaintance, has taken to you. Now I can tell you that is something, because it isn't everyone she takes to; and those she doesn't know about it immediately. Oh, she can be so terribly rude. Being straightforward, Mary calls it, and adds, she doesn't beat about the bush, and no shilly-shallying. As you'll find, Mary is devoted to her: she has really given her life over to her, and is bullied for her devotion. But, my dear, I must warn you, you must not let her dominate you. By that I mean claim all your attention, as she is apt to do with anyone she is fond of, such as Matthew. Oh yes. Do you know'—her voice dropped again—'she has fought me all my life for him. When I was younger, it used to trouble me greatly, but not any more. I understand her better these days. Yet I must admit, honestly, I find her a great trial at times. So, my dear, don't obey all her commands: gently but firmly put your own needs forward—I mean with regard to time spent with her—whenever you think it's necessary. But anyway, what am I talking about? Matthew will see to that because his needs, as you know, are greater than hers or any others in the family.'

'Yes. Yes, I know that, and I hope I can fill them. I'm determined to. I can say this to you now, Lucille'—here Elizabeth gave a soft laugh—'I just want to say I love him so very much.'

'I'm sure you do, my dear, I'm sure you do. And you have suffered a great deal because of it.'

'Oh no, no, not really. Although my feelings for him helped me at last to say no to that man, I know now I could never have gone through with the marriage.'

There was a pause; then Lucille said, 'When do you intend to marry Matthew?'

'It's not settled yet.' Then, suddenly putting a hand to her mouth, she exclaimed, 'It's not Sunday still, it's Monday! I should be at work. And Matthew too.'

'It's all right, my dear; he's seen to that. He's been on to the hospital and explained you're not very well, in fact that you've got a chill. He also contacted his own supervisor to say he could not be in until tomorrow.'

Elizabeth sighed and said, 'Oh dear, dear. I feel I'm putting everybody out. Sister won't be very pleased; and Matthew will be missed on his ward. I . . . I . . .' She paused and stumbled on her words, as she went on, 'I don't know what you think, but I feel that Matthew would eventually profit from completing his course, that he should have something more than me to keep his mind busy—even if we were married soon.'

'I couldn't agree with you more, dear, because as Granan once said to me in her wisdom, a man needs something more than the woman in his life if he is going to go on loving her. It takes some working out, that bit of wisdom. But as she also pointed out, love has its time-limit and it never succeeds if it claims the best part of twenty-four hours a day. As Mary would put it, and has done, "Keep a dog on a chain and it will some day bite you, but let it run, and it'll never do that." It's odd, isn't it, that our lives are based on sayings and proverbs? Everything we do can be capped or explained by one or the other.'

As Elizabeth looked at her she thought it wasn't only the old lady who was wise, this one was too, but she had come to her wisdom in a different school. From what she remembered of last night, Lucille had been sold into marriage by her selfish mother, whereas Granan had been loved, and by the right man. Of a sudden there again flashed into her mind the picture of a man's hand wiping the tears away from the face opposite her.

'Well anyway, my dear'—Lucille had risen to her feet—'come along, no more proverbs or wise sayings for the time being, it's action stations. We must go along to Granan who, I warn you, will be fuming because it is now almost eleven o'clock and you haven't shown your face to her.'

It was like two happy sisters that they went downstairs and along to the annexe to face the dragon, with Lucille saying in a whisper, 'What do you bet we find Matthew already there?'

* * *

And yes, they did find Matthew there. He had already taken the worst of the onslaught. Nevertheless, they too ran into a battery of verbal bullets, until Lucille said, 'I'm retreating,' and in unusually high spirits left the room.

It was almost an hour later and after much cross-talk that Annie Wallingham said, 'You two should get out. Matthew should take you up to the Mount'—she was looking at Elizabeth—'but you'll have to wrap up well. You should go straight away. Why not take that fellow of yours with you? Where is he now? I would tell him.'

'Oh,' said Matthew, 'he's gone into town to collect his sister, and they're going to the flat to pack the rest of Liz's things . . . But he'll be back shortly; he never wastes any time.'

'Except with his tongue!'

On this, Elizabeth and Matthew went out laughing.

21

Elizabeth was standing in the hall waiting for Matthew to return from having a
word with his father when Rodney appeared, saying, 'Well, I never thought you'd
join the camp so soon, and so quietly. I
didn't hear a thing and no one roused me.'

'Would you expect them to?'

'Yes; yes, I would. I happen to be one
of the family, in spite of some people forgetting it. Oh'—his tone now changed—'I
wasn't meaning you. I wasn't. I'm sorry'—
he put out his hand and gripped her
wrist—'I'm a surly brute. Believe me, I'm
glad you're here. Yes; yes I am.' He was
staring at her. 'It . . . it makes a difference.
You wouldn't understand, but . . . but it
does. Yes, I'm glad you're here.' Slowly she
pulled her hand from his grip, which

caused him to say, almost in a plea, 'Oh, don't say I've upset you; that would be another black mark against me.'

'You . . . you haven't upset me.'

'I haven't?'

'No. No.' She made herself smile at him.

'Oh well, that's all right then.' He too was smiling now, and she noticed how a smile changed his face: he could have looked attractive if it wasn't that he scowled so much.

'I . . . I understand you're going up the Mount.'

'Yes, I'm to see the view from there.'

'Oh yes, it's a lovely view. But it's more fun when it snows, because we use the sledge then and come down the side road right from the top. It's very exhilarating. I'll take you down when it next snows.'

Lucille now came into the hall and he said, 'It's great fun sledging down from the Mount when it's snowing, isn't it, Mama?'

'Yes,' Lucille said, and turning to Elizabeth, she added, 'They got me on that sledge only once and I said never again. It scared me to death. You run down on to a flat plain for a little way; then there's another drop, all of six to eight feet, and some of the foolhardy ones will go over that too.'

'It used to be great fun, though.'

Elizabeth looked at Lucille, who was staring at her son. For a moment Rodney appeared like some schoolboy who was recalling an adventure, and she knew that his manner was surprising his mother. But with Matthew's appearance on the stairs Rodney walked away, and Lucille turned to Matthew as he stepped into the hall and said, 'I'd wait for Jim if I were you.'

'Don't worry, I'll be all right: I'll have my guardian angel with me.' He put out his hand, and Elizabeth took it.

Lucille opened the door for them. 'Which way are you going?'

'By the annexe and through Granan's back yard. It's a shorter route,' Matthew said.

They had reached the end of the terrace and were stepping on to the grass when Matthew, quickly turning his head to the side, said, 'That's the car; I can hear it coming into the yard. I'll run to the other end and whistle him from there. He won't hear me this far.'

'No; let me,' Elizabeth said.

'What? And do me out of the only straight run I get in the day? They don't know it indoors, but I often do it in the early morning. Watch . . . watch!' He patted her cheek, then stepped on to the flagged path and began to run, using his stick as if it were a third leg.

She smiled as she watched him: it was marvellous how well he was beginning to cope with his disability.

When he reached the end of the terrace, he disappeared from her sight, and she knew he had dropped down on to the driveway to the farm.

For a moment, she stood looking about her: she had not, as yet, been to this part of the garden. A few yards ahead of her was the low wall framing the annexe's small back yard; to her left was a rough path she imagined led to the kitchen garden. She had seen this, but from the other end: it was a very large space, bordered on three sides by a seven-foot-high stone wall. Behind was a copse, headed within a few yards of her by an enormous old oak tree.

Matthew had told her about this tree. Reportedly, it was about two hundred years old, and around the foot of its girth was a rustic seat, made, she understood, by Matthew's great-grandfather when he was a boy.

For a moment she thought she would go and sit on it: truthfully, she told herself, she was still feeling very tired, and really was not looking forward to any hill-climbing.

Although her fear had somewhat lessened, she was still filled with a dread that seemed to consume her body. As she wondered whether she would ever be rid of it, she experienced a freezing sensation: her whole being stiffened, and she felt she was about to scream; then the sound was choked in her throat as the arm came about her, pinning hers tightly to her sides, and the hand gripping her jaw was like an iron fist; and there he was, looking down into her face, and she knew the moment for which she had been waiting had come, that moment when he would actually kill her.

'Surprised, Liz? . . . You shouldn't be: you know that no one makes a fool of me and gets away with it. You bloody, stinking tart, you! But I'm here to give you a choice;

and you have only seconds to make it. You come quietly back with me this minute or else, when they find you, even your blind bastard won't be able to recognize you.'

She was past dread, she was past terror; there was nothing she could do—he meant every word he said.

'Well? Nod your head.'

She did not nod her head for, as quickly as fear had frozen her, there now entered into her a rage that told her: right, she was about to die, but she wouldn't make it easy for him. She couldn't move her arms and, her body being so pressed into him, she could not lift her knee into his groin. But her legs from the knees downwards were free, and what instinct for self-preservation guided her foot, the toe of her heavy walking shoe, to his fractured shin she never knew. But for a second the pain loosened the arm that was about her and brought his other hand from her mouth and to his own face as he gasped; and at this two fingers of her left hand flew to her mouth, and with what air she could gather from her shaking body she whistled. It was loud, but soon strangled by his doubled fist hitting her full in the face.

Her head swam, and for a moment she seemed to go almost blind, but when she opened her eyes her momentary courage was again frozen into an ice-block, for there, flashing before her face, was the long open blade of a razor.

She knew that razor. His father had always used a cut-throat. He kept two of them in cases on the windowsill in the scullery. A leather strap hung on a nail to the side; and next to it was a narrow mirror. As a child she had looked on fascinated as Mr McCabe stropped his razor: up and down, up and down, up and down! And that was what the blade was doing, flashing up and down before her eyes. 'I'll mark you as you marked me, and in the same places.'

Of what happened next she was really not aware, except that he seemed to fling her off and that she was flying through the air . . . but after hitting the wall of the annexe yard she knew nothing more . . .

There was a pandemonium now on the terrace: screaming, yelling and swearing filled the air.

Clinging to Mike McCabe's back by an arm around his throat, Jim was aiming to reach the waving razor when the gardener Jones added his weight and the three of them fell to the ground in a writhing heap. Annie Wallingham's voice was screaming, 'Get ropes! Get ropes!' and the old lady was stopped from joining the men on the terrace by the strong arms of Mary and Bella holding her on the step.

Further along the terrace Peter and Lucille were holding back Matthew, who was yelling, 'Let me go! Let me go! Where's Liz? Let me go, I tell you.'

The three were pushed aside by two men rushing towards the still-struggling mass, one carrying a coil of rope.

'It's all right! It's all right!' Lucille was gasping now, 'I can see her. She's sitting by the wall.' She did not say that the figure she could just make out was, in fact, lying against the wall in a huddled heap.

It was Peter who, in a very firm voice, was exhorting Matthew, 'Stop it, Matthew! Stop it! You can do no good along there.' Then, his voice rising, he cried, 'Rodney is with Liz now. He is lifting her up . . . he's carrying her.'

'What!' The high exclamation came from

Matthew. 'He's carrying her? Why is he carrying her?'

'Hold it! Hold it!' Peter was struggling with Matthew now. 'You can't go along there. I've told you. Anyway, he's carrying her into the annexe.'

'We can go through the house.' Lucille pulled her son around, and Matthew knocked her almost on to her back when he turned and in a shambling run made for the front door.

Peter and Lucille followed and steered him into the house, and there Peter said, 'Take him along there while I phone the police and a doctor.' He had not added 'and an ambulance', but the head hanging over Rodney's arm suggested one would be needed . . .

Mike McCabe's legs were by now roped at both ankles and thighs, his hands tied together at the wrists behind him, so trussed that he cursed and yelled at his captors as he wriggled his upper body as though he would rise from the ground.

Only three men were now holding him down, because Jim was lying on his side on the edge of the terrace, his two hands, which were covered with blood, gripping the upper part of his leg. His trouser leg was wet, with a dark stain reaching to well below his knee. As Peter reached him, exclaiming, 'Good God! What's happened here?' he fell on to his knees beside Jim, who in a voice very unlike his usual one said: 'He slashed me with the razor.'

Jim had known what had happened to him from the moment the razor edge pierced his thigh and ripped the skin downwards. Strangely, though, he felt no pain now, only a bit sick and sort of faint. But he wasn't going to faint, he had never done so in his life.

Into the dimness a voice was saying quietly, 'It's all right. It's all right, Jim, old man; the doctor is on his way. Don't try to move, just lie quiet. The girls are going to wrap you up.' Peter took a strip of sheeting from Cook and put a tourniquet as tight as he possibly could over the gushing wound.

But Jim knew nothing of this; he had now gone into deep blackness . . .

When Matthew and Lucille entered the annexe sitting room, Matthew cried, 'Where's Liz? What's the matter with her?' And it was Rodney, kneeling beside Elizabeth on the rug before the fire, who said,

'A lot, I should say; she's unconscious,' and he added, 'Have you phoned for a doctor, Mama?'

'Yes, dear.'

Matthew made towards the voice of his brother, and when his hand touched Rodney's shoulder, he said, 'Get up! and let me down there.'

'You can do nothing; she's unconscious.'

'All right!' and Matthew's voice had a threatening edge to it. 'But get up and let me see to her.'

'What can you do? You can do nothing. It was I who saw her and carried her in.'

It was a swift movement: Matthew had thrown his stick aside and his two hands, gripping the back of Rodney's collar, brought him to his feet as if he were a puppet. And when he threw him aside, he would surely have fallen on his back had not Bella's stout form and Lucille's arms saved him.

Kneeling on the rug, Matthew was saying softly, 'Liz. Liz.'

He felt that her pulse, though low, was steady, and as his hands covered Liz's face, Granan, now by his side, said quietly, 'You can do nothing, my dear, until the doctor comes. She doesn't seem to be bleeding from anywhere. Her face is swollen; probably where he struck her. But I'm sure she'll be all right.'

During this short conversation Lucille had guided Rodney across the room and out into the corridor, where he now stood leaning against the wall. His face was white with rage; it seemed he was trying to speak but finding it difficult. When he did, his words shocked Lucille: 'I'll do for him one day. I will! I will!'

'Oh, Rodney! Don't say a thing like that. You should have got up when he asked you.'

'Asked me! He never asks, he commands. He's belittled me all my life. He's a big-head, a vain, conceited big-head.'

'Oh no, my dear, you can't say that. He's never bragged about the medal or anything.'

'Bragged!' Rodney's voice was almost a yell. 'What was it but brag when he refused to take his medal unless the other five got it too? He went to the highest and put his case before them. They had to be recognized because he could never have done the job on his own.'

'He was right, my dear, because two of them died in paving the way for him into that outpost; he could never have done it on his own.'

'Oh, Mama, you would take his side if you saw him murder me tomorrow.'

'Rodney! Rodney! Don't say things like that. You must talk with your father, or I will, about your attitude.' Then she swung around, crying, 'There's an ambulance outside, and there's more commotion; it must be the police. Come along and help me: they'll want to talk and ask questions, and your father will come downstairs . . . What'll happen next, I wonder.' She hurried from him, but in the hall she was checked, for there, halfway down the stairs, was her husband.

He was walking sideways, gripping the banister with both hands and with his two sticks hanging from his forearms.

'Oh, Richard. Richard. What are you trying to do?' She rushed up the stairs and, putting an arm about him, she brought one of his hands from the banister and, taking his sticks, she helped him down into the hall, where, standing upright now, he demanded, 'What the hell's going on?'

'I'll tell you, or Rodney will . . . Come along now into the drawing room. And Rodney!' She was calling now to where Rodney was at the front door. 'Come back and see to your father, will you? Tell him what's happened. I must see to things, and the girls are on the terrace. I don't know why.'

It was with some reluctance that Rodney obeyed her and took his father's arm, while Richard Wallingham demanded, 'Where's Peter? Get him!'

As if obeying her husband, Lucille ran on to the terrace, there to be amazed at the sight of two ambulancemen carrying a stretcher on which Matthew's man was lying, and to hear the doctor saying to Peter, 'Go with him! His people must be informed that they're taking him to Fellburn—it's the nearest. Go on, man!' And he actually thrust Peter up into the ambulance. 'Phone back from there; I'll see to the colonel.'

He now pushed roughly past Lucille, saying, 'Excuse me, Mrs Wallingham, but I must use your phone straight away.'

'What's happened?' she asked. 'Is it serious?' She was running by his side now, back into the house, and he answered

abruptly, 'Everything, I should say; it's
touch and go. That maniac's razor has
done its work well.'

Unceremoniously he picked up the
phone and dialed a number, then said
brusquely, 'Get me Dr Manning immediately. This is Dr Bell here.' His foot was
tapping the parquet floor as he waited;
then, his voice changing, he said, 'That
you, Ivor? This is David here. How's the
theatre? Clear?'

'Yes, just; within the last ten minutes.'

'Well, I'm sending you a man. He should
be there within a few minutes. He's in a
bad way. The femoral artery has been
slashed; he's lost a lot of blood, though
probably not as much as he might have:
the colonel's man did a good job with a
tourniquet. I'm at The Beavors. There's all
hell let loose here, a maniac with a cut-
throat. You know the colonel's son, the
captain who is blind? Well, it's his chauffeur and man who's got it. Anyway, as you
can guess, he'll need the theatre right
away—no dollying up if he's going to survive. Will you do it? I'd rather you than Os-
borne.'

'Yes, yes, of course, man. But what's it all about?'

'I don't know; but I shall before I leave. I've got to see the young woman the razor was meant for. She's the captain's fiancée. I'll call in on my way back, and wait for you if you haven't finished the job. I wouldn't have been here at all, they are patients of Peel's, only the police inspector, on his way here, saw me getting into my car after presenting Bruce Tollet with another son.'

'See you later then, David. Some time since I had a femoral artery.'

When the doctor put down the phone, he turned and looked at Lucille, who was now standing near the foot of the stairs, and when she neither moved nor spoke, he said, 'She's in the annexe, I understand?' Still she did not speak, but just inclined her head.

After giving her a sharp look, he left her and hurried along the corridor.

It was then she heard her name being called sharply from the drawing room. She sank down on the stairs as her trembling legs gave way. Then her husband's voice came again, 'Was that Bell out there?'

She still made no reply, remaining on the stairs, and there Rosie found her and exclaimed, 'Oh, mistress! You feeling bad? Will I call Mary?'

Lucille had to swallow deeply before she said, 'No, no, Rosie, I'm all right, just a bit tired.'

'Will I get you a cup of tea, mistress?'

'Yes, but in a little while. I'm all right now.'

She pulled herself to her feet, then walked across the hall into the drawing room to be greeted with, 'I knew it was you out there with Bell. Why couldn't you answer me? What's going on, anyway? Is everybody going mad? I could get nothing out of Rodney, only what he thinks about his brother.'

At this moment Matthew walked through the door and said, 'You there, Mama?'

He did not wait for an answer but went on, 'Granan wants you. They've got Liz to bed, and the doctor's examining her now. Have you seen anything of Jim? I can't find him.'

It was Richard who put in, peremptorily, 'You want *your* man, well, where is mine,

I'd like to know? I've shouted myself hoarse. His place is in the house.'

Both men were startled by a yell as Lucille shouted, 'All you two can think about is your men and what they can do for you. Well, I'll tell you where they are. They are both in an ambulance. Your man, Matthew, will be going straight into theatre, and you'll be lucky if he ever drives you again. By the sound of it, it's his funeral you'll be driving to in that big damn Daimler, because he is bleeding to death, having taken the razor that was meant for your Elizabeth. And *your* man'—she had turned to her husband—'has spent his time away from you managing to stem some of the bleeding with a tourniquet. And now he has gone in the ambulance with Jim Taylor to take him to Fellburn, where Dr Bell's friend must operate on him straight away if he is to save his life. Then he is to inform Jim's parents about their son. So that is what your two manservants have been doing . . . Satisfied?'

On this she rushed from the room, tears raining down her face.

Matthew stood as if frozen. It wasn't until his father's voice, very low and sad, came to him, saying, 'I'm sorry, Matthew. I'm sorry,' that Matthew moved.

Groping his way towards a chair, Matthew dropped on to it. 'If anything happens to Jim,' he said, 'I'll kill that man. Whether he is guarded in jail or in an asylum, I'll find him and I'll kill him.'

'Don't talk like that.' Richard's voice was still low. 'But I know exactly how you must feel.'

'You don't! You don't!' The words were grim. 'I could say I almost love that fellow.'

'Don't forget there is Elizabeth.'

'Oh, Father. You know what I mean. Behind your military façade you feel the same way about Peter; else why did you bring him out with you? Men like Peter and Jim were called tight-corner blokes in the company. Others they called not-so-tight-corner blokes, and there were many such among those that gave them orders, and they knew it.'

There was a pause; then his father said softly, 'Even tight-corner blokes can snap,' and this remark seemed to startle Matthew for a moment; but then he turned his head in the direction of his father's voice. Did he imagine that his father knew that he had snapped when he thought he had gone blind? That he had tossed his rifle to one side and a hand grenade to the other, and had been about to run, and would have, had he not been stopped by Jerry and Fox? They were the only ones who knew, and they had given out that it was his hand grenade that had finished those Germans still defending the bridge. No . . . his father couldn't have known—but his tone indicated that he, too, had personal knowledge of the tight-corner ones snapping.

He sat back in his chair, and again there was silence between them until his father said, 'Do you think you could make your way to the kitchen, Matthew, and ask one of them to bring us a drink?'

David Bell had donned his coat again and was now in the annexe sitting room, a cup of tea in his hand.

Annie Wallingham was sitting opposite him. She seemed to have aged still further in the last few hours. 'Will she be all right?' she asked now.

'That remains to be seen. She has re-gained consciousness, but she's still in shock. And one thing is sure, during the next few days she'll be in a great deal of pain: her left side is badly bruised from the shoulder to the knee. Her left arm was completely out of its socket, but I've fixed that. She has a large lump on the side of her head, but no cut. Her main physical trouble is going to be her face. It is swollen now but it'll be more so tomorrow. As for her mouth . . . well, it's a wonder her jaw isn't broken; the blow she received wasn't just a slap, but from a doubled fist. Yet, in time, these will all heal. From what you've told me, she must have got a great shock, in seeing not only that maniac again but also the razor: it must have shown her very clearly what he meant to do. And so I would suggest that she be kept very quiet. Talk to her, but don't expect any answer until her mouth heals. Finally, I would suggest you have a day and a night nurse in, because she shouldn't be left alone.'

'Oh, no, no!' Annie Wallingham's voice had perked up. 'There's no need for nurses; I can't abide them. Anyway I, and the others, will see that she's never left. There's Mary and Bella, and there's always Rosie from the kitchen. And I have nothing else to do but sit down all day. Then, of course, there is my daughter-in-law.'

He smiled wryly and said, 'And who's going to look after your daughter-in-law's domain? And your grandson, now that he's lost his man?'

She did not answer for some seconds, then she said quietly, 'Poor fellow. And he was so good for Matthew; he seemed to alter his life. I don't know what will happen there. He has Elizabeth, of course, but he was very fond of Jim Taylor. He stood up for him right and left, treated him as an equal.'

At this, David Bell got to his feet, and in a tone that held a reprimand he said, 'I think the war made all the men that were in it equal.'

It was another matter of seconds before the old woman said, 'I deserved that, Doctor, but I'm really of the same mind as yourself. One says these things without thinking.'

He smiled at her now and patted her arm: 'No need to apologise to me. You'd be surprised what I know about you and your thinking. And what *I* think is, you're a fine old girl, with the spunk of a dozen.'

If Annie Wallingham could have blushed she would have; but what she said was, 'I understand you are going straight back to the hospital. If you should see Peter, tell him to phone us.'

'Yes, of course I will, but I expect he'll do that in any case.'

She let him go. Then she sat down again and, shaking her head slightly, she muttered to herself, 'Damned silly thing for me to bring up, class,' and lifting her eyes to the ceiling, she added, 'See to him, will you? He's a good fellow, and his kind are needed, especially in this house. And not only by Matthew . . . no.'

Peter returned at nine o'clock, and all he could tell them as he faced his master, the mistress, Annie Wallingham and Matthew in the sitting room was that the doctor said it had taken longer than had been expected, and that, as yet, he could not give any opinion of the outcome. The waiting room, he said, had seemed to be full of the Taylor family and the mother and sister were being allowed to stay the night.

22

Five days later, Elizabeth still lay in bed. Her mind was clearer now; it had moved up out of the mist, but not out of the terror, the new terror that had replaced the old but which, in fact, had been there all the time: the terror of Bridget McCabe.

After she had regained consciousness and entered into a realm of pain which consumed her body and told her that she would never again be able to move her lips or open her eyes wide, and that her face had been altered for ever, she had nevertheless formed a plan that was to be a guard against her fear. She would never speak again, or eat, and so she would be able to lie in this bed, and there would always be someone with her to guard her; and they would stick the needles in her to deaden the pain, and they would put the cup with the spout on it to her lips, as they did in hospital, and drop liquid down her throat.

So she did not move until the third day, when twice she was caused to jerk in the bed. The first time was when the old lady lifted her pain-pulsing nose and caused her to open the slit that had been her mouth and painfully swallow two or three spoonfuls of beaten-up egg and brandy; the second time was of more importance, for the terror attacked her mind and, somewhere in the depths of her she cried, 'No! No!' against the voices wafting very quietly across her as her pain-racked limbs were being sponged.

'He'll be dead by now,' said one. 'He was such a nice fellow, was Jim. I had a thing about him. What Mr Matthew will do without him, God knows.'

She did not hear the other voice saying, 'Well, where there's life there's hope.'

Then they were sponging the thing that had been her face, and it was Rosie's voice she recognized saying, 'Her being conscious, d'you think she can hear what anybody says?' and the answer, she knew, came from Bella, 'It's not very likely, else she would have moved by now, probably sat up. Dr Bell says it's like a slight coma; she'll speak when she's ready to.'

The voices were now coming from the far end of the room. 'I'll never forget the sight of those five fellows lugging that maniac down the terrace in a canvas sheet and throwing him into the Black Maria. That young policeman on duty said yesterday that they're not keeping him in Durham, he's for the asylum, and he'll never be able to stand up to the charge of attempted murder, he's too far gone.'

There was the sound of the door being opened, and Elizabeth knew, without anyone speaking, that Matthew had entered, and that Lucille was with him.

Matthew had taken her hand and was saying, 'Hello, darling. Do you feel better?'

She peered at him through her swollen lids, and for a moment she had a great desire to speak to him; but she knew she couldn't, no more than she could lift her arm and put it round his neck. Her desire not to speak had taken hold, and she seemed unable to use her voice.

Lucille was at the other side of her now,

and as her fingers were stroking her cheek, she said, 'Oh, they are going down. You look much better this morning, Liz. Another few days will see a great change, and you'll be back to your dear self.' Oh no she wouldn't; never again would she be her dear self, never! She knew that what Mike McCabe had started his mother would surely finish. Lucille was saying, 'I had a phone call from your brother this morning, to see how you were. He'll be coming again next week.'

Her lips opened slightly: Phil had been here and she hadn't known? Well, she hadn't known much in those first few days, had she? Only that she knew now what it was to suffer indescribable pain.

She heard the door open again and Mary's voice saying, 'You're wanted on the phone, Mr Matthew.'

Lucille said, 'Go along, dear; I'll stay with her.'

Matthew paused for some seconds before he lifted up the phone. He guessed that the caller would be from the hospital, but dreaded the message he would be given.

'Yes? This is Matthew Wallingham here.'

'Oh, Captain, it's me, Cissie.'

'Yes, Cissie?' There was a slight tremor in his voice.

'It's good news, Captain. It was around eleven last night, about two hours after you left, he took a turn for the better. The fever, or whatever it was, went down, and Sister said to me ma, "He'll be all right now—he's got a fighting chance, and a fine constitution." That should have stopped me ma from crying. Anyway, now we're going home, Captain, and, as the doctor said, we should go to bed and sleep for twenty-four hours. You know, me ma couldn't sleep on that leather chair. But the first thing she'll do is have a bath. Funny, isn't it, sir? She wouldn't have one here.'

Matthew was smiling as he listened to Cissie rattling on. He knew it was reaction to her feelings, for neither she nor her mother had left the hospital since Jim had gone in. He broke in on her, saying, 'Have you seen him this morning?'

'Just for a minute or so; that's all they would allow. He spoke my name, and even grinned at me. He did the same with Ma. And he was about to say something about you—he said your name, like—but the nurse stopped him and hustled us out. But we are so relieved, sir, I thought I'd let you know.'

'Thanks, Cissie. Thanks indeed. I'll be along later.'

'Yes, sir. I thought you might. Bye-bye.'

'Bye-bye, Cissie.'

Matthew put down the phone, then, groping for the chair that was set near the telephone table, he lowered himself on to it, and putting his elbow on the table, he rested his head on his hand as he muttered simply, 'Thank . . . God.'

Dr Bell was standing near the window. It was some distance from the foot of her bed, and so it was only snatches she could hear of the conversation between him and Lucille; but what she did hear was, 'There's nothing at all wrong with her body,' and part of Lucille's reply, 'Stiff as a ramrod, wasn't she?' Then the old lady's voice saying, 'It would seem she's determined not to walk,' and the doctor's voice again, 'Oh, I know that, because whatever's on her mind . . .' Then his voice faded away until she heard, 'It'll be hospital and physio-therapy treatment.'

Now the doctor's face was hanging above hers, and his voice was brisk as he said, 'You are feeling better today, aren't you, Miss Ducksworth? No pain in the side, and your face is almost back to normal except for a little discoloration, so tomorrow you are going to take a little walk, aren't you, into Mrs Wallingham Senior's sitting room? She and the captain have both said they will play the piano for you, because music is very soothing, you know. And don't worry, my dear'—he was now patting her hand—'no one is going to ask you to talk until you are ready to do so. I am going now, but I am sure you'll be happy to know that Mr Taylor is up out of bed. Like you, at first he had trouble with walking, but every day he is showing progress. Goodbye, my dear; I'll see you tomorrow, when I hope to hear good news of you.'

Her body felt rigid. Once they had her up they would make her walk. And then they would take her outside. And she mustn't go outside, ever. He got her outside, and so would his mother. Oh yes, yes. She shut her eyes and sought to rid herself of the face that was forever looming before her and would, she felt, be there all her life.

'Don't worry, my dear.' It was Lucille now talking to her, and Elizabeth opened her mouth as if she were about to speak; but the words expressing her fear were buried too deep in her and she couldn't drag them to the surface.

'She's worried,' the old lady said. 'Give her a dose of her medicine; it'll soothe her.'

The medicine did soothe her, and she slept; but she didn't know for how long, only that she was awakened by Phil's voice saying, 'Oh, you look much better, Liz.' She turned her head and his name seemed to fill her throat, but she couldn't utter it. 'There's a difference since the last time I saw you. But anyway, I thought I'd better come up and tell you how things are. Mum is much better. It's as if she's had a miracle cure these last few days. Such a lot has happened, Liz.' He turned from her to Mary, who was handing him a cup of tea. 'Oh, thanks. Thanks, that is welcome.'

'Mistress says there's a meal for you whenever you're ready for it.'

'Oh, thank her, will you? I just want to

have a little talk with Liz here and tell her my news and then I'll be along.'

After draining his cup, he placed it on a side table, then he returned to the bedside and again taking Elizabeth's hand he said, 'You'll never believe this, but James McCabe and young Sam put Aunt Brid and her brother on the boat for Ireland yesterday. She was taken into hospital shortly after that madman started on his holiday. She had collapsed in the kitchen. And what d'you think? She has cancer, a kind that comes quick and sharp, no warning. It's to do with the ovaries, and it's a death warrant.

'Anyway, when she returned home she seemed a changed woman, James said, not a bark out of her, and she phoned her brother in Ireland. Apparently she wanted to go back and die there. The brother came over straight away and he talked to James. And for the first time James got the truth. He had always been given to understand that her father was dead. The brother said he had been in the local asylum there for the past thirty years. The old mother is still alive, and well into her eighties, but she still helps to run this small farm they have. The brother is a bachelor, and there is a sister at home who has never married. He seemed such a quiet man, so different from Bridget . . . Anyway, it turns out that the insanity on the father's side went well back. It has certainly broken out again in Mike.

'Don't shiver so, my dear. It's all right. It's all right now. The other one's now where he'll never trouble anybody again. Young Sam said to me he couldn't help but feel sad: he never liked his mother, but from the time she came back from that hospital, she never raised her voice, in fact she seldom spoke. And another odd thing, in fact two: Sam said she never went into her sitting room, not once; nor did she make one remark about Mike; and they don't know whether or not she knew what happened to him. Anyway, my dear, it's made a difference in our house. I'm sure Mum took to her bed because she was scared Bridget would come again. But when I left this morning, there she was up on her feet, and Dad looking a different man, too.

'Oh! What is it, Liz?' He rose quickly from the chair and held her shoulders.

'Don't cry like that. I thought you would be glad. Oh dear me!' He looked about helplessly. But there was no one else in the room. There was a bell-pull by the side of the bed, and he tugged frantically on it.

Almost immediately the door opened, and there was Mary, and behind her the old lady and the sound of shuffling footsteps. 'I don't know why, but she burst out crying. I had given her some news that I thought might please her.'

The room seemed packed. When Matthew pushed through to the bed and took the weeping figure into his arms, the cracked voice that came to the others, crying, 'Matthew! Matthew!' brought sighs of relief, even tears to their eyes.

It was the old lady who, patting Phil on the back, said, 'Young man, one cries when one is happy, and to my mind those are very happy tears.'

Matthew and Jim were sitting by the window in the narrow side ward. Jim was in pyjamas and dressing gown; Matthew was wearing his army greatcoat. They had been talking for the last ten minutes or so.

Jim was saying, 'That's marvellous news—she'll be all right now?'

'Oh yes. She's still a little shaky on her feet, but it seems that's natural for she's been in bed for almost three weeks. And now that her mind is clear and fear of that demon woman is gone, as Dr Bell said, what happens now is a convalescence of a few weeks' rest. Mama and Granan will see to that. It's odd, you know, but she talks quite openly to Mama, and Granan has noticed this and taken it philosophically; she says to me, "She talks to your mother but listens to me." '

'Will you go back to work now, sir?'

'I don't know, Jim. I shall have another week off to think. And Elizabeth has to think too; it's been a very trying time for both of us. And it's not going to be easy taking up work again, both our kinds of work.'

There was a pause, then Jim asked, 'How's the temporary going?'

'Oh,' said Matthew, 'very well. He's acting as a chauffeur should do, keeping his eyes on the road and his mouth shut, no chit-chat, no contradicting my opinions of this, that and the other. I know where I'm

going, and I'm helped in and out in the
correct way, and always addressed as a
captain should be.'

This Matthew had said unsmiling, and he
was now waiting for the usual response,
and when it did not come, there flashed
into his mind words his grandmother had
often said: 'Half in fun and whole in earnest'. 'But now,' he immediately added in
a loud voice, 'I'm bored to extinction. And
how long have I to put up with it? That's
what I want to know.'

He put out his hand across the space
and when it was taken, he gripped Jim's
firmly, saying, 'I do miss you, Jim. Getting
into that car is like getting into a hearse.
When do you think you'll be out of this?'

'A week, ten days at the most, they say.
I was down at the gym yesterday, and the
stiffness is going. They tell me I shall have
to use a stick for some time, but it won't
prevent me from driving a car.'

'Oh, we'll see about that. What we want
is to get you back home and into your new
abode, where you won't have any running
up and down stairs when you hear my
whistle.'

'But I've made it nice up there,' protested Jim.

'Well, you're now in what was the coachman's cottage at the end of the yard. It has two rooms and its own kitchen. The women have seen to it, all of them, supervised by Peter.'

'Peter.' Jim's voice was low as he uttered the name. 'I had him in the other day. It was after Dr Bell called. I wouldn't be here, he said, if it hadn't been for Peter, because in the vital ten minutes or more it took for him to get there, Peter had quenched the bleeding somewhat . . . It's difficult to thank a man like that, particularly so when he refuses to believe he's done anything out of the ordinary.' He laughed now as he added, 'When my brother Lance comes out—he's due about this time—I'll have to see him after he next clears a gentleman's dressing table and comes across a nice gold ring or watch. I'll have it inscribed "To Peter".'

They were laughing together now, and when there sounded a bit of a commotion outside the door, Jim said, 'Oh my God! That'll be Ma again; she never stops crying.'

'You're lucky to have such a caring family, Jim.'

'Yes, I know that.' Jim was now on his feet and holding out Matthew's stick towards him, then he went on, 'I've always been glad of that. But I never thought I would come across so many caring friends as I have done in your family, sir.'

'You owe my family nothing, Jim. One day I'll tell you what you've done for them, but not now, this isn't the time. I'll get away now and let your mother have her cry out. See you tomorrow.'

'Yes sir, see you tomorrow.'

PART THREE

PART THREE

23

Three weeks later, Elizabeth was lying on the sofa in Granan's sitting room. She had a rug over her knees. It had been placed there a few minutes ago by the old lady herself. Elizabeth had said, 'You're trying to make me into a retired old lady companion to yourself,' and it showed the regard in which she was now held in the household, especially in the annexe, when Annie Wallingham had answered, 'Well, what d'you think I've taken all the trouble over you for? And by the way, should you want anything at all, ring that bell for Mary. It's never used enough, and it's practically gone rusty, like the one in the bedroom. There're going to be changes in this house.' And at that she had gone off to her afternoon rest, leaving Elizabeth to ponder.

Going to be changes? There already had been. She herself had brought them about, causing much havoc, all through loving Matthew. But they had all been so wonderful to her. It was as if she were surrounded by love, such a love as she had never experienced before. Not from her own mother, or even her father. From Phil she had. Oh yes, Phil. Phil in a way had brought her back to life with his message that she need fear no longer. She was filled with happiness except—she paused in her thinking—there was that one small fear, to which she dare not put a name. Perhaps it was in her imagination . . . Yes, it must be in her imagination.

The door opened softly and Rodney came in. He had made a habit of popping in about this time in the afternoon during the period his grandmother took her rest, and more so these last two weeks when Matthew had been back at work. Matthew wasn't happy about taking up his training again, but Elizabeth had urged him to do so, pointing out that she herself would soon be joining him if she went on improving. It was as the doctor had said: she must not forget that within a few weeks she had suffered two bodily attacks, and more dangerous still was the fear they had engendered. This, too, had needed time to heal.

Rodney stood by the side of the couch and looked down on her as he said, 'How're you feeling?'

'Oh, so much better I feel a fraud to be lying here'—she pointed to the rug—'as I said to your grandmother, tucked up like another old lady.'

'She wouldn't like that. She hates to be looked upon as old. Have you seen the snow?'

'Yes. It isn't lying though.'

'No, more's the pity.' He now pulled a small stool towards the fire and, within an arm's length of her, sat down on it, his elbows on his knees, his hands hanging slack. 'I love the snow. We don't get enough of it here—it does something for me, you know.'

She looked at his face. It was bright, as if with excitement, boyish excitement, as he qualified this by saying, 'I should live where it snows three parts of the year.'

'It must make the farmwork more difficult, I mean for the animals and the hands,
when it's snowing.'

'Yes; yes, I suppose so, but that doesn't
affect me. When I was a young lad and
during the holidays, in the winter that was,
I used to pray for snow, and when it came
I would spend my days on the side of the
Mount. The times in a day I dragged that
sledge up were countless, but the reward
was coming full-tilt down that hill.'

She said, quietly now, 'Your liking for
snow doesn't seem to fit in with your feelings for the farm.'

He stared at her for a moment before
saying, 'No, that's true, but we can all have
dreams, can't we?'

He was waiting for her answer, and she
said, 'Yes, yes, we can all have dreams.'

'Well, the farm wasn't my dream when
I was younger. It just sort of happened that
way. It seemed something of my own,
something that I could manage, something
that I was good at; and I am good at managing'—and now his voice changed and a
bitter note came into it—'if given the
chance.'

She put in quickly, 'Will . . . will you

take your holidays in skiing resorts and places like that, now the war's over?'

'No. No, I shan't.'

There was scorn in his tone now, so she said, 'But you seem very fond of sledging.'

'Yes, but not among a mass of tourists.'

'Have . . . have you never travelled?'

'Travelled? Yes, of course I have travelled, before the war, that is. To France, Spain and the usual holiday places a child is taken to—not given the choice, just taken to—if I can call that travelling. But it isn't my idea. No jaunts to America or Canada. Oh, and certainly not to Australia.' His mood suddenly changed and he laughed outright now, saying, 'What I want is a mountain of snow to myself, and perhaps on the lowland I could farm there . . . goats or llamas or something like that.'

She laughed with him as she said, 'You were born a couple of centuries too late, I think.'

He nodded. 'Perhaps. But you . . . would you like to travel?'

'At one time I used to think I would, but my dream was always of deserts, because I thought deserts were completely covered with sand. On and on and on. Just sand,

sand dunes, sand. But deserts are not like that, are they?'

'How d'you know if you haven't been?'

'Oh, I've read quite a bit. I've learnt about them through travel books. I love travel books. I'm what you would call a fireside traveller.'

There was a pause, and during it she had to look away from his face. Then, his voice very quiet, he said, 'As I read it, you would like to travel, get away, go to strange places, exciting new places, snow-covered places—but you're hemmed in, tied . . . tied.'

'I am nothing of the sort, Rodney, and you are quite mistaken. I don't want to travel to faraway places, especially snow-covered ones. That's what I like most'— she now pointed to the blazing fire—'and warmth, homeliness.'

'You don't, not at bottom.' His words came from deep in his throat. 'You feel you must repay people for being kind to you, so you think what they want you to think. You're hemmed in much more than I am and you'll never get away from here. I could walk out tomorrow because I know what I want, and'—he bent towards her, his voice a mere whisper—'it isn't the farm.' He sprang up and actually kicked the stool to one side. Then he was gone, and once again her body was trembling: it hadn't been her imagination.

For a brief instant she felt that Mike McCabe was back in her life, and at this she sat up and threw the rug from her; and putting her hand across her eyes, she let her head drop to her chest. That was until the door opened again and brought her head jerking upwards. Then she breathed evenly once more when she saw it was Peter.

'What is it? What is it, my dear?'

'Nothing. Nothing. I . . . I felt a little dizzy. I . . . well, I thought I would try my legs out and . . .'

'I've just met Rodney stalking down the passage. He's been in here, hasn't he? Of course he has, and he's upset you.'

'No! no, he hasn't.'

'Look, Elizabeth.' Peter now took hold of her hands. 'If he annoys you in any way you must come and tell me. Now, do you hear?'

'He didn't! He didn't!'

'He did. Don't tell me, I know Rodney.

I've even been sorry for him at times, because in his younger days he was outshone by two brilliant brothers, and jealousy is very deep in him. So please, Elizabeth, do as I say. If he upsets you, and it's only by his talking that he can do it, you must come to me; whatever you do, don't give Matthew an inkling of it. They've always been at loggerheads, and if Matthew thought he had said one word out of place to you I wouldn't like to . . . Well, I'll say no more. Anyway, now lie down again and rest. Come on, put your feet up.'

She put her feet up and lay back, and he put the rug over her. Then, bending down to her, he said, 'You know your trouble? You're too nice.'

'Oh! Peter. And you know your trouble? You make people cry.'

'Don't you dare'—he straightened up—'because I don't want to get it in the neck from Captain Matthew Wallingham who, if my watch is right'—he looked at his wrist—'will be here within the next fifteen minutes, together with his peg-leg champion.'

Elizabeth laughed gently, saying, 'How is Jim really?'

'As usual: tactless, sharp-tongued and limping. That's why in the kitchen they've named him Peg-leg, and his retorts to this are not fit to be leveled at animals, never mind cooks and maids and such.'

'He's really a wonderful fellow.'

'Oh, don't rub it in, else I'll become jealous.'

'Go on with you.'

He went out laughing and she lay thinking. They were all so nice, so loving and caring, except—she paused in her thinking—well, she supposed she could put Rodney's attitude down to caring; but oh, she didn't want that sort of caring. She was beginning to fear him. Yet what could he really do? Nothing, for she and Matthew were to be married in June. Things were already being set in motion. Perhaps after that he would suddenly leave and go and find his snowy mountain?

Why did these things happen to her? Peter had said it was because she was nice. She wasn't always nice—at times she had a sharp tongue—but she was always grateful for kindness. However, it was gratitude, Rodney had suggested, that was drawing her into the family web. That pattern was like the one her mother had woven so that her own life shouldn't be disturbed. But it didn't fit in with this pattern. She wasn't marrying Matthew out of gratitude or pity, but through pure love and the knowledge of a love that was returned twofold. So nothing must come between them. Should Rodney upset her in any way again she would do as Peter had bidden her, she would tell him, and hopefully he would settle the matter with Rodney once and for all . . .

It seemed only a short while later that Matthew came into the room, crying, 'Where's that lazy individual who will neither work nor want?'

'She's here,' replied Elizabeth, 'and she's not going to get up.'

He now flopped down beside her and after a long warm kiss he said, 'How's it been?'

'Same as every day, killed with kindness. And you? How are things in the big world?'

'Oh, not the same as usual. There was great fun in the ward this morning when Danny was brought back from the gym wearing his new leg. Of course he can't get used to it yet, but you should have heard that ward when our dear Sister Grace said, "How does it feel?" and was answered with, "Feel? The bugger hurts!" Even Tony's bed rocked, and, you know, he hardly ever moves.'

Elizabeth was laughing as she asked, 'And how did Sister take it?'

'She was not amused. Oh, you know, I thought she would have laughed her head off and then gone for him; but no, she lectured him on his language. After she had gone, the little demon said to me, "She was the only one who didn't laugh" and I knew he had said it on purpose in order to hide his own particular feelings about what to him is a tragedy, as there'll be no more real football for the poor little fellow.'

'It's been snowing. Will you be able to get up to the Mount? Won't it be slippery?'

'Oh no: it hasn't lain long enough, and I'll put my boots on. Anyway, Jim must have his daily two-pennorth of fresh air, as he calls it, and Flossie her training. She's coming on. She answers to my merest word now, and as long as she doesn't see a rabbit she keeps close, even when I haven't got her on the lead. I'm looking forward to the day when she can guide me up there on my own. Not that I don't want Jim's company, but you know what I mean.'

'Yes, darling, I know what you mean, and she's a lovely dog.'

'Yes, she is, and she has very good taste because she likes you, and she doesn't like everyone that she comes across, either male or female. She'd have been put down years ago if somebody had had his own way.'

She didn't question this, but pushed him, saying, 'Go on then, because it's time for Granan to appear and have an afternoon cup of tea. You know what happens if she gets hold of you: she'll want a running commentary on your day.'

'You want to be rid of me?'

'Yes. Yes, I do. I see far too much of you.' She kissed him hard on the mouth and he returned her embrace before he felt his way out of the room. Then she heard Lucille's voice, saying, 'Jim's waiting for you, dear,' and Matthew answering, 'Right! Mama. I'm on my way.'

Lucille came in and on a deep sigh she let herself down into the armchair at the opposite side of the fire. Then with a short laugh she said, 'I'm getting into the habit of quoting Mary's proverbs and sayings to fit every situation I find myself in, and to-day's has been "Come day, go day, God send Sunday".'

'Been tough?' asked Elizabeth softly.

'You could say, upstairs and down. Richard had a great deal of pain all night. You know sometimes he feels nothing at all, and then his left leg will play havoc and we all know about it. Poor Peter. Yet he takes it in his stride, as he always has done. Well, that's upstairs. Now downstairs. Oh dear. Cook clipped Rosie across the ears and Rosie had a crying spell. This is all because, I understand, Cook says she won't learn. But the poor girl, after scouring pots and pans and running at Cook's bidding and helping Bella, hasn't much time to practice trimming pie-crusts while balancing the pie on one hand, so bang went the pie on to the floor. Fortunately it was only a small one, what Cook calls an individual. So I felt the one who needed the slap round the ear was Cook, but one daren't say that to one's cook.' Then as Elizabeth laughed she added, 'But they're all so good really. I don't know how they get through half the work they do. You know, before the war there were eight staff inside, but now there's the same amount of work, if not more, with the running up and down stairs. Yet they're all so cheerful. Anyway, by now I suppose Cook has made an enormous fly cake for their tea because it's known that Rosie could eat her way through any fly cake.'

'Oh, what's a fly cake?'

'Well, you've had pieces for tea, my dear, a number of times. It's simply two pieces of pastry with some dried fruit inside. The boys used to call them fly cemeteries.'

'Oh yes, yes'—Elizabeth was nodding—'they are lovely.'

Lucille now got up and went across to Elizabeth and sat down on the edge of the couch, and in a low voice she said, 'It's wonderful to see you up and about; but remember what I told you about being dominated and taken over. From now on, you should make a gentle stand. Look at yesterday and the fuss she raised because I wanted you to come down and have dinner with us—she herself wasn't up to what

she calls a sit-down dinner, which, when
my husband manages to get downstairs,
can be a bit prolonged. Remember, she insisted that you take your meal with her.
And it's difficult, I know, not to please her.
It took Matthew to get you out of her
clutches for an hour or so. As he pointed
out to me, the only time he has with you
now is when he gets back before she's finished her nap, or at weekends. Oh, she
doesn't mind him being with you, but it's
as long as you're both with her.'

Quietly now Elizabeth said, 'It's wonderful to feel wanted.'

'Yes, I know, my dear'—Lucille bent forward and took her hand—'but there are
others would like to share your company
too: I, for one, when I'm not flying hither
and thither; and there's also, you wouldn't
believe it, Richard . . .' She paused on her
husband's name. 'Well, the other day he
said, "I understand that Elizabeth can play
chess. I . . . I wonder, when she's well
enough, if she'll give me a game, because
that man there," and you know'—Lucille
gave a little chuckle here 'he was pointing
at Peter, "that man there knows as much
about chess as he does about flying an

aeroplane." And you know what Peter replied? "Well, sir, in that case I should be able to beat you hollow because I've had experience of flying," and at this my husband was gallant enough to say, "Oh yes; my memory must be going. It's age and other things, but don't start bragging about that experience." "No, sir," replied Peter meekly. It was very funny: I had to get out of the room before I laughed aloud, as there are occasions when some men don't like being laughed at.'

Elizabeth stared at this woman. She was a lovely creature. That was the only way she could put it. A lovely creature. And she was Matthew's mother and, as she had thought before, she had a feeling for her that she had never had for her own mother.

'And there's another thing,' Lucille was talking again, 'that inclined me to say, "Come day, go day, God send Sunday." My daughter Hazel phoned up and asked if we would have the children for a few days at the beginning of the Easter holidays, because they themselves have been invited to go on someone's boat, or something like that. Now I'm going to confess to you, my dear, that I'm not so very fond of my granddaughters Cathy and Lily. Cathy is eight and Lily nine and they have both been spoilt and are very precocious. Granan can't stand them. Once—it was two years ago—she spanked Lily's bottom until the child howled. Oh, there was a to-do; their holiday was cut short and, as my husband remarked, it wasn't often that anything happened in this house that pleased everyone. To make that story complete I must tell you why Granan used such force. The child informed Granan that she was an old cod-face and that her father had called her an old wizened big-mouthed hag. I can tell you there has been no exchange of words between that particular son-in-law and Granan since.'

Lucille was bending forward towards Elizabeth, and their heads were almost touching. They were both shaking with laughter. They could have been two sisters enjoying a family joke. Elizabeth took out a handkerchief and dried her wet lids, and Lucille, now standing up, still laughing, muttered, 'You can understand he does not visit the annexe . . . Aah!' She held up her hand. 'There's a rustle next door, I'm away. But you will be down to dinner tonight, won't you? There'll be only me, Matthew and Rodney.'

On the last name Lucille paused and said, 'I understand he called in this afternoon.'

'Yes; yes he did.'

Lucille seemed to wait for Elizabeth to say something more and when nothing was forthcoming she said, 'I hope he doesn't upset you at all.' And on that she went out.

I hope he doesn't upset you at all. Had Peter been talking to her? Again she recalled the memory of a man wiping away a woman's tears with his forefinger.

It came as a great surprise. It was mid-April and the sun had been shining all day, but during the night there had been a heavy fall of snow. The household woke up to a white world, and they couldn't believe it; the snow must be a foot deep all round the house, and looking up towards the Mount, it appeared as if they were in the Alps. The sky still seemed laden, so when another fall came about eleven Rodney was beside himself with excitement, as were the children, who had arrived with their mother three days ago.

It was Elizabeth's first meeting with a female relative of Matthew's, one who was soon to become her sister-in-law, and from the beginning it was evident that Hazel wasn't as enamoured as everyone else in the house seemed to be by this nurse person. The only good thing about her that Hazel could see was, as her own husband had pointed out, she would act as a godsend in that she was taking Matthew off his parents' hands. He must have become a burden to them, and his condition would undoubtedly keep him so for the rest of their lives. So, while Hazel didn't take to the rescuer, because of her husband's explanation of the situation she could see now why her mother was so pleased with the girl, because it wasn't everyone who would take on a blind man. And, of course, being a nurse, it would be two for the price of one, so to speak.

She had left her children with instructions to behave, yet as soon as the car door had closed on her the girls began their usual rampage through the house. That was, until their blind uncle shouted at them.

They didn't like their Uncle Matthew, but they liked Uncle Rodney. He would play snowballs with them, and today he was going to give them a ride on his sledge.

It was Saturday. Elizabeth had been back at work for a week, and she had

found life strenuous and very tiring because everyone wanted either to congratu-
late her on her engagement to the captain
or to probe about what had happened
when, as one brash nurse said, her ex-
lover had tried to cut her throat.

She was out for a walk with Matthew,
to get them away from those squealing
brats, as he said. Yet they were at the foot
of the Mount slope when one of them
came hurtling down on the sledge, sitting
between Rodney's legs, only to be tumbled
off as the sledge slewed round and slowed
up on the plateau.

Peter came slithering down the side
path towards them, saying, 'Were you
coming up? Your mother asked me to keep
an eye on them because you never know
what they'll be up to. Slide over the quarry
top, I wouldn't be surprised. But it is lovely
up there.' He looked at Elizabeth. 'You can
see for miles. You would really think you
were on the snow slopes abroad.'

The sledge had come to its hurtling end
about six yards away from them, and now
Rodney came towards them dragging it
behind him. 'Come to share the fun?'

When no one answered for a moment

he said, 'Come on. Come on.' Then, speaking to Matthew, he said, 'Bring her up, she's never seen anything like the view from the top. It's fine, isn't it, Peter?'

'Yes, I've just been saying so.'

'Well, come on then and see for yourself.' Rodney was looking at Elizabeth now. 'Oh, come on'—it was almost a plea—'the snow'll be gone tomorrow.'

And, thought Matthew, you'll be a different man. He had never understood his brother, and of course his brother had never understood him . . .

Cathy, now helping to tug the sledge upwards, was yelling her glee to her sister above them, and as Peter took hold of Elizabeth's other arm he said quietly across her to Matthew, 'Don't worry, Matthew; there's only another two days of them. That's something to look forward to. They'll be gone by Monday night or Tuesday.'

'Well, thank God we're at work on Monday. What d'you say, darling?'

And to this Elizabeth answered, 'I say with you, they're two very unlikable little brats.'

'Well put,' said Peter; 'I couldn't agree with you more.'

At the top of the Mount, Elizabeth drew in a long slow breath of air and looked about her, then said, 'It is lovely.'

'Anyone else for the high flyer? Not you!' Rodney pushed Lily. 'You've had more than your share. And stop that noise! Do you want to go down, Matthew?' The invitation sounded kindly, and Matthew answered it with, 'I wouldn't mind, but I'd like Elizabeth in front.'

'No. No.' It was Peter speaking. 'I wouldn't chance it, Matthew.'

'Do you think not, Peter?'

'I really do think not.'

'Well, what about me taking her down?' Rodney put in.

'No one's asked me if I *want* to go down,' said Elizabeth.

'That's right,' said Peter, 'nobody has. But would you like to? All right, Matthew?'

'Yes, all right with me if Elizabeth wants to chance it.'

She didn't want to chance it, but the brothers were speaking amiably to each other, not snapping, and her decision might keep the peace. So she said, 'I don't mind trying, but I've never been on a sledge of any kind.'

As she sat down on the sledge and felt Rodney's legs slide down her hips she heard Matthew say, 'Use the brakes, mind, keep the pace slow.'

'Who are you telling how to drive this sledge?'

Whatever retort Matthew might have made was lost in the rush of air, and they were away. Rodney had one arm tightly around her waist. His other hand was on a lever attached to the frame of the sledge. It was a wonderful feeling, a sort of flying through the air but down towards earth like a bird in gentle flight. That was until he moved the lever, and at this the flight became a rush; it was as though the sledge had left the slope. As they passed the spot where only minutes before it had stopped she heard herself scream, and now they were streaming over a sort of plain before they dropped, and with a rush of air into her body she knew that she had left the sledge and was rolling into a soft cushion of snow, held tightly in Rodney's arms.

She was experiencing fear as vividly as she had done when she had faced Mike McCabe with the razor in his hand, for now Rodney was covering her, kissing her passionately. She tried to tear her body from his, but it seemed glued to her with the snow. 'You can't go through with it,' he was saying. 'You mustn't! You're mine. I felt it from the moment I saw you. We'll go away. Damn the farm! I've got enough money to start again. I know you're just taking him out of pity. He's blind, he'll never be able to see you. You'll weary of him, I know you will. It's because they've all got at you; I know how you feel. You could love me; you do a bit. I'll make you. Yes, I'll make you. We'll get away. You've just got to walk out.'

Their heads were free and now, her body making a great heave, she brought a knee up through the soft snow and with that strange strength that had come to her on another occasion she slammed it into his groin. And now she was free and she could hear the commotion about them. She heard Peter's voice and Matthew's yell, and then she was being dragged upwards and all she could cry was, 'Matthew. Oh, Matthew.'

'It's all right, darling, it's all right. Take her, Peter. And you! . . . you! Where is he? Where is he?'

'I'm here, big fella, I'm here, and it's done now. It's done.'

Matthew put out his hands and grabbed at the air in front of him. Then, staggering through the drift-filled ditch, he found Rodney's shoulder, only for Rodney's fist to come out and knock his arm to one side as he yelled, 'It was nothing. She enjoyed it.'

Just as he had dealt with the sergeant, so now Matthew aimed for Rodney's face but caught him only on the side of the head.

Peter had left Elizabeth and was now pulling him away from Rodney, and when Rodney's doubled fist was raised he yelled at him, 'Leave over, you! You've done enough. Don't think we're all blind; you knew where the brake was. But you didn't use it, did you? . . . Don't come back at me, lad, else you'll get more than you bargained for.'

'Who d'you think you're talking to? What are you, after all? You're only a servant who's been given license in my home. I don't know what you're talking about; what happened was an accident. And anyway, I've come over that leap a hundred times and landed, as we did just now, in a snow-drift.'

'Yes, you have, but this time you had a purpose. As I said, we're not all blind.'

'How dare you!'

'Oh, shut up! You always were a sly, un-derhand bugger.'

Elizabeth, her shivering body now pressed tight against Matthew's, had never before heard Peter speak in such a man-ner. There was no gentle calmness about the man now; he sounded like any rough soldier might. Well, that was what he had once been, wasn't it? And thank God for it. He knew . . . he knew what Rodney was up to. Oh dear God, when was it all going to cease? Her voice a whimper now, she said, 'Take me in, darling. Please, take me in.'

It was as if she had spoken to Peter, because now he was at her side, loosening Matthew's taut arm from about her and saying, 'Come on. Come on. Let's get out of this.'

He now led them both through the knee-high snow and on to the path where the two girls were standing, for once silent. He said to them in a voice similar to that he had used to Rodney, 'Get inside the house and up to your room, and stay there until your grandmother comes to you. Get!'

They got, and at a run.

At the house they were met by Lucille who checked them, saying, 'Stop running! children. Stop running!'

'Oh, Grandma, they were fighting. Fighting. Uncle Rodney and Uncle Matthew. They were punching each other. And . . . and Peter was nasty to us and said we must go to our room until you saw us.'

Lucille stared at them for a moment, then said, 'Well, go on up this minute and do as he says. But first of all take those wet boots off.'

And now she went to the door and stood waiting, her own body shivering. Fighting. Well, she wasn't really surprised. It had to come into the open some time. And that poor girl. She seemed to cause havoc—but it wasn't her fault. Men. Oh! men.

She saw the three of them coming along the terrace, Elizabeth between them. But at the doorway they stopped and it was Peter who said, 'Take her to Granan's, please. We'll go round the back and get rid of our boots.'

She said nothing but took Elizabeth's arm and brought her quickly into the hall, shutting the door after her without saying a word to either of the men. Then, having pulled off Elizabeth's snow-sodden woollen hat and gloves and her overcoat, she said, 'It doesn't matter about your boots, we'll take them off when we get in.'

And now she led her quickly along the corridor and into the annexe and the sitting room where Mary was laying a table for tea. On the sight of Elizabeth she exclaimed, 'Oh! miss. What is it? You look like death. What's happened? Has she had a fall, mistress?'

'Let's get her boots off, Mary.'

Lucille pressed Elizabeth down on to the sofa and she and Mary proceeded to unzip the long calf-length suede boots and to chafe her feet. Then she said, 'Get a hot-water bottle, Mary, and make a strong cup of tea.'

'Yes, mistress; right away.'

Lucille sat on the couch next to Elizabeth and as she now chafed her hands she asked, 'What happened? The girls . . . they said they were fighting.'

'Oh! Lucille, I . . . I seem fated to bring trouble to this house.'

'You do nothing of the sort, my dear. There was trouble in this house long before you came, and some of it was through Rodney, and I am not blind, neither is Peter. Oh no; Peter has never been blind. I shouldn't use that word, but you know what I mean. It's Rodney, isn't it? But you don't need to tell me, I know. And another thing: I've never seen Peter look so angry . . . but he'll tell me what happened.'

'I . . . I can tell you, Lucille.' Elizabeth's voice was breaking. 'He purposely made the sledge go very fast so that it took us over the edge and into another drop.'

'Oh no!' Lucille put her hand across her mouth. 'He could have killed you.'

'No, no, that wasn't his intention. We fell into a deep snowdrift and . . . oh!'—she shook her head—'it doesn't matter.'

'It does matter, dear. Did he do anything . . . I mean, anything to you?'

'Oh no. No. It . . . it was just what . . . what he said.'

'In . . . in the snowdrift?'

'Yes . . . yes, in the snowdrift. I . . . I can't tell you. And please . . . please don't mention it to Matthew, I mean, repeat what I've just said . . . that Rodney talked.'

'No, I'll say nothing to Matthew. But you say he talked, and he probably told you that he loved you and that you shouldn't marry a blind man.'

Elizabeth's eyes opened wide; then she looked away, but was saved from replying by the door being opened and Peter leading Matthew in.

'Is she all right?'

'Yes, dear, don't worry. Come and sit down beside her.' Lucille had risen to her feet. 'She's a bit shaken and cold, but that'll pass. It isn't every day she finds herself in a snowdrift.'

'Mama!' Matthew was almost yelling now. 'She didn't *find* herself in a snowdrift, she was taken there! Plunged there by that maniac. If anything had happened to her, I tell you, I would have killed him. I could have, as it was; he was damned lucky I was unable to see him. Something must be done, Mama. We can't live in the same house. Something . . .'

'All right, my dear. I know something

must be done, but at the moment try to remain quiet. Something will be worked out, I promise you. But here is Mary with a cup of tea and a bottle. They're both comforters. There, my dear, drink this tea and I'll put the bottle on your lap until you finish.'

'Thank you. And please don't worry. I'm all right, it was just the cold.'

'And the shock. As if you hadn't had enough!'

Matthew's voice was loud again, and his mother, bending towards him, said, 'Keep your voice down, will you, or you'll wake Granan, and she only wants to hear about this and we'll have another explosion. Come along, Peter; the master'll be yelling his head off for you.'

Peter hadn't as yet spoken, and at Lucille's bidding he left the room without making any remark at all. Nor did he speak until they reached the other sitting room, and then it was in answer to Lucille's query of 'What really happened?'

'I'm sure he was trying his hand with her. Oh no,' he put in quickly, 'not rape. I shouldn't think so, but when I reached them their heads were above the drift and

I had to pull her out of his arms. She looked frightful, and it wasn't a look caused by ordinary fear after a fall. She could only gasp out Matthew's name. I pulled her out and took her to Matthew who was struggling along the drift. Then I went back to your youngest son and told him what I thought about him in no polite language. And he was about to go for me when Matthew lumbered on to the scene and tried to get at him. For a minute there was hell to pay between them before I could get Matthew away and back to Elizabeth who, I am sure, was on the verge of collapse.

'You know, you can't go on like this, one of them will have to leave.'

'I can't bear the thought of Matthew leaving; and yet now he has Elizabeth he's bound to, sooner or later. And the master will have to be told about all this business. I don't know how I am going to do it. I wouldn't want him to blame Elizabeth.'

'Leave that to me, my dear. The subject can be brought up and spoken about without touching a great deal on Elizabeth.'

Lucille put out her hand, and he took it and raised it to his lips. Then they stared at each other for a moment longer before, turning from her, he went out.

The result of Peter's diplomacy was that, later that evening, Rodney was summoned to his father's room. But it was he who got the first word in, saying, 'If you want a private conversation with me, Father, let it be private,' and he looked from his father to where Peter was busying himself at a side table on which stood an arrangement of bottles and jars.

'If I wish Peter to stay, he'll stay.'

'It's all right, sir,' Peter said, dusting his hands one against the other. 'I'll be downstairs until you are ready for me.' And at this he left them, passing Rodney without a glance.

Now Rodney continued, 'I don't know what you've heard, Father, but it was all a bit of fun.'

'From what I gather, from both Peter and my other son, the end of your exploit was certainly no bit of fun. You are quite used to throwing yourself clear of the sledge, you've had plenty of practice; but Elizabeth was your passenger, besides which she has gone through a very traumatic time of late, and the shock she got won't have helped her. Moreover, you seem to forget that she is a young lady who is soon to be your sister-in-law.'

'Young lady be damned! She's a nurse; and have you asked yourself why she is marrying a blind man? As I see it—with, I'm sure, many outsiders—it's through co-ercion.'

'How dare you talk in such a fashion! Coercion from whom? And let me tell you, I have the highest regard for her intentions. She loves my son and he loves her. He may be blind, but he is still an attractive man.'

'Yes . . . an attractive man who needs attention practically every minute of the day in one way or another; he makes the best of his infirmity and has caused nothing but trouble in this house since he came back into it. You'd think he was the only one who was wounded in the war and that everybody owed him something. Well, I owe him nothing.'

'No, you owe him nothing!' His father was shouting now. 'Only the fact that but for him and the likes of him you would probably now be a pig-swiller under Hitler.

Now you listen to me. There must be changes made here because he refuses to live in the same house as you, and his going will upset your mother more than a little. So I propose that you change your room and make an apartment of that room in the west end.'

'My God, no! That room . . . the isolation block? D'you remember what it was used for?'

'Yes, I remember well. It was used when you all had measles and such, and Nanny slept there. And as I recall, it's a large room with a pleasant view, and it has its own staircase to the back.'

'I won't do it. I'll be a laughing stock among the staff.'

'Not if you make this appear as your own decision. Well, it's either that or you convert your well-equipped office—and you have had it well equipped, and well furnished, if I remember from my visit two years ago—into a room where you can sleep. You were grumbling then about the work you had to do, paperwork and other things, and that you couldn't take time off because there was no one you trusted to take charge. If you remember, I suggested you acquire a manager, and turned the store room next door into a nice little flat. So there you have your choice. And now please leave me, for the reports I have heard about the supposed accident you have verified out of your own mouth.'

'It's not fair. I don't deserve this treatment. I . . . I have worked for you for years.'

Richard Wallingham's voice was a bark now. 'You have not worked for me for years, you have worked for yourself; and if you don't want to hear some further truths concerning that, get out of my sight this minute!'

When Rodney flung out of the room he almost collided with his mother, and all he said to her was, 'You're like the rest of them,' and at that he took the stairs in a series of leaps and dashed out of the front door, not bothering to bang it, as he might have done, behind him. This was accomplished by Bella, with a muttered 'Dear, dear! What a day! What a day.'

Upstairs Lucille was now standing by her husband's side. Her hand on his shoulder, she was saying, 'Don't agitate yourself, Richard, please.'

'Agitate myself? Oh, how I long to be on my feet, just as Matthew must long for his sight. There's no understanding in that one just gone. How is it he's so different from the rest?' Yet deep within himself, Richard knew he could answer that question, and that there might soon come the day when he would.

'Jealousy is eating him up,' he said. 'But then he's always been jealous of Matthew; even though Matthew is now a blind man the feeling still remains. Do you know what I did the other day, Lucille, after I had watched Matthew find his way from this room?'

'No, dear, what?'

'Well, I made it my business when I was supposed to be asleep to sit and keep my eyes closed for an hour, just to get the feeling of what it must be like to be blind. And, do you know, I could only manage it for half the time, for the blackness, interspersed with what seemed to me streaks and clouds of white light, became utterly unbearable. I groped for a book. I groped for my pipe, because I thought I knew exactly where I'd laid them, and for my reading glasses which are always to hand on the little table there. I leant towards it but for a time there seemed nothing there, and when I actually did put my hand on my glasses I dropped them to the floor. I tell you, Lucille, Matthew must have gone through hell before he was able to accept his condition.'

'Well,' she said softly, 'I think he did. He's admitted to me since that he thought he was going mad, and didn't mind because it took him into another world. That was until the kind nurse comforted him one particular night, and you know the rest. He said that Elizabeth saved his reason, and I'm sure she did. Poor girl, she has had to suffer for it. But now they're both so happy together and we're all looking forward to the wedding.'

'All except our youngest son, Lucille, and you've got to face up to that. All except him.'

It was a long moment before she said, 'Yes, dear, all except him.'

25

Another week had passed, and the atmosphere in the house had changed yet again. Mr Rodney had ordered that they clean out the west-wing room and move his things along there; then that his meals should be served there. As Cook had said to the rest of the staff, this had all happened since that sledge business and those two rips were here.

The little she could get out of Mary sounded as if there was a suggestion that Mr Matthew and Miss Elizabeth might possibly set up for themselves in Newcastle near their work, and that the mistress was upset and Madam was raging against Mr Rodney. And as Cook explained to Jim, who after all she considered was quite new to the family, Mr Rodney had always been a trial ever since he was a lad. There was no pleasing him, and even then you got little thanks for it. Not like Mr Matthew and Mr William. The girls, the mistress's two daughters, were in a way very like Master Rodney. And she had ended with, 'You're walkin' better, Jim,' and his reply was as expected: 'And aye, you're gossiping better than usual, Cook, but go on. Go on. You'll improve with time.' On such a quip he had been pushed out of the kitchen.

For Elizabeth, it had been an uneasy week. She'd had her work cut out to stop Matthew from following a plan he had actually voiced to his mother, that he should go into a hotel until Jim could find a suitable flat for them, where he could see to them. But knowing how much his leaving would hurt Lucille, she had said to him, 'Leave it, darling, for the time being. As arrangements are now you won't come across him; nor shall I,' and as she added the last words she had thought, And thank God that I won't.

During the week she'd had a long conversation on the phone with Phil and a few words with her parents. Her father had sounded much brighter, different. He hadn't asked her about coming home for a visit, but her mother had, even if it were only for a weekend; and to this she had replied, 'It's practically a day's journey each way, Mum, and I'm up to my eyes in arrangements for the wedding.' Her mother had made no mention of her forthcoming marriage, although Elizabeth had written a letter to them, telling them of it and hoping that they would attend, adding that they'd be made very welcome by Matthew's family.

It was Phil who said, 'I'm looking forward to your wedding, Liz. Just one thing I've got to know,' and he had laughed: 'will it be grey morning suit and high hat?'

'Oh no.' She had laughed back at him. 'We have both agreed, and his mother too, that it's going to be very quiet. Neither of us want any fuss.'

'That's wise,' he had said, 'and I feel sure, having met him, you will be very happy. He seems a grand fellow.'

'He is, Phil,' she had replied. 'He is.' And she had added finally, 'I'm so glad that you've spoken of it, because neither Mum nor Dad has referred to it.'

'Take no notice of that,' he had said. 'I know Dad is happy about you.'

But when she had put the phone down she was sure that her mother wasn't, and that, being made as she was, she would never really forgive her for the uproar she had caused in the family, even though, had it gone through, she would have been married to a madman, with a mother not far behind him . . .

Although by now she was over the shock of the sledge affair, as she thought of it, the fall into the snow and her wet condition had brought on a cold which she had doctored during the week in order to remain at work; but now it was Saturday again and so she could rest. Both Lucille and Granan agreed with her when she gently refused the invitation to accompany Matthew, Jim and Flossie up to the Mount.

When Granan said to Matthew, 'You take care up the top today, there are mists floating about,' he had replied: 'It's just to keep up Flossie's training, and Jim wants more tough exercise for that leg of his.'

'Well, in that case,' said Granan, 'I'll go up above and you can wave to me in between patches.'

'Well, it's one thing to know when you're not wanted,' said Matthew, bending over to kiss Elizabeth.

It would be only a short while before Lucille was to recall his words.

They were at the top of the Mount now and Matthew said, 'Is it clear?'

'In patches.'

'Let's go to where Granan can see us, and we'll start waving.'

Presently Jim stopped Matthew, saying, 'Here we are.'

At this Matthew raised his stick and waved it in the air and said to Jim, 'Are you doing your stuff?'

'Yes, yes, I'm doing my stuff. Not that she's interested in *my* wave.'

'Oh, I wouldn't say that; she's fond of you at bottom.'

'Huh! at bottom, yes.'

At this point Jim half turned and looked across the great expanse of land on which the sun was shining, and he exclaimed loudly, 'Good Lord! There's a hare. She's sitting on her hind legs, washing her face like . . . like a cat. Oh my God, Flossie's off! Call her! Call her, sir!'

'Stay!' yelled Matthew. 'Stay!'

'Oh, it's no use: she must've got the scent.'

'Well, go and get her, for God's sake! because you don't know where the hare will lead her. Of all things, a hare.'

'Are you all right?'

'Yes, yes, I'm all right. Go on!'

At a shambling run now, Jim made after the fleeing dog, but she was soon lost to his sight by a wave of mist that obliterated the sun. The sun, though, was still shining on Matthew; he could feel the warmth of it. He was also aware that there was someone walking towards him, and thinking it was Jim returning he called, 'Couldn't you find her?'

When there was neither answer nor further sound, he swung around and waved his stick from side to side, saying, 'Who's there? Who are you?' Then in a louder voice, he called, 'Jim! Jim!' and again, 'Who's there?'

Of a sudden he felt the bottom of his stick lifted upwards and his hand, holding the handle, thrust into his chest.

He gripped the handle more firmly now and pushed the end against whoever was holding it, but in a flash of terror he knew it was his brother, and he cried, 'For God's sake! Rodney, have sense.'

He now felt the stick being pulled round, and himself with it; then he was being pushed backwards. He let out a high scream of 'Jim! Jim!' and the next moment he was flying, his arms and legs outstretched like a bird, into nothingness.

When Jim came limping hastily out of the mist, he first heard Flossie growling, then saw her at Rodney's leg, as he tried to shake her off by thumping her.

'Where is he? Where's the captain?' he yelled.

'He . . . he fell over. I couldn't stop him.'

'Fell over? I heard him screaming. You bastard, you, I'll do for you. I will!'

'It . . . it was . . . I didn't. I did nothing. It was her, the dog. Get her off me. She rushed at him and . . . and he fell.'

Jim dragged the dog from him, but the animal continued to growl ferociously.

'She would never have rushed at him. You dirty rotten . . . ! Oh my God! My God!' Jim went as near as possible to the edge of the quarry, but although he could see the bottom where the great boulders lay he could not make out any object lying on them.

Quickly, he now fastened the lead to the dog's collar and, dragging her with him, he yelled back, 'I'll get you! D'you hear? If it's the last thing I do, I'll get you.'

When he reached the kitchen door fifteen minutes later, he was yelling, 'He's . . . he's gone over the top . . . fallen over the top!' He was now rushing through the room, the dog at his heels, to hear screams from the annexe and Granan yelling, 'He pushed him. I saw him.'

Unceremoniously he thrust his way into the annexe sitting room, there to see the old lady being held by both Lucille and Peter. And straight away she called to him, 'He pushed him. I saw it all through the 'scope. He pushed him. The devil in hell! He's down there, lying. Get the police and a doctor.'

Jim too began to stammer, 'Yes, he must have been pushed. Rodney . . .'

'Be quiet! Please, please be quiet,' Lucille implored.

'Shut up! woman.' The old lady now thrust Lucille away with both hands, crying, 'Your son has been murdered. I saw it, every motion of it I saw. Jim was running after the dog, and Rodney appeared out of nowhere, out of nowhere, and he gripped the stick. I saw it. I saw it all. But then the dog got him. The dog got him else he would've been away. I know he would . . . Matthew . . . Oh, Matthew!'

'She's right!' said Jim. 'He didn't fall; he screamed, he screamed for me. It was a cry for help. When he wants me it's always a whistle. And he's not lying among the boulders at the bottom. I looked. He must have been caught in the scrub on the cliff face.'

'Oh my God!'

'Steady. Steady.' Peter now pushed Lucille towards the old lady, saying, 'Stay with her. I'll . . . I'll phone for the doctor and the police. They'll know what to do.'

'Where's Miss Elizabeth?' Jim said.

'She's upstairs playing chess with the master. I'll get her after I've phoned. Now calm down, madam, calm down. When the police come we must tell them he fell over while Jim was away looking for the dog. It's up to you, madam, whether or not this becomes a public scandal. I'm sure the colonel wouldn't want it to be.'

* * *

Two separately roped figures were manoeuvring themselves from one clump of shrubs to another on the vertical face of the quarry. They were being directed by men up above, who were laying out the ropes. One climber was a bricklayer from the village whose hobby was rock-climbing, the other a young policeman with the same skills.

In the group watching from the quarry bed were Peter, Jim, Elizabeth and Old Joe, together with two ambulancemen, two other men from the farm and the gardener. But the most voluble of them was the dog, because Flossie would not stop barking.

'I've told you, Peter, that that dog will sniff him out quicker than any climber.'

'Yes, Joe, and get herself entangled, with that long hair of hers, in one of those thickets up there. And that'll be another one to rescue.'

'She's no fool, that dog. I know her better than any of you. She'll get entangled, yes, but she'll get out of it. She's begging with every bark to be let go.'

Jim, who was finding it difficult to hang on to the straining animal, turned to Peter, saying, 'He's right, Peter. And if she finds him they'll find her, too.'

Peter said nothing for a moment, then on a sigh: 'Do what he says, let her off; it's right, Joe does know her better than any of us.'

Immediately Flossie was released she stopped her barking; and when Elizabeth made a sound that was like a groan, Peter, whose arm had been supporting her tense body, tightened his grip on her, saying, 'There now. There now. It's true what Joe says, she is more likely to find him than they are.'

They were all watching Flossie now. One minute she would be on the top of a boulder, the next she would disappear into a cleft.

Then Joe, his voice vibrant now, said, 'There she goes!'

Flossie was clawing her way up through the rough scrub growing out from the lower part of the quarry face, but the higher she climbed the more she became lost in the thicker tangle of smaller scrub.

Once she stopped near one of the dangling men, who bent and patted her. Then he was following her, until she disappeared into a thicker and broader mass.

Now the man called up to those above him, and he could be seen to hover over the spot into which the dog had disappeared.

It would seem that he could see nothing; but then there came to those below the muffled sound of Flossie's bark, followed by more commotion from those at the top as they guided the second climber towards the first. What followed next was only dimly made out by those below. But they knew that the climbers had taken knives from their belts and were now hacking a way into the thicket.

The ambulancemen did not need to be given any direction. They picked up their stretcher and, saying to the three farm workers, 'Come on. We'll likely need all the help we can get,' they made their way to a position directly below the climbers and as close to the face as possible.

Jim followed them, but when Elizabeth tried to pull away from Peter's hold, he said, 'No. No. You'd only be in the way. They've got to come this way.'

'I'm a nurse! Peter. I'm a nurse!'

'Yes, I know you're a nurse all right, but you'll not be in a state to help anyone if you attempt to cross those boulders. It'll take those men all their time to get the stretcher back. Isn't that right, Joe?'

'Yes, you're right. And look, miss. Once they get him here, there's still quite a way to the road and the ambulance. You can see to him then.' He did not add, 'If he's alive.'

Was it hours or days or weeks she stood there, until she saw that the stretcher blankets were not covering the still, twisted form of her beloved, that his face was exposed; and by the look on that face she knew that death was not imminent.

26

Peter held the brandy glass to Lucille's lips and when she choked on it he said, 'Try another sip, mistress.' She did so; then he poured a good measure out for the colonel, and this was thrown back almost in one gulp. Then Richard Wallingham, looking up at Peter, said, 'What have we bred, Peter, and why?'

'It's a question I can't answer, sir.'

'Both my mother and Jim Taylor can't be wrong, can they?'

'No, sir.'

There was a long pause and then Richard asked, 'Where is he now?'

It was a hesitant reply. 'I . . . I think, according to Cook, he . . . he's attending to a dog bite.'

'A dog bite?'

'Flossie got him by the leg.'

There was another long pause, then Richard said, 'You know something, it's a dreadful thing for a father to have to say about his son, but at this moment I could wish he would get rabies and die from it.'

'Oh, don't! Don't!' The cry came from Lucille.

'Well, what if your favourite son dies? Is his murderer to be let off scot-free?'

At this Lucille sprang up and fled from the room.

There was silence between the two men for at least a full minute, then Richard Wallingham said, 'Go and see if she's all right, Peter. She won't be, but try to explain to her how . . . how I feel. Will you?'

'Yes, sir; yes. And yourself, try not to worry. I'm not a praying man, never have been, but all I can say now is, the only thing we can do is to pray for Matthew's survival.'

She had been sitting in the nurses' rest room for three and a half hours. Matron Johnson had come and talked to her; the ward sister Isabel Fowler had come and talked to her; and the Sister Tutor Grace

Foster had sat with her for over half an hour. They had all been so kind, but the one she was waiting for now was Dr Venor.

The doctor had not allowed her to stay in the side ward while the nurses prepared Matthew for the theatre, but he had come to her since and told her that they had found a deepish cut in the side of his head and that his left leg was broken below the knee, but despite this, and several bruises, the doctor had said he was holding his own. And this phrase had stayed with her since. He was holding his own. He was holding his own.

One of the ward nurses entered the room carrying a tray on which there was a cup of tea and a plate of biscuits. 'You won't believe it, Liz,' she said, 'but I've just discovered that our dear Sister Fowler is human. You know old Peggy in the end bed, and her little bottle that she keeps in her bag that nobody's supposed to know about? Well, Sister took it out and quietly offered it to me to put a few drops into your tea, and old Peggy never said a word. So here it is. How much do you want?'

Elizabeth shook her head and tried to smile.

'Well, when I take it back to Peggy, I'll kiss her, begod! if I don't, as she herself would say. And who knows, I might also plonk one on Sister Fowler's brow.' Her voice now changing, she added, 'I'm sorry to the heart about this and all you've gone through. We all are. You'd never believe it, the whole hospital's rooting for him. The only thing we can't understand is how he managed to fall. I mean, he had that cute driver fellow with him, and his dog. How did they let him fall down a cliff or whatever it was?'

She waited for an answer, but none was forthcoming from Elizabeth who, after sipping at her tea, said quietly, 'Thank Peggy for me.'

'I will, love. I will.'

Yes, they'd all be wondering how, accompanied by his man and his dog, Matthew could have fallen over a cliff. Well, they would never know . . . that was, unless he never regained consciousness. Then they would have to know. Oh yes, they would have to know then . . .

It was a good half-hour later when Dr Venor came into the room. He was actually smiling as he said to her, 'He's all settled and comfortable now.'

'How is he taking it?'

'Very well. Very well. The head injury was the worst, but they've seen to that. The only thing is'—his smile widened—'he's bound to have a definite hangover when he comes to. But there's always morphine, isn't there, Nurse?'

'Yes, Doctor. There's always morphine.' Her voice was trembling on the verge of tears when she said, 'His . . . his leg?'

'Oh, they've set that; and as far as can be gathered there's no internal injury.'

'He'll . . . he'll be all right then?'

'Well'—he paused—'he is a strong man physically, but he's had another shock. We can only hope that he will weather this. Being a nurse you will know that the next day or two could be crucial. But if care and attention and . . . and your presence'—he paused here and inclined his head towards her—'can help him, then he will recover. Oh!'—he put his hand on her shoulder—'try not to distress yourself further. Like the rest of the hospital staff I, too, am deeply sorry about this, and so near your wedding day. I understand from Sister Fowler that she does not expect you to return to work next week, because you too have had your own share of shocks lately.'

'I'm very grateful, Doctor.'

'It's nothing. It's nothing.'

He was about to bustle out when he turned to her and said, 'That man of his is a bit of a nuisance. He's got the hall tiles worn out with pacing backwards and forwards. I had to prevent him from entering the theatre block.' Then in a softer tone he added, 'Such devotion is rare these days, but, nevertheless, take him home with you.'

She did not say, 'It's he who'll have to take *me* home,' but after a moment she followed him out, then went to her ward to thank the sister and the staff before hurrying along to the side room where Matthew lay.

Two nurses were in the room and they remained still while she stared down at the bandaged head lying on the low pillow. The face was deathly pale, and she groaned inside, as she had when she first saw him on the stretcher. She did not touch the hand lying near to her on the counterpane, for, had she attempted to, she knew she would have gripped it.

Without making any sign to the nurses, she turned and swiftly left the room and hurried to the hall where she said to Jim, 'What happened when you got the mistress home?'

'I . . . I didn't stay to hear much, only that the colonel can't get his mother to keep her mouth shut.'

When Bella let Elizabeth and Jim into the hall, Peter came from the drawing room and hurried towards them. He did not immediately ask, 'How did you find him?' but said, 'They're in there, waiting to hear your news.'

'I . . . I want Jim to come in with me.'

'Yes, yes of course.' There had been no hesitation in Peter's voice; then he turned to Jim and said, 'The colonel was wanting to see you, anyway,' and, his voice dropping to a whisper, he added, 'You must tell him what happened, but without any frills. Keep your own opinion to yourself. Just state the facts. You understand?'

Jim nodded and said briefly, 'Aye, I understand,' and followed him and Elizabeth into the drawing room, where Lucille, hastily rising from her chair that had been set near her mother-in-law, said, 'You're back! Oh . . . how . . . how is he? What did they find?'

'Lucille! Please, sit down and let them get their breaths. Sit here, Elizabeth.' Richard pointed to a chair to his left side; then, addressing Jim, he said, 'Take a seat, Taylor. Take a seat.'

Jim did not say, as he was supposed to, 'Thank you, sir,' but went and sat on a straight-backed chair that was set near a glass cabinet full of china.

When Lucille, again looking at Elizabeth, said, 'Would you like a cup of tea, dear?' the colonel almost barked her name, *'Lucille!'*

'All right! All right!' she retorted. 'You won't allow me to ask how my son is, so what am I to do?'

At this point Annie Wallingham demanded, 'Tell us, girl.'

So Elizabeth briefly described all she knew, ending with, 'We'll really know nothing more until he regains consciousness. As the doctor said, it depends upon his reaction to this further shock.'

'Did you see him?' asked Lucille tentatively.

Looking at her, Elizabeth said softly, 'Yes, Lucille, I saw him, but as you know, nobody looks well after an operation.'

'He'll survive?' This came from the colonel. 'I'm asking this of you, not as Elizabeth but as a nurse. What . . . what is your real opinion? Please give us the truth.'

'Oh'—she lied now, and with conviction—'as far as my knowledge goes, I'm sure he will survive his physical disabilities at any rate; but, as the doctor said, we'll not know the result of the shock until he regains consciousness, and then perhaps not for a few days after.'

'Thank you. Thank you, Elizabeth.'

The colonel now turned his attention to the stiff-faced young man sitting some way from the group, and he said, 'I know, Taylor, that my son is very fond of you, in fact he looks upon you as a friend. He is a man who has been in command of a great many men and he knows men, and the fact that he can call you friend proves to me that you're a man worthy of his respect, even, I may add, if you don't show that respect to others. But that's another point. Now I want you to tell me and those present here, and without any of your private thoughts on the subject, exactly what happened this morning when you were up on the Mount. My mother's version is that she actually saw his younger brother grip his stick, then seem to wrestle with him before pushing him towards the edge of the quarry and so over. She came downstairs screaming when you came in with the news of what you had seen. Now, in plain words, tell me exactly what happened as you know it.'

In plain words Jim told them what he knew had happened and how he had been called from chasing the dog by Mr Matthew yelling his name twice. He had been running through mist, but it was clear when he reached the top of the quarry that Matthew had disappeared. At this point he could not bring himself to mention Rodney by name, but said, 'Flossie was biting into your younger son's leg. The dog had apparently come back on her own in a roundabout way.' Jim could not now resist adding his own opinion here with a statement that was damning: 'It is evident the other one was trying to make his escape, but the dog had stopped him.'

There was a long pause until Annie Wall-ingham's voice said, 'There. What did I tell you? And the fellow's right. The other one, as he put it, was trying to make his escape down the hill.'

'Mother!'

'Well, you've been doubting me, thinking I'm in my dotage.'

'I never doubted you, Mother, but I wanted confirmation because this is a very, very serious matter—it couldn't be more so—and I have a duty to perform. So, Lucille, we will have that cup of tea you were suggesting a moment ago. No, don't get up, dear, we'll ring for Mary; but one last thing before you do that. I will say to you all that if Matthew should die I will hand my younger son over to the police. In any case he will not be able to stay in this house. My mind has been busy during these last few hours of waiting and I have made plans for him. I shall say no more at present, other than just this.' He was looking straight at Jim now, and he said, 'You are a vital part in this affair now, and I trust that you will not pass the information on to anyone until I give you leave.'

Jim stared back at the stiff-faced man

sitting upright in his chair, and what he said was, 'The apparent looseness of me tongue does not represent the real quality of me brain, sir.' On this profound statement he rose from the chair and, looking now towards Lucille, he said, 'I'll tell Mary about the tea, ma'am.'

Richard closed his eyes and lay heavily back in his chair, and he did not open them again until his mother said, 'Say what you like about that fellow, Richard, he's got more up top than comes out on his tongue, as he said, and he's not to be looked down on.'

'Who's looking down on him?'

'You are, and you have; but we won't go into that now. Just tell us what's on your mind . . . I mean about your plans.'

The colonel eased himself up just the slightest, then, looking at his wife, he said, 'You remember Francis Waterford?'

Lucille thought a moment before she said, 'Yes. Yes, the people in New Zealand. The one who used to send Christmas cards every year.'

'Yes, the one who used to send us Christmas cards every year. Well, his father happened to be a cousin twice removed from my father. My father, as I understood, met this cousin a few times and liked him, but the family did not want him to keep up any connection in that quarter because—oh, let it be whispered'—he was shaking his head slowly from side to side—'there was a strain of Maori in the family and at that time it was not to be recognized. Mixed blood. Well, my father's cousin had two sons, and it was the eldest, Francis, who sent the Christmas cards; and, if you remember, there was always an open invitation written with them for us to visit them. I, unfortunately being the grandson of my grandfather, remembered the strain of Maori blood, so did not respond, and it's a few years now since the cards ceased, isn't it?'

'Yes, yes, Richard. About five or six I would say. The last came just before the war.'

'Yes, before the war. But one of Francis's sons joined the war because, if you remember, New Zealand declared war on Germany immediately after we had, and thousands of New Zealanders fought in North Africa and France; and they were fine soldiers. Thousands of them died, too, and Francis's younger son was among them. I recall I had the decency to send him my condolences, but I've heard nothing from them since. I only know that they have a large farm and that they live in the North Island. But we haven't their address. You haven't kept it, have you, Lucille?'

'No, Richard, I'm sorry, I haven't.'

'Well, it can easily be found. Peter?'

'Yes, sir?'

'You know how to go about these things. Get in touch with New Zealand House in London; I'm sure they will help you. Say that I want to trace a relative. The full name is Francis John Waterford. I can't think that there'll be all that many Waterfords there, yet you never know. But he farms in quite a big way, I understood, in cattle and sheep.'

'I'll do that right away, sir.'

After Peter had left the room Annie Wallingham demanded of her son, 'What can he do for us at this time?'

'He can, I hope, Mother, allow my younger son'—he could not bear to mention the name Rodney—'to pay a visit with the intention of setting himself up in farming there. He will know nothing of the reasons for the request from me and I'm sure he won't be told by the culprit. If Rodney does take this opportunity then it is up to him what he does with his life. Alternatively he will be handed over to the police to face a charge of attempted murder. However, should Matthew die, there will be no such choice: he will be handed over straight away.'

Lucille now asked quietly, 'Why are you picking on New Zealand, Richard?'

'Because, my dear, I want him out of the country. I'll never feel happy for Matthew until there is a great distance between the two of them, for there's something in my son that was also in Elizabeth's previous suitor. Do you see my point, Elizabeth?'

For the first time Elizabeth spoke, saying, 'Yes. Yes, Colonel. I see your point. I know how you feel about this, and as I'm the cause of it . . .'

'Don't talk like that, girl. Don't talk like that! You are not the cause of it. We are the cause of it, this family, and it is only myself who can really understand why, and I'm too tired to go into that now.'

Mary brought in the tea tray and, after placing it on a side table, she looked at Lucille, saying, 'Jim has given us the good news, mistress. We're over the moon, we are, we're over the moon,' and with this she went out.

Lucille handed one cup of tea to her mother-in-law and the other to her husband. Then, taking the third one to Elizabeth, she put it beside her before looking into her face and saying cryptically, 'Well, I'm over the moon, too. Aren't you?'

27

It was two days since the operation. Matthew had been heavily sedated for the first twenty-four hours; now he was conscious, but in such pain that he was asking himself why they did not give him morphine. His head was aching with a dull thumping pain. His leg too was hurting and he wanted to move, but somehow he couldn't. Where was everybody? He went to move his hand and felt it being held; and when a voice came to him, saying, 'Hello, darling,' he repeated, 'Hello, darling.' Then he wanted to move and turn on his side, but he couldn't. That voice was Elizabeth's. Where was he? Don't say . . . don't say he was back in the hospital. The war was over. Jerry had gone and . . . But now there was a voice in his head crying loudly, *Jim . . . Jim . . . Jim . . .* Who was Jim? He wanted Jim. But who was he? Where was he?

'Lie still, darling, lie still.'

There was that woman's voice again, a girl's voice. Yes, of course, it was Elizabeth's voice. There was something wrong with his head. If they would only give him something for this pain. He opened his eyes, then remembered that it was no use opening his eyes. Yes, it was coming back to him now: it was no use opening his eyes, he was blind. And Jim? Jim? Jim was his friend. Jim drove him. What had happened?

'Nurse! Nurse!'

'Yes, my dear. Lie still. Would you like a drink?'

He thought it had been Elizabeth talking, but this was a different voice; he was in hospital again.

'I'm dry.'

'Here you are then. It's just a straw. Suck on it gently.'

Who was she talking to? Suck on it gently? He wanted morphine. Gratefully he drank, then slowly lifted his lids. There was something wrong with his head. He was dreaming again. Yet he had been drinking through that straw. But he was dreaming that he was in a mist and could see far off the sun shining on glass. He wished they would give him some morphine. He closed his eyes again. Then once more he opened them, quickly now, and blinked. The far light was still on the glass. What glass? What light? He was imagining he was seeing things. It was this pain. Oh, he wanted a painkiller. 'Nurse! Nurse!'

'Yes, I'm here.'

'May I have something? My head is so painful.'

'Yes, my dear, in a short while.'

'No, now. Now. I'm . . . I'm so tired.'

'Then go to sleep, darling. Be quiet now. Be quiet.'

What were they talking about? That was Elizabeth's voice. Where was she? Why didn't she speak to him? There was that queer light again, it seemed to be in his eyes. It was hurting him. It had moved now, it had become dark in parts. One dark part kept moving back and forwards. Why didn't it stop so he could see the light on the glass again? Go to sleep, she had said; go to sleep. He was dreaming, dreaming.

They had pricked his arm; the pain was easier now. He would go to sleep. Yes, he would go to sleep.

The nurse standing beside Elizabeth said, 'They do go on after coming round, don't they? But he's doing well really. His pulse has strengthened. The cutters-up seem satisfied. It's what's going to happen in the next day or two, isn't it?'

'Yes, yes.' Elizabeth nodded her head. She didn't want to talk, she just wanted to sit by his side and hold his hand. He must be in a great deal of pain. The nurse said kindly, 'He's sound asleep now. Why don't you go and take a rest? He won't come round again for some hours, you know that.'

Yes, she knew that, and the nurse wanted rid of her. She could understand that too, because when anyone was sitting by a bedside you always had to disturb them to take temperatures and blood pressures and so on.

'Why don't you go out and have some lunch? It's hotpot in the canteen; it was quite tasty. Charlie Fox took your watch-dog in there a short while ago. By, he's got a tongue, hasn't he, that one?'

Elizabeth's silent nod confirmed this, and she left the ward and made for the waiting room where she knew she would find Jim. The minute he saw her, Jim threw down the paper he was reading and said, 'Everything all right?'

'Yes, so far, Jim. Yes. But I'm feeling terribly tired, and as he's . . . he's had an injection and won't wake for some hours, perhaps not until this evening, I thought I'd slip back to the house and perhaps get an hour or two's sleep.'

'Aye; that's a good idea, miss, because, as Peter said this morning, you were up at three o'clock and in the kitchen making tea. He was up himself because the colonel was having one of his bad nights. I don't envy him his job.'

'Well, in his place and with a certain person we both know you would do the same.'

'Aye,' he gave a short laugh now, 'you're right, miss, I would.'

She almost fell asleep in the car, and as soon as she laid her head back and was quiet Jim stopped his chattering.

Last night she had only managed three hours' sleep, and the previous night less

than that, but now her tiredness was getting the better of her and this morning she
had known that if she hadn't been careful
she would have nodded off even while sitting by Matthew's side.

They no longer had to approach the
house by the farm but could drive in
through the main gate, for several turfs had
been removed and the drive extended to
make this possible.

It was when Jim opened the car door
to help her out that he saw she had been
dozing, and, taking her arm, he led her
along the terrace to the front door. When
she said, 'I'm all right, Jim, thanks. I really
am,' he replied: 'You're not all right.' Pushing the door open and seeing no one in
the hall, he led her along the corridor and
into the annexe, where he knocked on the
sitting-room door before taking her in.

To the old girl, as he thought of her, who
was now struggling to get up from the
couch exclaiming, 'What is it?' he said, 'It's
all right, madam. It's all right. She's only
tired, dropping with sleep. A hot drink, I
should think, then bed. And . . . and Mr
Matthew is all right. He's had a jab, she

said, which will keep him asleep until this evening. I mean an injection, like.'

'Yes, yes. Thank you. Thank you. Sit down, my dear, sit down. I'll ring for Mary.'

'Have a good nap, miss.'

Jim turned and went out, to be met by both Lucille and Peter, and it was she who exclaimed, 'What is it? Have you brought Elizabeth back? Is she ill?'

'No, ma'am, only very, very tired—practically slept all the way in the car. As Peter there will tell you, she was up half the night. A few hours' sleep and she'll be on her feet as right as rain. The old lady is seein' to her.'

Then they all turned as one as the sound of raised voices came from the drawing room. Peter took Lucille's arm and led her back to the stairs, saying, 'Go on. Go to your room and lie down.'

Turning now to Jim, who was looking at him enquiringly, Peter said, *'He's* in there; and the colonel's reading the riot act. Go to the kitchen and have a drink of something. I'll let you know the outcome.'

'Do. Do that. I'll be very interested.'

Jim's head was moving slowly up and

down, and to this Peter said, 'You're not the only one.'

After Jim had crossed the hall towards the kitchen, Peter went to the drawing room door and, standing to one side, he listened to the colonel saying, 'You'll do as I say, because if you refuse there's only one alternative, whether Matthew lives or dies: to hand you over to the police. If he dies there are two witnesses to prove that you murdered him; if he doesn't die, there are still two witnesses to prove that it was your intention to kill him. So you go to New Zealand and you take up your life there, farming or whatever is offered.

'Yesterday, through the New Zealand office in London, I got the address of Francis Waterford. The Waterfords were connected with my grandfather's family way back, so this morning I made it my business to phone that gentleman. I understand that there has been a standing invitation for my people to visit New Zealand and his extensive farm. No one ever took it up, but I enquired if it was possible for one of my sons to buy some land in his quarter, or perhaps a small farm, and he sounded very agreeable to the idea. He lives in the North

Island, where the land is very fertile and business is brisk in cattle and sheep and a number of other trades. He said he would welcome . . . his term was "any of my stock". I cannot tell him that I am duping him by sending him one who is a disgrace to the name of Wallingham. But he will hear nothing from me about your past, and it will be up to you to prove there is some decency still left in you.'

'I'll not go. I'll not do it. I'll prove it was an accident. I can. I will.'

'You can't, and you won't, and you know it.'

'I . . . . I haven't the money to set up a new farm on my own.'

'You have the money. I am no fool. You have been quietly feathering your nest for some time. I don't know how long it was before I came home that you started, but you have stacked away quite sufficient to enable you to buy a small property. But having said that, I will also give you half the amount I had left to you in my will. This will be paid in quarterly sums through my lawyer for as long as you remain in New Zealand. There is a condition to my generosity, which is that you remain in contact with Francis Waterford's family after you get there. You might feel inclined to turn up your snobbish nose at what you find, because there is mixed blood somewhere along the line: that is why my Christian grandparents only deigned to keep up the acquaintance rather than seeking friendship. But let me tell you this: if it wasn't for the New Zealanders and their fighting forebears coming in their thousands to our aid—and dying, too, in their thousands—you, my pampered son, would at this moment be in a different position.'

'I won't do it. I'll find a way.'

'Yes, I thought you would say that, and I know what you mean. You will slip off quietly; you have your own banking account. Apparently you think there is nothing to stop you doing that because at bottom you think all I have said is merely talk. Well, by now you should know that I'm not given to long speeches, and this is the longest speech I think I have ever made in my life, and the bitterest. So let me warn you, if you carry out your decision to slip away I'll immediately inform the police, and I tell you, I mean every word I say. I'll give you until tomorrow morning to come and tell me that you are packed and ready for New Zealand. Now get out of my sight. Go!' The last word was a yell.

28

It had been about a quarter-past two when Elizabeth had lain down; it was six o'clock exactly when she awoke to the chimes of the grandfather clock on the stairs, but at first she wasn't aware of the time. It was still light, so she stretched herself before throwing off the rug that had covered her. Then, sitting on the side of the bed, she looked at her watch, and this brought her to her feet almost in a jump. Six o'clock! She had thought it was about four! Oh! goodness. She rushed to the bathroom now and sluiced her face with cold water, drew a comb quickly through her hair, picked up her coat and hat from where she had laid them on a chair and hurried down to the annexe sitting room, there to see Lucille sitting on the couch with her mother-in-law.

'Where d'you think you're going?' Lucille got to her feet and, taking the coat and hat from Elizabeth, she went on, 'Sit yourself down, girl.'

'It's six o'clock. I . . . I never thought I would sleep that long. I must get back.'

'You mustn't get back.' Lucille actually pushed her into the armchair. 'I myself have only been back this last half-hour. Jim drove me in at three o'clock and I left at five. He is sleeping peacefully and they are all very happy with the results so far. So there's nothing to worry about: he is no longer unconscious or suffering from the anaesthetic.'

'Oh, yes, he will suffer. The anaesthetic has an effect on some people for days.'

'Yes, Nurse. Yes, Nurse. Thank you for telling me.'

'Oh, Lucille, I'm sorry.' They were clasping hands now and laughing when Annie Wallingham said fretfully, 'If anyone were to speak to me I would know I was still here.'

'Oh, Mrs Wallingham. Oh.'

'Oh, for goodness' sake! girl, stop calling

me that! Be like the others, insult me behind my back but to my face please do
what they do, the hypocrites, and call me
Granan.'

As they laughed gently, the thought
passing through Lucille's mind was: How
wonderful it is to be able to laugh. But I
don't know how I can after what Peter told
me took place. Richard must be torn to
the heart. As Peter had said, the colonel
had meant every word, and he had never
spoken so long at one go in his life, or
with such vehemence. It had had its results, for it hadn't been more than an hour
later that Mary came to her and told her
that Mr Rodney was packing his cases,
and she knew that at the news she had
only just stopped herself from saying,
'Thank God.' She'd had to remind herself
that he was still her son and that he was
the last one who had swelled her belly,
only immediately to remember she had
been bitterly unhappy and unwell at the
time, and had hated every moment of
those nine months of carrying him. Was it
all his fault that this had happened? No,
because she had never been able to bring
herself to show him enough love. Nor had

Richard. Yet Richard should have understood his youngest son, because he himself had been brought up without love.
Granan and the general had thought of no
one but themselves, after losing their beloved younger sons. But why hadn't they
then turned to Richard? Granan had joined
the general in India, whereas she herself
had never gone out of her way to join the
colonel but had stayed at home to bring
up the family. Had she then ever shown
any love to Rodney? No; and he had, in
a way, followed in his father's footsteps—
but only in a way, for his father was above
cold-blooded murder. Oh, she was glad, so
glad that he was going. She hoped he
wouldn't come and say goodbye to her.
That would be too much to bear, because
her guilt might get the better of her.

'You're star-gazing, woman.' Her
mother-in-law's voice came at her as if
from far away, and she blinked her eyes
and said, 'Yes, I was a bit. I was thinking.'

Now Annie's voice was low as she replied, 'Well, don't, my dear. It'll get you nowhere. Tomorrow will come and be over,
and the next day too, whether we're here
or not. What has to be will be. Richard has

done the right thing, the only thing to make life possible not only for you but for all of us in the future. Now, that said, let's get down to practical matters. I told Mary that as soon as I rang for her it would mean that you, my dear Elizabeth, had risen from your beauty sleep and she was to bring in a tray with a substantial tea on it because I knew you wouldn't be staying here for dinner.'

Elizabeth's instinct was to get up and throw her arms about the wizened little woman sitting opposite, but she sat still, only bending forward a little as in comic chastisement she said, 'One of these days I shall tell you what I think about you.' It had been a good imitation of Cook's voice and the old lady's rejoinder, 'And I'll be waitin' for you, aye I will that,' came in a voice that was definitely that of Mary.

'You two should form a duo; there are plenty of variety shows that would jump at you.'

A short while later Mary reported back to the kitchen that she couldn't believe it, but it made her heart glad because there was the three of them actually laughing . . .

well, not really laughing but smiling audibly, as the old general used to say.

It was turned eight o'clock that evening when Jim left Elizabeth at the hospital gates and, as had been arranged, went to visit his mother: he'd be back, he said, at nine o'clock on the dot.

When Elizabeth reached the side ward where Matthew was lying she was surprised to find a nurse standing outside the door, and terror struck at her heart for a moment, for there came to her the sound of voices from inside the room. But the nurse soon reassured her: 'Everything's all right,' she said, 'but I've to tell you that you can't go in yet awhile, he's being . . . well, he's being examined. Dr Venor has just gone back to his office. He told me to tell you to go there, he wants to have a word with you.'

'Are you sure Ma . . . I mean the captain is . . . is all right?'

'Yes; yes, miss, take my word for it. He's all right. At least he's better than he was. Oh yes, he's better than he was.'

When the nurse smiled broadly Elizabeth turned away from her; she was puzzled and her walk almost turned into a run as she made for Dr Venor's office. In one way, she was surprised that he should still be here at this time of night: she understood he usually went off duty about six.

In answer to her tap on his door, he called, 'Come in. Come in,' and as he rose from his seat behind his desk he was smiling at her.

'Sit down. Sit down, Nurse. I . . . I have some rather startling news to tell you. I don't know how far it will progress, but at present it is good news, so please don't look so anxious. You see, it was shortly after five o'clock, I understand, when the captain woke up, at least as much as he was able to after the sedative he had been given. Well, the story goes as I'm telling it to you. He asked for a drink, and when the nurse gave it to him he suddenly pushed it away, saying, "There it is again! There it is again! It's on the window!" and he pointed towards the window, then he almost knocked the glass of water from the nurse's hand and actually yelled, "It's a light! It's a light! In the distance, it's a light!" The nurse rang the bell for Sister, and together they had to stop him from thrashing about in the bed, because his leg was plastered and he could have hurt himself further.

'When he insisted he could see the light on the window Sister rang for another nurse and sent her for me. Well, when I arrived they were actually trying to hold him still in the bed because he had almost loosened the bandage on his head. I said to him, "What is it, Captain? What's your trouble?" And he said, "Trouble? Trouble? The light on the window in the far distance. The light on the window."

'Then,' went on Dr Venor, 'I spoke to him sternly, saying, "You must calm yourself. You will do yourself an injury, and the light on the window will go and you won't see it again if you keep thrashing about. Now, you understand me, Captain? You under-stand what I am saying?" And at this he almost became limp and whispered, "Yes. Yes." Then again he was endeavouring to stir when he said, "But there was a light on the window."

'I told him I was sure there was and that if he promised to lie still the light would remain there; but that if he thrashed about it might upset his head so much that the light would disappear. At this he seemed to understand my meaning because he lay quietly.

'I went out and phoned Mr Carey. He's the eye surgeon. I knew this was the day for his visits to the General Hospital where he operates, and I managed to catch him just before he was leaving and explain the situation. He seemed very interested and said he'd be here as soon as possible. He arrived about half an hour ago, together with a young doctor. He tested the captain as much as he could under the circumstances, and he says it is quite definite that the sight is returning, but we must all take it slowly. Oh no! my dear. Sit down again. Don't cry like that or you'll make yourself ill, too.'

'I'm sorry. I'm sorry.'

'Don't be sorry, just be glad, as I know you are. But don't expect miracles right away. We had understood that he lost his sight when a shell burst close to him, but that his eyes seemed to have suffered no physical injury. What has probably brought back the sight is another shock, this time when he fell over the cliff and struck his head on a boulder. One shock has counteracted the other. Not feasible, you might say, but it is. You follow me?'

Yes. Yes, she followed him. Oh, how she followed him! The wonder of it was too much to take in. She even thought that if he got his full sight back he would have Rodney to thank for it. Then she chided herself for her twisted way of thinking before saying, 'His . . . his family will be overjoyed. May . . . may I see him later?'

He paused before saying, 'Well, I will enquire. I'm going back there now. You go to the rest room, my dear, and I'll come and see you there.'

She had to wait only twenty minutes before Dr Venor returned, when he said, 'I'm sorry, my dear, but Mr Carey says it would be better if he is again slightly sedated and is not further disturbed tonight. And you will understand that for the next day or two he must be kept quiet, which means, unfortunately, no visitors. There must be no excitement.'

'Yes, Doctor, I understand. You are a very kind man, Dr Venor, and, as the saying goes, you hide it under a bushel.'

'Oh, Nurse. I am not used to compliments, not even kind words. I am generally a receptacle for complaints, misunderstandings and, in some cases, abuse, so when someone pays me a compliment I do not know how to accept it gracefully. You need practice in such things!' At this he held out his hand, saying, 'Thank you, my dear, and good night.'

He now opened the door and she paused for a moment on the threshold and said, 'Good night, Doctor, and my thanks again.'

She went to the call box in the hall and rang up the house because she felt she must tell them the news straight away, she could not let them wait until she got back.

The voice on the other end of the phone said, 'Yes? This is The Beavors,' and she exclaimed, 'Oh, Peter! Peter.'

Peter's voice came back rapidly, saying, 'What is it? What's happened?'

'Oh nothing. Nothing wrong. Only good news. I want to have a word with Lucille.'

'Can't you tell me? I'm in the colonel's room . . . Yes, go on, Elizabeth, please tell me. The colonel is anxious.'

'Well, I . . . I don't know how to put it. I'm shaking with relief: The doctor has just told me that Matthew . . . well, they think he can see a little. He has been terribly excited twice today about some light that he can see and the eye specialists are with him now.'

'Oh, that is simply marvellous. Marvellous!'

'But wait . . . wait.' Elizabeth's voice was calmer now. 'This is only the beginning, the doctor warned me. They will have to take it slowly to find out . . . well, how much of his vision can be restored, or is restored, and above all he must be kept quiet. So I was advised not to trouble him tonight, because they're putting him straight to sleep. And no visiting for the next two days. I'm . . . I'm on a cloud at the moment, but it's so thin I fear I might fall through. We'll all just have to be patient. But I just had to tell you all straight away because Jim is not picking me up until about nine. But the signs are very hopeful.'

'Hopeful? They're marvellous! Oh, wait till I tell them.'

'But, Peter, be careful. The doctor had to warn me about my excitement. But go on now and tell them. Bye-bye for the present.'

'Goodbye, Elizabeth. Goodbye.'

After putting the phone down Peter said to the man who was sitting in the bed, straining forward, 'Matthew . . . Matthew can see a light or something. The specialists have been with him and by the sound of it they'll be attending him for the next day or two, which means no visiting. But isn't that marvellous news? What an end, sir, to an awful day!'

The colonel didn't answer him. His head was back, his eyes were closed, and it was some time before he said, 'Yes. Yes, you're right, Peter. It's put a different aspect on things. But it isn't finished. You've got to take that package along to Rodney.' He pointed to what looked like a bundle of letters wrapped in a waterproof case.

'Oh yes, I'll do that now. But if you'll excuse me, sir, I must go and tell the mistress and Madam first.'

'Yes, yes, of course.'

He was half-way down the stairs when he saw Lucille making her way along the corridor and he called, 'A minute! a minute! I've got news. What d'you think? Just what d'you think?' He was standing on the last stair and looking down into her face. 'Elizabeth's just been on the phone. She's terribly excited naturally and rather garbled, but what I can make out is that, well'—he stopped here—'I'm rather garbled myself. But Matthew can see, my dear. Matthew can see. Just a little light. But he has to be kept quiet and as yet there can be no visiting. Oh please, please!' He stepped down the last stair and steadied her, saying, 'Don't give way, but go along and tell Madam. I'm on an errand.' He held up the package.

'He can see?'

'Only . . . only a little. Elizabeth warns us, as I suppose she's been warned, that it's early days and likely they've got to go slow to find out just how the eyesight will develop. Nevertheless, he can see light.'

Lucille was standing with one hand gripping her throat, the other holding Peter's hand, and he said, 'Come on. Come on, my dear. I'll come with you to tell Madam. She'll sleep without her pill tonight on this news.'

Bella, who just a minute ago had entered the hall from the kitchen, now turned about and ran back into the kitchen and cried at Cook and Rosie who were working

at the table, 'You'll never guess! You'll
never guess what I've just heard. Mr Matthew can see, he can actually see! Miss
Elizabeth's been on the phone. I heard Peter say he can see light.' She now pressed
both her hands into her bosom as she exclaimed in awe-filled tones, 'Isn't that a
blessing from heaven on this troubled
house!'

Her mouth agape, Cook said, 'Never!
You're sure?'

'Of course I'm sure, Cook, I've got the
ears. They've gone to tell Madam.'

Cook left what she was doing at the table and flopped down into a chair near the
fire. She was about to say something to
Bella when she turned and looked at the
wide-eyed and open-mouthed Rosie and
cried at her, 'Well, you were about to take
his coffee up, so why don't you get along
with it and bring the dirties down or you'll
never finish the night.'

Rosie grabbed up the coffee tray, and
used her buttocks to push open the door
that led into a passage and the back
stairs. On the landing it was her foot she
used to announce her entry into the long,
sparsely furnished room. As she laid the

tray down on the end of the table she couldn't help but cry her news aloud: 'What d'you think, Mr Rodney? They've just heard that Mr Matthew can see. What d'you think of that, eh?'

The man sitting at the other end of the table stared at her, and the stare took the smile from her face and brought a sober, even frightened note to her voice as she said, 'I'll . . . I'll take your tray, sir,' and, leaning over, she pulled his dinner tray towards her; then, picking it up, she raised her lids a little to glance once more at him before hurrying out.

Eeh! he looked terrible, devilish. In a way, she had been sorry for him, well, just at times, 'cos everybody was against him. But not now: what they said must be right, but now she daren't think what they said; all she knew was that from the look she had seen on his face he could kill anybody.

Back in the room, Rodney stood looking down at the tray of coffee. He had the urge to take it and throw it crashing against the wall. So he could see, could he? God! To think that *his* action, *his* retaliation for all the injustices he had put up with from that

same one, had given him back his sight!
This was the final blow. The swine would
be able to see her now. And to think he
could have got away with it if it hadn't
been for that damned dog.

He looked down at his leg. Nobody had
come to see to it; they hadn't even asked
the doctor to look in. It could have been
poisoned. If he could get at that animal
this minute he would see that it bit nobody
else, and that *would* be a little bit of jus-
tice. Oh, yes, yes. He'd show them he
wasn't finished yet.

In fact, he was no longer against going
to New Zealand; they knew nothing about
him there, his father had promised that
much. The family sounded a rum lot, but
they would likely be pleased to meet an
Englishman who had a proper business
head on his shoulders. He could make
himself agreeable when he liked, and that's
what he would do. He'd make himself indispensable to somebody out there, because he was convinced he'd make his
mark, especially amongst people who
knew nothing of him.

Suddenly the door was thrust open

again. Rodney did not rise to his feet as Peter approached.

As he put down the package on the table Peter said, 'Your father wishes you to have these papers. They contain confirmation of your future allowance from him. The matter has been taken up by his solicitor, who will get in touch with a New Zealand bank. Also there is the confirmation that a berth has been arranged for you on the *Orontes* sailing from Southampton the day after tomorrow. The colonel asked me to say it is a six-week voyage, by which time you may have sorted yourself out and decided on your approach to your new relatives who are waiting to welcome you.'

Quickly now Rodney rose to his feet and it looked as if he was about to spring at the older man; instead he said, 'Don't you dare talk down to me, you common, crawling individual! What were you but a private from the lowest ranks? and you've wormed your way round Father, and now Mama too.'

At that moment the only thing Peter was thankful for was that Rodney hadn't placed his mother first, for that might have intimated that he had more than a little knowledge of the situation between them. But he said, 'For two pins I'd put my fist into the middle of your pasty face in such a way that you wouldn't be able to see for a good part of your journey ahead.'

In fact, now his hand did shoot out as if he were about to carry out his words, but it was to grip the front of Rodney's shirt and pull him forward for a moment, and then to thrust him back against the fireplace wall.

They stood glaring at each other before Peter said, 'God! how I want to slap you down. Always have, since I first came across you. But I'll leave it for somebody at yon end. It will surely happen one day. Oh yes. The New Zealanders are like the Aussies, they'll smell you for what you are, then God help you.' And on this he turned about and went out.

It was around eight o'clock the next morning when Peter, coming down after giving the colonel his early-morning tray of tea, saw Bella waiting for him at the foot of the stairs, and she said, 'Peter, Old Joe asks if he can have a word with you.'

'Where is he, Bella?'

'He was outside a minute ago. He'd been talking to Jim, but Jim's having his breakfast now.'

Peter went out by the front door and along the terrace, and there he saw Joe standing at the open doors of the new garage admiring the Daimler, and he called to him, saying, 'You wanted a word, Joe?'

'Oh aye, Peter.' And Joe came hurrying towards him. 'He's gone . . . he's gone.'

Peter didn't ask who had gone, but said, 'What time was this?'

'About half-past six. I was surprised when a taxi drew up in the yard, but before I could ask the fellow what he was after at that time Mr Rodney came downstairs from his office. He must have brought his cases down there last night, and he handed them to the taxi man. Then he brought down two more cases and an overcoat. He didn't take the slightest notice of me—I needn't have been there, but I was standing not far from the bonnet of the car. Before he got into it he said to the man, "Just wait a minute." Then do you know what he did?

'Well, he walked up past the big barn

to the small barn where we'd put Flossie's kennel, and I saw him take something out of his pocket on his way up. It was something small because I couldn't see it. And then he opened the door, and stood there. Now if Flossie had been in he would've heard her bark. Oh aye. If it had been Mr Matthew, she would've been all tail wagging, but on sight of Mr Rodney her bristles used to rise. She was never a dog that would crawl on her belly to one who had beaten her. She never forgot it and she would've barked if she had seen him, and so she wasn't there. I saw him pause for a moment, then bang the door and put whatever he had in his hand back into his pocket. And when he got back to the taxi, there he was facing me. And, Mr Peter, I tell you that in all me long life I've never seen anybody look at me as that man did this morning. You can't paint it, no matter how you put the features, and I've got no words in me head to describe how he looked at me. Then he got into the taxi without a word and went off. And you know, it takes a lot to make me shiver, but I stood there shivering.

'The mind is a funny thing, a very funny

thing. You know, during the war I used to take Flossie home with me sometimes at night 'cos she was lonely, and Phyllis . . . well, she always had a soft spot for her. So last night something told me to take her home, and this morning something told me again not to bring her in, and I left her happy, sitting by the kitchen table waiting for Phyllis's titbit, which was milky porridge. Phyllis always has her porridge made mostly with milk, and Flossie loves it. Strange, Mr Peter, but God guides in some way, because whatever he had in his pocket this morning would have meant the end of Flossie. I don't know whether it was a little gun with a silencer, you know—you can get them—or it was some poisoned meat, but it was something. Well, it's over. And now I'd like to know what the master wants doing. I mean, what's going to happen.'

'Oh, I can tell you that,' said Peter softly as he placed a hand on Joe's shoulder. 'He's well aware of the fact that you know that farm better than anybody else and he wants you to see to it. And he knows you'll have help from Ben and the new fellow Strickland. Is he all right?'

'Never better, Mr Peter, never better, and very willing.'

'Well, the master says you're to take charge. Don't do any work yourself, but employ another couple of hands, because the lambing's coming on and you'll need more help.'

'I'll do that, Mr Peter, and with pleasure. But as for running the farm, well, the seasons see to that; apart from accidents the farm runs itself. But I'm gonna tell you one more thing, and I don't suppose you'd like the master to know about it. But there must have been a lot of paper pushed into the boiler fire this morning, 'cos there was more than usual smoke rising from the chimney when I came in. I went upstairs to his office. There was nothing there in the little cubby-holes—you know, where all the bills and things are kept—nothing but the ledger. And you know, I hadn't much schooling, but with the little I had I learnt to read and write. Me readin' was better than me writin', especially where figures were concerned, because they rammed the times tables into you in those days; and there's been more than once, usually on market day, when he's been gone at night, I've had a look into his office and at the ledger. Now I know about markets and their fluctuations, as they're called. When things are plentiful the prices can drop down to the bottom of the well, but there's other times—oh aye, there's other times—well, as I've said about me figures, I know how many beans make five, and on a market day I never saw an entry in that ledger that tallied with the prices at the market, or the receipts in one or other of the shelves.

'Well, he's gone, Peter, but he's been fleecin' the master for a long, long time and his pockets must be well laden, I can tell you. Now you can keep that to yourself as between you and me, 'cos I wouldn't want it to distress the master.'

'Well, Joe, I can tell you this, I don't know to what extent, but the master hasn't been blind to everything that's been going on down in your quarter.'

'No?'

'No, Joe, he hasn't, because according to him who's just gone, he reads the papers, local and otherwise, and he knows the state of the markets. He couldn't believe that the farm was only just holding its own.'

'Well, well!' said Joe now. 'I'm glad to hear that, 'cos I would hate for him to be thinkin' that I was sneakin' about.'

'He'd never think that of you, Joe, because he holds you in the highest regard.'

They stood looking at each other for a moment, then, patting the old man's shoulder, Peter said, 'It's all in your hands, Joe. It's all in your hands now.'

Joe was about to turn away when, a joyful look on his face now, he said, 'What d'you think about Mr Matthew's turn of events? Now I ask you, isn't that something?'

'Yes, it is, Joe, it's the greatest news.'

'We'll be on tenterhooks now to hear how he's getting on.'

'You'll hear, Joe. You'll hear.'

'Aye. Aye.' The old man turned away and his walk was quite brisk for a worn-out seventy.

The news that his younger son had left his home for good and all brought from the master only two words, 'It's over'; but from Lucille, 'I . . . I didn't expect him to come and say goodbye, but I can't help but feel sorry for his plight'; and from Annie Wallingham, 'Well, he saved his neck, and, in a way I'm sorry for that, but now we can get back to normal.'

29

It seemed that all night he had been fighting against the effects of the sleeping tablet: he remembered rousing a number of times, when he had told himself that there was something he must do before sleep overtook him again. But now he was really awake, because he could hear the voices of the nurses. He recognized them as two of the day staff, including the cheeky little one—no nonsense about her. Why he should think of her as little he didn't know—perhaps it was just that her voice gave him the impression she was shorter than her partner, who giggled at times and patted his cheek and said silly things. The shorter one was saying now, 'I bet we have another day with him; he should be slapped down. Look how he

went on last night. He only stopped because Mr Carey went for him and told him
that if he didn't stop his thrashings about
he'd be back where he had been for this
long while and all the good would be un-
done, and that he must remember he was
still a sick man.'

And now Matthew heard the taller one
giggle and say, 'I nearly burst my sides
when he came back with, "Shut up, you!
I am not a sick man. I can see, d'you hear?
Get on with it." Eeh! no one speaks like
that to Mr Carey, but he got on with it.
Eeh! I could have hugged him.'

'Oh, I can see you doing that. You're like
the rest of them, half barmy about him, but
Ducksworth got in first. She'll be along
shortly. Not till after ten, though. I give her
that much sense 'cos she knows the routine. Pull that end tight.'

During this discourse they had been
changing the top sheet on the bed, and
now, their arms around Matthew's back,
they gently lifted him further up the pillows,
and as they did so Matthew slowly opened
his eyes and saw close to him, but through
a slight mist, a round face topped by a
bunch of fair hair on which was perched

a white starched cap, and in the sweetest
tones he could muster he said, 'From what
I can see of your face, Nurse, you are what
they call a sharp-tongued little piece.' It
was almost a squeal of laughter that came
from the other side of the pillows, but he
went on, 'If you decide to slap me down,
then I will slap you back. Understood?'

There was a long pause. It seemed that
the bed was shaking; certainly the short
nurse's body was quivering, and her answer came in as low and sweet tone as
his, saying, 'Fair enough, big-head. And, as
you say, I am a sharp-tongued little piece
and have sense enough not to be taken
in by magazine heroes, captains or otherwise.'

Slowly and painfully Matthew now
turned his head to the other side, and in
spite of the pain that was racking him at
that moment he wanted to cry out aloud
with joy because he could also see this
girl's face, which was further away from
him; it was still through a mist, but nevertheless there it was; it was longish, and
she probably had brown eyes to go with
her mass of dark hair. Her skin looked
tanned; perhaps it was the mist. His voice

still soft, he said, 'Have you any idea, Nurse, what the sight of you is doing to me?'

'Oh! Captain.'

She couldn't go on any further, and he said, 'All I'm waiting for now is, not some painkillers, although I could do with some'—he had turned his head once more to the little figure—'but the sight of'—he paused—'Ducksworth.'

'Well, you've got a wait before you,' was the retort. 'First, I'll see Sister about the painkillers, then you'll have breakfast and a wash, which you really should have had before we made the bed, but we were told not to disturb you. As if anyone could disturb you.' She now began to tuck the sheets round his shoulders and when, looking into her face, he said very softly, 'Will you come to my wedding?' she exploded, 'What!'

'You heard me. Will you come to my wedding?'

'But . . . but why me?'

'Because, my dear, if I wasn't marrying my beautiful Elizabeth, it would have had to be you, because of your soft voice, your warm tender ways, the gentle touch of your hands.'

There was another high, almost hysterical laugh from the nurse standing at the foot of the bed.

'You cheeky monkey! If you were only a little bit better I would slap you across the chops.'

'And that's another thing,' put in the weak voice of Matthew, whose head was now sinking into his pillow. 'Your choice of words is perfect. Nurse'—his voice was fading slightly—'I'm . . . I'm only teasing. Be . . . be your dear self and get me those pills, will you? I don't know what they've done to my . . . blasted leg, but it's giving me hell. Yet I'm so happy I could sing, that's if . . .' His voice trailed away, and when his upper teeth caught his bottom lip the little nurse said quickly to her partner, 'Go and tell Sister he needs a painkiller.'

Now bending over Matthew, she stroked the wet hair from his brow, and when his lips moved and he attempted to speak again, she put a finger on them, saying gently, 'No more now, laddie. Take it easy. There's a long day ahead of you. Sister'll be here in a minute. Close your eyes. That's it, close your eyes; the pain will soon be gone.' Then she added, 'And you can tell me what you think of me again.'

Elizabeth was standing with Jim in the general waiting room. They were the only people there and she felt she couldn't leave him until someone came to tell her that she could now visit the patient. Jim was saying, 'D'you think they'll let me in to see him for a minute?'

'I will see that they do. Just hang around in the corridor.'

He took a step away from her and looked her up and down and said, 'By! I've got to say it, miss, from head to toe you look beautiful.'

'Oh! Jim. I am not beautiful. I pass . . .'

'If you were one of our crowd, I would say shut your . . . for politeness' sake I'll say mouth; and quoting my grannie, "Beauty is in the eye of the beholder," like the woman said who married a cross-eyed man.'

Elizabeth laughed. 'You've twisted that one around a bit to suit yourself, haven't you?' she said. 'Doesn't it go: "It's everybody to their taste, said the woman who kissed the cow"?'

And Jim joined in with her laughing now; then, his face serious, he said, 'You know what I'd like best in the world at this minute, or the next few minutes, or whenever it happens? It would be to see his face when his eyes light on you for the first time.'

'Oh! Jim, be quiet. I don't want to go in there dripping tears.'

The door opened. The nurse who stood there smiling said, 'The way is clear.'

Elizabeth did not smile back at her; her face was straight; she felt nervous.

Jim followed at a short distance behind them . . .

Matthew was lying on his back, but his head was turned slightly towards the door. When it slowly opened and as slowly there came into the room a golden figure, it was as if his heart stopped for a moment because he had to gasp for his breath. She stood with her back to the door. He did not speak, but with one slowly raised hand he indicated that she should move down to the foot of the bed, which she did. And he looked at her. The mist was very thin:

he could make out all the detail of her, from her beautiful hair crowned with a small peach-coloured velvet hat to her beautiful face. So, so beautiful. Different altogether from what he had imagined, for no imagination of his could ever have come up to the reality. And the golden suit falling to the shape of a slim body; and then the legs, the long legs that Jerry had first spoken of and that he had felt near his. But again nothing could compare with the magic of seeing. He closed his eyes for one second. That was his Liz standing there, that beautiful, beautiful thing. Without haste his arms lifted upwards towards her, and without haste she came into them and, positioning herself on the side of the bed, she held him as she had done once before, and his head lifting painfully from the pillow was pressed into her neck, and again she felt the warm wetness of his tears . . .

It was a full ten minutes later when there was a rustle outside the door and in bounced the little nurse. 'Well!' she said, 'got it all over?' She looked to where Matthew was lying back among the pillows with his right arm twined around Elizabeth's forearm, holding her in a very awkward position on the side of the bed, and she said, 'He's making you look as comfortable as a donkey in a drawing room. Here! sit on this chair, and you, let loose of her arm.'

Laughing gently, Elizabeth removed her arm from Matthew's grasp and, sitting down gratefully on the chair, she said, 'Thanks, Nurse.'

There was a low murmur from the bed and Matthew said quietly, 'Don't make any mistakes, my love; she's not a nurse, she's got hands on her like the feet of a Corporation horse.'

'Oh, Matthew.'

'Oh, don't you worry, don't take any notice of him. Common, he is, like that one outside who says he wants to see him. Is that right?'

'Who's outside?'

Matthew's voice had changed as he appealed to Elizabeth, and she answered softly, 'Jim.'

'Oh, Jim. Yes, of course I want to see him, and instantly.'

'You would, he's your type.'

When the nurse left the room, Elizabeth,

now shaking with her laughter, said, 'Since when, Matthew, have you spoken to a nurse like that?'

'Since, my darling, she was the first face my eyes really saw. I don't know how long ago that was—two, three, four days—my head is still muzzy.'

'Not more than two days ago, darling.'

'Well, we've travelled together a lot since then if it's only two days ago. She's wonderful.'

'Yes, by the sound of it I should imagine she is.'

The door opened again and back came the nurse in question, followed by Jim, whom she announced by saying, 'This is the fella who wants to see you.'

Jim walked to the foot of the bed, then along it and up the other side, and he and Matthew stared at each other for quite a while without speaking. Then Jim said, 'All right?'

'All right, Jim. Fine.'

So this was Jim. This was what he looked like, the man he had cried out for, the man who was his friend: Jim! Jim! In his head he could still hear himself screaming the name.

From Jim's stance he realised it was difficult now for him, who was never lost for
words, to find any to meet the situation.
What he decided to do was to take up the
old game, and so he said, 'By the way,
that little body over there, the dumpy one
pretending she's doing something at the
medicine table, her name is Nurse Marshall, and she and you should get on well
together—like you, she doesn't know her
place.'

'Huh!' It was a loud 'Huh!' but still the
little nurse did not turn round.

'Aye, well,' said Jim, sensing the situation. 'How d'you do, miss?'

Gladys Marshall turned from the table
and, looking at the sturdy young fellow,
said, 'I do very well, mister, when I'm in
decent company, but being in a hospital
you meet all kinds of people, and patients
come and go, and some you would wish
would go sooner than others, if you follow
my meaning.'

'Yes, I do, Nurse, I do indeed.'

When the nurse turned back to the table
Jim looked at Matthew and said quietly, 'I
suppose I'll have to be lookin' for a new

job, as you'll be wantin' to drive your own car now.'

'Oh, certainly, certainly. Well, what d'you think?'

'Just what I said, sir, you'll be wantin' to drive your own car and I'll be out of a job.'

'Well,' Matthew's voice came slowly now, 'there's that in it. Yes, there's that in it.'

At this point Elizabeth's voice broke in, saying with some authority, 'He'll never be out of a job as long as I need a car, because I would never feel safe with anyone else driving me.'

'Thanks, miss,' said Jim now. 'I'll sign up with you any day, and be glad to. Some folks are very ungrateful.'

'Yes, they are, Jim, I quite agree with you.'

'Elizabeth Ducksworth!'

'Yes, Mr Wallingham, you were saying?'

Matthew gave a deep sigh before weakly saying, 'Nurse Marshall, do me the kindness to get rid of this fellow, will you?'

'Well, as it's the first civil request you've made of me I'll do that for you.' She now looked at Jim, and he back at her, and there was merriment in both their faces; then Jim took the hand that was being held out to him from the bed and when Matthew said to him, 'Get me out of here as soon as possible, will you, Jim?', Jim answered in the same vein, 'I'll do me best, Captain, I'll do me best.' Then he added, 'I can't wait for the day.'

When Jim and the nurse had gone, Matthew lay quiet for some minutes, gripping Elizabeth's two hands. Then he said, almost in a whisper, 'I'm a lucky fellow, Liz. What I would have done without that man these past few months I don't know.' Then, his tone lightening, he said, 'Of course, on the side there was you.'

'Darling'—her voice was serious now—'you've had enough joking for one morning. Now what you must do is lie quiet because your mother . . . mama . . .' she kissed him gently before going on, 'is coming in for her turn to be with you. She's been so patient. You said a moment ago you were lucky to have Jim, well, let me tell you I feel as lucky to have made friends with her, and friends we are. She'll never act as . . . well, as a mother-in-law, never.'

'Mother-in-law.' He brought one of her hands up to his cheek. 'How soon?'

She rose to her feet. 'We're not going to discuss that, not at this moment, nor for another week or so.'

'How long will it be before I can stand?'

'That depends upon you and how good you are. Now I'm going to leave you, my love.'

'Just . . . just one minute or so more, darling. I . . . I want to ask you something. Do . . .' There was a long pause. 'Do they know how it happened?'

There was another long pause before she answered, 'Yes, they know how it happened.'

'Jim . . . Jim would have told them?'

'Yes. And your grandmother told them too.'

He stirred in the bed, and she put her two hands quickly on his shoulders and said, 'Now, now, lie still, please. She was at the telescope, you remember? waiting to see you wave. It was very misty but she saw it all happening.'

'Dear God!' Then he asked quietly, 'Where is he?'

She seemed to consider for a moment,

then said, 'Well, I should imagine about now, if he's travelling straight there, he should be on the train heading for Southampton and the boat, *Orontes,* that will take him to New Zealand.'

'*New Zealand?*' The words came high.

'Yes, New Zealand, where I understand your grandfather had distant relatives, big farmers. The colonel has been on the phone to them about his son who wishes to travel and set up his own farm. It was all done very diplomatically.'

'And he complied?' The last words were a whisper.

'Not really, but it was either that or— Look! I'm a fool telling you you must keep quiet, then talking about something that should not be discussed for weeks ahead. You are safe, my love. There's only one thing I'd ask you to remember about this whole dreadful affair. Through him you have your sight back. Just think along those lines. Now, I am really going this time.'

She put her lips on his and he tried to hold her tightly to him; then as she released his hold and stood away from him, his eyes tight on her, he said, 'I adore you.'

She went hastily out and, now almost blind herself with tears, she bumped into two figures standing not far from the door.

'Oh, don't take on, miss. He's well, he can see. Life's ahead of you both. I was just telling Nurse here, there's not another one on this earth like him, not only for you but for me an' all.'

Nurse Marshall put in briskly, 'If you've upset my patient I can report you. You know that, don't you?'

'Yes, Nurse. Yes, Nurse,' said Elizabeth, laughing now through her tears; then she added, 'His mama, as he calls her, will be here this afternoon.'

'Oh, what a pity! I'll be off this afternoon. I'd have loved to hear him call her Mama— he'd have never heard the last of it. You'll be back tonight?'

'Yes, of course.'

'Good. I can hold it over him as a threat, to keep you out if he starts any more of his antromartins,' and turning away she went back into the room, leaving Elizabeth to ask on a laugh, 'What's antromartins, Jim?'

'The same as divil's fagarties: kicking up a fuss.'

On their way out of the hospital Elizabeth remarked casually, 'She's a nice girl, that nurse, isn't she?'

'Ooh!' This was uttered on a high note of surprise. 'What are you suggesting, miss? She's not my type. Not with a voice like that.'

'I wasn't suggesting anything, Jim . . . but you never know.'

'I do, miss. I do.'

They both got into the car laughing.

30

His homecoming was a very emotional one.

His father, pulling himself painfully to his feet, held him close while neither of them spoke a word. His grandmother's reaction, as was to be expected, was different: 'I believe; help thou my unbelief. At this moment I say God is good.' As for his mother, she leant against him, her arms around his waist, her head on his chest, and through her tears she cried, 'Oh my darling, my darling.'

Elizabeth stood aside. Her face was wet, her throat was choked, and when Matthew's voice broke in with a cracked sound, 'Isn't anybody going to offer me a drink?' seemingly in answer to this demand the door opened and Peter entered. His face was alight, and he was bearing in his arms a large tray on which were two decanters and a number of glasses; and his words seemed to sing as he said, 'Welcome home! Welcome home!' Then as he placed the tray on a side table he remarked to no one in particular, 'Jim is outside. I told him he would be welcome.'

Before Matthew could reply, his father cried in a loud army voice, as if in command, 'Don't stay out there, man!', at which they all laughed. Then the door opened and Jim entered the room.

Automatically, he took his place by the side of Matthew's chair, and in his usual manner he said, 'Why didn't you whistle?'

'I didn't have a chance,' said Matthew, followed by much laughter and then the raising of glasses: 'To Matthew. To Matthew. Welcome home.'

Some minutes later, it was Peter who said, 'I'm sorry to disturb the party, Mr Matthew, but they're all on edge in the kitchen, just waiting for you. Old Joe and Ben are there, too.'

When Matthew rose to his feet, saying, 'I'll go now,' the colonel said to Peter, 'Take a couple of bottles with you.'

* * *

It was Annie Wallingham, as usual speaking her mind, who said, 'I've never known The Beavors, during its long existence, have so many visitors in one day. And all supposedly so well-meaning, when all the time the intention was to get to the bottom of why Matthew should have fallen down the quarry, while attended by his chauffeur and the dog: And wasn't it strange that Rodney should have left for New Zealand at the same time?'

To one of the earliest callers, the family's supposed best friend, Ted Henderson, Peter had given a reason for Rodney's departure by saying, 'Oh, it wasn't hasty at all. It had been on the cards for months— Mr Rodney had been corresponding with a half-cousin who was anxious for him to join in the farming community out there, and the bookings on the liner had already been made.'

Peter knew he hadn't been believed, but what did it matter? The information he had given would likely set another rumour around, one that might be all to the good . . .

It was late that evening when Elizabeth

and Matthew said good night to each other in the little sitting room. It had been a long day and Matthew was tired. But as they sat, in each other's arms, on the couch, he suddenly said, 'Today I think I've seen every face I ever knew in these parts. But there's one missing, who was prominent in my life. That's Jerry. I can't understand what's happened to him. Can you?'

'No, you would have thought from what's been reported in the last few months of the happenings in this house that he would have contacted you in some way.'

'Yes, it's odd. I think we must look into it.'

'Yes, we will, darling, but now you're very tired, you've had more than enough for your first day out. And there's so much to talk about. But you're not doing it tonight. So come on, up you get. Jim's waiting for you in the hall.'

'Oh yes. Lord! I forgot. I forget everything when I'm with you. Do you know that?'

'No, I don't. But you can tell me about it tomorrow. I am Nurse Marshall now, so

come on and get your body up those
stairs.'

Their embrace was long and tender, and
they said no more, but went out and into
the hall where Elizabeth passed him and
his two sticks over to Jim, whom, as usual,
he greeted uncivilly, saying, 'I don't need
you, you know,' and received the reply,
'No, I know you don't, but you're stuck
with me and you'll just have to put up with
it.'

At five o'clock on the following day Peter
went to Jim's room with the message that
the colonel would like to see him in fifteen
minutes' time.

'See me?' said Jim. 'The colonel? He
sent the message? Not Mr Matthew?'

'No, not Mr Matthew, Jim. He generally
just whistles.'

'Aye. Aye, he does. What's it all about,
d'you know?'

'Yes, yes, I do, but I'm not in any position to inform you what plans the colonel
has.'

'Oh my! Oh my! You sound on your dignity.'

'Yes, I'm very much on my dignity at the present moment, Jim.'

'Something happening to you? I mean . . .'

'If you mean am I going to get the push? No.'

'I never meant any such thing, and you know it. But there seems to be something fishy in the air. I've hardly seen the boss all day.'

'No, you wouldn't. He's been closeted with his father and Madam most of the day.'

'Is the colonel in bed?'

'No, he's not in bed, he's in the drawing room, waiting for you. Now why are you looking like that?'

'What am I looking like?'

'As if you're going to blow your top.'

'Well, I've felt like it. I haven't had so much time on my hands for weeks. I saw more of him in hospital than I've done since I brought him back.'

'Oh, dear, dear. I must tell Mr Matthew that he should do something about that.'

'Come off it. Don't take that tone with me. You know you can't.'

Peter laughed and turned away; then,

looking back over his shoulder, the grin still on his face, he said, 'You are definitely one in your own line, Jim Taylor.'

Definitely one in his own line. What did he mean by that? That he was odd man out? Well, one thing he was certain of, there was something up, and the quicker he was enlightened the better . . .

Fifteen minutes later Bella announced him into the drawing room by opening the door and saying in formal tones, 'Jim Taylor, sir.'

Jim looked at the company awaiting him. There was the colonel, sitting in his basket chair; Peter, standing by his side in what appeared to be a permanent position; and to the left of him sat the mistress; then facing her son on the opposite side of the fireplace was the old girl; next to her was Miss Elizabeth, and naturally who would be next to her but the captain. It looked like a committee meeting. The only thing missing was a table running down between them.

'Sit down, Jim.' Matthew was on his feet now and pointing to a chair that seemed to head the two rows of people. There were only six of them altogether, but to Jim they looked like a full boardroom.

'There's been a lot of talking and discussion going on in this house since you brought my son back yesterday morning.' The colonel was looking at Jim, then went on, 'We want to talk to you about changes we wish to make'—again he paused—'and to see if you are agreeable.' The colonel actually smiled now as he added, 'Those are my son's words, "to see if you are agreeable", not to tell you what we want or what we plan, but to see if you are agreeable.'

'And you don't like it put that way, sir, is that it?'

The question seemed to startle them all, and it was the old girl, as Jim thought of her, who now made them all laugh gently by saying, 'Here we go! Here we go!'

'No, I wouldn't put it like that, but that's the way he wants it.'

Jim looked at Matthew, who moved his head as if to say, 'Behave yourself.'

The colonel was speaking again. 'Whether you are aware of it or not, Jim Taylor, I am still the head of this estate— and, by the way, I have been requested to use only your Christian name as others do. I find this difficult, and you can understand that, I'm sure.'

'Oh yes, yes, I can, Colonel, especially coming from you, yes; so I don't mind being called Taylor.'

The colonel closed his eyes, then in a voice in which there was a slight crack he said, 'I am pleased to accede to my son's request in most things, so to keep the peace I will address you in future as I do my other old hands on the farm, by your Christian name.'

When Jim answered to this, 'Very kind of you,' he omitted to add, 'I'm sure.'

Along the two rows there was a movement of heads, except the colonel's which was inclined downwards.

'Well now'—the colonel's voice was brisk—'no more fencing. It is like this. My son, I am told, never wanted to go into the fighting forces. From the beginning he would have preferred to deal with the land, to be a farmer as he puts it. Now, since his sight has returned, that wish can be granted. He intends to run the estate himself, and also to establish part of the land as a market garden, not only to grow vege-

tables but also soft fruits, and to plant or-
chards. And he envisages some long
greenhouses. This will entail a lot of extra
work, for which he will need an assistant
manager. My son suggests he offer you
this post. You have had some farm experience, and he seems to think you are quite
capable of managing whatever we take on;
and this I can in no way dispute.'

There were no words from Jim Taylor.
He simply sat staring at the colonel in
blank amazement. Then, his head jerking
towards Matthew, he said, 'You're finished
with the hospital do, then?'

'Yes, Jim, I'm finished with the hospital
do.'

He now addressed Elizabeth, asking,
'What about you, miss?'

'I'm finished with the hospital job, too,
Jim.'

'You are? I thought you were gonna be
a sister?'

'Oh, that was open to debate. You can't
be a sister until you step into somebody
else's shoes.'

'Like that, is it?'

'Yes, it's like that, Jim.'

Now it was the old girl's voice piping in

again: 'She'll still be able to use her nursing training, for Mary won't be able to handle me much longer on her own. And then there's my son here. He needs some nursing attention, and now and again Peter needs a hand, too, not to say a little more free time. So there's nothing being done out of kindness here. As you can see, we're all out for ourselves.'

'Oh! Mrs Wallingham.'

'What are you laughing at?' The old lady had turned to Lucille, and to the surprise of her husband Lucille said, 'It's wonderful to hear return gunfire.'

The colonel looked at his wife: she was a new woman these days, different. He had never really known her. Was it too late? Almost. Almost.

He was brought back to the present by that Taylor fellow saying, and even with some humility, which was surprising, 'This lot is much too big for me to take in all at once. I'm really lost for words.'

'Never!' snapped the colonel now in a definite army tone, to which Jim replied: 'Well, as you say, sir, never! But there's always an exception and this is it, because lifts like this don't happen every day—I know that much about life—and me being who I am, I can't at the moment see why such a one has come my way, except that I like to drive a car and I've looked after somebody for whom I'd work for nowt. But it's a big reward, and how it'll work out will have to be proved.'

'Yes, yes, it will, and it'll be up to you.'

To this statement of the colonel's the reply was, 'Aye, and at times it'll take some doing, because as me da would say . . .' He stopped here, and the colonel said, 'Well, go on and tell us what your da would say.'

For the first time there was a grin on Jim's face and he said, 'And use such language as I'd lose me new job before I'd started? Not me, sir, I've a little bit more up top than that.'

'I'm pleased to hear it,' said the colonel. 'I understand you come of a big family?'

'Nine of us, sir. Five lasses and three other fellas, and they're all all right, decent workin' lot. Well, that is except me eldest brother, Lance.'

There was a pause before the colonel said, 'Well, what ails him? Can't he work?'

'Oh yes, sir, but at his own particular job,

and it's one that forces him to take a holiday now and then. To put it plainly, sir, he's in jug.'

'In jug? You mean . . . ?'

'Yes, sir. He's along the line in Durham. And that was a mistake, the first and only one, he says, he'll ever make in his life.'

There was quite a stir in the room but no word came from the colonel until Jim said, 'Oh, I haven't hidden anything, sir. I told Mr Matthew all about him in the first place. He's a decent enough fellow otherwise.'

'What has he done that he should be imprisoned?' The voice that now came from the colonel sounded again like that of the soldier.

'Just tidied up a lady's dressing table, sir.'

'What?'

'Just what I said, sir. Hates untidiness, he's what me da calls a tidier-upper. When he happens to go into a room and he sees a lady has left all her bits and pieces scattered over the dressing table, he can't bear it, he just tidies them up.'

Matthew's head was deep on his chest, his hand was gripping Elizabeth's. Her other hand was across her mouth. Lucille's face was a contortion. As for Peter, his forearm, which was resting on the leather-pillowed top of the basket chair, was shaking visibly. The expression on the colonel's face couldn't be defined. Only his mother's face appeared ordinary, except for the glow in the eyes, and she asked now, 'What did he get for tidying up?'

'Well, ma'am, he got a year. He blamed himself, because normally he never does a job in this part of the country, he says it isn't worth it. But he was at a hotel and he happened to pass a bedroom whose door was open, and he saw a really untidy dressing table. It was dinner hour, and he assumed the occupant would be downstairs; so he walks in and tidies up the place, only almost to scream himself when a woman steps out of the bathroom stark naked. However, being the gentleman he is, he grabbed up a coat that was lying across the bed and put it round her. But, as he said, it was a waste of his time, for there through the door came the hall porter and the manager. By the way, none of the family knew anything of this for some time, for he never stays at home on his infrequent visits, and always uses a different name when he stays at a hotel.'

When the spluttering died down, the colonel asked, 'Has he always been in this . . . er . . . er . . . business of tidying up dressing tables?'

'Yes, sir, since he was fourteen. He laughs about that first time, because when he skimmed down the drainpipe, there were two bobbies waiting for him, and one happened to be a joker, who said, "You should never come out the way you go in, laddie," and being the bright lad he is, he answered, "Then why didn't you tell me before I went up?" He wasn't afraid of the bobbies, but he was of me da, who skinned him alive. That was after me ma finished with him.

'But he's travelled a lot since then, sir, and learnt a lot too. He's been educated.'

'Educated?' The colonel's eyebrows were raised.

'Yes, sir, I mean educated. He talks well; he dresses well; he can pass himself in any company. And he's well read. Whenever he travels he reads. Which is odd, because he ran away from home when he was six-teen, and I don't think he had opened a book until then. We never heard anything of him for more than four years.'

'Was he in a gang?' demanded Granan.

'Lance in a gang? No, madam, not him. Lance is his own man. But no—that isn't quite right. From the little he's told me, he's got a boss, but he doesn't call him boss, that's my term for it, he refers to him as "my friend Mr Goodbody". They both travel a lot. What I've worked out in my own mind is that Mr Goodbody is a jeweller in his own right. I guessed this when he let drop the word "shop" one day. And I also think that Lance worked legitimately as a traveller—he often used to go over to Holland before the war, and, you know, there was a lot of diamond business that went on there and no doubt will again now. But in between times, I'm sure he's cleaned up some very untidy dressing tables nearer home, even private safes that are untidy too. And who would have suspected Mr Goodbody's assistant, I ask you, madam? I should imagine Mr Goodbody and he were able to do a lot of groundwork. Of course, they weren't often seen together. Reading between the lines, I know that Mr Goodbody had a villa somewhere in France before the war, and will doubtless go back there now.'

'It's unbelievable.' The colonel was shaking his head.

'It's true, sir, every word of it.'

And now the colonel, looking at his son, said, 'You do pick your friends from peculiar families, Matthew. Here is our future assistant manager to the estate telling us he has a brother who is doing time for being a'—he paused—'a tidier-upper. And then there is Fox, who, so you have told me, was a wonderful man, the only one in your company who could produce a tank, a jeep or a goat stripped and ready for the spit, following the mere suggestion that such a thing was necessary.'

It was Jim who was grinning now as he looked at Matthew and said, 'Was Charlie one of them, sir?'

'Yes, Jim, the best of them. Well, your brother may have been a tidier-upper; Charlie was a picker-upper.'

Jim's grin widened as he said, 'I'll have to have a crack with him one of these days.'

With a note of irritation in his voice now, the colonel said, 'Get me to my feet, Peter, and let us eat. That is, after my son closes this meeting with his announcement.'

Matthew gripped at the sticks at his side, then rose from his chair, and looking at Jim, said, 'We have finally made the date for our marriage—the twentieth of August, Jim, and I hope you'll do me the honour of being my best man.'

Jim was truly lost for words now. After all, Mr Matthew had two brothers-in-law, and then there were the Hendersons, the McArthurs and the Taggarts, all well-known families, all with young fellows in them. And those not counting the Raeburns, with a bishop and a lord to boast of! But he had chosen him, Jim Taylor. No, he couldn't find a word to say. He could only look straight at Matthew, utterly speechless for once. That was until Matthew said, 'Also we would like you to join us for dinner tonight by way of celebration.' Still Jim did not speak, but he shot a lightning glance towards the colonel, and Matthew put in, 'My father agreed with the invitation.'

'So that being that,' said the colonel in a colonel's voice, 'let us for heaven's sake eat.'

And now Granan spoke up, as she was

being helped to her feet: 'And I second that, with one request only, Mr Taylor. Please do not come out with any more of your tales during the meal: I don't want to choke. So let's away.'

They paraded away slowly, Peter assisting his master, Lucille on one side of her mother-in-law and Elizabeth on the other, purposely leaving Matthew and Jim alone together for a moment. And when Jim made no effort to speak Matthew held his hand out and said, 'I could never have chosen a better. And I want all your family to come as well. So come along, man, come along.'

It was a very merry meal. As Bella remarked to Cook, 'I can't remember ever hearing so much merriment in this house.' And, being diplomatic, she added, 'Such praise for your splendid effort too.'

It wasn't until the meal was over and they were about to make their way to the drawing room for coffee that Jim looked across the table at Matthew, saying, 'Me ma visited our Lance last Sunday and it looks like he might be let out a month or so earlier for good behaviour. Would he be included in the invitation?'

If Annie Wallingham had been eating she certainly would have choked, as surely would the others; as for the colonel, he was forced to sit back in his chair.

Even Matthew couldn't answer for a moment and Jim went on, 'Well, I thought I'd better ask 'cos me ma'll be on hot bricks if he makes his way in unexpected like. I just wanted to make sure.'

The colonel, now actually rubbing his eyes, turned to his wife and said in a serious tone, 'Lucille, see that your dressing table is tidy, will you? And, Mother, do you still keep your tiara in your own jewel box and not in the safe?'

'Yes, I do, Richard. And when he comes I'll take him aside and show it to him. That's after we have had a crack. By the sound of it I think he's the only type in my long years I haven't as yet had a conversation with. And to meet a tidier-upper of dressing tables is something to look forward to. And now, for God's sake, let us see if we can get through the coffee stage without choking.'

31

It was the nineteenth of August. It was a cool evening following a surprisingly hot day. They had walked through the gardens and were now sitting quietly on a small bench next to the pool in the rose garden. Elizabeth's head was resting against Matthew's shoulder, and his right arm was around her waist, his other hand holding hers. 'This time tomorrow,' he said, 'we should be in London, and the following day on our way to America. Can you believe it?'

'No, darling, no, I can't take it in, less still that tomorrow is to be our wedding day.'

His grip tightened on her waist and he pulled her closer, saying, 'I've dreamt of it;

it's kept me awake at night. From two o'clock tomorrow afternoon you'll be mine.'

'I've always been yours, darling, always, ever since I held you in my arms when I was forty-nine.' For a moment they laughed together; and then he said, 'Have you really thought about what it all means?'

'Oh yes, my love, as much as you, and wanted it as much as you.'

'You couldn't possibly. It's been tough at times, especially since I saw you for the first time. You were a golden light, and like that you've always remained and always will.'

They sat still for a moment until she said, 'In a way I wish tomorrow were over. It's funny, but at first it was to be just a small affair, a family affair. Now has it grown to such an extent that I doubt if the marquee will hold them.'

'Well, it's your fault; you shouldn't have so many admirers.'

'Admirers!' she repeated. 'Mum and Dad and Phil—admirers! Three of them! All the rest are in your squad. Apart from your sisters, their husbands and their children, there are at least thirty from the family's close friends in the neighbourhood. Then there's all Jim's tribe.' She laughed here. 'Aren't you glad, darling, we've got Jim?'

'Glad? Add to that pleased and thankful.'

'And there are fourteen of his family besides the tidier-upper.' Laughing, they clung together again for a moment until Elizabeth said, 'I am dying to meet the famous Lance, aren't you?'

'Well, I promise you, dear, he won't be a bit like what you think of as a burglar; but that's what he is really, a burglar, and in a big way at that, I should say. Do you remember that night when Jim first introduced him to the conversation in the drawing room? I'll never forget it as long as I live. I recall waking up laughing in my sleep at the sight of Father's face. Now *there* you have a changed man, and Mama too is happier than I've seen her for years. But that is because she's got you. She loves you, you know.'

'And I love her too, very much, oh yes, and not only because she's your mother. I never think of her as a mother-in-law. I don't know what it is. Perhaps because at first we needed each other, just to talk to. And I can talk to her, just as I've done from the first to Granan. Oh, who could help loving that old rip? You know, she's just dying, really dying to meet the tidier-upper. It's a funny thing to say, darling, but in a way she's not unlike Jim, is she? I mean, there are no half-measures with her: she says what she means.'

'Yes, but I tell you what has troubled me. It's the sight of Jerry. He has changed, hasn't he? And I can understand, too, his fear of going into the darkness.' His tone was now low and sombre. 'It's a dreadful place to be, Liz. Not unless he has experienced it in some form can anyone understand it. Up to a point he had, just having the one eye. But when that too became affected . . . oh, I can understand his fear only too well. It's put years on him. But Jackie's nice, isn't she? I would say she's another Ducksworth, the very wife for him. And her people are very good, finding him a place in their factory where he can be of use. One thing we must do when we come back, we must keep in touch with them, have them here often.'

'Oh yes, Matthew, yes.'

'How many will there be altogether? I've

been too busy outside with Jim and the rest to go into numbers.'

'Well, there'll be that lot there, on the farm. Also our little staff from indoors, not counting six from the hospital: Matron, Sister Fowler, Sister Grace, Dr Venor, Mr Carey and Nurse Marshall. Oh yes, Nurse Marshall. Even if I hadn't invited her you would have had a request from Mr Jim Taylor concerning her.'

'No!'

'Yes. You are so taken up with yourself, Mr Wallingham, that you don't notice these things happening under your nose.'

'I am so taken up with you, Miss Ducksworth, that you blot everything and everybody else out.'

To this there was only one appropriate response, and when at last their lips parted he said softly, 'I love you so much, Liz, that I am fearful, and I realise for the first time that love doesn't always bring happiness. There are so many tangents: anxiety, doubt, disbelief, all these things. Anxiety in case anything should happen to you; doubt that you might stop loving me; disbelief that it is happening at all, that the joy, ecstasy and wonder are just a dream. At times I have to shake myself and say no, it's no dream, it's reality; and yes, it is painful, but that's part of loving.'

'Oh Matthew, Matthew. I'm not worth all that. I'm not.'

'Leave it to me to say what you're worth. I tell you what I'll do'—his voice now held a note of laughter—'I'll get Tommy Dodds to pick a high note up the scale and name it after you.'

'First, though, you are going to play the piano for me. Please, Matthew, don't put it off any longer. It would be the perfect wedding gift for me, to hear you play at last. And just think how it will please your grandmother.'

'Oh! all right. Yes, you're right, my darling, it is time for me to have a crack at it. Apart from you and Granan, Tommy is always on at me about it too.'

'Well, we'll tell him about it tomorrow. He'll be here with his wife; he was so pleased with the invitation. And while I'm thinking of numbers, there will be some people from the village as well as those from the estate cottages. Your mother has their names down, and they'll all be here for lunch in the marquee.

'So it is all ordered, and Cook hasn't had a hand in it. For once, as Granan said, we shall see her in a hat and coat, specially bought for the occasion. How long has she been here?'

'Oh, years and years; she must be in her middle sixties, if not her late sixties. She came here as a kitchenmaid, I understand, when Granan was youngable, as she terms it.'

Again they were quiet for a moment, and then he said, 'I'm looking forward to seeing William. We were two of a kind, you know, more like twins, although he's older than me. He seems to have done fabulously well in America. Fancy sending us that gold-plated dinner service. Twelve pieces of everything. As I look at it I feel guilty that anyone can afford to buy such a gift! It would keep an ordinary couple of families for the rest of their lives, and in comfort.'

'Strange, you know,' said Elizabeth, 'but I thought the same when I saw it, and I asked myself when on earth we would use it.'

'Oh, we'll use it, and if the farm goes broke under my management, we'll sell it

and it'll pay off the debts and the mortgage.'

'There isn't a mortgage.'

'No, but there might be by the time I'm
finished, and with the ideas that Jim is putting into my head for new crops, from shal-
lots to asparagus. You're shivering, darling.
Come on, let's go in.'

She had shivered because a funny feeling had passed over her. She remembered
that not a few yards away was the seat
she had made to sit on when Mike
McCabe's hand had come over her mouth
and his razor had flashed before her eyes.
He was safe for life where he was, and
his mother was dead, and Rodney Wallingham had been exiled, you could say, to
New Zealand. And all this had happened
through her.

No, she wouldn't think like that, for, because these things had happened, a man
who was blind was seeing again, and the
house had come back to life. An old lady
was happy because her beloved grandson
was with her and could once more see her;
his mother was happy because she had
made a friend she could talk to; and the
colonel had become a different man, a

softer man. Then there had come into their lives a man named Jim Taylor, who had become not only a loyal friend to the family but also a laughter-maker. That too, in a way, had all come about through her, so she must look upon it that the dreadful things that had happened in their own time brought forth good.

As they were making their way slowly back to the house, Lucille was emerging into the passage from the kitchen where she'd had a last word with Cook about the timing of the house party's breakfast for the next morning. Entering the passage from the other door, she saw Peter. They stood a moment smiling at each other, then he said softly, 'Are you happy tonight?'

'Yes, Peter, yes, you could say I am happy . . . almost. And you?'

'Yes, you could say too that I am happy . . . almost, and mainly because you are so.'

Their hands met, for not more than a second; then in answer to her 'Good night, Peter,' his reply came softly, 'Good night,' but 'my dear' was almost inaudible.

For a moment he stood looking at the

closed door and recalled the first time their hands had touched. It was in the library. He had been sorting out some books and looked up to find her standing near, staring at him. The look in her eyes then told him what had been in his heart for a long time. He had risen from his knees and gone to her; and she had held out her hand to him, saying, 'I look upon you as a friend, Peter,' and he had replied softly, 'And I you, mistress.'

'And it must remain so.'

'Yes; yes. It will be as you say. We are friends for as long as you wish.' And so it had been . . .

Lucille made her way to her husband's room. He was sitting up in bed, his hands lying idly one on top of the other on the counterpane. He greeted her with, 'All settled then?'

'Yes, dear; thankfully they're all tucked up.'

'It's been a long day for you.'

'Yes,' she agreed, 'but it'll be longer tomorrow. Wait! Richard, do you hear the piano? Matthew is playing—playing for his future wife.'

'You are happy for them?'

'Very. Oh, very. And you, dear?' She looked at him.

'I am happy for them, yes, but envious.'

She walked along by the bed until she was near his hands, and then taking one up she held it and stroked it gently as she said, 'Why are you jealous of their happiness?'

He stared into her face, then said quietly, 'Because it is something that I've never myself experienced. You didn't love me as she loves him. Nor did I understand the real meaning of love or what a girl like you needed at that time. You had been hurt, then had been pushed on to me, and I wasn't big enough inside or even knowledgeable enough to know how to treat you. You didn't love me then, and I don't think you've ever grown to love me. At least until recently, when I've detected a certain difference in you.'

'Oh, Richard. Richard.'

'Don't . . . don't cry, my dear. Please don't cry. You have been such a good wife to me, and patient with me. I've been boorish at times, and still continue to play the colonel in civilian life. But of late I've been looking at things and people differently. I've had time to think things out and also to listen. Come, come, my dear, no more tears. Don't let me make you unhappy tonight.'

'You have never really made me unhappy, Richard. I have been unhappy because I knew I had failed you. I hadn't given you the love you deserved, the love that you needed, because I do know, from what I picked up early in our marriage, that all your mother's love and the old general's had been given to your two brothers. But after they were killed your parents did not turn to you, as they should have done. And you must have felt more than ever bereft. I should have understood this, but understanding only comes with years, and as you say so truthfully, I have been different of late because I, too, have been thinking differently, much of it having been brought about by Elizabeth, and not a little by our new retainer by the name of Jim.'

The latter remark caused him to smile and he said, 'Yes, by the name of Jim. I'm telling you this, and reluctantly, my dear, that I recognize that that fellow has more real brains in his head than all the rest of this household put together, including me.'

'Well, I wouldn't quite agree with you

there, my dear. Brains perhaps, but mostly wit. He knows his power. He can make one laugh. I have grown very, very fond of him, maybe brought about by knowing that he would give his life quite willingly for Matthew.'

'Yes. Yes. That is something for me to be jealous of too. Yet I don't know . . . there is Peter. Peter has given his life to me.'

'Oh yes; yes, he has, my dear. Peter is a very, very good man.'

He looked her straight in the face as he said, 'Yes, I know that, Lucille, only too well: Peter is a very good man.'

She moved closer up the bed now and, bending, she put her lips to his; it was a long, long time since they had been there. He held her to him, and as he did so she murmured softly, 'I have grown to love you, Richard. Late in the day, perhaps, but I can say now, as I have never said before, that I do love you. And if I may'—her voice dropped lower still—'I would like to lie beside you tonight.'

To this he made no reply, not a word, but pressed her head deep into his shoulder.